THE EXPEDIENT WIFE

R. S. HAMPTON

Copyright © 2025 by IstanbulMiami, LLC

Ebook ISBN 979-8-9985116-6-0

KDP Print Paperback ISBN

Print Paperback ISBN 979-8-9985116-7-7

Audio ISBN 979-8-9985116-8-4

Cover Design by Nick Castle

Marketing Design by Emily Gervais, Ebb Studios

All rights reserved.

This is a work of fiction. Names, characters, business organizations, places, and incidents other than those clearly in the public domain are either the product of the author's imagination or are used fictitiously. Any resemblance to actual persons, living or dead, events, or locales, is entirely coincidental.

No part of this book may be reproduced in any form or by any electronic or mechanical means, including information storage and retrieval systems, without written permission from the author, except for the use of brief quotations in a book review.

Without in any way limiting the author's and publisher's exclusive rights under copyright, any use of this publication to "train" generative artificial intelligence (AI) technologies to generate text is expressly prohibited. The author reserves all rights to license uses of this work for generative AI training and development of machine learning language models.

For Ayhan.
Without you, none of this would have been possible.

INTRODUCTION

All characters in this novel are fictional. Many of the locations depicted are accurate; others are entirely fictitious. Explore the cities in Türkiye and determine the accuracy for yourself. Perhaps you will also fall in love with this country.

I traveled to Türkiye before the first Gulf War, as a U.S. Air Force wife, landing at İmir's Çiğli Air Base early one morning, as did Quinn. Growing up in the rural South, this first trip overseas changed my life. I nervously spent the first few days scanning the crowds of people from my hotel room window as they navigated the wide seaside Kordon. With a simple morning walk, I met the fig vendor described in this novel, and that experience gave me the confidence to begin looking for an apartment.

With no translation app and no base for housing, I was thrust headlong into a very different culture, learning to communicate with smiles, laughter, and pictures. I found the Turks to be a warm and helpful community. I felt safe and accepted.

Now married to a Turk from Istanbul, we live on an off-grid, remote mountain farm in Türkiye for much of the year. The Expedient Wife came from my wanderings through Istanbul's

Grand Bazaar, İmir's seaside, and other cities and villages throughout the country. I hope you enjoy the start of Quinn's journey in Türkiye. I know the country will change her life as much as it changed mine.

R. S. Hampton

PROLOGUE

EXPEDIENT | ik'spēdēənt |
adjective
(of an action) convenient and practical,
although possibly improper or immoral
noun
a means of attaining an end, especially
one that is convenient but considered
improper or immoral

New Oxford American Dictionary

1

QUINN

Something is wrong. Landing in Türkiye, as the U. S. Air Force cargo plane rolls to a stop in the dark of night. Even though my husband promised to be on the tarmac at this small Turkish training base, he isn't. My hands fumble as I try to unbuckle my safety harness. With my stomach in knots, I snatch my backpack and head forward as an airman opens the door.

While this is not my first trip outside the United States, it is my first exposure to the military world. Every cell in my body is jittery as I thrust my head out the airplane doorway and look toward the bottom of the steps.

There's no Harris.

"Let me help you, Quinn," Marty, the airman, says as his hand latches onto my bag. "Get you going on that second honeymoon." As Marty grins at me, a blush creeps up my neck. Even though he and I are now friends, having yelled back and forth over the airplane engine noise for ten hours, I'm still embarrassed at my newlywed status. Before I can take a step outside, he takes hold of my arm and thrusts something toward me.

"Your husband wanted me to give you this once we landed,"

he says, handing me a small package. "He told me it was important."

I give him a quizzical look and unwrap it. The box contains a gold cartouche on a thick gold chain, a rectangle several inches long and half an inch wide, with Arabic script on the front. This romantic gesture was what initially drew me to Harris. I extend the ends of the chain toward the airman, and he helps me put it on.

"Just doing my part for the newlyweds," he says, giving me a wink.

"Thanks, Marty."

He tosses my overstuffed duffel to another airman on the ground, and I take my first step outside. Breathing in the warm August air, I scan the dark for movement. The end of the summer in Charleston is miserable, and I am immediately thankful for the significant decrease in İmir's humidity. My heart lurches with exhilaration for several beats despite my worry over Harris.

After descending the rolling staircase, I step to the side as the ground crew unloads the cargo. Bouncing from one foot to another, I wait, staring out into the blackness while fondling the cartouche. It is heavy against my chest, but the chain is long enough for it to be hidden under my blouse. While I love my new husband, who is generous and thoughtful with presents, I can't get used to him being late for everything. My mother taught me that being late is the highest disrespect you can pay to someone.

Ten minutes pass. I squint into the blackness after checking my watch for the thousandth time. He still isn't here, even though he told me he would meet me "right on the tarmac." Çiğli Air Base—pronounced like *chili,* Harris said to me in Charleston—is a small airfield about an hour from the center of İmir. Harris insisted I enter the country here, but gave me no explanation other than this was "standard Air Force procedure."

Even though I am new to the military community, nothing about this place—with only two concrete buildings and one hangar—makes me think this is standard. But even though Harris is a bit unorthodox, I do trust him, and the thrill of having a partner who treats me as an equal is huge. The nearest airman takes a step toward me.

"Ms. Durand, ma'am, let me take that for you." He reaches for my duffel. "It's a hike to the passport office. Just wait over there. They are sending someone for you since the Major hasn't arrived yet."

"I've got it. And it's Quinn, remember?" I remind him. "You guys need to ditch the ma'am thing. You're making me feel old." I breathe in the warm air laced with a tinge of salt and jet fuel. At almost forty, I am not above carrying my own luggage.

Out of the dark, a smirking Turkish guard saunters across the runway toward the plane. A machine gun strapped across his chest, he grasps the rifle with his wiry arms, muscles protruding in relief in the dim glow of halogen lights. A shiver crawls up my spine.

The soldier gestures across the tarmac at a building roughly a football field's distance away with the tip of his barrel. After an affirming nod from the closest airman, I head toward the soldier and his gun, refusing to appear frightened, even though the nerves in my neck twinge every few seconds. Squaring my shoulders, my back ramrod straight, I force my tired body into my invisible lawyer suit, a permanently ingrained habit. I've had to deal with demanding clients and annoying judges, and now, it seems, a husband who is irritatingly late in a foreign country in the middle of the night.

I glance back at the soldier, the twinge in my neck more insistent. The soldier frowns as he points the gun's muzzle at the building to my right, and I adjust my direction. My stomach clenches. I feel more like a prisoner than an arriving passenger. Gripping my duffel, I adjust my backpack higher on my shoulder. Within the last few months, I've sold my condo, closed my law practice, and winnowed my belongings into these two bags. This trip is not how Harris described it, but it is too late to turn back now.

Outside the Passport Control building, the soldier stops, and I step through the door. I nod as I pass him, not comfortable testing my new Turkish. He gives me a sneer in return. *Welcome to Türkiye.* I drop my backpack on the counter of the concrete room, my duffel on the ground. The stern visage of the creator of the current Turkish Republic, Kemal Atatürk, hangs on the wall. The room smells of cigarette smoke.

A burly passport officer's intense brown eyes meet mine, and a bead of sweat slowly trickles down my spine. A wide strap stretches diagonally across his chest, holding a machine gun on his back. With a grimace, he adjusts the strap. My body stiffens, hoping his discomfort is with the gun and not with me. Without a word, he extends his open palm, and I place my crisp new passport and a copy of Harris's orders in it. These are required for me to accompany my husband to his new overseas location. The officer squints as he looks at my passport, then compares it to Harris's paperwork.

I hold my breath. The single name on my passport doesn't match the married name on the orders. I knew it would be a problem, but typical of Harris, he blew it off. The officer stops what he is doing to light a cigarette.

Would my Mexican marriage license help or hurt? I have no idea. I stick my hand in my bag, then withdraw it as the officer speaks. My lawyer brain reminds me to produce information only when requested and to refrain from making assumptions. Harris assured me that everything would be fine.

Right, buddy. That's not how my life works.

"Quinn Durand." His words roll out with a heavy accent as he squints at my passport.

"*Evet.* Yes," I respond in both languages.

He looks at the orders. "Quinn Robicheaux." Not surprisingly, he butchers the Louisiana name.

"Yes. I am the same person." I pull out my phone and pull up a translation app. My jet lag and the stress of Harris not being here are affecting my ability to talk to this man.

His expression says he isn't sure he believes me. I run my fingers through my hair as he flips through the pages of my Durand-not-Robichaeux passport. Abruptly, he pulls a large wooden stamp, a messy blue ink pad, and a page of rectangular stickers from a drawer. Flipping to the back of my passport, he rips off a sticker from his stack and then stops his hand mid-air. His expression is at once curious and concerned.

"Visa?" he whispers to himself, re-attaching the sticker to the original sheet. I lean over the counter toward him, trying to spot the problem.

"*Üzgünüm.*" I use the word I know for 'sorry,' and shrug. While the color on my visa is not as vivid, I see little difference. Maybe the words? So what if Harris included the visa? A jolt of fear shoots up my spine. This is not America, and I have no control. Will this officer refuse me entrance to the country over a stupid sticker?

My skin goes cold. Before I can respond, he pulls the gun in front of him. The barrel swings toward me, and I scramble backward to get out of the way. Before I can decide whether to flee or stay, he lifts the strap over his head and noisily drops the gun on the counter, the barrel pointing directly at me. I duck in front of the counter. I close my eyes and hold my breath, asking myself if I can really be shot for having the wrong sticker. When nothing happens, I slowly stand, legs shaking, and take several silent breaths to slow my racing heart.

Using a finger to stretch his collar from his neck, the man chuckles as he loosens his necktie while his other hand pushes the gun away. My nerves clearly entertain him. I heave a sigh of relief as he again removes the sticker from the sheet, this time placing it over the sticker in my passport.

As his hand covers my passport, the officer squints at something behind me. I turn with a smile, my heart racing as I expect to see Harris. Two men are outside, walking toward the door, both in formal U.S. Air Force Class-A dress.

Neither is Harris.

As I focus on the Americans again, the younger man's uniform looks freshly dry-cleaned; his jacket is crisp, and his pants have sharp creases. The older man's uniform seems as though he'd slept in it, and perhaps more than once. Lines of fatigue cross his face. I am sure Harris sent them to retrieve me, and I grasp my backpack in relief. This is so typical of him, and I hate it. Why come if he can send someone else, even for his wife? I glance at the passport officer. His eyes remain squinted, his brow furrowed in concern.

An uneasy feeling begins to settle in the pit of my stomach.

"Mrs. Robicheaux? Mrs. Quinn Robicheaux?"

Harris's name rolls from the younger man's lips with ease, as if he had been pronouncing New Orleans names all his life. He steps toward me with his hand outstretched, but stops short, rudely forcing me to step forward to complete the handshake —a tacky power move. I shake his limp, sweaty hand and paste on the friendly lawyer smile I reserve for the courtroom. And jerks.

"Quinn Durand. Harris was supposed to meet me here over an hour ago. Where is he?" I look around the man's shoulder, expecting Harris to come through the door, spouting his usual laughter and bravado.

As I wait for a response, the Turkish officer moves from behind the counter to stand next to me, his eyes flicking between me and the two men, my passport in his hand. I look at the younger man first, then the older one. The Turk's hand slides down the counter next to his rifle, and the tension between the men is now thicker than the humidity I left behind in Charleston.

My lawyer's smile fades. Ignoring me, the younger man glares at the Turk, and the two men continue to size each other up. The American is taller and broader, almost identical in physique to

Harris. He is physically superior to the Turk and thirty years younger, yet the Turk's expression remains impassive. He pulls the rifle toward him as if daring the younger man to come at him.

The hair on the back of my neck jumps to attention.

"Gentlemen?" I use my courtroom voice. "Where is my husband?"

"Ma'am, I'm so sorry," says the younger officer, giving the Turk one last glare. His blonde hair is the same color as Harris's, and his accent is the same, so much so that he could be my brother-in-law. The queasiness in the pit of my stomach increases. He places his hand over his heart as he introduces himself.

"Captain Theodore Maynard, U.S. Air Force. Your husband was my logistics partner and my friend. We go way back." He gives me a slight smile as he gestures to the other man. "This is Air Force Chaplain Major Don Stone."

"Mrs. Robicheaux..." Stone hesitates as he shifts forward and grasps my right hand in both of his. His clammy touch makes my skin crawl. He smells like he needs a bath.

"Durand. My last name is Durand. Tell me where my husband is and when he will be here." With the last word, my brain suddenly kicks in, and the introductory details plow through the jet lag. This man is a chaplain. The mental slap comes as I look into Stone's steel gray eyes. I know the words before he says them.

"Ma'am, your husband was involved in a helicopter accident several days ago. I'm afraid..." His voice trails off at the end.

I interrupt. "Accident? Take me to him." I clutch the chaplain's sleeve and begin pulling him toward the door, my eyes begging him not to say the words I know are about to come. He refuses to move.

"Ms. Durand. I'm very sorry. Your husband didn't make it."

2

QUINN

Stone's words slice my heart open like a jagged hunting knife. It takes me several long breaths before my heart calms, my tears stop, and my brain re-engages. Still, my knees give way, and the Turkish officer catches me and lowers me into a chair. As the Americans stand in front of me, the Turk hands me a tulip-shaped glass of tea and motions for me to drink as he heads back to the teapot.

"No. Harris is not dead. He can't be." I whisper aloud, more to myself than to the men, before addressing them directly. "What happened?" I look from Maynard to Stone. Stone had omitted "in the line of duty" from his death notification. Neither man speaks, so I try once more to regain a semblance of power.

"What was Harris doing in a helicopter? Was this some logistics trip?"

"We do not know his exact location before the crash, where he was going, or where he had been," Stone says, "and there was confusion about the cause of death. Then, there were notification issues. We sent a man to Major Robicheaux's last known address on file in Charleston, but it was vacant. It took us some time to track his movements to you."

The room spins as sweat breaks out across my forehead. The cigarette odor is cloying. I move back awkwardly, trying to find the chair. Stone shifts toward me to keep me from falling, but the Turkish officer, once again, catches me and lowers me slowly into the chair. I take several deep breaths to tamp down the nausea and fight the tears.

I refuse to cry in front of these men. Stone's words float around me as I grip the arms of the chair, shoving my emotions into the mental compartment I use when a trial is going bad, and my anger threatens to take control. The tears refuse to obey me, though, and I can feel them slowly rolling down my face.

"When did this trip occur?"

Maynard interrupts before Stone can answer. "Harris arrived in Türkiye three days ago."

"No," I say, "he didn't. You have the wrong man," I say. "Harris has been in Türkiye for two weeks. I watched him board the plane and then watched as it took off." I squinted at them. "Also, we've been married for several months, so why couldn't you find me? Don't your computers keep up?"

I stand and grab my backpack, reaching for my duffel. "Take me to him. I want to see his body."

Stone reaches for my arm, causing me to stop.

"Ma'am, he..." I hear a slight Texas twang. He falters as if he doesn't know what to say. Why not? Isn't this his job?

Maynard interrupts again. "The helicopter crashed. There is no, a..." he hesitates, "...body for you to identify. Even if we could take you to identify something, all the information is classified. We're waiting on the forensic report, but unfortunately, it may take a few days. I'm very sorry for your loss. I can assure you that if there were any information we could give you, we would."

I collapse back into the chair. The anger, the despair, and the gut-wrenching pain are all shrouded in shock that feels like a wet wool blanket thrown over my body. I lived through the death of my father years ago and then, more recently, my mother. Now, my husband? My heart races, overpowered by the anxiety of never seeing Harris again. I grapple to restrain myself from bursting into a full-blown crying jag.

A hand nudges me, and I look up to my right. The Turkish officer hands me a cloth handkerchief. I accept it, but mentally refuse to use it. Keeping my control is all I have left.

Maynard squats by the chair to be at my level. "By the time you're back in the States, we'll have absolute verification and get it to you as soon as possible." His voice is soft, a lame attempt to be comforting. "We've received orders from the local commander for your return on the next flight out. I assure you, we're looking out for your best interests."

He looks at Stone, who nods in agreement.

The States? I married Harris to take me *out* of the U.S. That he already had orders to Türkiye had been a plus for me. We made plans for life as military nomads, both of us wanting to travel with no thought of settling down anywhere until we were old. There is no physical address to provide to the Air Force for shipping our belongings, and no stateside location to which we can return. They cannot force me to leave, even though my blood pressure pounds in my temples at the possibility that, as a military dependent, they very well might have that power over me.

"Look, I have no intention of going anywhere until I know what happened to Harris. I won't leave without him. I need to see him with my own eyes and claim the body—if it's him."

Stone tries next, his voice more forceful than Maynard's. "Ma'am, there's nothing more you can do here. Your plane has a scheduled departure in a few hours at Menenderes airport. You'll want to be on it."

The single grain of strength left in me expands, filling my entire body. I stand, placing the tulip tea glass on the counter before I lose control and throw it at Stone. Slinging on my backpack, I bend for my duffel, taking thirty seconds or so to gather my thoughts. I swivel to face the two Americans, my resolve suddenly shifting into a slow, angry boil.

"Gentlemen," I say, my Southern drawl accentuated by the rising tide of emotion I fight to contain. "I'm not getting on another plane. I just got off that one." I point to the cargo plan still being unloaded on the tarmac. "You've provided no proof my husband is dead, and I'm not going anywhere without Harris's body, dead or alive, classified or not."

Chaplain Stone reaches to take my hand, but I angrily pull it away. A quick flash of anger crosses his face.

"Ms. Durand, there is no choice here." Maynard's voice is like a parent speaking to a petulant child. "You are an unaccompanied spouse of military personnel on foreign soil. We are concerned about the validity of your marriage and whether you are entitled to military benefits for surviving spouses, especially considering Major Robicheaux's involvement in dubious activities."

Validity of my marriage? Wait—dubious activities?

"What horseshit. Don't you dare talk trash about my husband." I spit out my words in a furious torrent. "And I don't need your damn benefits. After he finishes," I point over my shoulder at the passport officer, "processing my passport, I'm out of here."

Papers instantly rustle behind me. I turn to watch the officer scoop the wooden stamp in one large hand and open the ink pad with the other. My stomach jumps with each thump of the stamp on my passport. A large, dark blue circle bleeds ink over the visa. He stamps the orders, then the other paperwork, page by page, my heart lurching with each one.

Thump, slam, thump, slam, thump, slam.

While my head says Harris's death might be possible, my heart refuses to believe it. Would the U.S. government fabricate lies if he weren't dead? Probably not, but the identification could be incorrect, particularly since the investigation is ongoing and there is apparently no physical body. In the States, having a body is crucial. My legal brain whirls to come up with answers.

When finished, the Turkish officer waits for the ink to dry and then gathers my papers, the passport on top. He slides the stack to me across the counter, then reaches for the cigarette smoldering in the ashtray. He sucks in, exhales to his left, and glares at Maynard.

"I am Mehmet." His gaze flicks back to me. "I am sorry for your husband. Should you need, I am at your service, *hanım efendi*." He bows slightly as he places his right palm over his heart.

"Welcome to Türkiye."

3

QUINN

Inspector Bora Karataş lets out a soft belch as he pulls out a cigarette, lowering himself into the chair in front of his *patron's* desk.

"Ms. Durand is, how do the Americans say?" he says in Turkish. "Ah, yes, a firecracker. And you owe me two hundred lira."

Chief Inspector Sedat Özbek leans back to let his second-in-command update him on Quinn Durand's entrance into the country. Both men are exhausted at three o'clock in the morning, but Sedat needs the information for the report to be on his superior's desk by seven. Hakir Demirci, Sedat's boss, is the chief of the organized crime department at Emniyet Genel Müdürlüğü, the Turkish National Police (TNP). After working for Demirci for fifteen years, Sedat knows his report cannot be late. The man takes no prisoners.

Because his assignments are project-based, he receives orders from whoever is in charge of the problem he is tasked with solving, as well as from Demirci. For nine years, he and Bora successfully navigated the political intricacies of working in various departments and agencies across Türkiye. They can be on loan to another *EGM* department or receive direct orders from MİT, the

Turkish National Intelligence Organization. Successfully dodging physical bullets and political arrows, they are almost as far as either expects to go.

This case, however, may bury them both.

Smelling strongly of tea, cigarettes, and sweat, Bora taps the end of a cigarette against his opposite palm and places it unlit in his mouth. He more than likely has been smoking nonstop since he left the *Çigli* airfield. Sedat listens as Bora continues with his report, disregarding the typical formalities insisted upon by the other higher-ups in the organization and not worrying about what his subordinate is wearing. The two men are beyond this.

"Why do I owe you two hundred lira?" Sedat asks.

"She's not what we thought or what you thought. She's not one of the casino groupies and isn't a—" Bora didn't finish the sentence.

"I will see for myself," Sedat responds, believing in only what he can see. This unwavering insistence causes issues in many areas of his life, including religion and confirmations of death. Unless he sees the person identified as dead, they are not dead. It is that simple.

"I would expect no less," Bora says, laughing while jumping up to pace the room. "And you will not believe who those idiots sent to tell her,"

"I'm sure I do not know," Sedat responds, "but you are too excited. Too many cigarettes and too much tea, I think."

"They sent Maynard and a priest. Can you imagine? *Maynard.* Why would they send *him* with the priest?" Bora sits. "I had to stop talking in broken English. The weasel knows I am fluent. He stayed quiet, a clear sign he is up to something."

Sedat grabs the receiver on his desk phone and orders them tea, more for himself than Bora. He leans forward in his chair, elbows on the desk, clasping his hands, in his classic thinking pose.

"Tell me about her," he said. "How did she react when they told her that Robicheaux was dead?"

"Just as you would expect a wife to react. She almost fainted. I had to catch her from hitting the floor, as those stupid Americans had no courtesy. When she got her feet back under her, she made it clear she didn't believe her husband was dead. Just like you, she wanted proof, but they had none. Honestly, I was surprised. She is refusing to leave until they provide more conclusive information."

Sedat tries to contain his irritation at Bora, first for comparing him to their mark and then for breaking protocol again. His friend rarely follows the rules, preferring to go along with whatever happens at the moment. Some days, Sedat wishes he could be that impulsive, but then he would not be the chief inspector. He feels obligated to chastise his friend even though it will do no good.

"You were too close to her, Bora. She was to be in and out in only a few minutes, quickly so she would not recognize you on the street if you came close later." Sedat gives Bora a stern look, but his friend ignores him, as usual. "What proof does she want?"

"His body," said Bora. "And she swears she will not leave until she gets it. And what was I to do? Her husband didn't show, and then the two idiots arrived. She was very upset." Bora looks at his feet instead of at Sedat. "And as you can expect, Maynard did not like me being there."

Sedat is surprised that Maynard did not openly identify Bora in front of the woman. With Maynard's involvement, his superior will insist that proving the woman's relationship with organized crime will be a snap. Sedat hopes so. Chasing this woman has already wasted his time.

Following Durand, in İmir, no less, is beneath him as a chief inspector based in Istanbul. The task should have been assigned to one of the rank-and-file officers in İmir's police department, not the Chief Inspector of Counterterrorism. Yet he had to be punished for his mistake.

Sedat had chased Harrison Robichaeux for the past two years, coming within less than an hour of arresting him before the man was killed. Demirci insists he pays for that mistake by doing foot soldier duty until the woman leaves the country, or is in jail. Sedat's *patron* prefers the latter.

Sedat curses under his breath, something he rarely does. This is all he needs: a grieving foreign widow who is not cooperating with her government and most likely will not cooperate with his. This is especially true when neither country is entirely sure the bits and pieces of the body found are Harrison DuPries Robicheaux. One week is not enough.

"Do you think she is involved?" Sedat asks. "Did she know Maynard?"

"Do you want the official response?" Bora looks pointedly at the telephone, then at the large print on the wall that decorates the room. Sedat watches Bora scan the room, which serves as their temporary office in İmir, before he responds.

"It was swept an hour ago, Bora." Sedat opens his drawer and pulls out a black box smaller than an iPhone. He switches it on and tosses it to Bora. "Check the room yourself."

Bora walks around the room, but the machine stays quiet. The man is Sedat's opposite, believing his feelings even when given conflicting physical evidence. Sedat cannot discard his friend's reactions as the man's "gut" had saved them more times than not.

"I don't think she has anything to do with this," Bora responds. "She left the plane excited to see her husband, and when he didn't appear, she was worried. This is not one of your hooker types, the ones Robicheaux dated before. This one is a real person and, at the moment, a bit destroyed."

"You didn't answer me." Sedat snaps. "Did she know Maynard?"

The Expedient Wife

"No." Bora shakes his head. "If she did, she hid it well. I also give her high marks for immediately picking up that Maynard is a jerk."

There is a gentle knock at the door.

Sedat softly chuckles as he waves the sleepy tea boy into the room. Once the tea is served, he stuffs ten lira into the boy's shirt pocket, ten times the cost.

"Go home, *oğlum*. Sleep well, child. I will tell Emre you will be late tomorrow." Sedat scribbles a note and hands it to the boy. "Give this to one of the men at the front desk, and someone will take you home."

Bora continues when the door is closed. "He made her angry, trying to be a friend."

"Start at the beginning and give me the details."

Sedat has no time for politeness. When he needs information, he needs it immediately. His staff and, of course, Bora are used to it. However, when he interacts with the world, his abruptness is not well-received, so he forces himself to adopt an aura of charm. He sips on his tea as Bora fills in the details and his impressions.

"I can't believe he married her right under our noses," Bora says.

"The background file on her arrives tomorrow." Sedat looks at his watch. "Well, today. She won't be anything but a simple housewife, I'm sure. Given the photos of how messy he is, Robicheaux needed a maid and a housekeeper."

Bora nods but wears a strange smirk that Sedat can't read.

"What?" Sedat asks.

His friend's face grows smug. "I will let you see for yourself how ridiculous that statement is."

"Were you able to get the apartment information into their system?" Sedat asks, ignoring Bora's jab.

"Robicheaux had already added it, I assume," Bora says. "I checked that while waiting on the plane to land. There is so little security there for a military organization. I am always surprised by how easily I can access their systems. It appears he never suspected you of anything other than being the landlord."

"Of course, he didn't. You know I do nothing halfway." Sedat looks away from Bora as he prepares to write his report. "Anything else?"

When Bora doesn't respond, Sedat looks up at his friend, who is wearing a kilometer-wide smile.

"I cannot wait for you to meet her."

4

QUINN

Outside, I stop to suck in a large breath of warm night air. Across the tarmac, a soldier leans against the hangar, and I shiver at how alone I feel. My skin feels strange, and I crave a shower, a bed, and a redo on this entire day. Insisting no taxi will come at this time of night, the Americans escort me to a dusty olive-green sedan. I peer into the darkness as we exit the airfield gates, wondering if I should tell them to turn around.

Hell no.

There is no way I can live with myself if I don't find out what happened to Harris. I'd finally summoned the courage to fall in love after being jilted at the altar years ago. I'd given up the career I'd worked so hard for, and set out on an adventure I'd dreamed of for years. Harris promised me a marriage of excitement and travel; I refuse to give up now. Harris wouldn't want me to. Denial is the first stage of grief, but if he were dead, I know I would feel it.

Maynard turns from the front seat to face me. "Ms. Durand... may I call you Quinn?"

I nod. *Who cares what he calls me?*

"Major Stone and I have your best interests at heart here. Harris was a terrific guy. He and I graduated from Loyola and joined the military together. I loved him like he was my brother."

I listen, wondering why Harris never spoke about this *brother*.

"I know you are in shock over Harris's death, but there's no need for you to stay in Türkiye. The Air Force can transfer his body back home."

I don't respond, silently staring out the window into the darkness, wishing the man would stop talking.

"Tonight, you'll be at the Kordon Hotel in the Alsancak neighborhood of İmir, the downtown area. If you don't know, the Air Force allows a two-week stay at the hotel until military personnel can find a permanent residence." He turns to face forward. "In our investigation, we learned Harris rented an apartment. Your household goods and unaccompanied baggage arrived. I'll pick you up from the hotel tomorrow, and we'll see what needs to be repacked."

Ordinarily, I would chafe at a man I've just met ordering me around like a subordinate, but right now, I don't care. Just because he gives me an order does not mean I will cooperate. I've always been a loner and a renegade. I won't stop now. However, it was a surprise that Harris rented an apartment. That was to be my responsibility since he would be working. The bigger surprise was that Harris's *things* had arrived. Everything I owned had been sold or given away. Harris assured me that's how the military rolled, and his personal things were also limited to bags he could carry. But I don't say this to Maynard. It is none of his business.

JUST BEFORE DAWN, I am awakened by a haunting Arabic voice that blasts from outside. With only a few hours of sleep, I'm confused for a moment in the dim light. With so little rest, my brain is a swirling vortex of questions. Screwing my eyes shut, I feel like I'm underwater as I put my hands over my ears, begging the call to prayer to cease. Finally, with a *click-thump* of a microphone through the loudspeaker, it stops.

When I open my eyes, the worn-out hotel room with its threadbare carpet and dusty blue curtains gives me a jolt of sorrow that cuts through the lead blanket of exhaustion. I force my feet over the side of the bed and head for the bathroom out of habit more than need, before collapsing into the single armchair.

He isn't here, and he won't be. I close my eyes again and feel his arms around me and the warmth of his lips as he trails little kisses along my shoulder. I see his face from our wedding day, the delight in his eyes as he holds me close, twirling me around in his arms after the minister had pronounced us husband and wife, *marido y mujer*. The scenes are so vivid I can smell the flowers I'm holding and feel his fingers as they grasp my face for a kiss. I open my eyes to look into his.

He isn't here.

A torrent of emotions rages upward and outward, and I grab a pillow and scream into it over and over and over until there is nothing left for me to feel other than the loss. My new life is crumbling around me. Violent hiccups begin as the sobs stop. Removing the tear-soaked pillow from my face, I wipe my eyes and flop back on the bed, unsure of what to do. Harris cannot be dead. I would have felt something if he'd been killed. Some other poor woman lost her husband, not me. Yes, he has irritating traits, such as always being late and leaving his clothes on the floor. But those things aren't important. Harris loves me. I know that with every ounce of my soul. He would never leave me like this.

I force myself to stand. Another look around the shabby hotel room, and I want to climb back into bed and pull the covers over me. But I'm not in Georgia, safe and sound. I'm in Türkiye. And my husband is missing. The only way I can find the apartment is through Maynard, but I hate feeling so helpless and dependent on others.

Stone's allegations from the night before about my marriage taunt me. If I return to the States, I will be shut out of the investigation and become the poor, grieving widow with a host of unanswered questions. If I stay, I will be the thorn in the military's side, more likely to get attention and answers. I climb back in bed and close my eyes. Visions of the balcony where we stood on our wedding day, with the azure sea just beyond the rail and the crashing waves below, play in my mind. It was the most romantic wedding a couple could imagine.

As the bedside clock flips to six a.m., my memories shift. I had been in love once before. Our wedding day was the weekend after I graduated with honors from college. I had always strived to be the perfect daughter for my parents, even though my mother never exhibited one ounce of pride in me. My hair was in a romantic updo, adorned with flowers and beaded hairpins. My face looked like something from a magazine. And my dress—I was wearing the wedding dress that every woman dreams of, with mounds of lace, a long train, and a veil to match.

With my veil affixed, I rose at the knock on the dressing room door, knowing it was my mother, the person walking me down the aisle in place of my father, who died when I was fourteen. But it wasn't.

Standing alone in the hallway was my fiancé, in jeans, boots, and a ratty t-shirt rather than the custom tuxedo we had purchased for him together two weeks prior. He smelled like a distillery, his hair unwashed, eyes bloodshot. I couldn't speak. The realization of what was happening hit me like a collapsing wall of bricks.

"Quinn, I'm sorry. I can't do this," he said.

"Why?" At least he had the decency to tell me to my face, rather than just doing a cut and run, or God forbid, by text.

"My parents..."

"Ah. We're back to the part where I'm not good enough for you." *And you, the chicken shit that you are, couldn't tell me until now?*

"Well, it's more than that. I've been seeing someone..." His eyes could not meet mine.

"Who? For how long?"

"She'll fit better, Quinn. I don't want you to have to face my parents every Sunday and deal with their attitude. I can't fix that. And my father has set me up to take over his business. We won't be able to avoid them."

"Who is it?"

"Quinn..." I already knew. It was the girl he'd dated in high school, whose father owned most of the town where he'd grown up, the small-minded girl whom his mother had always wanted him to marry.

"You never loved me?" I didn't want him to say it to my face, but I had to know.

"Quinn...I..." He looked at his boots rather than at my face, and it told me everything I needed to know. No, he didn't love me, probably hadn't, but didn't have the guts to say it to me until now. I was the substitute.

Since then, I'd kept myself at arm's length or further, never letting myself open for the pain I knew would come, even with the constant pushing by Trudy, my best friend in law school. I dated while in Atlanta, but never found anyone I felt confident wouldn't hurt me again.

Then my mother's cancer returned, and I moved home to South Georgia. The men in Glensboro were hunters, fishermen, or farmers. The only single professional was a CPA who bored me more than watching paint dry. Charleston, where Trudy lived, and its possibility of reasonably intelligent men were hours away, and Atlanta was even further.

The local bar's term for me was "frigid." Part of that was because of their egos. Even though I had a general practice that covered everything from divorces to real estate, I repeatedly won in the courtroom against them, and they didn't like it one bit. As a result, I was branded a renegade. Yet always being alone, both personally and professionally, got old, and when my mother died, I'd had enough.

The phone on the desk rings. The bedside clock shows it is ten minutes before eight. I ignore it, but it does not stop, and I finally get up and answer it.

"Durand."

"Hello, Quinn." It is Maynard. His voice is too friendly for such an early morning, especially without coffee. "I located your apartment and will pick you up in about half an hour. Is that enough time?"

Damn. He beat me to it. I shouldn't have gone back to bed. I agree to the retrieval time and location, and cut the call.

Until the body is ready for transport, I can stay in Türkiye, but I don't know how long that will be. A week, maybe. My legs start to crumple under me again. I don't know what's wrong with me. I stood firm through being jilted at the altar and through both of my parents' deaths. This isn't like me.

I make my shower as cold as I can stand. When I've had enough, I get dressed. Maybe if I keep moving, my brain will stop its relentless chatter. And my soul will stop aching. But I know neither will happen. My mind is chastising me for relying too much on Harris to save me and not relying on myself.

Putting on makeup to hide the dark circles under my eyes, my thoughts go back to Trudy and her constant push toward Harris. If she and her cousin had not pushed me to date Harris in the first place, I wouldn't be here. But I cannot push this off on her. I'm the one who married him.

This is a disaster. I'm clearly not meant to have people close to me. They either leave me—or they die.

5
QUINN

Breathing in the sea air slowly and deeply, I regain control. Regardless of what this man expects, I will do whatever it takes to discover what happened to my husband. He pulls away from the curb, heading along the seaside.

"How was your room at the Kordon?" Maynard asks. "I admit it's not the best place, but it's what the military provides here." I'm instantly thrown back into the South, with his folksy, sycophantic small talk, as if we had not met the night before over my husband's death. His eerie resemblance to Harris strikes me again.

"One night at the Kordon Hotel is enough if you ask me," he continues, oblivious to my staring and far too wrapped up in the sound of his own voice to notice my thinly veiled disdain. "It's bad enough to come overseas to Türkiye for a PCS, but when they dump those poor little enlisted wives in that ratty hotel and make their husbands go straight to work, it's just not right, you know?"

No, I don't know. Harris explained to me on the day he received his transfer orders that there was no base in İmir. All military lives "on the economy," meaning apartment living scattered across various neighborhoods. He would go to work in a standard office building, and the PX, the military department store, and the commissary, the grocery store, were also in regular storefronts in the city. I would need to learn Turkish quickly, he said, and suggested several apps where I could practice and also find an online tutor.

"PCS?" I ask.

"Oh, sorry. Permanent Change of Station." He stares at my backpack. "Where are your things? Your bags?"

In truth, I had forgotten, but I couldn't tell him that. He already considers me a useless object that must be shepherded and sent back to the States.

"I wanted to see the apartment before lugging everything there," I mumble quietly. He nods, my answer satisfactory, as he returns his attention to the traffic.

"We can get them later," he says. "You might be right. With Harris, no telling what to expect." He chuckles as he hands me several pieces of paper. "I stopped at the FLO office and grabbed the info they had."

"FLO?" I ask. It seems this man's entire vocabulary consists of acronyms.

"Family Liaison Office," he says. "They help military members with the logistics of a move. The apartment address is in there. Can you look for me?"

"You said his furniture has arrived?" I ask as I unfold the pages.

"That is what I was told," he says. "It's either listed on the paperwork, or we will find out when we get to the apartment."

I scan the first page and see a Turkish address at the top, under a heading for "Current Address."

"Please translate this address," I say. "I can't figure out the Turkish." I show it to Maynard, who looks at it quickly, then back to the rush hour traffic, intermittently lurching forward.

At a red light, Maynard points to the first words on the address line. "This is the name of the street." He points to more names. "Next is the name of the apartment, see? The first number is the building number, and the second, after the slash, is your apartment number."

The traffic light turns green, and every car around us beeps its horn, and I twist around in an attempt to see why.

"Ignore the beeps. It's how they talk when in cars. The traffic lights sit too far back from the intersection. The first few cars can't see it, so the others honk when it turns green." He grins, then nods at the paper. "I know where this street is. We're not far away."

It all sounds so logical. I scan the rest of the first page and flip to the next. Under the "next of kin" contact, I search for my name. It isn't there. I flip to the next page.

"Why am I not listed as his primary contact?" I ask out loud, reflexively. "And who are all these women?" I scan further and see the names of his parents next to a Nashville address. It should say, New Orleans. These pages are like a junk pile of errors. I go back to the page and re-read the names.

"Wait until we stop, and I'll look." Maynard shakes his head, but his neck is a rosy shade of pink. I squint at him, trying to figure out what he's hiding, then continue to read, flipping quickly through former addresses and what I assume are assignments.

Several miles through heavy traffic, Maynard turns down a steep hill into a neighborhood of apartment buildings stacked like dominoes down the hillside. He stops the car in front of a modest four-story building.

"Here, let me see." He reaches for the papers, and I hand them to him. Suddenly, his face is now bright red.

"What's wrong?" I'm not sure I can take much more in a twenty-four-hour period.

"Harris didn't tell you he'd been married before?"

"No. Girlfriends, many. Marriages, none."

"I don't know how to tell you this, but he's been married

several times. The women on this page—" he points to four names in a row—"are his ex-wives. See the designation here?"

I snatch the page from his hand and stare at the names, feeling the blood drain from my face. "Wives, plural? There are *four* of them?" I blink, then stare at him as if he's grown two heads. I look back at the page, unable to keep from shouting. "What the—I'm wife number what? Five? These are his *wives*?" I go back through each page. "Wait. I'm not listed here at all."

I glare at Maynard, who has the decency to look chagrined.

"Now you understand why Major Stone says your marriage was in question," he said sheepishly. "While I knew you existed because Harris told me, I didn't know your last name or anything about you until we tracked you down from the orders listed with the base in Charleston."

He takes the paper from my shaking hand and puts his palm over mine. "Two shocks in one day," he said, attempting a consoling tone.

"No shit," I mumble, removing my hand. I look at the apartment building, then back at him. "What else am I about to discover in there?"

He shrugs. "I knew Harris well. There are stories behind these other women that are unlike yours, but yes, they were still his wives. But you know what? That's history. Let's get into the apartment and at least get you moving toward home and the future."

Here we go, the anticipated shove back to the States. He returns the papers, and I fold them, biting the inside of my cheeks with my teeth as I stuff them into my backpack. We get out of the car, and I take deep, calming breaths to steady myself, but they are not helpful. Harris's alleged death and his four previous wives, all in the space of a single day, is just too much.

Maynard steps to the front door of the building and scrutinizes the names on the door plates, then pushes a buzzer. A woman's voice answers loudly in Turkish, and after a short discussion, he returns to me.

"There's no spare key," Maynard says.

"You didn't get a key?"

"No." He shakes his head. "Harris probably had his set, and your set is most likely inside the apartment. I arranged for the landlord to meet us."

I hear Harris's ex-wives laughing at me from my backpack, and a shudder runs through me. I thought I knew my husband, but it's very clear that I don't, and Maynard's inadequate explanation doesn't help. I am mortified and angry, and my inner critic begins to rant mercilessly. *Why did you even get married? You knew something like this would happen.*

I was tired of being alone, tired of my job, and tired of never being able to live freely, given the small-town rules. I always followed those rules at the beginning, trying to be the upstanding attorney, a "somebody" in my hometown, and someone my mother would be proud of. But I hated my job. Practicing law in a small town is like herding sheep. When people fight, especially over minor issues, they often lose all perspective.

Because of my Asian grandmother, my father's mother, I have been considered an outcast my entire life. In a southern state, even a diverse one like Georgia, I was called "Slanty Eyes" and tormented regularly. Even graduating third in my law school class, I was shunned by many large law firms because of my heritage. And then there was the gossip, of which my mother was the queen. It grew worse every year, and fleeing to visit Trudy in Charleston became a routine weekend activity.

I shift uneasily as Maynard sits on the entry stairs to the building and motions for me to sit next to him. My leg bounces impatiently as I twist a curl of hair with my fingers, vowing to go through every blasted acronym on those pages—even though I am terrified of what I might find.

6

SEDAT

Sedat and Bora sit in companionable silence. As they wait, their spotter confirms by radio that the target spent the remainder of the night at the Kordon Hotel and was just retrieved by a man in a military vehicle. Sedat's Turkish employee at the American vehicle depot routinely installed trackers in the U.S. vehicles once the Robicheaux investigation focused on İmir. The men listen to the Americans' conversation, watching as the olive-colored sedan pulls into a parking space uphill from the apartment Sedat had rented to Harrison Robicheaux. Conveniently downhill, Sedat's unmarked car is parked under a plane tree, hidden behind a rectangular garbage container.

"We need to talk about Bülent," Bora says, looking at Sedat.

As usual, Bora refuses to focus on the task at hand, and Sedat's entire body tenses at the statement. He mentally recites the Turkish numbers from one to ten to prevent himself from saying something he might regret.

"We will not discuss my father," Sedat responds. "I stay away from any investigation of him and his businesses at Demirci's insistence. My father has been a petty smuggler for as long as I can remember. It does not matter this time whether it is counterfeit cigarettes, untaxed liquor, or whatever else it might be."Sedat flicks his hand toward the olive-colored sedan. "Keep your mind on our current target."

As usual, Bora gives a loud *huff*, raising binoculars to his face even though they are close enough to see the Americans without them.

"You're such a grouch lately," Bora replies. "I will be happy when we are done with this woman."

For almost a decade, Sedat has never told Bora the truth about his father. Bulent Özbek is a petty criminal who aspires to be the "big man" of his mountain village. Sedat's hometown sits north of Istanbul, five kilometers from the Bulgarian border. His father is an elder and respected leader, although that respect comes from fear rather than admiration. In truth, his father is a nobody.

When Sedat was a child, he and his mother were beaten regularly, whether for sport after a night of drinking or for a perceived slight over dinner, his mother's clothing, or how the house was kept. Bora views his family as the most important thing in life, and Sedat understands this. With a loving wife and three beautiful girls, Bora's life is chaotic yet idyllic, mirroring the halcyon days of his friend's own childhood with his nurturing parents. Sedat's upbringing and subsequent relationships were the complete antithesis of each other. Sedat's youth had been anything but sheltered and naïve, and he knows, without question, that Bora would never understand. Sometimes, he did not even know how he had reached this point in life without landing in prison. Had he not scored the highest on the police academy exam, he would not be.

Sedat looks toward the car and then up to the third floor of the apartment building. As the landlord, he has his own set of keys. The day before, after the confirmation of Robicheaux's death, he had authorized a full search of the apartment, instructing his staff to leave things as they found them. Unfortunately, the team found nothing Sedat could use in his investigation. What Robicheaux had obtained from the card game in Russia had either been burned in the crash or sent to his wife, his new target.

Since Sedat's mother had not used the apartment across the street for years, arranging the rental had been easy. When their surveillance revealed Robicheaux was looking for a two-year residence several weeks ago, Sedat paid a Turkish worker at the U.S. military housing office enough to ensure this location was the only choice available when the major asked for the list of military-approved apartments. He put the lease in his mother's maiden name, Gökçe, and used the same surname when introducing himself to the unsuspecting Robicheaux. He would do the same today to the man's wife.

Sedat feels a bump on his upper arm. Bora extends the binoculars.

"Take a look. I don't want you to be surprised and screw the investigation when you meet her because your poker face is so deplorable. You are so sure of what she is, and this time you're mistaken."

"Was I ever a problem in an investigation?" Sedat asks. "That is you, not me. Unlike you, we are lucky that Maynard has never seen my face."

Bora shoves the binoculars at him. "Just look."

Sedat takes the binoculars and adjusts the focus as he watches the tall, blond man skirt the front of the vehicle to open the passenger-side door for an attractive woman. He had bet Bora two hundred liras that the woman would be either a casino whore or another U.S. agent, Robicheaux's typical choices. Still, Bora had insisted in the middle of the night that she appeared to be neither.

Playing the role of her new landlord, he is ready to make his own assessment. Robicheaux's reputation was that of an international thief who had never been caught, and Sedat is curious about the woman this man had married. When the U.S. Air Force assigned Robicheaux to Türkiye, because of his persistent association with unsavory figures, he had become Sedat's problem. With the thief's death, he is now saddled with his wife.

Sedat argued with the Chief over his involvement, insisting that Robicheaux was only a glorified petty thief, not a member of any mob, and not part of any organization they were currently attempting to dismantle. With pressure being applied from above, Demirci insisted that Sedat be certain. Demirci's boss believed Quinn Durand worked closely with her husband, leaving Sedat no choice but to act accordingly.

If Sedat is lucky, things will fall into place easily. If she has what he needs, she will be deported or jailed by Sunday, and the information Demirci demands will be on the man's desk first thing Monday. Sedat intends to be on his sailboat *Özgürlük*—"Freedom"—headed toward a long-needed vacation in the Aegean by Monday afternoon.

Bora and Sedat watch as Maynard buzzes the intercom at the front door. Away from the vehicle, there is no sound, and Sedat watches their mechanical movements in silence. The woman's face shows disappointment as the pair makes themselves comfortable on the steps of the apartment building.

"It is time," Bora says, reaching for the binoculars. "What do you think?"

"She is attractive, but that is irrelevant. The woman can still be an idiot. This tells me nothing."

"I promise you, she isn't," Bora snorts. "Once you meet her, you will understand. Maybe you could pick up on these things more quickly if you had a more active social life."

"Do not belittle my personal life." Sedat adjusts the binocular vision and studies the woman. Long, black hair spills over the shoulders of an athletic body graced with ample curves. He scrutinizes the purple half-moons under her eyes on a makeup-free face. In that respect, Bora is correct. She appears, at least superficially, to be grieving.

"Aren't you going?" Bora points toward the apartment building.

"Let's see what they are saying first. Grab the directional wand from the back seat."

7

QUINN

Sitting on the front steps of the apartment building, Maynard and I wait for the landlord. It appears to be an ordinary middle-class neighborhood in a large city. A taxi stand is at the bottom of the hill. Unoccupied drivers lounge around a backgammon table, cigarettes in every hand. A small market sits up the hill, and a park is across the street. Trees shade rambunctious children, their unbridled peals of laughter and the heavy clangs of playground equipment drown out the muffler of an occasional vehicle.

I break the silence. "Captain, you don't think he's dead?"

"It's Ted." Maynard's head whips around so he's facing me. "I promise you, Harris and I are old friends. We can drop the formalities." He squints at me, confused, and asks. "What do you mean? Of course, he's dead. We got the report."

"You just told me that Harris *has* the keys. Not had. Has."

"I misspoke, Quinn. Believe me, Harris is dead."

Yet they only had a "report," not a body. He will not be dead to me until I see him with my own eyes. Right now, however, I want to get inside the apartment to be "home" for a few hours, in the place Harris picked for us, surrounded by his things to ground me. A lump of pain rises in my chest, and I fight it.

Nope, no tears. I mentally picture four beautiful women, sirens conjured by my mind from merely a handful of names on the contact list, laughing at me in a group photo. The growing ache in my heart threatens to rise further still as I recall Harris's betrayal, but it is cured in place by the white-hot heat of humiliation. It does the trick to stop my tears.

A tall, athletic man in a business suit turns the corner and strides up the hill towards us. He does not look much older than me, about forty-five, and has a fashionable two-day beard. His straight hair is the color of dark chocolate and touches his shoulders. He appears to be of French or Italian descent, and his stiff demeanor and exotic features exude competence. He stops in front of me and smiles with formal politeness.

"Mrs. Robicheaux?" The man bows slightly, placing his hand over his heart. "I am Sedat Gökçe."

"Quinn Durand." I stand. "Harris Robicheaux's wife." I extend a hand.

"*Hoş geldiniz,*" he says politely as he takes my hand. "Welcome to Türkiye."

"*Hoş bulduk,*" I say, giving him the appropriate response learned from my language apps. The man's eyes squint at me carefully before his face relaxes, and he smiles. I think he is surprised I have learned some of his language.

"Ah, yes. Ms. Durand. Please call me Sedat. Follow me. I will open the door for you to see into the apartment. Excuse me. For you to go into the apartment." He addresses Maynard, then me. "My English is not good. I am sorry."

I return the smile. "No, your English is fine."

As I follow his broad back up the steps and into the building, it is the first time I feel—no, the second time, after the passport officer—momentarily comforted in this horrible situation. Why? I don't know. Maybe it is his chivalry or impeccable manners, the opposite of Maynard's. We ride the elevator, and I hear people talking on the stairs, the Turkish words fading as the elevator rises. After religiously working on my Turkish for hours each day with a tutor, I'm pleasantly surprised to find that I understand the basics of what I'm hearing.

At the front door to the apartment, I watch as Sedat repeatedly turns a long silver key, each level of the lock clicking loudly in the marble hallway. After the sixth or seventh turn, the door opens slightly with a final click. Extending his hand for me to go first, I enter a small foyer. A door to the kitchen is directly in front of me, the living room is to the right, and a hallway is on my left. As the landlord enters the apartment, he promptly removes his shoes and places them neatly against one wall. I remove mine, but Maynard ignores us and strides into the living room in his combat boots.

Two walls of windows and a balcony wrap around the left corner of the living room. I am drawn to the balcony, and I stand outside with Maynard at the railing. I gaze at the sprawling view of the entire city surrounding the bay like a horseshoe. Ferries crisscross the water, and seagulls fly at eye level in groups of threes and fours as the water sparkles in the sunlight. This apartment couldn't be more perfect, and I'm forced again to stop the tears.

A twang of pain runs through my chest as I think of Harris and me living here together. I want Maynard and Sedat to leave. Emotions clamor to get out, and I must deal with them alone. I step back inside. Sedat clears his throat, and I turn to face him.

He fidgets. "If you will excuse me, please, I must go to—ah—for making your key to the door. Your husband received the key; I did not make another before coming here. Will you stay, please, until I finish this? Then we must discuss the lock."

"Yes, I will be here. Thank you so much for your help." I do not understand what is so different about this lock that it warrants a serious discussion, but it is his apartment, and I need a key. I turn to Maynard. "I will call you from the hotel when I return to get my things or with questions," I say, trying to squelch my dismissive tone but not succeeding.

"Quinn, let me stay and help you pack all this," Maynard responds. His voice reminds me of a petulant five-year-old. "There may be things that involve the military that you won't know how to handle." He thrusts his arm toward the boxes stacked haphazardly around the room, most of them already opened and some unpacked. "This is chaos. You've already been through a lot today, and I know Harris would want me to help you." He steps closer to me, invading my bubble of space.

"No, I'm fine." I take a step back. "Right now, I need…" I close my eyes and breathe, unable to say anything. Maynard grabs my hand and gives it a light squeeze. I open my eyes to find his face in front of mine, and I jerk backward.

"I understand," he whispers, ignoring my obvious discomfort at his sudden proximity. "I'll check back later this evening and let you know if there is anything new about the accident."

He gives me a polite smile and turns to leave. I close the door behind him, seeing that he has kicked my shoes from where I placed them by the living room door. I collapse onto the living room couch, wrapping myself in a familiar sweater that smells of Harris's cologne, and let out the sobs. I am alone again.

This will be the third time I've lost someone I love to death. An aggressive cancer ravaged my father's body quickly and snatched him from me when I was just a child. I had thought nothing could be worse, but little did I know that years later I would live through my mother's prolonged, agonizing decline, and her final surrender to an illness that took her two years ago. And now Harris's death, and its ambiguity, prevent me from entering the grieving process.

For me, Türkiye may as well be no man's land. The Universe has decided that I am entitled to only brief periods of happiness followed by death.

I drag a dining room chair to the balcony and sit for a long time, trying to let my heart and mind rest. My stomach rumbles, telling me my body needs food, but I'm sure that whatever I eat will only come back up. I head to the bathroom and splash cold water on my face. On autopilot, I grab my backpack and head for the door. I must retrieve my things from the hotel before I collapse. As I open the door, I stop. I have no key and no idea when the landlord will return. As I begin closing the door, a hand curls around it and shoves it open toward me.

Maynard is standing there, carrying my duffel bag from the hotel, a smirk on his face.

"What are you doing? Why are you carrying my bag?" I ask. "And why did the hotel let you take it?"

He steps toward me, again, too close for comfort. I am forced to look up because of his height and proximity. I'm not a small woman at five feet seven, and I won't give in to his power play. I am sure that whatever he wants will not be in my best interest because I can feel it. I snatch my duffel and toss it down the hallway, continuing to block the door.

"What do you want, Captain Maynard?"

"It's Ted, remember?" He grabs my arm to stop me from slamming the door in his face and shoves his way around me, his smile wide and plastic. "I thought we were friends."

He isn't my friend, and I doubt he was Harris's, either. When I don't respond, he starts talking again. "We should discuss some things about Harris, including your alleged marriage."

Alleged. Here we go. I point to the living room, and we sit.

"How well did you know Harris before you married him?" he asks.

So much for being Harris's best friend; otherwise, he would know everything about me.

"How is that any of your business?" I rub my temples and wish for a cold drink of water.

"What do you know about his position with the military?"

I give him a bored look and don't respond, waiting for him to explain why he is here. I glance at my watch and then look back at him, my eyebrows raised for the next question.

"Quinn, are you aware that Harris was about to be brought up on charges?"

A chill crawls up my back. "For what?" Instantly, I feel my body shift into professional mode. I will gather as much information as possible, but I will neither admit nor deny anything.

"Theft of government assets and military secrets." The answer rolls out casually as if it's not a big deal. This man has just accused my husband of treason, punishable by death.

A mental war begins within me, whether to protect myself or push him for information. If his assertion is true, I need a lawyer immediately. Specifically, I need a criminal defense lawyer with experience in white-collar crime and additional expertise in military law. Although I worked in a courtroom for ten years, I handled civil cases, not criminal ones. The handful of criminal cases in my first years of practice did not prepare me for this. It isn't like riding a bike. I'm not just rusty. In criminal matters, I am unqualified.

Yet, the accusations against Harris are not the point. You can't charge a dead man. Maynard must believe I am involved in whatever Harris has done and intends to threaten me. I can feel it. My beleaguered brain reminds me to keep my mouth closed as a possible "person of interest."

"I don't know what you're talking about." He needs to be a mushroom, in the dark and only fed crap. Besides, I've been with Harris every day for months. We just got married, and we were inseparable until he left for Türkiye. I don't see how he could have done anything within the last two months without me knowing about it.

Yet Maynard's smile would make the Cheshire Cat proud. He leans back in his chair, balancing it on two legs. Who is this man, really? And how does he know of possible charges against Harris?

"I can't believe you're innocent in all this. You were married to him. Or was your marriage fake?" His smile fades as he shifts forward in his seat. "The JAG office says he was involved in a criminal escalation of activities over the past six months. The Department of Defense contacted the JAG corps because the exact time of the last incident coincides with your..." he pauses and leans further forward with a sick grin on his face. "...wedding day."

An incident on my wedding day. The looming migraine I've managed to keep at bay threatens to crash into the center of my brain like a tidal wave.

"Cut to the chase and stop insinuating." I resist the urge to rub my thumbs over my temples.

"I'm not insinuating anything. You were, and still are, part of Harris's operation. His partner."

Me? I've never even received a parking ticket. I need to maintain control even though he is accusing me of being an accessory, a criminal.

To treason.

Punishable by death.

"I don't believe you," I say. "Prove it."

8

QUINN

Maynard leans toward me again, his voice soft but urgent.

"Look, Quinn. They are accusing Harris of stealing military secrets. I'm trying to protect you here. The exact words of the guy I talked to? 'Harrison Robicheaux is a thief, a liar of the highest order, and most definitely a traitor.'"

I refuse to believe it. The Harris I know is none of these things, yet I'm hit with an instant sting of betrayal when I remember the four wives of whom I had been blissfully unaware. My blood pressure pounds like a jackhammer in my head. I stare at the damaged corner of the ugly gilt coffee table, trying to process what's happening.

"On a related note," Maynard waits for me to look at him, "the Turkish Council of Forensic Medicine conclusively identified Harris's remains. They were called to help when the U.S. military examiners couldn't arrive from Germany."

Maynard pulls several photos from his cargo pants pocket and lays them gingerly on the table. The color photos show a blackened body on a morgue table, dental records, and several blackened teeth.

He taps an index finger on the corner of a photo. "You wanted conclusive proof of death. The dental records match."

An invisible baseball bat slugs me in the stomach. Even though Stone had been clear that Harris was dead, I hadn't wanted to listen then, and I don't want to hear it now. My hopes and dreams for the future were pinned on Harris, and for the entire day, I trusted my intuition that he was still alive.

But Harris is dead. And if I am to believe Maynard, a traitor.

"And your proof that he is a traitor? Or a thief?"

I look at the black, charred mass in the photos. My stomach lurches, but I'm able to suppress the nausea. I've seen the same type of photos in case files of electrocution accidents. Maynard's voice is filled with fake concern, his words enunciated carefully.

"Quinn, with Harris dead, the JAG insists that the DOD's search must shift."

To me. He doesn't say the words aloud, but the insinuation is clear. Ted Maynard, the Department of Defense, and maybe the entire U.S. military believe I am an accomplice. *Damn it, Harris, what in God's name were you involved in that could incriminate me?*

"Look, Quinn, not only are these serious charges, but there's missing classified information that Harris has. The DOD wants it back. Finding it for them is the only way you'll get through this."

Ah, finally, the point. He thinks I have something, and whatever it is, he wants it. I sit back in the chair. My mind is whirling, and fear is preventing me from thinking clearly. I breathe slowly and force myself to consider all the possibilities.

Has. Again, he's using the present tense as if Harris is still alive. My heart skips a beat.

"What is this missing information?"

Maynard leans into the couch, his arms resting along its back as he crosses one leg over the other. He thinks he's in charge now, and I will roll over in any minute. Despite my frayed nerves from the seriousness of his allegations, I bite the inside of my cheek to keep from laughing. The internal chuckle allows my brain to finally shift into gear.

"A disk. A file or a spreadsheet that makes no sense to you. A letter with codes you don't understand. They will detain you if you don't provide it by the end of the week."

"Detain me? How?" I ask.

"If you're lucky, it will be house arrest. Otherwise, they will take you to the base at Incirlik and lock you in a cell or let the Turks hold you in a cell in Diyarbakır jail. That's a nasty place. Don't let it get that far. You don't want to see the inside of a Turkish prison, trust me."

He pauses, thinking that I'm that stupid. Diyarbakır Prison was closed and converted into a museum. I'll go through every box in the apartment and find these documents—or whatever—if they are here. But I won't give him anything. I don't trust him.

"You need to find the documents by next Monday. That's when they expect Harris's body to be released, or the remains of it anyway."

Five and a half days to find a tiny needle in a country-sized haystack. Knowing how much Harris traveled, the haystack could be the entire world.

"And what does this information relate to?"

"That's classified and a matter of national security." His voice is condescending. "It's even above my pay grade. But they showed me this." From his other pants pocket, he pulls several pages and unfolds them.

"This is the federal indictment against Harris. He used military funds for high-stakes gambling, which, as you know, is theft of property of the United States military, along with conversion. Then there are allegations of conspiracy with Russian actors, illegal due to the war in Ukraine. There will be more when a federal prosecutor finishes the indictment."

Maynard is well prepared and uses effective lawyer-speak, but it still doesn't ring true. If I am a traitor, in league with my dead husband and hiding military secrets, someone from the U.S. government or military would have already detained me immediately at the airport or maybe even before I left Charleston.

I scan the illegible signature on the last page. It hovers over the typed name of a Washington, D.C., federal prosecutor, not a military one. I scan the document for anything that could tie the accusations to me. There is nothing yet, and that is not the point. If Harris can hide four ex-wives from me and pass off what I now suspect is a fraudulent passport without so much as a blink, there could be anything lurking in the prosecutor's files.

Am I a traitor? No, but I understand all too well that "innocent until proven guilty" is applied at the discretion of the powers that be, and in this case, those powers are high-ranking military officials. If they think they have something to pin on me, I know I'm in for one hell of a fight to prove otherwise. I've seen too many clients in this position. My reputation is all I have, and it will be ruined. Whoever selected Maynard to scare me had chosen wisely. I am terrified.

But I am innocent. And at this point, I'm angry as hell.

9

SEDAT

Sedat adjusts in his car seat, carefully listening through the earbuds as the woman in the apartment sobs. He sits woodenly so as not to show his subordinate how the sound affects him. Bora, as usual, is oblivious. The man talks rather than listens, an irritating habit that Sedat cannot get Bora to break.

"How did your meeting go?" Bora asks, pulling out one earbud and picking up a soft drink can from the holder.

Sedat puts an index finger to his lips and points to the receiver resting on the dashboard, but that does nothing to stop the man's chatter. One day, he will tape Bora's mouth and force him to stay that way until the man can remain quiet.

Meeting Quinn Durand was unsettling. Even in the face of what is genuine grief, her defiant independence surprises him. Yet her influence over him is more than that, even though he cannot identify what is bothering him. He has no idea how to act around Quinn. He wonders if his basic English and bumbling professor persona were too, as the Americans say, "over the top." When he returns with the keys, he must pay closer attention.

Sedat has had limited relationships with women, only his

suffocating mother and his clingy sisters, who look to him for everything. He doesn't know how to read any woman outside his family, especially an independent one. At the police academy, Sedat stopped dating to focus on work. Later, his undercover assignments prevented him from forming any serious relationships. While Bora and the rest of his team believe he has relationships occasionally, he doesn't. He does dinners, vacations, and concerts alone. He has several female friends who accompany him from time to time when he is unable to attend an event alone. Confiding in Bora ensures he will talk to others in his department, and Sedat refuses to allow his personal life to be the topic of office gossip.

"Maynard is back. Something is wrong." Sedat motions for Bora to stop talking. "He just told Quinn that her husband was to be charged."

Bora grabs his dangling earbud and stuffs it in his ear. "That man is such a blatant liar. Who knows if what he's telling her is even true?" He looks at Sedat as he talks over Maynard's voice. "Where did you hide the microphone? It is working very well."

Sedat waits for another lull in the conversation. He will explode if the man does not stop talking.

"I dropped it inside one of the small pockets of her backpack when she was on the balcony." He glares at Bora. "*Saçmalama.* Shut up, Bora, and listen."

Bora squints as he concentrates on the conversation, looking out the windshield as if he can physically see the two people talking inside the building. Their technology is mid-level, and the reception is good even ten blocks away.

"He is laying it on…" At Sedat's angry look, Bora stops mid-sentence and points to the receiver.

"Possibly," Sedat says. "He intends to frighten her, but is pushing too hard. She has only just arrived. He should use more finesse with this woman."

Bora lets out a bark of laughter as he points to Sedat. "So it went well, then. I told you she pushes back. You liked her, didn't you?"

Sedat looks away, refusing to give in to the man's taunts. He wants Bora to be silent so he can concentrate. He must hear Quinn's voice to catch her reaction to Maynard's lies. He wishes he could be in the apartment with her, slap Maynard, and stop this needless manipulation.

"Will she believe all this garbage?" Bora asks.

"And being with the woman for less than thirty minutes will tell me this?" Sedat lets out an exasperated huff. "I do not know."

He reaches for the door handle before catching himself.

"Maynard's behavior is unnecessary," Bora says, "but if we intervene, it will destroy any chance of us getting close to Quinn. You know this better than I."

Sedat leans back in his seat and listens to things he cannot see but only imagines. He looks at Bora. "I believe we are the only ones," he says, "who knew exactly what Robicheaux was up to and Maynard's possible involvement. But it is only because we put two years into this damned investigation. I am ready for it to be over."

They listen as Quinn shifts closer to her backpack.

"Maynard has to create a scenario serious enough to scare an intelligent lawyer, I think," Bora says, "to get her to either make a mistake or give him what he wants. What I find interesting," he continues, "is that Maynard has no idea if Robicheaux's wife is truly involved."

"Robicheaux must have stopped confiding in Maynard for him to need to push her like this," Sedat replies. "But, if he obtains the information we need from her, it will make our job easier. If he bungles it, the job still should be easier, as she will need someone to turn to."

Bora turns to him, pointing to the receiver, one eyebrow raised. "I think he just bungled it."

An intelligent woman will not yield to threats. Sedat knows

he must tread carefully to have any hope of gaining her trust; to befriend her disingenuously would require quite the duplicitous dance. He wants to be upfront with her, question her, and then put her under surveillance, but the chief has vetoed any initial interrogation or confrontation. His boss wants them out of sight, behind the scenes. Sedat hates games like this.

"We should be ready for the next step," he says.

Bora points to the large food basket in the car's rear seat. "I'm ready when you are."

Sedat removes the earbuds, stuffing them in his coat pocket, and reaches for the door handle.

"Good. Deliver it tonight." He hands Bora a folded card. "Put this note with it, where I invite her to dinner, and let me know what else you hear. I will meet you at the office after I deliver the keys. There is no need for you to wait for me."

10

QUINN

A strange chirping noise startles me. I'm so tired, and I've lost track of time. The chirp erupts again, along with harsh rapping on the heavy steel door. I struggle to my feet and look through the peephole. Sedat is checking his watch, a frown on his face. I pull my dirty hair back into a ponytail, then open the door.

His eyes are brown, almost black. Behind thick, black-framed glasses, his dark eyes take me in slowly, lingering on my wrinkled T-shirt, grubby jeans, and puffy eyes and face. I'm struck with the contrasting memory of Harris's cobalt eyes, and a wave of devastation washes over me. I turn my back on my landlord, even though it's rude. I'm about to lose it again, and I use my fingers to pull at the corners of my eyes and stop the tears.

Embarrassed by my emotions, I straighten my clothing. I am in my own home, having just received confirmation of my husband's death and allegations that he was a traitor. I can look any damn way I want. I turn around, and Sedat is still standing at the front door, waiting for me to invite him in with an expression of curiosity and concern.

"May I come in?" A pronounced Turkish accent marks his

British speech pattern. He has changed his clothes and is wearing a lightweight jacket, a white dress shirt, navy slacks, and leather shoes. He exudes a quiet efficiency, a calmness that relaxes me, the same reaction I had earlier.

"Certainly."

Entering the apartment, he again removes his shoes, this time revealing bright yellow socks patterned with blue sailboats. When I cannot hide a smile, he clears his throat to get to business. I try to block the living room with my body because it looks like a bomb exploded. His eyes widen at the mess as he dismissively waves his hand toward the living room.

"Moving is *çok zor*," he says, acting as if the mess is expected. "Too difficult." He looks at the door to the opposite apartment and then quickly closes the front door. He points at the kitchen.

"Shall we sit?"

I follow him, and he makes himself at home, pulling the keys from his pocket and placing them on the small table.

"I consider myself a friend of your husband after bargaining so heavily with him over *rakı* about the rent. He is a fascinating man. He insisted I make sure everything about the apartment was to your liking while he is away."

I'm hurt that Harris told him he wouldn't be here, but didn't tell me. The hurt pokes at my heart, warning me that the blubbering is about to begin again. With so many questions, I won't be able to ask even one without breaking down.

He pulls a business card from his wallet, and I take it. Underneath his name are "Professor" and "Istanbul University." I assume there is a campus in İmir, since Istanbul is five hours north by car. Or maybe he's on sabbatical. Right now, it's not important. I plaster my "don't let the jury see you sweat" smile on my face.

"Thank you for checking on me."

He continues. "I am sorry, I was moving too quickly before. I remembered I had another set of keys at home, even though it took longer than making another set..." He shrugs his shoulders, his hands out in front.

"Harris told me nothing about the apartment," I say. "Did you bring a copy of the lease with you, perhaps?" The look on his face says I've caught him off guard for some reason.

"I can supply a copy for you," he responds casually, "if you cannot find Harris's copy."

I nod. "It is probably in a box. I'm sure I will find it." I break the uncomfortable silence because I need his help. "The water heater looks to be from the eighteenth century. Can you show me how to use it? And also the stove in the kitchen."

"Yes, certainly," he replies.

I threw a lot of words at him quickly, yet he had no problem understanding me. I squint at him, trying to understand what has changed, but he turns and heads for the bathroom. He pauses at the bathroom door, then rakes his fingers through his hair as if nervous. I give him more space before following him into the room.

The bathroom is huge, even larger than a typical American one. It is more of an all-purpose utility room, with built-in cabinets along one wall, a double vanity, and room for a large, ancient water heater and a washing machine. I listen as he tediously teaches me how to use the ancient water heater and how the washing machine must drain into the bathtub.

"I was to schedule the plans to make changes in the apartment, but your husband was insistent on renting this way." His English is halting again, and his expression suggests an apology. "It is old, I know. But my mother liked this big room."

"Now that I know how things work, I'll be fine. Can you show me the stove? And anything else you think I should know?" Even if I'm booted from the country at the end of the week, a hot shower and the ability to cook will be welcome benefits.

"Yes, the kitchen and one more thing. Come with me, please."

Sedat strides back to the front door and holds out his hand. "Keys, please."

I hand him back the keys.

"To properly lock this door, you must turn this second lock repeatedly, see?" He shifts so that I can see what he is doing. "I believe you refer to this as the deadbolt. There are six turns you must make. It is a steel door, and if you lock it properly, nothing can get through this door."

I nod and wonder what he did for a living in a prior life—something in the military, probably. Or maybe teaching is only a part-time adjunct position, and he has another occupation. He is a born military commander or a corporate leader, perhaps. Whatever it is, he is used to giving orders and training people.

"If you forget your key, Ms. Durand, and shut the door, the first simple lock will engage." I nod again, watching him point to the smaller lock. I'm accustomed to doing things myself, and I wonder why he thinks I need to be instructed in this manner.

He catches my eye and continues. "It will be easy to lock yourself away from home. If I am in Istanbul teaching, I cannot help you." His expression is stern, as if I were a five-year-old. "This key," he wiggles it in front of my face, "is extra. You must hide it somewhere or arrange to keep it with a neighbor you trust. The little one," he shows me a gold key, "is for the front door of the building."

The lecture is complete, and he hands me the keys.

"I understand." I don't know anyone to give the spare key to, but I will only be here a week if the Air Force forces me out of the country. No, I won't let that happen. I can't, but I cannot tell this man my plans. I look at the city's flickering lights on the other side of the bay, and a longing wells up inside me. Before it's too late, I extend my hand, needing him to leave me before I'm a sobbing puddle on the floor.

"Thank you for your help, Mr. Gökçe." I drop my hand and try not to look as awkward as I feel.

"*Hayır*—excuse me—you must call me Sedat." He sounds offended.

"Yes, of course—Sedat. Please call me Quinn."

He reaches for the door handle and then drops his hand. "Excuse me, did Harris not explain how to pay for the electricity, the gas, and the water delivery? I told him these things, but we drank a lot that night."

Will he never leave?

"Also, did he contact the television and internet company for you? Please give me your number." He reaches out as if to take my phone and insert his information.

"Sedat, I arrived from the States early this morning." *Was this still the first day?* "When I get a cell number, I will call you."

Only the first day, and I am tired of the sordid details of Harris's secret life. Or maybe it was only a secret from me. Hoping Sedat will get the hint, I glance at the half-opened boxes in the living room. Instead, he waits, his head slanted slightly to one side, and a professional smile on his face.

"Now that Harris is gone," I begin, "I think I am only here to ensure that I return our furniture and belongings to the United States. Since I don't know how long I need to stay, I must determine what to do about the lease and its terms." I prattle, and a pained expression moves across Sedat's face, something I can't identify. He holds up his hand to stop me. I must be talking too fast for him to keep up.

"Excuse me. What do you mean by "Harris is gone?" Creases form on his forehead as he scowls. "Are you getting the divorce so soon? He says you were only recently married."

"You don't know?" I ask softly.

"*Afedersiniz.* Sorry, excuse me, please. Know? I do not understand." He squints at me and cocks his head.

"Harris was killed in a helicopter accident."

Shock replaces the confusion. He stares at me, and then an

expression I interpret as pity slowly starts and intensifies. He steps backward as if I'm diseased.

"No." His voice is even harsher and demanding, and I wince at his tone. Observing my flinch, he becomes earnest, and his voice softens.

"I must help you. Please accept my, how do you say—eh—condolences. A foreign woman should not be alone in Türkiye, and I must not leave you with this condition." A pained look spreads across his face again. His emotions seem all over the place, something we now have in common.

"Thank you, Sedat, but I don't need help." I reach for the door handle, but he is not ready to leave. He is standing as if he is a soldier, shoulders thrown back, his feet apart, his eyes searching mine as if preparing for me to collapse on the floor with a wail. If he waits much longer, I'll undoubtedly comply. He crosses his arms over his chest.

"Yes, you need my help. Things are very different here from America. You must trust me. I will help you, but I must wait until tonight. Will you be comfortable waiting until that time?"

I start to protest again, but he raises his hand to stop me, the military commander in charge.

"You must let me to help you. You should not be alone where you know no one." He hesitates as he opens the door. "I will come again tonight."

I silently nod, then close the door behind him, unable to handle one more thing. I sink to the floor, wishing I had someone to talk to about all this, someone I could trust to confide in. But until I understand what Harris was involved in, I can trust only myself.

11

QUINN

At noon, a woven basket stuffed with kitchen supplies and Turkish food awaits me on my doorstep, raising my hackles. I don't know anyone here besides Maynard. While an apology is in order after our conversation, I'm not sure a gift basket is the appropriate gesture. A folded card is tucked between a loaf of artisan bread and a jar of olives.

Welcome to the apartment.
We can discuss what you need to live in Türkiye at dinner tonight.
Please meet me at the top of the hill at 8 pm. Enjoy the food from my country.
Sedat

In the basket is a small bag of French Roast, a grinder, a loaf of bread, several bags of cookies, crackers, and sweets. Another note at the bottom informs me that I can purchase fresh fruit, vegetables, and milk at the market located up the hill.

After several cups of black coffee, I leave my apartment with a new outlook and walk downhill toward the taxi stand rather than uphill to the market. My need for cash and a SIM card is more pressing than my need for food. My stomach flops when the familiar military green sedan pulls up beside the curb.

Why would Maynard think I wanted to see his face again today, and how does this man have so much free time? Expediency prevails. He can help me find the mail, locate a Citibank, and get a SIM card for my iPhone faster than I can. So, he wants to prove he is Harris's old college buddy and my new best friend? Right now, regardless of his threats, I'll indulge him.

Maynard leans over, grins, and barks out the open window. "Came to check on you, and here you are. Saved me the ride up that rickety elevator. Hop in."

His attitude reminds me of a boy I dated in high school. The guy was a smart ass with no manners, and my parents detested him.

"I'll gladly ride to Alsancak, Captain Maynard." I give him a polite smile, hoping to avoid any discussion about criminal charges or my return to the States.

"Oh, for Christ's sake, call me Ted. You'll see I'm practically family." *I don't think so.* "I know yesterday was hard, but we'll get through this. I promise I'm here to help."

Not wanting his help, I nod and look out the window. This man loves hearing himself talk. I want to slap a hand over his mouth so he'll stop.

"Where are you headed?" he asks, pulling away from the curb.

"To get the mail, find a bank and a place to buy a SIM card." If Harris were to receive any important mail, I needed to get it before Maynard did—if he hasn't already.

"Ok, the APO is up first," he replies.

What would the military do without its acronyms?

He continues. "It's short for the Army Post Office, although the Air Force uses it too. Can't use the U.S. Postal System here."

I don't tell him I already know this. I'd rather he know as little about me as possible. I pull the FLO papers from my backpack.

"Can you identify the other acronyms on here?"

I hold out the pages, but he turns the corner onto the bayside highway and ignores my question. Once he is out of the roundabout, he glances at me, and I brace for more accusations.

"How is your apartment?"

I blink twice at the innocuous question. "It's fine. Lonely without Harris, but otherwise, it's okay."

Lonely is an understatement. I miss my husband, his banter —and mostly his body—even if he is an *alleged* liar and a serial cheater. Until I find proof of both, the jury is still out. I'm not looking forward to sleeping alone tonight in Harris's bed. It will be worse than the two weeks apart in the United States. At least there, I expected to see him again. Today, I want to see him again, if only to hold him one more time before I strangle the life out of him.

Maynard gives me a sympathetic look. "Yeah, it's hard not having that loud mouth of his. He always had a joke, a story, something."

"If you don't mind, I'd rather not talk about Harris." Maynard focuses on the traffic, although I can see the muscle in his cheek flex as he grinds his teeth.

The post office turns out to be a dilapidated concrete box. The clerk is a nondescript man in his early thirties, wearing camouflage fatigues and a T-shirt, with a bored-out-of-his-mind expression. He doesn't follow Air Force dress regulations, but who cares? Not me. He's just a postal clerk, and I need Harris's mail. Maynard seems to make the postal employee nervous. At least this time, there's no standoff like at the airport.

Harris was weird about electronic transfers of any type. He never used digital bank transfers, but always insisted on paying and receiving refunds by check or cash. He used snail mail for anything important. I, on the other hand, want everything to be digital. After running a law office, I'm not too fond of paper. A virtual post office receives my mail, actually several—one in

Savannah and another in Miami—where each piece is scanned and sent to my inbox. I set them up the week before I left, just in case I needed a backup. And now I'm happy I did.

I complete a form, and the clerk gives a cursory glance at my U.S. driver's license. Never looking me in the eye, he tells me the box number and hands me a key. I find the mailbox around the corner and pull out handfuls of crumpled envelopes. Returning to the clerk, I ask for something large enough to hold the mail. He retrieves a plastic bag from under the counter, unloads what looks to be his lunch from it, and hands it to me.

Maynard hovers too close, as usual, forcing me to turn my back on him for privacy. I load the mail into the bag when an envelope catches my eye. Harris wrote my name in fat blue Sharpie across the front. I hold the envelope, staring at the royal blue words, and my pulse races. I flip it over.

A missing postmark and no return address let me know the letter was not mailed. Either the clerk opened the back with the key, or Harris stuffed it in the front. I flip the envelope over, nervous to read what is inside, and grab the corner to open it. Maynard's breath tickles my left ear, and my skin crawls as if attacked by midges.

"Is everything okay?" he asks, looking over my shoulder. This man needs to learn the definition of "personal space."

I shove the envelope in the bag and step sideways away from Maynard, far enough to check out the mail clerk. While I don't think the clerk is the type to participate in subterfuge, with a simple bribe, he wouldn't think twice about adding an envelope to the pile. And while anyone could have added this envelope, the handwriting is Harris's.

Maynard leans in. There is no way I am reading anything from Harris in front of him. If he wants to be my "friend," I will play along and get things done, but that is all.

"Everything's fine," I say, and head for the door. "I need a Citibank ATM for Turkish lira. And I need a SIM card."

Maynard strides ahead, and I follow ten paces behind like a subservient housewife to irritate him.

"I guess Harris told you to pick that bank since there are two branches near his office."

I stop and stare at his back. I've banked with Citibank for years, long before I met Harris. Did he think I had no life before my husband?

He flips his hand to the opposite side of the street. "There's a Turkcell phone store down that way. Here's the bank." He points to the Citibank on the corner.

I use my Citigold card at the ATM to pull the daily limit in Turkish lira, using my body to block Maynard's view. I wait for the ATM to spit out the lira. I'm unsure what to do if I cannot clear Harris's name or my own, but if I have to run for my life, at least there is cash in my savings. But where would I go? Right now, the scared little girl inside me wants to throw in the towel and figuratively run for the hills. The woman standing in front of the bank, however, wouldn't dare run without a good reason, but stands her ground.

When I finish with the ATM and stuff the enormous stack of bills in the bag with the mail, Maynard slides quickly away from me as he lights a cigarette, acting as if he hasn't a care in the world. He did everything possible to see the bank screen with my information.

"Phone store?" I ask, wearing my professional lawyer shark smile.

He points to a telephone store down the block. It's a standard cell phone store, featuring a blue color scheme with yellow accents, rather than the hot pink colors of my former carrier in the States. Otherwise, it looks the same. So far, so good. Harris said being in a foreign country was not a big deal. So far, it isn't. Maynard and the landlord think I need their help, but I've been independent my entire life. Why rely on men now?

Telephone service was the one thing that Harris and I argued about before he left. He insisted that since we would no longer be living in the U.S., we did not need telephone service from the States. He swore it was more practical to use SIM cards in each country where we lived. What had already seemed like a substantial compromise now felt as though Harris wanted me cut off from the world. I will kick myself forever for giving up my lifelong phone number.

After an easy discussion with a young clerk who speaks English, my phone is ready for use. I need to contact Harris's parents, discuss returning Harris's belongings with them, and then call a friend at the Federal courthouse in Georgia. I leave the store with my SIM and a hotspot in my backpack, ready to make these calls and do some courthouse research. It's time to ditch Maynard. He wants to know what is in the mailbag on my arm, and I'm not going through the mail with him anywhere near me. He watched the bag's every move this entire time.

"Thanks for the ride in, Captain Maynard." I throw up my hand in a polite wave as I start to step away. "I'll walk back to the apartment from here."

Maynard's face is angry as he rushes toward me, his eyes on the bag. "Quinn, it's two miles. I'll drive you." He steps toward me with a menacing look.

Nope. I'd rather walk across hot coals. I take a step back.

"I'm sure you need to get to work," I start to turn away as slowly and politely as I can, but he grabs my upper arm, holding me in place.

"Aren't you worried about—"

I cut him off. "No." I pry his hand from my arm. "Let me go."

A Turkish man, leaning against a storefront window and smoking a cigarette, watches us as if we are on a reality TV show. He shifts as if to walk toward us and intervene. I will not stand on a public street in a foreign country while Maynard threatens me and comments about my false indictment, even if the audience may not comprehend the conversation.

"Ms. Durand, I am speaking to you," Maynard shouts after me, a half block down the street.

I keep walking, determined to show him only my confidence, not the nervous jitters bouncing up my skin. A man who looks like the passport officer from the other night exits a market across the street and steps off the curb, walking toward Maynard. I'm sure it is my memory, reminding me how much he distrusted Maynard. Now I know why.

"Quinn Durand!" he shouts again. "You cannot walk away from a military officer. You are the guest of the Air Force here."

Yeah? Watch me.

I turn toward the bay before he can scream at me again, making another left on the Kordon toward the apartment in Mithatpaşa. Still unsure he hasn't followed me, I step into a dress store and pretend to browse for a few minutes until my jitters stop.

With no sign of Maynard. I fish in my backpack for the landlord's card to cancel dinner, but Sedat doesn't answer the call, and his mailbox hasn't been set up. A taxi passes me, and I almost flag one but don't. I need time to walk and think.

The city had planted palm trees in large, irregular holes in the sidewalk, which, in my world, are personal injury hazards. The downtown neighborhood of Alsancak looks like Tampa. I walk past intricately carved stone buildings and narrow alleys with cafes and shops, then cross the busy street at a traffic light.

I stop and look at the sea. For the first time, the weight of Harris lifts from my shoulders. The envelope with blue Sharpie in the bag screams to be opened, but I'll wait for the privacy of the apartment. I don't want the world to see me completely unravel over what I read from Harris.

I see why he was excited to move here. Sunshine, the sea, and palm trees were part of his internal operating system, and he loved water as much as a fish. A wave of grief washes over me, but I shove it back, refusing to cry in public. The anger is there, but so far, I've buried it. I feel sorry for the person with me the day that anger explodes.

Women push baby strollers next to the seawall, and young couples sit on benches, lost in each other's eyes. An open cafe smells of grilled meat and French fries. People are everywhere, enjoying the outdoors, enjoying their lives, and a calmness descends. They are just normal people. As Harris says, I will be fine.

A rough-hewn wooden cart clatters by in the opposite direction, mounds of grapes in a rainbow of purples, greens, and reds on its flatbed. Other vendors pass by, smile or nod, and stop to offer me samples. I thank them but decline until a short little man offers me a deep purple fig the size of a tangerine. He pulls it apart and extends half toward me, beckoning me with his Turkish words and hand gestures for a taste. Figs are something I cannot turn down. My mother grew them in our backyard, and their scent brings back memories of home. I bite into the explosive sweetness, and the man gives me the other half of the fig, delighted with my laughter. He refuses my money until he understands I want a dozen more to take home.

My phone rings. I shift the bags of figs and Harris's mail to my left hand and swipe the phone with my right, looking at the word UNKNOWN CALLER on my screen. A violently painful feeling in my stomach desperately believes it will be Harris.

12

SEDAT

While the food basket was a ploy, he had been insulted that she did not immediately call to thank him. That is what a Turk would do, but he had no experience with an American's standard of etiquette. He realized he was foolish when he pulled up the national telephone database for foreigners, and her name was nowhere on the list. She'd told him she had no phone.

His second cell phone rings, but it is a number he does not recognize, and he lets it go. After a few minutes, the same number calls again. He had only given the number to Bora and Quinn Durand, and Quinn does not have a phone. It is Bora calling, telling Sedat that he witnessed Quinn voluntarily getting into Maynard's vehicle, despite his earlier threats to her that day. There is no reason for her to be with Maynard, but Sedat has to admit that the man is the only person she knows in İmir, despite his dangerous nature. Sedat knows his anger will get the best of him if he gets near Maynard. Leaving the surveillance to Bora, he begins to tackle the files arranged in piles on his desk.

Just before one o'clock, Sedat wearily pushes away a stack of reports as his phone rings. Glancing at the caller ID, he puts Bora on speaker and rests the phone on his desk, grateful for the break. He removes his glasses and rubs his eyes, tired from the tiny print and the poor copy quality of the reports after a night of no sleep.

Bora's voice floats toward him. "She is captivating. I love this woman."

Sedat resists rolling his eyes. "Where are you?"

"Alsancak. I've been behind them all morning. The first stop was the American military's post office, then a Citibank machine, and now a Turkcell office. Neither suspects I am close, so don't harass me about being recognized. She picked up a bag full of mail, got a large stack of lira from the machine, a six-month SIM card, and a wireless hotspot."

"Did you get the numbers from Turkcell?" Sedat asks.

Bora rattles off both Turkcell numbers, and Sedat writes them down, realizing the number he has just been given is the one that has called him twice in the last hour. The Turkish government allows foreigners to use local SIM cards for up to six months. He assumes the hotspot is for her computer at the apartment, but he will confirm that tonight. Sedat wonders why she needs an extended SIM card when she is only staying for a week. He doesn't like where this is heading.

"What is her American number?" Sedat asks Bora.

"There is not one," Bora responds. "She gave them an unlocked iPhone with no service."

"Interesting." Sedat wonders why Robicheaux would send his wife to a country without cell service in today's digital world unless neither of them planned to return to their country. He needs to learn her intentions. Staying in Türkiye might imply her guilt. It will be easier for her to hide funds in this country than to transfer them to hers.

"What has she done that is so enthralling?" He is sure the woman is simply walking down the street. Bora is easily excitable.

Bora begins laughing. "Maynard has no manners. He got ugly with her, and she left him screaming right there in the street."

"Screaming? Did she injure him?"

"No, only his ego is shattered." Bora lets out a loud belly laugh. "Have you ever seen a man scream at a woman in public? Such embarrassing behavior. Maynard was unhappy with her because she would not ride home with him. He tried to stop her from leaving him, then yelled at her repeatedly as she walked away."

"Did she appear frightened?"

"Not in front of him, but later, she went into a store where she stayed for about ten minutes. I think she was hiding from him and collecting herself."

"So she doesn't trust him now, you think."

"Not any longer, but there was minimal conversation today. Your microphone works well, so I'm sure I didn't miss anything. She was finished with him once she found the things she needed."

"You are still following her, I assume."

"Correct. She is on the Kordon, walking toward Mithatpaşa. She has tried to make several calls, but whoever it is has not answered."

Sedat would answer the next time.

"Why doesn't she take a taxi or a minibus?"

"No clue, but I think she is trying to relax. She is watching the people and the food vendors carefully. She made the fig man laugh with her antics."

Sedat smiles wistfully, wishing he had met this woman under other circumstances. The thought disappears as he looks at the Turkcell numbers Bora gave him. He needs to focus. This woman is his target.

"Stick with her. Let me know if you encounter any issues. Also, please let me know when you return to the apartment. I will take the evening shift for dinner. Select two officers to handle the overnight and get a good night's rest."

"Will do."

If Maynard has upset her, Quinn may try to cancel dinner with him, as most women in his experience would. He taps the number to return the call, ready to stop that from happening.

"Hello?" Her voice is breathless as if she has been running. The street sounds around her are loud.

"Ah, Mrs. Quinn calls me from a number I do not know." He tries to keep his voice friendly. "How may I help you?"

"Yes," she responds. "This is my new cell number. I wanted to be sure you had it now that I'm your tenant and not Harris." The noise of the vehicles makes it difficult for him to hear her.

"Is there a problem I need to help you with now? It sounds as if you are running."

"No, there is no problem. I'm coming home and wanted to talk to you about tonight."

"If there is no emergency, I must go now. I am unable to hear you very well. I will see you tonight at the restaurant next to the park. Eight o'clock, please."

She would not dare stand him up for dinner.

13

QUINN

Rounding the corner in front of my neighborhood market, I stop at the sight of Maynard perched on the top step of the stairs to my building. Again? Now what? I shudder at having to face him and duck into the market to give myself time to think. Every hour brings something new about Harris that I don't want to know. What is it going to be this time? And when will this day end?

I stuff my shaking hands into my pockets and as I start to use my shoulder to open the market door, a college-aged boy opens the door for me on his way out. Smells of roasted nuts and ripe sheep's cheese float around me, but as the door clangs shut, the street sounds disappear, and silence surrounds me. I'm the only person in the store besides the man behind the counter. I close my eyes for several seconds and breathe slowly as I hide behind a rack of chips.

Opening my eyes, I remember I need food, even for a week, and a dozen figs and a gift basket won't be enough. Shopping will calm my nerves before I face Maynard again. Grabbing a basket, I find eggs and milk, then search through fifteen types of olives and a mountain of cheeses. I select several large tomatoes and add apricots and plums. Having stalled long enough, I head for the cashier. I return the older man's smile as he rings up my purchases, his messy apron stretched across his broad stomach.

"*Burada yeni misiniz?*"

My brain freezes, and I cannot recall the Turkish I frantically studied in the U.S. I knew '*yeni*' meant 'new,' but that was as far as my memory would take me today.

"*Ben anlamıyorum*," I don't understand, I tell him, slowly sounding out the syllables.

"English?"

"*Evet, lutfen.*" Yes, please, I responded in Turkish.

"You are new here?" Just the sound of those simple English words lifted my spirits more than I thought possible. It was such a simple thing, this brief attempt at conversation, a connection with another human who was not out to ship me off or put me in jail.

"Yes, I moved to an apartment down the hill."

"American?"

"*Evet.*"

"Welcome. *Benim adım* Adnan. I am Adnan." He places his hand on his heart and gives me a slight bow.

"My name is Quinn." I copy him and put my hand over my heart, then reach across the counter and shake his proffered hand.

"*Çok teşekkür ederim.*" I hope my nervous pronunciation is correct, but he appears to understand my thanks. He smiles, and I grab my bags and then stride out the door. The man has given me confidence. If Maynard wants to give me a difficult time, I will pummel him with fresh eggs.

"Quinn, I was worried about you walking home. I needed to be sure you made it." Maynard stands as I approach. He grinds his cigarette into the sidewalk with his shoe, making me cringe. Doesn't the man use garbage cans?

"I am the same as I was an hour ago. Just fine." I keep walking.

Gripping the handles of the grocery bags knuckle-white, I pretend he is invisible.

"Quinn, wait." He's annoyed with me, but he can get over it. I turn my back to him and set down the bags, using the short key to unlock the outer door.

"Can I come inside?" he says.

"Thank you for your help, but I still have things to do." I try to keep the sarcasm from my voice. "As you know."

Hearing him climb the steps to the front door, I shove the door with my foot as the lock clicks open. Grabbing the bags, I step inside the building foyer, and the door snaps shut. As Maynard reaches the door, it slams in his face.

"Sorry," I tell him, lifting both hands with the full grocery bags. "I'll get through this on my own."

Unfazed, Maynard yells through the glass door.

"Look, Quinn, we need to talk. The DOD will obtain authorization to enter your apartment. You won't be able to stop them."

With the apartment's steel door and lock? I doubt it. According to my new landlord, no one will get in unless I let them. I ignore Maynard and carry my bags to the elevator. His shout penetrates the glass door, and I jab the elevator button once, then again. His face is beet red when I glance at him. Something in me needs the last word. When the elevator finally arrives, I prop open the door with a bag and walk to the glass door. I look directly into his eyes.

"If any American thinks they can question me or search my apartment, tell them to bring a warrant."

Inside, I put away the food as I eat another fig. My heart racing, I dump the mail from the bag on the living room floor, snatching the envelope from Harris. It holds something lumpy, and I jam my finger under the flap and rip it open.

Yeooowwch.

Something from the envelope hits the floor. I suck on the paper to ease the pain of the cut on my finger. The words in royal blue Sharpie jolt through me as Harris's spidery handwriting covers the page. I bend down and pick up a disk from the floor. Inside the envelope, there is a note.

Quinn, you will get a package explaining this. DO NOT TRUST ANYONE. Do not read the disk. Hide it in your necklace. I promise I will come for you soon. All my love, H

I sink to the floor, my emotions ripping like a waterspout through the waves before it crashes to shore. My heart leaps with excitement, only to crash when I realize I have no idea when the note was written. While I love Harris, faking his own death—if that is what this is—borders on emotional abuse, yet my heart is relieved that he is still alive. The rest of me? Every ounce of me is furious that he is making me go through this insanity.

The letter raises more questions than answers, and something about its tone bothers me, even though I'm not sure why. Inspecting the disk, I am curious to see what is on it. It is too small to fit in my computer, but too large for my phone. I carefully place it and the letter under my iPhone on the table so the breeze from the open balcony door doesn't blow them down the hall. Collapsing on the couch, I pull the necklace over my head and inspect it. Instead of a solid gold piece, there is a thin crack around the edge that I overlooked before. Finding the catch, I press it, and the back pops open. Grabbing the disk from the table, I carefully place it inside the cartouche and close the back. It fits.

I grasp the long, rectangular pendant in my hand. It is an ingenious hiding place. After placing the necklace over my head, I sink into the couch as I picture Maynard and Stone. They lied to me, and it explains why Chaplain Major Stone had such difficulty with the death notification.

I run my fingers over the blue Sharpie-inked letters on the envelope. Harris left me notes all over our apartment in Georgia, written in the same sprawling script, always in blue Sharpie. His notes were loving, funny, and tender, wrapped carefully and tucked into my duffel. There's no need to pull them out to compare. Harris wrote this.

Why didn't those men search the mailbox? Maybe they did, and then Harris added his envelope after their search. I look at the front again. If someone forged his handwriting, they are good at it. I saw Harris's handwriting every day for two months, identical to the note. The words resemble Harris's style, and the handwriting bears a striking resemblance to his. Yet, the visa issue at the passport office is a reminder that anyone can fake anything.

Desperately, I plow through the rest of the mail, searching for another letter, a note—anything written in Harris's distinctive blue scrawl. Nothing.

I must access the disk. If I play his game, I will be blind. He did not know me well if he thought I would play along. He lost the right to tell me what to do once he involved me in this escapade. Dread fills the pit of my stomach. This disk must be what Maynard is after and what keeps him hovering like a honeybee over a coneflower. It certainly explains why he stupidly continues to talk about Harris in the present.

I grab my laptop and scrutinize its sides and back, taking out the disk and comparing it to each slot. Even the smallest space is too large without an adapter. My exposure to computers is basic at best. I know enough software to run a law practice, handle accounting, and prevent unauthorized actions by a secretary, but I am far from being a programmer or a hacker.

I grab the hotspot from my backpack and connect my computer to the internet. Searching with Google Maps is difficult. In English, the results are minimal. I use the translation app to find a store that sells an adapter. The words are not translated correctly because the results return a hairdresser, a convention center display, and residential apartment fronts.

I need help. I flag the most likely stores, then fold Harris's note and put it in my wallet. Placing the disk safely inside the pendant, I ensure the back snaps securely, then place it around my neck and lock the double clasp. It drops to the top of my cleavage and hides under my clothes, something a spy would use. My heart rate increases, and I fall into the chair. My husband may very well be a spy, but he—or I—need to clarify the thief and traitor bit.

Harris's warning could be from a dead man. I wrap my hand around the pendant, grasping for something to keep the magic of the man I married alive in my head, regardless of how lonely I suddenly feel, and then how angry I am at him. Jerking myself out of my despair, I search the Federal Court system's PACER website for Harris's name, thankful that my login and password are still active. The system reveals nothing, proof that Maynard is lying. Yet the entire action may depend on an as-yet unconvened grand jury. Or because Harris and I are definite flight risks, with us already overseas, the Feds may have sealed any indictment. There are too many possibilities, and I need someone on the inside.

I grab my cell phone and call the federal court clerk, a friend from my monthly book club in Charleston, a group that is more fond of wine than books.

"Hey Tammy," I say into the phone. "How are you? How are the girls?"

An excited Minnie Mouse voice blasts through my speaker. I lift the phone from my ear and lower the volume.

"Girl! I thought you had cleared out. You left work weeks ago."

"I'm already overseas, just cleaning up a few final things. Can you check your system for me? I can't find anything in PACER, and I need to be sure nothing's left hanging."

"Well, sure, if I can. What do you need?"

"Just see if there's anything in my name. While you're at it, make sure no one's suing me, or I'm not under criminal indictment," I laugh, pretending it's a joke while hoping she will be thorough in her search.

Tammy's laugh comes through the phone. "Give me a second." She pauses and then asks, "Is everything okay?"

"Oh, sure. You know me—just paranoid about making sure everything transferred correctly." Hopefully, she won't call me out on this because I rarely worked in federal court, and she knows it.

I hold my breath and wait. This is only one jurisdiction, and the U.S. lacks a nationwide searchable system. With Harris roaming about the world, there aren't enough hours in the year to call or search every jurisdiction. With no Interpol contact, I'm at a loss.

I hear the clatter of Tammy picking up her phone. "Nope. You're all clear. I don't know why you think you wouldn't be. You're not one of our routine offenders who shouldn't have been licensed."

"Thanks a bunch, girl."

"No problem. If I get wind of anything coming through, I'll call you. Is this your new number?"

I keep my response light and carefree. "Yep. That would be great. Just text me. It will save you the ridiculous fee. Tell everyone hello the next time you guys meet, will you?"

"Will do. Good to hear from you."

Hearing Tammy's thick Southern accent makes me think back to Trudy, and how she had talked about Harris the day she'd met him.

"He's perfect for you, Quinn!" she gushed at me over the phone. "You have to meet him. Why don't you come down this weekend?"

"Trudy, I'm finishing up a trial. Can't we talk about this later?" My mind was on the man I had cross-examined earlier that morning, who had lied on the stand. I had ripped him apart, and by the end of his testimony, the judge declared summary judgment, an automatic win for me, and the end of the trial. I was in the middle of drafting the order for the judge's office and only half-way listening to what she was saying.

"He really wants to see you. Get your butt down here." She kept babbling about the Air Force, his last trip to Italy, and his plans for Türkiye, where he was to be stationed next.

"Trudy, I'm not interested right now. I've—"

"No excuses," she interrupted. "You're not listening. He travels extensively and is actively looking for a wife. You can stop working. Travel. Do whatever you want. For God's sake, Quinn, this is your ticket to get out of that rat-infested hole you're in!"

"I'm not wife material. We've been over this."

"You let that stupid redneck put you in a box." Trudy's voice was exasperated. "It's time to get over that, Quinn."

Her excitement for the rest of the week had been infectious. Yet it hadn't dawned on me until now that neither she nor I checked up on him, like we usually would have. I got caught up in the moment, in the excitement, and in a man my best friend thought was "perfect for me." Had I been that oblivious?

Yes, I had.

I look back at my computer screen. A target letter from a prosecutor outside Georgia is possible and will give me notice that I am a target of an investigation. Just the thought of such a letter makes me nauseous. Opening my iPostal account, I search for a letter with no return address or from any court. Nothing. I check my attorney's state bar account. I am correctly listed as licensed but inactive, and there are no flags against my record. I am wasting time. Until a prosecutor files something against me or I am arrested, I will be Harris's clueless widow.

I grasp the gold pendant in my hand. Now, I must get into this disk and determine if I'm a felon.

14

SEDAT

"Anything interesting happening?" Sedat asks when he taps his phone to accept Bora's call. He had been listening to the sounds from the recording, but Quinn, unfortunately, did not talk to herself aloud. Other than traffic and seagulls, there was not much to hear.

"Maynard is back. She's avoiding him in the market."

While Bora was watching their target in Alsancak, Sedat called his superior and requested permission to install video surveillance throughout the apartment. If the Turkish National Police wants Quinn, he argued, this is the most efficient way.

Since Sedat held a power of attorney for his mother, Demirci granted permission to install video and audio monitoring in the apartment without hesitation on the day Harris signed the lease. Sedat watches as the small screens of each room pop up on his monitor, connected by the video feed. The tech installs a microscopic camera in every room except the bathroom. The Chief insists on monitoring *every* room, even the bathroom, but Sedat refuses to allow such surveillance, especially since others on his team will review the tapes. He has no intention of having a peep show for his men.

Returning the extra apartment key to Adnan, the tech leaves the market just as Quinn appears. Sedat holds his breath as he hears the tech hold the door for Quinn as she enters the market. While the boy is talented, he cut it too close this time. Sedat listens through his earbud in the opposite ear to his phone as the sounds of shuffling replace those of the outdoors, until he hears Adnan's voice. He listens to the conversation between his operative and Quinn and conveys the information to Bora.

"She is about to come out now," he says to Bora. "Monitor what she is doing for a few minutes until I talk with Adnan. Have the guys ready for this evening."

"I've scheduled them for ten tonight," Bora replies.

Sedat then calls Adnan on his desk phone, leaving Bora's connection open on speaker on his cell. He listens through the earbud as Maynard attempts to access the apartment building. It was times like these that Sedat wished he could clone himself.

"What a polite woman," Adnan says. "She is trying to use her Turkish. Not so much the typical American, I think."

"I think she deceives you, old man," Sedat responds. Adnan, his uncle, has been on the force longer than Sedat has been alive, and he has more experience than any of his other team members. The older man is due to retire but refuses to leave, insisting that the boredom of retirement will kill him. Sedat uses him in places like this, where his experience is invaluable, but the risk to his uncle is minimal.

"*She* is the *target*, not your new neighbor. Anything else?"

"No," Adnan replies. "She purchased some small items, enough for a few days. Nothing remarkable."

"You'll need to cover her apartment from either the market or the park for the rest of the day," Sedat says. "I will take over at seven tonight and pick up the apartment key. Call me at the office if she goes out before then."

Bora suddenly laughs out loud. Sedat cuts the call with Adnan and focuses on Maynard's shouting through the earbuds.

"She let the door slam in his face," Bora says. "He is bleeding. This is too much. I love this woman."

Sedat cannot help but smile. "I have her from here. Coordinate with Adnan and take the evening off. See you tomorrow."

Opening his laptop, Sedat tracks Quinn as she enters the apartment, and a jab of guilt runs through him. Even though he has conducted surveillance many times, watching this woman feels wrong; yet, given the short timeline, this is the most practical way to resolve the situation. With the pressure from his superior, he has no choice.

She puts away the food and then begins sorting through the mail, searching for something. Sedat watches as she picks up a small disk from an envelope that has fallen to the floor.

"Ah, here it is. That has to be what he stole at the card game." Sedat leans toward his computer and speaks aloud to himself. "It looks too small to fit her computer."

He watches as she fiddles with a necklace, taking it in and out from underneath her shirt twice. As he quickly makes his tenth tea of the day, he wonders how Quinn could have so much energy without sleep when she has to be jet-lagged. Has she used the entire bag of coffee he left in the gift basket? As he settles in with his tea, he abruptly sits up, splashing tea on the front of his dress shirt.

Where in the hell is she going now? Why did he think this woman would be like any other, stay home in her comfortable apartment, take a nap, and deal with her grief? As he reaches for his keys, Adnan calls.

"Your target is on the move. Your backup team is in play."

"Thank you, Adnan," Sedat replies. "I will follow from here. Stay in contact, please."

"*Kesinlikle, patron.* I am here."

15

QUINN

"Nothing this size?" Maynard's deadline is pushing me forward, even though it has only been less than twenty-four hours since I arrived. I hold up the disk to the man behind the counter, looking for a gadget I can use. I'm in Alsancak, hoping the very center of İmir will be where I find what I need.

"*Hayır.*" No. He shakes his head and heads for the door, motioning for me to follow as he points down the street. The store he directs me to is claustrophobic, with every type of electrical item strung from floor to ceiling and covering the twelve-foot walls. This clerk also shakes his head at the disk. I pantomime my question of where to go next, and he does precisely what the last man did.

I am wasting time.

The last thing I ate was a fig, but I don't recall the exact time. It's now three-thirty, and I am starving, with dinner not until eight. Seeing a cafe across the street with a large patio, I sit at an outside table for two under a pergola of pink, orange, and yellow bougainvillea. I scour my phone for a computer shop. I am used to finding everything I need from Google Maps back home, but that doesn't seem likely here.

"What would you like to drink?"

My head pops up at the heavily accented English, and I place my phone face down on the table. The waitress is a twenty-something with smooth olive skin who sports no make-up. Her brown eyes are curious under thick bangs, and her long black hair hangs almost to her waist. She points to the menu written in Turkish on the wall.

"Something to eat?" she asks. "A sandwich or a pastry? There are salads if you like, or soup."

"Coffee," I respond, unable to read the menu, "and a sandwich. It doesn't matter what kind."

She nods, returning quickly with a Turkish coffee and a cheese, parsley, and tomato sandwich.

"Do not drink the thick part on the bottom." I look at her curiously, then down at the cup. With a spoon, I feel the thick layer of coffee grounds at the bottom of the cup. Jet fuel. I needed this in law school. I take a sip and close my eyes. Heaven.

Opening them again, I see the waitress smiling as I enjoy my coffee. "Can you help me with something?"

"*Tabii ki*. It would be my pleasure."

I look around to see if anyone else can hear me as I lower my voice. "I need a computer store specializing in accessories or parts."

She nods. "I cannot help you, but Arzu can."

"Who is Arzu?"

"Em, she is a person who, I guess you could say, knows everything about computers." Her expression tells me that her description is not exactly correct, but I am too desperate to care. I need to know what is on this disk.

"Where do I find her?"

Her smile stretches across her pretty face. "I will try to reach her for you. She lives close to here."

I thank her, then sip my coffee as I devour my sandwich. As I think of ordering another, I wonder why her response seems too easy. Harris has made me paranoid about everything. I see nothing unusual with the car or foot traffic on the street. The cafe windows, though, are too dark to see inside. I need to get better at this spy crap if I'm going to sneak around.

A loudspeaker's clicking interrupts lunch as the Arabic call to prayer blasts from the buildings. To my surprise, no one stops what they are doing to pray.

The outline of a man stands inside the cafe doorway, just out of sight. As I focus, he appears to be facing me, watching me, and the hair on my arms stands at attention. I casually look around, but the people at the other tables appear to be regular customers.

Their indifference means nothing. If the past day has taught me anything, it's that looks—about anything—can be deceiving. I need to find the computer store's location and start moving. I stuff the last bite of my sandwich in my mouth and finish the coffee.

A lanky girl, a few inches taller than me, with wavy brown hair past her shoulders, approaches, then plops down at my table, tossing her leather backpack in an adjacent empty chair. She dresses like a computer nerd with black jeans and a T-shirt with an unfamiliar band's logo. The words "computer hacker" cross my mind, and I understand the server's description.

This girl looks to be in high school. She raises her hand as I yell over the melodious voice, signaling me to wait until the prayer ends. Pushing her long bangs away from her face, she uncovers a mischievous smile. When her face is revealed, I notice she is older than I thought.

The voice on the loudspeaker finally stops, followed by a *clang* and a *click*. I scan the doorway to the indoor part of the cafe. The person is still there in the shadows. I'm guessing it's a man simply from his height. If he comes any closer, I'll bolt.

"Are you Arzu?" I ask. Over her shoulder, I see the man in the doorway step outside and walk toward us, then pause. He looks away when I stare at him. He is about six feet tall, wearing a brown suit and dirty black shoes. His belly strains the buttons of his dress shirt, fighting with the belt that holds up his baggy pants. He takes another step toward us. I wait to see if he heads toward the patio or the street. He doesn't turn toward the street.

My leg jackhammers the closer he gets.

"Yeah, sure, maybe. Seda says you needed a little help?"

My attention returns to Arzu. Her English is excellent, with only a little accent, and Harris's warning not to trust anyone pops back into my head. My sensors are on full alert as the man comes closer. They could be together.

I stand, gather my things, and paw through my bag for my wallet, dropping enough lira on the table to cover my bill plus a generous tip. At the edge of my periphery, I see Arzu's quizzical look, then the shake of her head as she shoves back her chair and grabs her backpack.

Across the room, Seda gives Arzu a questioning smile, then looks at me. I stare at the man and then back at the server. She seems to understand. Just before the man reaches my table, Seda, holding a tray full of dirty dishes, moves in front of him.

The man's focus is entirely on me. As if part of a comic symphony, the entire tray of leftover food, half-finished drinks, and dirty napkins tips toward him. Seda steps back, avoiding the crash. Amid the table, chairs, and gawking patrons, the man slips, sprawling on his back in the center of the patio.

I sprint down the restaurant's steps and across the street, winding through narrow alleys to avoid a tail. To catch my breath, I duck into a boutique, shifting close to the wall behind a mannequin, smiling at the store clerk who raises an eyebrow at my strange behavior. I don't know what else to do. Whoever is following me is most likely an expert.

I spot an internet cafe across the street and dart inside, then slam two hundred liras on the counter for the ten-minute minimum. Sitting in the back, I look at the worn-out desktop computer. Its slots are no smaller than the ones on my laptop. Removing the disk from the pendant, I wrap it in a clean tissue to prevent losing it, and put it in my pocket. I wait until the boy at the counter is free, then approach the counter. He looks up from a book he is reading.

"Something is wrong?"

I pull the tissue with the disk from my pocket. "Have an adaptor for this?"

"It is a memory card." Why does anyone younger than thirty think that the rest of us are technologically ignorant?

"Yes." I resist the urge to roll my eyes. He fishes around in his backpack, retrieving several gadgets, and tries unsuccessfully to load the disk.

"*Yok.*" After one last gizmo, he tosses the items into his backpack. "No correct size."

"Where can I buy something?"

"Not possible. The store will not sell. You will need help."

"Really? Why?"

He cocks his head to the side. "It is too small. I call my friend to help you, possibly. Maybe."

I hesitate. Another friend. Is this a standard Turkish thing to call your friend when you need something? Can I trust this one? It doesn't matter. I must know what is on this memory card. He clears his throat, waiting for a response.

"Yes, please call."

The boy digs in his jeans pocket, pulls out a cell phone to make the call, then drops it into his backpack.

"Twenty minutes. I will find you." He flips his fingers, dismissing me to return to the computer in the back.

"Thank you." I bet he doesn't treat his mother this way.

I browse the internet. When I look up, Arzu is staring at me through the open door of the internet cafe, shaking her head and sneering as the counter boy motions to me. I'm not sure this is a coincidence.

Arzu flips her bangs away from her face as I reach the door. "Big stunt back there."

I examine the girl with more care. Her pale green eyes return my stare with anger and mistrust.

"Seda may lose her job because of you."

"I promise you," I insist, "I was only trying to get away from that guy."

"Who is he?" She is belligerent. "And who are you?" With one hand on her hip, she grasps her backpack strap with the other. Her thumbnails at the corners are scabbed from severe biting. She isn't as much of a bad guy as she wants me to believe.

"I don't know who he is. Do you?" I reply, keeping my voice at the same level as hers. I won't let her bully me. "What can I do to help Seda? It wasn't her fault." I pull the disk from my pocket and extend it toward her. "I need your help to find out what's on this."

"He has explained what you need." Arzu points to the boy behind the counter, pushing my hand away. "My fee is two hundred American dollars." She holds out her hand for the money.

"For a simple adapter?" I try to keep the shock of being railroaded from my face.

"You Americans are rich," she replies. "Go ahead. Prove me wrong."

"It isn't worth two hundred dollars, and you know it." She is Turkish, so I have to haggle, something ingrained in their culture.

"Fifty dollars, and I need an ATM. I don't carry cash." I shift my backpack higher on my shoulder and look toward the door.

"Then let's go. The man you need to see is waiting for us."

"Just tell me where to go…"

Exasperated, Arzu stops outside the door, raking one hand across her scalp in frustration. She is the picture of an overgrown pixie in Doc Martens boots.

"He will not help you without me, and with a disk that size, he is the only one who can," she responds. "As you can see, everyone in İmir knows I am the fixer for problems like this. Either you want my help, or you do not. But you wasted my time twice today."

With no other options, I gesture for her to lead the way, feeling like I am walking into an abyss.

16

QUINN

Arzu raises her right eyebrow as if daring me to question her abilities or status as a computer hacker emeritus. We are located down the block from the internet café, heading towards a row of ATMs from multiple banks. I try not to smile as I picture her with pointy ears, sharp teeth, and fairy wings until I remember she wants two hundred dollars.

"Two hundred dollars is ridiculous," I blurt as I try to match her pace.

She keeps walking. "One-fifty."

"No, Arzu, fifty." My words spit out like arrows. "That's all I'm willing to pay." I stop, and she turns to face me. Her impish gaze scrutinizes me as she scowls.

She lets out a huff, then walks again. "Okay. Fifty."

At the ATM, I withdraw her money. Arzu is halfway down the block when I pocket the cash and the receipt and run to catch up. We turn the corner, pass the Hilton near the APO and the bank, the area I was in earlier today, and head for the bay.

"Where are we going?" I ask.

"*Karşıyaka*," she replies, spitting out the word.

"Where is that?" I ask, pulling out my phone to find the map again.

She bats her hand at my phone and points across the water. "We will take a ferry. No worries."

"Who is your friend?" I am determined to gather as much information as possible from her. Given the day thus far, I need anything I can get.

"Do not ask me questions about my friend. He will not like it. When we get to his shop, do not speak unless I ask you to."

"Why?" I ask. A twinge of fear rolls in my gut. "If I travel to the other side of the bay, to a neighborhood I've never heard of, I'd like to know who I'm going to see." I paused for a second. "And who I'm with as well. All I need is a tiny adapter, for God's sake."

She stops and turns toward me, hands on her hips.

"You Americans," she mutters, her boot tapping in irritation. Her face tells me she is thinking about how to respond. But she doesn't. She walks, and I hurry to keep up.

"I am a graduate student in Computer Engineering at the İmir Institute of Technology. And before you ask, I am twenty-eight years old, and yes, I know—I look twelve. I've heard every definition of elf possible." She stops once more. "Why do you ask so many questions?" she asks. "I don't want to know your name or what you are doing, and you do not need to know my business, so stop it."

We walk in silence to the ferry pier. I spot the Kordon Hotel several blocks away, and a wistful pang hits my heart, evoking the memory of when Harris and I planned to explore İmir together. Then, a wave of bitterness hits me, and I shove him from my mind.

I pay for the ferry tickets without her asking, another unspoken jab at what Arzu considers money-grubbing Americans. Boarding, I feel trepidation about the old, rusted boat and the lack of any safety equipment, except for ancient life jackets hanging from the ceiling. The vibration of the diesel engine rattles the handrail, and I hold on as the boat leaves the pier.

"Never been on a ferry in İmir?" Arzu eyes me with concern.

"My first ferry in any city," I reply, wondering if I'm already turning green. "I don't do boats. Motion sickness."

"I will get something to help. Wait here." She returns with a tulip-shaped glass of hot tea in one hand and a round, pretzel-like treat covered with sesame seeds in the other.

She points to the opposite shore. "Keep looking toward that side of the bay. We will be there in fifteen minutes. And we must get your fear under control. You reek of it."

I almost spit out my tea. "Fear? I'm not afraid. It's just water that makes me sick."

Arzu lets out a laugh before she lowers her voice. "It's not the water. It's you. You've been terrified since the cafe. If I can see it, so can he. Grow a backbone, Miss America. You will need it."

Several blocks from the ferry pier, a sign for *Buca Bilgisayar* hangs awkwardly over the sidewalk. A thick layer of dust covers the front windowpane, and the computers and parts on display are from the prior century. Arzu sees my skepticism.

"He does not sell computers. He does other things...." Her voice trails off.

"So he's a hacker?" I ask, not caring that I'm badgering her for information she doesn't want to give.

Her hand is on the door, and she turns back to me. "No more questions or ridiculous labels. Don't worry. Your little disk will be a piece of cake for him."

She pushes through the old wooden door, and a bell tinkles overhead. No one is at the counter, but the sound of a chair scraping across a floor comes from behind a dark blue curtain in the doorway. A hand pushes the curtain aside, and a man in his mid-thirties walks to the counter, speaking to Arzu in heavily accented Turkish. He looks as if he has just rolled out of bed. A geometric circular tattoo covers half of his neck, sliding toward his shoulder and under his T-shirt.

I look around the room. Several photos hang on the wall, one from Sochi and another from St. Petersburg, making it easy to guess where he's from, but I've never met a Russian, so who knows.

After speaking with Arzu, he looks at me carefully. My gut tells me to watch out for this one, and as Arzu previously suggested, I throw on my invisible coat, tuck my fear down tight, and return his stare. There is no introduction of me to this man, or vice versa.

He looks at me. I wait.

He holds out his hand, silently requesting the disk. I pull it from the tissue, and his tattooed hand takes the disk, placing it in a square plastic gadget. He grabs a laptop sitting on the counter, boots it, and then turns the computer to face me. He hands me the gadget and points. I insert the end into the USB port.

The screen flashes with a login and password prompt. When I don't immediately start typing a response, a message appears, letter by letter, with a roaring-lion logo.

"*Unauthorized use destroys in thirty seconds.*"

The login and password sections are in the lion's mouth, both sections blinking in bright yellow. After two seconds, another line flashes:

"*Tick Tock.*"

Panicking, I flip the computer around to the Russian. He reads the screen, his face alarmed. Instantly, he jerks out the black plastic box from the USB port. He slams the computer closed and shoves the gadget and disk toward me. I snatch the plastic box with the disk and stuff it in my front jeans pocket.

Before my hand is out of my pocket, he is around the counter, my arm in his huge hand, gripping it like a vise. He shouts angry words I don't understand at Arzu as he shoves me toward the shop's front door. Arzu wedges herself between the Russian and me, forcing him to release me. I stumble backward and slam into the front door of the shop. His face is red, and his voice is so loud and abrasive that I'm not sure if he's speaking in Turkish or Russian.

I run to the sidewalk, not waiting to find out, and stop several doors down. The Russian steps outside and shakes his fist at me, then disappears inside the store. I stand mortified on the street, waiting. Arzu steps outside. Her sly grin makes me relax, but only just a little. For the first time in my life, I feel exceedingly naïve.

She walks toward me with a sneer. "You did a poor job hiding that fear, Miss America."

I blink but don't respond. She is right. I'm terrified not only of the Russian hacker but of this entire situation my husband forced upon me.

"No login and password." Her words are a statement, not a question.

"No." I nod my head toward the computer shop. "Why was he so angry?"

She ignores my question and asks another of her own. "Do you know what is on this memory card?"

"If I did, why would I need to do all this to open it?" I cannot keep my voice down.

She squints at me as if trying to assess the truth of my response.

"Where did you get it?"

"In the mail."

"Do you know the person who sent it to you?"

"My husband."

Arzu blinks, and her face screws into an angry scowl. "Why do you need me? Or my friend? Your husband should be able to open this for you. My friend is furious about this."

I look across the bay toward Alsancak, trying to keep my face emotionless. I don't know when Harris wrote the note or when he delivered it to the post office. The military says he's dead, but Maynard acts like he is alive. My angry heart says he's alive because of the letter in my wallet, yet I will follow the military line until I know for sure. There is no need for her to know the truth, especially when I don't know what that truth is.

"Because he's dead." My eyes drop to my feet.

I've caught Arzu by surprise. Her eyes flash toward the computer shop, and she steps toward it, then turns and pulls my arm in the other direction.

"Come with me," she says. "We need to talk. This is serious."

I follow her to a tea garden several blocks from the computer shop, away from the ferry pier. The green garden is dotted with a dozen small tables under a massive grape arbor. We take a seat among a scattering of patrons. I let Arzu order, turning my face into the breeze and closing my eyes.

I open them and try again. "What's the deal with the Russian?"

Arzu refuses to look me in the eye. Her fingers tap on the table. This disk is a can of something worse than worms, and I want to know what will slither out once it's open.

"My friend believes you are trying to trap him in something with this message."

"How?" I ask.

The waiter delivers two glasses of tea, and she waits until he leaves, focusing on her glass.

"He would not tell me anything, just mumbles about a Bulgarian group, and now I'm curious. I know he left Russia because of some gang, so he knows more than he's telling. What work did your husband do?"

I hesitate for several seconds before I respond. It would take Arzu less than five minutes in this town to figure it out for herself. It may be a city of millions, but İmir acts like a village.

"Harris worked for the Air Force."

She leans back and takes a sip of tea. "Why did he send this memory card to you?"

I force myself to hold her gaze. "I don't know."

This isn't entirely a lie, just somewhat.

"Do you know where he would hide a login and password?" she asks.

"No," I respond, glancing across the bay toward my new apartment.

Arzu's eyes narrow. "You are not telling me the whole truth." She waits for me to deny her statement, but I don't, so she continues.

"Do you have an email address?"

"Of course. Why?" I ask.

"Did you check it for mail from him?"

"Of course. Do you think I can't handle routine email?" My irritation is taking over my side of the conversation, and I mentally remind myself to chill.

"Given the warning on this disk, I'm sure he emailed you something that you won't recognize. Something that looks like spam, possibly."

She leans back in her chair, tossing the last finger of tea as if she's drinking tequila. "Come on, we need to see."

"And if there's nothing?"

"I do not know, Miss America. We will decide then." She stands and motions for me to follow.

"Where are we going?" I throw a stack of lira on the table, assuming it is the proper amount. The rate changes so frequently that I'll need to check it daily to avoid shortchanging the staff when I can't wait for the bill to arrive.

"To the internet cafe on the next block to use one of their computers since we cannot use my friend's."

"Why can't I use my phone?" I ask. "I bought a Turkish SIM."

"After what we learned about your little disk, someone could track you with that phone."

My heart jumps into my throat. Trying to retrieve information from this disk is like playing Whack-a-Mole with spies.

"Someone like who?" I ask, not wanting to know.

"Like the nasty people who put that message on your disk."

Spy games territory again. Only worse.

17

SEDAT

Texts roll through Sedat's phone so quickly that he has to silence the notification dings. He puts in an earbud, monitoring his team in one ear and using his desk headset to monitor the microphone in Quinn's backpack, which he placed there along with a tracker. Bora is beside him, giving up his rare time off to help monitor Quinn.

The backup team reports by radio. Quinn is searching for something in electronic stores but is not finding what she needs. Their report coincides with what he is hearing through his headset. He can hear her ordering food. Then, the ezan obliterates anything she says, and there is confusion before he can understand what is happening. His team reports a dispute at a restaurant. Quinn has run.

Sedat's team loses her, and he is glad he trusted his instincts. He checks the tracking app on his phone. The blue dot appears frozen as if it has stopped working. Either there is a glitch in the system, or she has discovered the tracker in her backpack. He hopes it is the former. He can hear her through the microphone, so he doubts she has found his equipment.

Quinn is breathing heavily as if she is running. Sedat is

unconcerned. If he remains patient, she will disclose her location verbally. He knew the moment he met her that he would need to keep a close eye on this woman. Even though she is wasting valuable hours that could be spent elsewhere, once she received the disk, she became his priority. He cannot afford to lose her location. Her breathing slows, and after some shuffling and unintelligible conversation, the background noise falls quiet, and then he hears the sounds of a keyboard clicking.

Sedat leans toward his partner.

"Bora, while I listen, contact the technical department again for the most advanced tracking capability. I want a better one than whatever this is that I'm using now." Tonight at dinner, her equipment gets an upgrade. "After that, can you go back and pull the background report on Quinn? I don't remember any training in avoidance techniques. Did I miss something? Or is she just lucky?"

"Let me call them, then I'll look," Bora responds. "I don't remember any training of that type either."

After the argument with tech over the requested equipment, Bora pulls up Quinn's background document on his computer and begins scrolling, shifting in his seat so that Sedat can see along with him. After several minutes, Bora shoves his rolling desk chair away from the computer.

"I am not finding anything. She is a lawyer with no intelligence background and squeaky clean. There are no charges, not even traffic tickets. She comes from a small town in Georgia, wherever that is. Let me cross-reference with the reports from Robicheaux."

Knowing that might take time, given the thickness of Robicheaux's file, Sedat wonders where else he could obtain information on Quinn Durand. As he makes a list of questions for his research assistant, he hears familiar sounds over his earbud. He calls the lead on the backup team, but before he can speak, the officer begins a rapid-fire report.

"*Patron*, our people are everywhere. We will find her, I promise." The tone of his lead is crisp and professional, yet Sedat can hear the underlying stress from losing his target.

"Zeki, do not let there be a next time." Sedat tries to keep his voice friendly. His team responds better to positive reinforcement than to threats. He rechecks his app, and the screen is no longer frozen. The blue dot slowly pulses inside a building. He pulls up a map on his computer screen, shifting his headset and readjusting his microphone.

"I have her location. I will text you. It is my fault for underestimating this target. I ordered better trackers and will resolve this tonight, so you won't be in the dark the next time. Notify me when you locate her."

He cuts the call and, after texting the internet cafe's location, stretches in his chair, focusing intently on the sounds coming through the earbuds. There is movement, an introduction, and then a conversation begins with another woman.

"Who is this Turkish woman?" Sedat questions aloud. He looks at Bora. "Contact the backup and see if anyone on the team recognized anyone at the restaurant where Quinn ate lunch. Apparently, from the conversation, this woman was there."

Sedat focuses on a spot across the room, straining to listen to the two women.

"They are heading to Karşıyaka." He communicates this to Zeki and then turns to Bora. "You must go. The next ferry leaves in ten minutes, and I need eyes I trust."

The two men have worked together for so long that they have developed a system of sorts. One needs to be in direct contact with any target they are watching. The other performs any research, interference, and coordination with backup teams. Bora is best at physical tracking. When direct interaction is required, Sedat uses his people skills. Sedat has no idea how they formulated this system, but the two complement each other, and with their system, neither has to bear the full brunt of any investigation.

Sedat watches his friend get ready to leave, knowing he has only made it this far because of Bora. The office is only two blocks from the ferry terminal. Bora can be there in less than five minutes at a casual stroll. He stands, pulls on his coat, and checks his pockets for his wallet, phone, and earbuds.

"I'll tell your new research assistant to hunt for this woman," Bora comments as he heads for the door. "Text me as much as you can."

"Of course. Once they are in sight, loop me in. Remember, she has seen you. Stay out of sight."

Bora steps back inside the office, grabbing a gray tweed flat cap. "Will do." He checks his watch. "I need to run to get there ahead of them."

The backup team reports that the two women are in sight, and Sedat continues to listen, trying to understand what Quinn is up to, while waiting for Bora to arrive.

"Arzu Tekin," a woman says as she enters the room. Her laptop is open in her hands. Sedat nods to the research assistant, a recent graduate from the police academy. "I'm looking for her information now." Within a minute, she turns the screen for Sedat to read. He calls Bora, hearing seagulls in the background.

"The woman with Quinn is possibly a computer hacker with a questionable background in the U.S. I assume Quinn needs her to access the disk she got in the mail."

"The woman with her looks like a college student," Bora replies. "I'm logging back into the system now. I'll text you when I see where they're headed."

As they listen to the conversation, Sedat becomes increasingly irritated by the seagulls, the rumbling diesel engine, and the chatter of passengers. He is thankful when the women stop talking and quietly finish the ferry ride. Once the women leave the ferry, he hears a tinkling sound coming from a nearby shop door within several minutes. His phone lights up with a call from Bora.

"This is not good, Sedat. Do you remember that Russian we arrested a few years ago for hacking into the finance ministry, but couldn't make the charges stick? You know, the one trying to get money for that offshoot of ISIS."

"The one with the tattoo on his neck? What was his name?" Sedat asks.

"Yeah, him. They just went into the computer store he uses as a front. I don't know what she's doing, but she is way out of her depth here, Sedat." There is silence for a few seconds, and then Bora continues speaking. "I can't see inside. No one has washed the windows in twenty years. There's no way I can go in. What are you hearing?"

"They aren't talking," Sedat replies. "Wait, there's yelling. Some problem, and the Russian is pissed. He is yelling at Quinn. Walk on in case they come out."

"Moving."

Sedat conveys the conversation to Bora. "The Russian is screaming that Quinn has jeopardized his entire operation by bringing in a disk from a competitor. He sounds more afraid than angry, shouting about 'Aslan.'"

"Aslan?" Bora says. "Do you think he's referring to —"

Sedat interrupts, his voice concerned, as they both know the group of Bulgarian ruffians using that name.

"Exactly. The Lion. A big problem if whatever she has is theirs."

"How in the world could this American woman be connected to those asshats?" Bora suddenly stops talking, and Sedat hears movement. From experience, he is also quiet, not wanting any inadvertent sound to cause a problem for his partner. He hates not being there this time. Next time, he will be.

Bora's voice is soft, almost a whisper. "She's out of there fast and heading back toward the ferry. Ah, she's stopped. I think she is waiting for the Tekin woman." He hesitates, then continues. "And there she is. They are talking on the sidewalk. Clue me in."

Sedat hears the women now, talking about the Russian's problem with the disk. "Bora, they are heading to a tea garden. It might be the one that is two blocks past you by the water. Heads up."

"I'll loop around. Let me know if you hear anything interesting. I'm unable to get close. The restaurant is outside, and there's nowhere to hide."

Sedat listens to the conversation while the women drink tea. He agrees with the Tekin woman that Quinn is not telling the truth.

"Bora, they are going to another internet café."

"Why? Wouldn't a hacker take her computer with her? These two seem to be very unorganized. Are you sure this woman is a hacker?"

Sedat looks pointedly at his research assistant. The woman mimes permission to speak.

"Speak, Yasemin."

Sedat turns on the speaker as the assistant recites Arzu Tekin's family history of protests and arrests, her undergraduate degree in computer science, a master's degree from Middle East Technical University, and details of her celebrated research assistant position at a prestigious university in California. Her position went south after allegations of theft between competing professors, and she was subsequently dismissed from the school. Tekin's record remained cold for several months until she registered as a student at the İmir Institute of Technology.

"Is she a hacker?" Yasemin asks rhetorically, "Probably not. Could she be? Absolutely. She graduated from METU as the top student in her class and received a full scholarship to the school in California. Her life is trashed in the United States; she is rebuilding her reputation. If nothing else, she is—what do the Americans say? A loose cannon."

18

QUINN

Harris's instructions tell me not to do precisely what I'm doing, yet I follow Arzu to a different internet cafe. I pay for the minimum rate for an hour at this new place called Space. The walls are black, with glow-in-the-dark plastic stars on the ceiling. Mobiles of the planets move slowly around their orbits in the dim light overhead. I feel like I'm in a kid's playroom.

The place smells of cigarettes and mold. The predominant sound is the clatter of keyboards. As I pass through the cubicle rows, heads nod to music through headphones and earbuds. A desktop on the right side of the room looks the most private, and Arzu follows me, grabbing a chair from the adjacent cubicle.

Logging into my Gmail account, I see forty-two new emails, the majority spam. Arzu reads over my shoulder as I scan each for a sign from Harris, checking all the senders' addresses. The last address is a jumble of letters and numbers; I think it is spam. I move the mouse to delete it.

Arzu's hand slams over mine. "Open it," she says.

"If it's spam and blows up my account..."

I stare at Arzu, and fear hits me. Is she a spy? Is sending

cryptic emails to an unknowing spouse standard spy protocol? I blink and look back at the screen and the weird email address, and then think how stupid that last thought sounds.

"Why this one? What makes it stand out to you?"

"It isn't selling you anything, asking for money with a fake invoice, or announcing you won a billion dollars. It's too much of nothing." She nudges my hand. "Open it."

The body of the email is blank. I click out of the email, search my spam folder for anything similar, then reopen it, unsure what to do. Still nothing. It's just an empty white page. I look at Arzu, and she shrugs. Curious, I click on the body of the email in the white space. Nothing.

As I move the mouse again to click away from the inbox, a single letter appears, then another. One at a time, letters appear until there are five words in Harris's favorite color of royal blue: WHEN WAS THE FIRST TIME?

The question blinks, then underscores and dashes appear beneath it, waiting for a date, just like the one on the disk. What the hell? First, the microscopic disk, the cryptic letter, and now this. A niggle of fear starts at my neck and shoots down each arm. If Harris is dead, who will I be talking to if I continue?

"Put in the date." Arzu points to the screen as her leg jiggles double-time beside me.

"Not so fast. How did you know this would happen?"

"It's sort of standard."

"Standard where?" I ask, almost blurting out, *in the spy world?*

"Standard when people want to hide things or block things. So what's the date?"

I'm not sure if I can trust her. I turn back to the screen and squint as I try to understand what date will open the gates to whatever hell is behind this. If this is from Harris, I need a date significant to both of us, something only we know. I start with the day we met in Charleston. Nothing happens. I use the European format for that date—still nothing. I input our first formal date.

The cursor continues to blink. My frustration grows, but at least no Mission Impossible-style warning appears like the one from the disk.

Desperate, I enter the date we made love for the first time. The phrase and date fade. My heart races as my fear turns to shock, then a punch to the gut when my brain finally engages. This has to be from Harris. No one else knew this date. It would be impossible for someone to know what we'd done at the secluded top of the mountain in the snow that night. It was a spur-of-the-moment trip, and we hiked in the snow for a mile. If someone followed us, we'd have known.

Losing Harris rushes through me again, coupled with the fear of walking into a spy novel with more angry Russians. I run my hand over the necklace under my T-shirt and stare at the computer. A second phrase appears: BELIEVE THOSE WHO ARE SEEKING THE TRUTH. The words blink. Chills crawl up my arms. There is no doubt that this word game originated with Harris, yet my husband has never played this type of game. He was an in-your-face guy, saying what he thought about anything and everything. He told me he hated games and hated puzzles even more. Who is behind this?

Hoping that the ratty computer chair isn't infested with vermin, I lean against its back as I search for memories of Harris gambling or playing any game. There's nothing except the mental picture of his ex-wives clinking glasses of fruity drinks with umbrellas while standing on a Mexican beach, laughing their butts off. *Some compassion, ladies?*

I don't actually know what he likes — liked —or didn't like.

Nor whether he is dead.

The computer beeps, and a digital stopwatch appears, beginning to count down from thirty seconds. I focus. The screen prompts me to complete a phrase attributed years ago to Andre Gide, a French novelist. Harris considered the writer one of the most important of the twentieth century. We talked about Gide, his lifestyle, and his work over dinner at a restaurant in New Orleans. I remember that night because the expensive bottle of cabernet Harris ordered cost more than our airfare for the trip.

I rapidly type in the words to finish the quote: DOUBT THOSE WHO FIND IT

A thrill rushes down my spine as my response is replaced with a link. My hands shake as I click on the link. The computer logs into an email system I've never seen. A simple inbox appears with only one item: a video file. When I click on it, Harris's face appears. After another click, the photo expands to the entire screen. Instantly, there is my loving, funny, crazy, and impulsive husband.

He laughs and starts talking.

"Q, you are so predictable. You always check your email, even though it's been a month since you sold the firm. You need to get a life, you know?"

I stop the video, pulling earbuds from my backpack. I turn to Arzu. "I need to hear this alone." She nods and rolls her chair away, pulling out her earbuds and connecting to her cell phone. I'm surprised, as Arzu doesn't appear to be the type to give anyone space.

I put in my earbuds and click the video. Harris resumes talking.

"I'm about to get on a helicopter." My heart lurches, and dread settles over me. My shoulders sag as I lean in toward the computer.

"There's an envelope for you in the APO mailbox. Inside is a disk I won in a card game. It's important that the disk gets into the right hands."

His face shifts from his usual, happy countenance to a worried frown.

"What is on this disk is dangerous, Quinn, and worth a lot of money. It is a new form of weapon, and every idiot in Europe and the Middle East wants their hands on it. In the last two days, they've

followed and threatened me. I'm recording this because I may not make it to you, and I want you to know how much I love you."

His face is now a mixture of sadness and despair. The finality of his words brings tears of fear, not just for what he's involved me in, but also grief for our love, because I know it's truly gone.

"You're receiving this because I'm dead. Yeah," he laughs as the shock slams into me, *"there's no way to say that easily. I'm sorry."*

His expression softens to the one he wore all those nights looking at me from his pillow. I grip the edge of the desktop, willing this video to be a joke, but Harris keeps going.

"I never thought I'd go this young, but with the life I've led, it's not unexpected. You'll hear many things about me soon, most of which will be true. But a lot won't be. When I started our relationship, I'll admit, I had a different plan, one I'm not proud of. But you changed me. I decided to be a better man when I met you that day in Charleston. If anyone tries to tell you that isn't true, they are a liar."

"So, thank you for marrying me. You gave me the happiest months of my life. I truly wish we had escaped my past life, moved to an island in the Pacific, and grown old together."

I stifle a sob. From the corner of my eye, I see Arzu shift. I extend my arm toward her, my palm up like a stop sign.

"I'm sorry you're caught up in my mess, but whatever is on that disk needs to get to the right group of Americans. And that's the problem. You won't know who the good guys are, and unfortunately, I'm not even sure myself, to be honest. I've even been sabotaged by my partner, Burt."

He runs his fingers roughly through his hair.

"I'm being chased, and now that I'm dead—that feels so weird to say—they will chase you. This video is as secure as possible, but I'm worried it will lead them to you. You'll need to decide for yourself who you can trust. Just be careful. The ones that look the most helpful are usually the vipers. As smart as you are, I know you'll make it through this."

Harris places his palm against the screen, and without hesitation, I do the same as if he's alive, and I can feel his hand through the void.

"Quinn, I love you. I always will. Please be safe and remember Mexico."

He kisses the palm of his hand and places it back on the screen, and before I can react—he's gone.

19

QUINN

I'm desperate to replay the video, but the email disappears in a fantastic trick of spy tech. Harris is truly dead this time, leaving me trapped in the world of James Bond. I collapse into an ugly cry and try to hide the snot and tears from Arzu. She shoves me aside and starts clicking. I paw through my backpack for tissues, but there are none. I drop my head on my arms and cry.

The clicking stops. Arzu's hand rests on my shoulder. I sit up, dab the tears from my eyes with my arms, and wipe my nose with my T-shirt tail. I look at her with hope. She shakes her head, her green eyes filled with compassion.

"The email is gone, and there is no way for me to retrieve it," she whispers.

"He's really dead." My voice is so soft that it forces Arzu to lean close to hear me.

"I thought you knew this?" she asks.

"The military told me he was," I respond with a sniff, "but I didn't believe them."

She pulls a small packet of tissues from her back pocket and hands them to me.

"Why?" she asks.

"My gut said he was alive."

I take a tissue from her and blot my eyes. This entire day is about to pull me under. I need to get myself together and fast. The drama of more tears will have to wait until I'm locked in my apartment.

Apartment. Dinner. I'm supposed to meet Sedat, the landlord, for dinner in two hours.

I take a big breath and steady my heart. At least I know what Harris and I had was real for both of us. As much as I hate him right now, I miss him. And, regardless of his past, I know from the video that his death was not an accident.

And his killer is now focused on me.

"What do you want to do?" Arzu asks.

I look at my hands as I clutch the tissue. "Right now, I just want to go back to my apartment. Can you find a way to access the information on this disk? There has to be a hacker that isn't frightened like the Russian." I could try guessing the dates like with the video, but I cannot risk making an error and having the disk erased. Since Harris wasn't the creator, the dates would be random anyway.

She nods and hands me my backpack, and I follow her out the door and into the sunlight like a dog kicked repeatedly to the curb. Back on the ferry, Arzu leads me to a quiet corner at the front of the boat and away from other passengers.

"Can you tell me what he says?" she asks.

Throughout my career as a lawyer, I have trusted my instincts. Everyone has this ability, but most don't consult their intuition. People are always in their heads. My instinct tells me I can trust Arzu. Yes, my gut also told me Harris was alive. I look at her for a full minute before I respond.

"The information on the disk is dangerous," I whisper. She leans toward me. "Harris didn't know what exactly was on it. I'm to give it to an American I trust."

"That should be easy. There are many Americans here."

I laugh softly. "Yes, but I haven't met one I trust."

Her pixie face is back, eyebrows raised. "What will you do?"

"Help me find someone who can read the information on this disk. Then I can decide." I respond, then shift my body toward her. "The military insists I'm part of whatever this is about. I'm not. Harris told me not to access the information on the disk, but I have to. I won't know how to clear his name, and mine, without knowing what I'm dealing with."

I sit back and scan the people around me. It is difficult in this country when I cannot tell who is a friend and who is a foe. I turn back to Arzu.

"My husband was most likely killed for whatever is on this. If you want to walk away now, I will understand."

I pull two hundred dollars from my bag.

Arzu lets out a snort. "You are such a princess, Miss America. Walk away? You don't know who you are talking to, but you will. Put your money away and give me your phone."

She types, adding her cell phone number to mine as she walks me to a taxi stand.

"You have your address to give to the driver?"

"Yes," I respond, "but I will walk. I need to think."

"It might be safer for you to think at home."

"Yeah, I know, but I can't live that way. Call me when you've found someone."

When Arzu leaves me, I feel very alone. Although loneliness isn't new to me, it has become more acute since I saw Harris in that video. According to the map on my phone, it will take me half an hour to walk home. The first few blocks, I feel like I'm walking in a fog, and my teeth hurt from the slow grind back and forth. I wander down the sidewalk, not focused on where I'm going, until I notice a bench next to the soothing water and collapse onto it. I need to think, but my heart aches, and my brain won't function.

I grasp the pendant. The feel of the warm gold against my skin brings me back to reality. Whether or not Harris loved me, his choices have thrust me into a dangerous world of military, spies, hackers, and murder. I fumble in my jeans and find the disk, removing it from the adapter and inserting it back into the secret compartment of the necklace. The plastic gadget goes into my backpack, in a zipper pocket next to my passport.

I can do this.

I need coffee beans to make more Turkish jet-fuel coffee, but I've finished Sedat's gift bag. Pulling up Google Maps, I trudge toward the *Kemeraltı Çarşısı*. The crowded cobblestone shopping bazaar is sure to have a shop that sells whole beans. Following the dots on the map, I survey the worn buildings. Rows of skinny storefronts line the sidewalk. Apartment balconies jut from their upper floors. Most Turkish stores are smaller than those in the United States. They are single narrow stone boxes with tall ceilings, a single glass windowpane, a front door, and a thousand years of history etched into every inch.

I have limited knowledge of history, and what I do know is courtesy of a single college semester of required World History. As an elective in my senior year, I chose Middle Eastern history and politics, focusing on the past two hundred years. The class sparked a fascination with all things surrounding the history of this area, but my Southern conservative world frowned on different cultures and religions. Harris unlocked that hidden dream to explore while promising me the world.

But the price is too high. He's dead, and if Maynard is to be believed, I'm about to be jailed.

I stop and recheck the map, my brain still arguing with itself. There is nothing to stop me from chucking all this, giving Maynard the disk, and going somewhere other than America. But I can't. I fell in love with Harris, trusted him, and married him. I will never be free if I don't discover what is happening here. Unleashed and alone, my irritation with Harris surfaces again, but I shove it down. I need a break from the constant mental ping-pong.

The scent of cinnamon, then cardamom, wafts in the warm air. A spice shop displays burlap sacks of various spices in colors ranging from rust to red, brown, green, and gold. Next to it, a shop holds a rainbow of silk scarves folded in squares and stacked twelve to fifteen feet high. I'm curious about what happens when a customer wants to see a scarf on the bottom, but I don't ask. A chocolate shop with multi-colored candies and chocolates is wedged next to a patisserie loaded with cakes, desserts, and pastries. The smells make me pick up my pace for the coffee.

A rooftop of white canvas sails shelters the street from the sun and rustles in the afternoon breeze. I wind deeper into the narrow passages as the chatter of the women shopping around me reassures me that someone's life is normal, even though mine is not.

Rows of young lambs, newly plucked pink chickens, and gaping sides of beef hang heavily in shopkeepers' windows. I notice their lifeless, hollow heads and awkwardly splayed, stiff limbs dangling flagrantly on display behind the glass. I feel the vacant eyes of the dead animals watching me as I pass by.

My skin prickles, and all at once, I want to run. I pick up my pace and pass massive baskets of seafood on ice; fish, squid, mussels, and a menagerie of unidentifiable slimy things from the sea that assail my nose. A few women pick among the fish, bargaining with the shopkeepers, but I don't stop to watch.

According to the map on my phone, I'm near the coffee shop. The hairs on my neck stand on end, but no dead animal eyes are staring at me now. I turn a corner and look for a familiar face, but I don't see anyone. I shrug it off, but my focus is waning under a building cacophony of noise. The shoppers' incessant mindless chatter drowns out my thoughts, along with the vendors' negotiating with customers at the top of their lungs or barking wisecracks at each other.

Above the hubbub of jumbled sounds in the busy market, I cannot concentrate. This is making me nervous. My craving for coffee and solid food, along with the shock of Harris's video, is making me paranoid. I try to ignore my anxiety, but chills travel over my arms. I walk faster and turn to glance behind me.

Two men in suits are following me, making no attempts to hide that I'm their target. I walk a half block, then stop in front of a shoe store, pretending to admire a pair. I check the reflection in the glass. The men also stop, light cigarettes, and talk to each other. They ignore me as they watch the crowds of shoppers.

I must hide somewhere until I figure out what to do. Picking up my pace, I weave through the shoppers and casually look at colorful items that catch my eye. I go in and out of shops but purchase nothing.

We slowly play this game for fifteen minutes until I duck into a small copper shop, its rear door propped open for air. Without a word to the proprietor, I hold my index finger vertically before my lips and step out the back exit into an alley, closing the door softly until only a crack is left. My body shivers in fear, telling me that Harris was right. I'm in serious trouble.

My stomach's rumbling threatens to reveal my hiding place as the two men enter the store. Neither man's suit fits, and their leather shoes are worn and scuffed. One has a mustache, the other is clean-shaven. The beardless one is the same man I saw at the restaurant where I met Arzu. How could he possibly know I would get coffee? My first thought is Arzu, but unless she is also following me, she thinks I am on my way home.

I peek through the crack between the door and the frame. The men exchange harsh words as they quiz the shopkeeper. Their accents sound more like the Russian at the computer store than the Turkish I've heard.

I can't see the shopkeeper to gauge his response. My hands grip my backpack so hard that my fingernails cut into my hands.

The men's flailing arms and pointing fingers combine with the rapid conversation. Finally, they leave the store. I close my eyes and sag against the outside wall.

Heavy footsteps rush toward the door. I slink further down the alley, ready to run. The door squeaks open about an inch. Fingers appear from the edge of the door. A hand slowly pulls the door inward.

It is all I can do not to scream.

20

QUINN

The men have come back for me.

I scour the alley for an escape route. Three separate doors open into it; otherwise, it is walled at the end with no exit. My heart beats so hard I am sure it will bounce out of my chest. I rise and prepare to slam the door on the person, reaching for the handle.

The proprietor pops his head around the door. I laugh, flooded with relief.

"*Iyi misin?*" His face is worried. He wants to know if I am all right.

"*Evet. Teşekkür ederim,*" I respond, happy that I understand him. With my affirmative response and then an apology for hiding in his store, he grins under his thick mustache. He walks down the stairs and stands outside with me.

"*Peki bu adamlar kimdi?*" The proprietor wants to know who the men are.

I don't know, and tell him so. "*Bilmiyorum.*"

"*Kanadalı mısın?*" He wants to know if I am Canadian.

"*Hayır, Amerikalıyım.*"

Properly identified as an American, I thank him again and reach for the door. He shakes his head and motions for me to wait. Striding across the alley, he bangs on the back door of another shop. After a minute, a thin old woman opens the door. She wears a colorful pink headscarf edged with delicate, crocheted flowers. As she talks, the flowers bounce around her head. She cackles when the man finishes his explanation, and her gray eyes catch mine with a wink.

She grasps my hand and pulls me into her shop. With a smile, the copper man bids me goodbye, and the door closes behind me. The old woman pulls me through a busy dressmaker's shop. Seamstresses work in a large room filled with floor-to-ceiling bolts of colorful fabric.

We wind our way through the machines and then reach a display room at the front. She grabs a large scarf, like the one she is wearing, and, using a mirror for my benefit, artfully ties it to cover my hair. Motioning me forward, I hold up my hand for her to wait. Probing in my backpack, I pull out a wad of lira and hand it to her. With a laugh and a few Turkish sentences in a dialect I don't understand, she shoves my hand away, and I return the money to my bag.

"Bir dakika." I point to my phone, needing a minute to consult my map. She nods and waits. Her shop opens onto a major street, and I get my bearings. With an enveloping hug, the old woman sends me off with a cigarette-worn cackle of laughter, and I step to the sidewalk. Scanning the street, I don't see the men. The borrowed scarf helps me blend in, although it is still evident, especially if someone notices my running shoes, that I'm a foreigner.

At the first intersection, I hail a taxi, thankful for small favors and Turkish conspirators. The faces of the men following me won't be forgotten, and my hands are still shaking with rapidly subsiding adrenaline combined with fear.

I don't know who they are, but as Harris predicted, the chase has begun.

And dagnabbit, I didn't get my coffee.

21

SEDAT

Sedat sees her trudging up the hill toward him at ten minutes to eight. She called his number twice after leaving the ferry, but he refused to answer, knowing she would only cancel dinner with him. He must get close to her to get the information on that disk. Yet that isn't the only reason he wants her here. Something inside him needs to see her.

She is tall for a woman by Turkish standards, with long black hair and a hint of Asian heritage, evident in her eyes and skin. As she gets closer, her makeup cannot hide her exhaustion and the paranoia that has resulted from whatever her husband told her in the internet cafe, followed by the chase through Kemeraltı. From the microphone in her backpack, he caught Quinn and Arzu's conversation in Karşıyaka, but when they started with the computer, after a long silence, there were only sobs.

From the conversation afterward, he gleaned there was a video from Robicheaux. He needs to recover that video, but the possibility is slim. Yet if it can be done, his technology group, already onsite, can do it.

He scrutinizes her as she approaches. If she is an actor, she has terrific control over her body language and demeanor. Even the color in her cheeks appears to be playing its part. A skilled artist can adjust these things, but Sedat does not believe she is that. He sees what Bora insists she is: a distraught woman caught in circumstances beyond her control. And he hates that he will only add to those circumstances. Guilt rises in his gut like acid, but he shakes it off. He has had many targets in his life. This is just one more, and there will be others after her.

The smell of food from the restaurant behind him cloaks the neighborhood. When Quinn reaches the cafe's outdoor seating area, Sedat rises to greet her, pulling out a chair next to him. He forces himself to appear happier today, less intense, to help the woman relax. Unless she trusts him, he will never reach his objective.

The evening breeze lifts the ends of her hair, and she touches a necklace or something hiding under her blouse. Her stomach rumbles as she reaches the table. She gives him a wan smile.

"Hello, Sedat."

"Did you forget to have food today, Quinn? Did I not send enough for you?" Sedat extends his hand formally, and her shake is firm and confident. Desperate to touch her, he has to force himself to let go of her hand. He motions to the chair beside him, but she sits across the table.

"To be honest, I'm starved. Thank you so much for your kind delivery. Everything is wonderful. I have enough food now for an army. How much do I owe you?"

"Please do not offer the money." He keeps his voice upbeat after the insult. "We do not do this here in Türkiye. The food was my gift for you, to show you my country." He flashes a quick smile, and she visibly relaxes. He motions toward the menu on the cafe's wall and sees her blush.

"I hate to act like a tourist, but is there anything with pictures?"

"No worries. If I may, I will order for you. The food is simple here, but it is good and homemade. Is this your first experience with Turkish food?"

"Yes." She scans the restaurant's lush outdoor setting. "This is my first time in a Turkish restaurant."

He laughs. "Are you afraid of my country? Türkiye's food is the best in the world. Here for an entire day and no food? What have you eaten?" With the look she gives him, he recalls what she has been through today. He realizes that, of course, she has most likely not eaten at all.

The waiter appears, and Sedat jokes with him in Turkish as he orders. He refuses to allow this woman to wallow in misery because of her lying scoundrel of a husband.

"Excuse me, but I am rude not to explain," he says as his phone buzzes with a text. "The waiter will bring you tastes of everything in the restaurant." He looks at the text and then back at Quinn. "Please excuse me. I must respond to this. We will talk about the apartment then."

He leaves the table and heads inside the restaurant. Bora's text says only CALL ME. Sedat taps the number for his partner.

"Yes, Bora. What is it?"

"How is your dinner?"

"Excuse me? You interrupt what I am doing with a target to harass me?"

"This isn't a target, and you know it. She is such a beautiful woman. You have no experience in this area. And no, your mother and sisters do not count. I am calling to offer you my years of experience and help you navigate this challenging time. I am listening, but you are not exploiting this opportunity."

"Enough, Bora. Don't call me again." Sedat ends the call with mental plans to strangle the man once he returns to the office. Returning to the table, he nods politely to Quinn and retrieves documents from his briefcase on the floor beside him.

"I am sorry for the interruption. This is the contract for your apartment. I knew you could not read Turkish, so I went to the *Noter* and had it translated." He hands her the contract and the attached translation.

"Thank you very much," Quinn says, looking at the document. "I appreciate your thoughtfulness, Sedat. Can you please tell me how I should pay the rent? I will only be here briefly and do not want to cause a problem. Do I pay in American dollars? Turkish lira?"

Sedat grits his teeth when he understands Robicheaux has told his wife nothing.

"The apartment has been paid in full for this year," he responds as his phone buzzes with another text. He checks to be sure it is Bora. He ignores the text on his office phone, then turns it off and drops it into his briefcase.

Surprise crosses her face. "What do you mean by this *year*?"

Sedat shrugs as her face turns to dismay. "In Türkiye, for people not from our country, collecting the year's monies before a tenant may occupy the apartment has always been the practice. We also do it with business properties. It is normal."

Quinn looks frantic. "Is there a possibility of getting the money back?" she asks.

Sedat shakes his head, trying to be polite. He would not allow a refund, even if it were detailed in the contract. His personal phone buzzes in his jacket pocket. He looks at the text, thankful it is in Turkish and not English.

"ARE YOU SITTING NEXT TO HER? TAKE HER HAND, MAN. HELP HER THROUGH THIS DIFFICULT TIME."

Sedat will kill Bora for this. He returns his focus to Quinn.

"I am sorry, it is my friend. I have told him I will talk with him later, but he is impatient." He places his phone on the table face down. "No, getting money back is not possible. The money has been spent, and the contract does not allow—how do you say—a refund."

She places her fingers at the corners of her eyes to stop the tears. Sedat can see she is wrapped in a sadness so strong that it feels smothering, even to him.

"Didn't you and Harris plan to stay in Türkiye for two years? Is there a problem with this?"

"There isn't a problem. I don't know what to do at this point. I can stay if the military allows it, but they may not."

"The American military? Why do they care if you live here? Especially if Türkiye allows this." Sedat's attempt at casual conversation is wearing. Both Maynard and the chief of the Turkish National Police want her out of Türkiye by Monday.

She stares across the park until he becomes concerned.

"Quinn?" Sedat looks at her. "Is there something wrong?"

Worry is etched in the lines on her forehead. "No. Everything is fine. As you say, Harris and I planned to live here for several years, and I will adjust to being without him. Please excuse my emotions. It has been a difficult day."

"I understand. What may I do to assist you?"

The waiter interrupts with a large tray loaded with small plates of food.

"Sedat, will others be joining us?"

He shakes his head, not understanding. "No, it is for us only."

The phone buzzes again. This time, Sedat turns this phone off and shoves it in his briefcase. Being completely unreachable is against department regulations, but his partner will not give him a moment's peace unless he does.

A laugh bursts from her, causing him to smile and look up.

"Is there something wrong?"

Her face eases, and she grins at him. "There is enough food here for five or six people."

"No, no, no. It is normal. You should taste everything. How else will you learn about the food if you do not try it?"

He gestures to the waiter to unload the tray and assists in placing the food on the table in an aesthetically pleasing manner. Sedat explains each dish to her: lamb kabobs, grilled eggplant, onions cooked with spices, two types of salad—one with cucumbers and tomatoes, the other with greens—and numerous plates of vegetable dishes, which he calls mezes.

"Please eat. Try them and tell me which you like for your dinner."

Not allowing her to protest, he waits until she selects the roasted eggplant, the walnut-and-roasted-red-pepper *ezme*, a sample of the ravioli called *mantı*, and kabobs. When full plates arrive, he digs in enthusiastically, encouraging her to follow suit, hoping the food may help revive her. After several minutes, he breaks the silence.

"You must consider my offer of assistance in Türkiye, Quinn. Harris would be angry with me if I left you alone." He leans back in his chair, taking a break from the food. "Your husband was such a funny man." He motions to the waiter and asks for glasses for a toast and a small bottle of *rakı*. "Türkiye can be a difficult place in the beginning. A woman should not be alone here until she can be certain of herself."

"Thank you, but I don't want to cause you trouble." She reaches across the table and pats his hand like a child. Sedat feels a jolt pass through him at her touch. She jerks her hand away, her face embarrassed, and places it under the table in her lap.

"Please do not concern yourself." Sedat keeps his demeanor light-hearted and relaxed, even though his entire body is now on edge. "There is no problem here. You are a recent widow alone in a new place. I will be sure you have a good start in my country. You should see the wonderful people, taste the luxurious food, and see the magnificent scenery."

Sedat sits back in his chair, mentally chastising himself for exaggerating. She will see through him if he keeps this up.

"Sounds like utopia," Quinn says.

"No, we have many problems. But we also have many things that are not found in other countries. I will have to show you."

The waiter returns with four small glasses. He fills two with cold water. Then he opens a bottle of clear alcohol and fills each glass halfway, adding two ice cubes. The drink turns into a milky cloud as the ice melts.

"This is *rakı*, our national drink." Sedat raises a glass for a toast. "To Harris. A funny man whose life should have lasted much longer. May you live the life."

She touches the necklace below her throat as she returns his salute, then takes a sip. He watches her face as the licorice-flavored ice-cold liquor slides down her throat, followed by a wince. He wishes she had worn something more revealing so that he could see her necklace.

"Live the life?" she asks, clearing her throat with a cough.

"Would you prefer something else to drink?" Sedat asks. "Rakı is not for everyone, I know."

"No, this is fine, thank you." She plants a fake smile on her face. Now he knows she is a poor actress. She detests the taste of *rakı* and cannot hide it.

"There is a saying in my country." He takes another sip of his. "You must live the day extremely, ah, completely without the next day's worries."

"Live in the moment," she responds quietly.

Sedat is pleased she understood. "Hmmm," he muses as he takes another sip.

She looks at the cloudy glass of *rakı*, grasps it, and returns his salute, downing the entire drink to avoid the taste.

"Close enough."

"Now, Quinn," Sedat says between bites, "where is your bank so I can be certain you know how to pay for your electricity, telephone, and internet?"

Enough of Bora's relaxation efforts and "getting to know each other." It's time for business.

22

QUINN

The waiter refills my *rakı*, but after the kick from the first glass, I pace myself. My paranoia does spike a bit, though. What is it about me that makes men think I am helpless? Or is it something else?

"Sedat, honestly, I'm unsure how long I plan to stay. With Harris gone, I haven't decided what I will do." The strong alcohol has loosened me a little too much, and I force myself to avoid the subject of the bank. Why is where I bank any of his business? It seems a bit nosy to me.

His movements are very measured now. He sits back, places his fork on his plate, drinks water, and uses his napkin. His thoughts travel across his face while he pretends to watch the children play in the park. His dark eyes are no longer warm and inviting; they appear almost black, and his sullen gaze is neither hostile nor friendly. I squirm slightly in my seat, unsure if I will like this new version of Sedat. I take another drink of *rakı* for fortification.

"Excuse me, please. May I ask a question?" he asks.

Does he know how much his eyes change when he is serious?

Or is it something else that makes him appear so instantly aggressive?

"Yes, certainly." I stop eating and steel myself, placing my fork on my plate as my chest tightens. I wait for him to blurt accusations against my husband and accuse me of being a spy, just as Maynard did. But why would he? He's my landlord, not a spy.

"Why did you come to my country? Should you not have remained in yours?"

Mr. Nosy again. My chest relaxes, and I force the rest of my body to do the same. I rub the back of my neck, unsure if I want to reveal this information to a stranger, and decide to give him a sanitized version. I study the tea that has just been delivered to the table, not wanting the caffeine to keep me awake once I crash, but needing it to withstand his questions.

"Harris and I wanted to use Türkiye as a base and then travel worldwide when he could take leave. He had been to so many places, and I've been nowhere. I just wanted to catch up and experience the world as he had. I think I still want to do that."

"If you stay in Türkiye, will you continue working here?" he asks.

"It will be difficult to have a job as a lawyer here. Your system differs from mine, and I am not sure of the licensing requirements. As I said, I don't know what I will do."

His pushing brings reality to the surface—I am alone and have nowhere to turn. I watch people going in and out of the market across the street until I am sure I can control the sobs threatening to surface. I've never been one to cry, but today has changed me. My foreseeable future is bleak, and the tears consistently hover in the background.

"Excuse me for asking too many questions. Please accept my apology."

A sense of fairness makes me apologize in return. "I didn't mean to unload my troubles on you."

He pushes his tea away and leans toward me. "I believe you should only think about one day."

"Do you mean one day at a time?"

"Yes, you must think about one day, the next day, and then the next, but only one at a time, not altogether."

Dessert appears; I have four to taste, even though I am as full as a tick. He selects a creamy cup that looks like rice pudding and digs in. There is nothing wrong with this man's appetite. He must be a runner to burn all the calories he has consumed just tonight. I shift the conversation away from me.

"Sedat, are you from İmir? Your business card says you are a professor at Istanbul University."

"I am from Istanbul and teach economics at the university."

He takes another bite as I nibble on something sweet that looks like a bird's nest with melted cheese.

"I am on summer break," he says. "I have some business here in İmir, and of course, I must assist you with the apartment."

"Did you live in the apartment I am renting?"

A pained expression passes over his face, but only for a second.

"No, it belongs to my mother. I manage it for her."

That explains the taste in furniture. Before I ask another question, Sedat signals to the waiter and pays for dinner. After my initial faux pas regarding money, I did not offer to pay. The extra food is boxed for me to take home, and Sedat grabs his briefcase with one hand and motions to me with the other, pulling me from my chair.

"Come, let us walk. I will find you a nice bottle of wine, and you will go home and sleep with your jet lag."

"I thought that was what your 'lion's milk' was for."

Sedat lets out an explosive laugh as he takes my arm, escorting me to the street. He lets go of my elbow and heads for the market. As I watch him walk ahead of me, a wistfulness for

Harris blooms inside me. I am exhausted and want Harris to hold me as I sleep. But this man isn't Harris, and I don't know why he brings up these feelings in me. The two men are very different from each other. While my husband was an extreme extrovert, traveler, and partier, Sedat appears more intellectual, a man who understands things without me having to say. A car blows its horn, breaking my introspection, and I continue out of its path and across the street to the neighborhood market.

"Thank you for the dinner and the extra food," I tell him as I catch up. "I don't cook very much, and having food prepared is a luxury. Thank you for listening. I didn't realize how much I needed to talk to someone."

"I am very pleased to listen to you anytime. You are an interesting person." He reaches to touch my upper arm, then drops his arm with a slight smile.

"I will take your advice and try to take one day at a time from now on, beginning tomorrow."

"Ah, tomorrow we will go to my bank. You will need a Turkish account to pay your utilities. I can only assume you have an American account, and the government no longer allows the opening of Turkish accounts just with a passport. You will need someone to—ah—represent—this is not the correct word—for you."

I can see him mentally checking his calendar.

"I will introduce you to Hasan, and you will start the account for the monthly expenses. Your lease requires you to have the utilities open. It will be easier for you to use a Turkish bank for these. Then I can take you to a wonderful restaurant in another part of the city. I have no meetings in the afternoon if you are not busy."

Do I need a local to vouch for me? Many countries do this with internal business transactions, so I understand what he is saying. I have had several foreign real estate clients, and this was one of the initial questions they always asked. But for a personal checking account?

"Sedat, this is not necessary. I promise you. Just text me a list of the things to be done, and I will take care of it."

He brushes off my words with a backhanded sweep as he returns his wallet to his inside suit pocket.

"Bah. This is not a problem for me. Let me help you."

While I appreciate the food and his offer to help, this isn't what I want. I don't need anyone's pity and don't want another man breathing down my neck. While Sedat feels he needs to help me navigate the Turkish system, I don't. I want to be left alone to wallow in my grief. I will figure out what to do with the disk hidden in the necklace clutched in my right hand. His forced schedule will waste an entire day in Maynard's very short week.

I stop and face him in front of the apartment building, and his face is filled with pity. I already hate being pitied as a widow.

"Sedat, you don't have to take me on as your charity case. I will learn to do the basic things very soon. You are a busy man. I can do this, I promise. You don't have to feel sorry for me. I decided to come here and must be responsible for my actions."

His body stiffens, eyes shifting to black again, his tone indignant. My body instantly reacts to the early warning of his eyes, bracing for an abrupt order.

"*Hayır*. I do not feel sorry for you." Then he goes silent, looking at me intently but with concern. He sighs, letting go of a long breath. "This is not true. I do feel a little sorry. If it were my wife..." He leans toward me, his voice quiet. "Quinn, I know you are a strong woman. You must know that every strong woman needs help at the some time. Let me to be your help."

I notice that when he's nervous or upset, he adds unnecessary words to his sentences, and while it's a bit endearing, I still don't want his help. I approach the front door as he hands me the bottle of wine he had selected at the market.

"Thank you, Sedat. Can I call you tomorrow about the bank? I'm afraid my jet lag has caught up with me."

Ever the gentleman, he nods, his hand placed over his heart as he responds.

"*Tabii ki, bekliyorum.*" He must see from my tired confusion that I don't understand. He immediately responds in English.

"Absolutely. I will be waiting for your call."

23

QUINN

After two glasses of the lovely wine from Sedat plus the two glasses of *rakı*, I quickly fall into a deep sleep, only to wake up at four, my mind desperately needing to know what is on the disk. I want to ask Arzu if she has found another way to open the disk, but it's too early to call. I get out of bed, pace the living room, and then give up and go outside.

On the balcony, I lean against the rail to listen as the first call to prayer begins. Most of the moving boxes are open. After preparing the Turkish teapot, I start at one end of the apartment and scrutinize each box. I need to be sure there are no backup files I've missed, no other disks, and nothing else suspicious. If I cannot find anything, no one else will either. The disk Harris sent me is always hidden in the necklace until I find another solution.

A red enamel box with Chinese lettering across the top covers the bottom half of a three-foot square packing box. It is so heavy I cannot lift it, so I tip the carton on its side and slide it out. It isn't locked, and I lift the creaking lid.

Inside are Harris's essential files on paper. Who keeps paper files anymore? I know of only one paranoid senior partner in the largest southeastern real estate law firm who keeps every piece of paper in his practice, renting two massive warehouses to hold every closing file for his thirty-office law firm. And apparently, my husband is the only other American person I know who wants paper.

Sitting cross-legged on the floor, I search through the files. Most contain invoices in different languages and items from the past, to be discarded. I fumble with a folder, and life insurance policies spill across the floor. Two older policies list his mother as the only beneficiary. Two have me listed, obtained the day after we married. I hear the quartet of divorcees squawking about their missing policies, and I mentally give them the finger.

I set aside the policies, reaching for another full box. A brown envelope, which I'd almost missed, rests at the bottom. Inside is a business card for a bank manager in Istanbul, with multiple addresses. There's also an ornate antique key on a ring, along with another smaller key that appears to be for a safe-deposit box.

Scrutinizing the antique key again, I pull up reverse search images on my computer. The key seems similar to those used on iron gates in Istanbul. I pocket the three items and unpack the remaining boxes. I don't find a will, although it may be in the safe deposit box or a military file.

My back aches, so I stand and stretch. While waiting for the delicious-smelling tea to steep, I sit on the balcony with my computer. Uber in Türkiye is in partnership with taxi companies and is heavily watched and regulated by the government. I'll have to fly or take a bus if I don't rent a car. Istanbul is located five hours north, making flying the best option, especially with low-cost airlines. Sedat will offer to drive me, but my gut says involving him will open a different can of worms and more nosy questions.

Later, just before 7:00 a.m., I call Arzu. She picks up after several rings and cryptically tells me to meet her at the Konak Clock Tower, two blocks from the *Kemeraltı* shopping area, where

I was followed yesterday. This time, rather than walking, I head down the hill, catch a minibüs, watch others hand up their cash for the ride into downtown, and follow suit.

Stepping out of the *minibüs* in Alsancak, I wait near the flower vendors at the clock tower, overwhelmed by the scent of the bunches of narcissus piled in front of one of them. Twenty minutes later, Arzu saunters off a big red bus and heads my way, totally unconcerned about leaving me waiting alone, until I remember she has no idea I was followed here yesterday.

I am sure she is here out of curiosity, yet significantly, she is the only one in my world who has not sought me out. We sit at a small cafe tucked in one of the many twisting passages of Kemeraltı, devouring a "village breakfast" consisting of an entire farm: tomatoes, cucumbers, ham called *pastırma*, black and green olives, sliced artisan bread, pastries, honey, and eggs. Arzu orders Turkish coffee for both of us. Since my last attempt was a disaster, I asked her to take me to a coffee vendor after we finished.

Harris's warning not to open the disk has driven me crazy since our ferry ride across the bay, and I ask Arzu about the risks.

"It is too dangerous, Quinn. With the timer on, if you attempt to open it yourself, you will erase all the contents, and I don't know what else you may trigger. I think you should leave it alone until we can find another solution. I have someone in Istanbul who might be able to help you, but I don't have an easy way to reach him. You will have to be patient."

"Patience is something I don't have, Arzu." We are down to five days on Maynard's timeline of when the feds will jail me.

"There is nothing I can do," she says. "In a large city, you would think there would be someone to help, but there isn't. It is too risky here, particularly with your friends watching every step you take."

"What friends? What are you talking about?"

"You are a very popular person, Quinn."

"Stop talking in circles." I stare at her.

"Don't you know?" She leans forward, and her voice drops to a whisper. "Men are following you everywhere you go."

"Yes, I know. I was followed yesterday. At first, I thought I was paranoid, but they followed me into a copper shop, and the shopkeeper helped me escape."

"Followed openly?" Her face goes white. "You saw them? What did they want?" As I suspected before, she isn't as badass as she wants me to think.

"I didn't understand anything they said." I shrug, trying to appear unconcerned. "I'm an American citizen. They won't touch me." The thought of my government slamming me into a Turkish jail cell passes through my mind, causing a shiver to zip down my back.

Arzu shoves her chair back from the table. She shakes her head at me.

"You are the most stupid person I have ever met or the most naive."

"And you can determine this after twenty-four hours?"

"*Kesinlikle evet.* You most certainly are. At least two groups are following you, possibly a third."

"What? That's crazy." I shake my head, not believing her for a second. "There were only two men."

"Crazy for you, yes. But I know what I see and hear."

"Hear?"

"I listen to people. I pay attention."

"And what do you see and hear, Arzu?" She is scaring the bejesus out of me.

"You have something they all want. There is war talk if they don't get it, even though I don't know what "it" is. Also, a lot of money is missing, stolen from some nasty men at a Sochi card game, plus other bad deals involving your husband."

She sits forward and talks quietly, concern written on her face.

"I visited the Russian to apologize. He is too valuable a

contact to make him angry. I had to know why the disk—or you—angered him so much. He told me some of these things, and then I checked with several other friends and learned more of the same story. I realized he wasn't angry. He was scared. The logo on your disk? It is from a dangerous group from Bulgaria. The Russian warned me to avoid you, insisting you are trouble."

"And you owe me fifty dollars." She extends her palm toward me. "I had to pay him for wasting his time."

"Okay," as I reply, digging in my purse for the money, "but that doesn't tell me what I have and why they want it."

"Your husband won the disk in a card game from a drunk. A taste of the contents is scheduled to be revealed next Wednesday. After that, a twenty-four-hour auction will award the disk to the highest bidder.

"Who is running the auction?" I ask.

"No one knows who they are."

"How can they auction off something they don't have? Auctioning off something unknown looks like a huge scam."

"I don't know, Quinn, but it explains why these people follow you. Also, according to the Russian across the bay, the mafia types who lost that money say it was to an American gambler who bragged he was from New Orleans. Is that your husband? My friend is sure they've also heard about the disk and want in on that action."

The twinkle in her eyes brings a smile to my face. The risk interests her the most.

"Besides the men wanting the disk and the money, who else is following me?"

"The Turks, but I don't think they want anything. They're just keeping themselves in the loop." Her face quickly turns skeptical. "I'm curious," she says. "Why do you trust me to help you?"

"Because I came to you, remember? Plus, you are the only person who has not asked me anything other than money or demanded information about Harris." I paused. "Well, maybe not my landlord."

"Your landlord?"

"Yes. He's Turkish, of course. He gave me food, brought me the apartment lease, and now insists that, as a widow alone in a foreign country, I need his help.

"I wouldn't trust anyone, Quinn, although he is probably looking for something else." She gives me a sly grin and a wink.

"That's not going to happen," I say. I hesitate, then decide I need to know. "Should I trust you?"

Her face transforms into the pixie from when we met, and then she grows serious.

"Probably not."

"Why?" I ask.

Arzu grows silent, pushing at the cuticles on her thumbs until I reach across and stop her.

"Because I've been in your place."

"How so?"

"I was labeled a thief by two competing professors at Berkeley."

"In California?"

"Yes. They were both vying for the latest in artificial intelligence. Of course, now their work is old news, but at the time, that code was cutting-edge. The notes of one vanished, and he accused the other of theft. Because I worked as a research assistant for both, I was accused of helping one over the other."

"Did you steal the notes?"

"No." She shakes her head. "While they could not prove my guilt, I could not prove my innocence. They dismissed me from the program and sent me home when my student visa expired. No other school would accept me with the accusations hanging over my head. The top of the tech community is small, and it did not take long for my troubles to follow me here. The schools in

Türkiye would not give me credit for the Ph.D. work I completed in California."

She sucks in air, filling her lungs, and then blows it out, looking away from me in embarrassment.

"You shouldn't help me, Arzu." The girl has her own problems and shouldn't be involved in my drama. I can't ask her to add more controversy to her reputation. "I don't know what's on the disk," I continue, "and I don't know what you will be involved in when we discover what it is. I've been given a deadline to find this information. If I don't produce it, according to this one American, I'll be jailed here or deported and jailed in the U.S. You must do what your friend says and stay far away from me."

Arzu shakes her head. "I'll take my chances this time. I don't think you should do this alone. Besides, you promised to pay, and I need the money."

"You'll get out if it's too much?"

"Believe me, I will do anything to keep from getting trapped like that again."

I cannot force her out. When she looks back at me, I return to business. "Who can hack this disk?"

"There's a boy in Istanbul. We can't just call. He doesn't work that way."

"I need to go there anyway."

"Really, why?"

"You say I shouldn't trust you, so I won't. Go with me to Istanbul and help me find your contact. And for God's sake, we need to negotiate a daily rate. I don't want you to hold me hostage for a huge amount once all this is over."

"I have to reschedule some things." She opens her iPhone and then looks up at me. "You'll need money for this boy."

"Let's get my coffee while you tell me how much for you and the boy."

"No, you don't pay for me until you get the results. It's my reputation. Don't worry. I won't charge you an amount that is too much, but I must confirm if he can do this work first. But you can pay for your coffee and our breakfast."

24

QUINN

"Speak of the devil," I say quietly as irritation flows through me. Maynard lounges at a cafe table at a restaurant several doors down and across the street. I can feel my heart rate climb, knowing he isn't here by accident.

Arzu follows my gaze, then squints at me. "Who is this man?"

"The American with the deadline I just mentioned." I stand, reaching for the lira in my backpack. "We need to go."

My cell phone rings with Sedat's name. I tap the screen, and he begins talking before I can say hello. Arzu tugs on my sleeve to get me walking as I talk, looking over her shoulder at Maynard.

"We have an appointment with Hasan in the shopping district of *Kemeraltı* at nine o'clock this morning. Will that be acceptable to you? If so, I will change my schedule." His question is more of a directive than a request.

"Sedat, I can do this—"

He interrupts. "No, you cannot." His voice is impatient. "I explained this last night. Please meet me outside Garanti Bank, located in the middle of the block on *863 Sokak* in *Kemeraltı*. I will see you there."

I'm left holding my silent cell phone, and without looking to see if Maynard is following me, I run down the crowded street to catch up to Arzu.

"What is happening?" Arzu asks.

"My landlord is helping me open a bank account at a Turkish bank."

"Do you have a Turkish citizenship card?"

"No."

She snorts a laugh. "It's not possible unless there is a bit of *rüşvet*. She rubs her fingers and thumb together and gives me a wicked smile. "Let me know how he does this. I can always use a contact on the banking side."

"A bit of what?"

"A bribe." She weaves in and out of the shoppers, taking turns quickly and moving in and out of stores. When she repeats this pattern several times, I understand she is trying to lose Maynard. We stop abruptly outside the coffee vendor.

"He's a professor, Arzu," I reply, breathless. "I don't think he's the bribing type. He seems to be a nice guy, just a bit nosy."

This time, Arzu lets out a belly laugh. "This is your second day, yes?" She points back to where we came. "And you're being followed everywhere now. Remember that things in this country are not what they seem. Would you like me to accompany you to the bank? I can be sure he doesn't cheat you. I promise I will not charge too much."

"Yeah, so you tell me. Concentrate on the boy in Istanbul. I can handle my landlord and the idiot Air Force officer."

Arzu follows me inside the coffee shop and waits while I load up with several bags of whole beans. I also grab a *cezve*, a copper cup with a handle, for making Turkish coffee on the stove, and an electric grinder. Arzu walks me toward Garanti Bank but leaves me a block away.

"Let me know when we're going to Istanbul. The faster, the better." I remind her.

"Yeah, yeah. You Americans and your schedules. I will call

you if I can arrange something. We may have to go there and see." She waves as she rounds the corner, heading for the bus stop.

I window shop down the block, checking for Maynard in the glass as I try to ignore the condescending glances of older women and the outright leers of their male contemporaries. People have no problem staring here, but I can't get used to it. I check myself in a store window's reflection as I try to spot Maynard.

I'm wearing a comfortable summer dress, my hair is pulled back in a conservative bun, and I'm wearing minimal makeup, much like the women my age around me. Reaching the bank early, I wait outside the front entrance. I try to melt into the wall of the building to avoid the crowd of shoppers as I wait for Sedat.

Nothing is wrong with my appearance. I'm simply a fish out of water.

25

QUINN

Sedat carries himself like a commanding general, dressed in an expensive gray suit. When he sees me, he is again the charming man from last night's dinner.

"Good morning, Quinn. I see you are rested."

"Thank you for dinner last night. The food was fabulous." I don't tell him I've been up since four or that I'm planning a trip to Istanbul.

Entering the bank, we receive effusive greetings from the branch manager. As I am introduced to Hasan, I can't help but observe how the banker reacts to us as if we are royalty, and Sedat is the king.

"Sedat, I have a Citibank account. This isn't necessary," I say softly, not knowing if Hasan speaks English. I want to know *why* Hasan is so readily willing to do this for me, especially when Arzu says it isn't legal.

"You will see its purpose in one minute," he responds with a wink.

Hasan ushers us to his office for tea and a profusion of desserts. After what appears to be a social conversation between the two men, the banker begins asking for my personal information as he sets up the new account. I squint toward Sedat as I respond to the questions. I'm uncomfortable giving out the details in front of Sedat, even though I shouldn't be. I assume Harris had to provide the same information on the lease application.

Within minutes, despite Arzu's assertions, I have an account in a Turkish bank. Hasan's tutor session at the ATM reveals that I can use my debit card and a PIN to pay all utilities, the Turkcell bill, and any other account I wish to link, without having to log in to my computer.

"These types of transactions are impossible at an American-based bank, even in Türkiye," Sedat says. "Türkiye does not use checks, and any American checks may be rejected."

I look at the ATM and immediately remember that Harris's military packet explained that all Americans had to use cash. Accounts in Turkish banks could not be obtained without Turkish residency or citizenship, and American banks could not be used for Turkish expenses. I watch Hasan shift from one foot to the other on the sidewalk and realize he is nervous.

My paranoia increases, as do my questions.

Who *is* Sedat? His business card from last night says he is a professor. As I scrutinize him while he talks with Hasan, I see that he looks very military again. He stands to attention, his hands clasped behind his back, his back ramrod straight. Unable to keep up with their rapid conversation, I politely wait for them to finish. My mind returns to the memory card, and I try to be careful as I look around for anyone, especially Maynard, who may be watching me.

I don't see him, but that doesn't mean he isn't there. As I turn back to the men, Sedat is waiting, his face questioning.

"Did you need something?" I ask. He smiles politely, his demeanor professional, and I realize Hasan is waiting for something.

"Your mind is elsewhere, I see. Is everything at the bank

acceptable to you? Is there anything else Hasan can do for you? Cash possibly? I have ensured he always gives you the best exchange rate." His hands remain clasped behind his back.

"Everything is great." I step toward the banker with my hand extended. "Thank you very much for your help." Hasan shakes my hand, and his relief is tangible as he disappears inside the bank.

I have a million questions, but I keep silent. I'm not sure Sedat is the right person to ask. Maybe it is Arzu's insistence that people are spying on me, or that I will abruptly bump into Maynard at any minute, or the Russian hacker who hates me, or the two men from yesterday. She's right. I'm way too popular at the moment.

"We will go to the restaurant now. I cleared my appointments for you, so—" He stops his imperious tone mid-sentence. "Is this possible for you? Is your afternoon free?"

My phone rings.

"I must take this call." I hold up my index finger as I have seen Sedat do several times, and walk far enough away so that he cannot hear my part of the conversation.

Arzu skips any pleasantries. "Meet me at the *otogar* at six tomorrow morning."

"There has to be a faster way than the bus. I'm running out of time."

"It would help if you told me these things. But, ah, no, we are not friends, you say. I am paid, so your unexplained deadline is logical for you."

"Zip it, Arzu. Is there a faster way than the bus?"

"Of course, there are flights hourly from Menderes airport, and they are less than fifty dollars, but the boy is unavailable until tomorrow evening."

"That works. I have things to do. How long is the flight?"

"An hour. Then, another hour on the train to downtown. Where do you want to go? It's a big city."

"I'll talk to you about it tomorrow. Can you get tickets for late tonight or very early tomorrow morning? Text me the link for mine, and I'll pay you for both tomorrow."

"Of course. Text me your complete name and the passport number." The call abruptly finishes just as it began. I pull up the security copy of my passport on my phone and send Arzu the information. When I return to Sedat, he is finishing his own call.

"I'm very sorry, but I do not have time for a long lunch," I tell him. Something has come up for later today."

"Another time for that restaurant, then." He looks irritated rather than disappointed. "I will tell my friend we will come another day. We can walk to a cafe for coffee, and then I will take you to the apartment."

Sedat removes his suit jacket and rolls up his sleeves. He strolls through Kemeraltı and continues toward the clock tower. On *Cumhuriyet Bulvarı*, we walk by the seaside. After a block, Sedat pauses, holding my elbow to stop me from walking past him.

"What are you doing?" I ask quietly.

He releases me and bends, pretending to tie his shoe, lifting his foot to rest on the seawall as he casually looks to his left and right. Tendons stand out on the back of his neck. Then he straightens and walks again.

"There are two men behind us." Sedat's voice is deceptively calm. "Do not look behind me, and do not look alarmed. If you do, they will know we have spotted them."

I run my fingers through my hair, a nervous habit developed in law school, and then, catching myself, drop my hand to my side as we walk. Looking across the large bay toward the city on the other side, I spot two men in my peripheral vision but don't dare shift my gaze. From this distance, I'm unsure if they are the same two men from yesterday. I touch his arm, and he glances at me but continues walking as if we are out for a midday stroll.

"This happened yesterday."

"What?" The word snaps at me. Even though his voice is low,

Sedat's face flushes with irritation as he jerks to a stop for a second, then continues.

"I don't know if it is the same men," I respond casually, trying to hide my uneasiness.

"You were followed, and you did not tell me this?"

"I don't know if they're the same men," I say again, my apprehension less well disguised this time. For a second, he sucks in his cheeks and turns his head to stare at my profile, then returns to his military bearing.

"What do we do?"

"We walk." His voice is tense but controlled. "And hope they do not move closer toward us."

I glance at the side of his face. A vein rises at his temple, showing completely restrained anger. Seeing him this way makes me nervous.

"What if they do?" I ask.

"We run." He stops and turns me to face him. "Do whatever I tell you, Quinn. You cannot go in a different direction or let your anger take you. This is not your country. Do not stop and yell at them and point your fingers at their chests like you Americans do in the TikTok videos."

I can't help it. I laugh, and he smiles. He removes his owlish professor glasses, puts them in his pocket, and becomes serious again.

"You will follow my directions. Please do not push me on this."

"I will. I want to get home in one piece. No pointing or yelling, I promise."

We pick up the pace, winding our way along the seaside. Sedat laughs several times as if I have told him a joke, turning toward me as he determines the distance between the men and us.

"They are getting closer. We need to move off the seaside and into the apartments."

Sedat nudges me to follow him and grabs my hand as he zigzags through three lanes of stalled lunchtime traffic to the other side of the street. I hear the men's feet pounding on the pavement behind us. Sedat pulls me into a run. We sprint across a side street, jog one block uphill, then turn farther into the neighborhood, climbing a steep incline.

Behind us, one of the men huffs words into a portable radio as he runs.

I am too out of shape for an uphill walk, much less a run. Breathless, I try to get Sedat to slow down.

"I think they are police. Shouldn't we stop?"

I read stories last month of American tourists who had fallen foul of the Turkish authorities by running rather than answering questions. Still slogging behind Sedat up the hill, I risk a look at the men and see shoulder-strapped guns under their flapping coats. Handguns in Türkiye aren't as common as in the U.S.

Sedat pulls me up the hill after him. "Do not stop. If they were police, they would have identified themselves by now."

Ahead is a large cross street with traffic. We arrive at the intersection just as a taxi rolls to a stop at a neighborhood stand. Sedat grabs the back door handle, opens it, and shoves me in headfirst. He ducks inside after me, yelling in Turkish at the taxi driver.

The taxi screeches away from the curb. I twist around to look at the two men standing on the sidewalk, desperate for another taxi, but nothing appears. They throw up their hands, pointing at each other as they grow small in the distance. I turn around. Sedat's calm is a facade. His eyes are black tunnels, and he's twisting a large onyx ring on his middle finger, as if mentally counting to one hundred to quell his temper.

"Wait, Sedat. Let me explain."

26

QUINN

We arrive in front of the apartment, and I know Sedat will not let me out of the taxi alone, but will expect a detailed explanation. I try to pay for the cab, but he shoves my money back into my backpack.

"Stop being ridiculous. Please go into the apartment. We must assume they know where you live."

He follows me inside the building and into the apartment. After he deadbolts the door, he strides to the living room window and stands with his back to me. I go to the kitchen for water. I return and hand him the glass, sensing he is about to explode. Sedat has been nice, trying to help me and make my life easier. I owe him an explanation.

"Why have men been following you, Quinn?" Sedat still stares out the window, refusing to look at me.

"This involves Harris. Now that he is dead, things I didn't know are coming to light."

"Like what?" He shifts forward, holding the glass so hard I think it will shatter. His stare drills into me. I take the glass from him and set it on the dining table.

"The American Department of Defense suspects he was a spy

and a thief and that I'm his partner. I've learned that Harris angered quite a few people, and there are several groups after him for stolen money."

I join him, staring at the bay. Do I tell him about the disk? He just saved me from two thugs. My gut still says no.

"Do you have the money he stole?" he asks.

I can feel him studying my profile for a reaction.

"No." I turn and sweep my arm at the mess: boxes and their contents scattered around the room in complete disarray. "I've looked through everything here. There's no money." I stare at my feet, then catch myself. Of all the clients I have caught in lies, I should know better. Body language is always the giveaway.

He squints at me. "There may be no money, but you found something else." He gives me a slow grin.

"I found some keys and a business card for a bank in Istanbul."

"Ah, so he hid the money. Do you need me to go to the bank for you?" He relaxes slightly and walks over to sit on the couch. His faltering English is now as smooth as a British native's. I stiffly control my facial expression even though it feels like a million buzzing bees are stinging me from inside. The suspicions I had at Garanti Bank have now doubled.

"No, I can go myself." I force myself to smile.

He picks up his phone, swiping as he checks something. "I will take you. We can go tomorrow."

"I don't need a ride. I can do this myself."

He laughs softly. "You are the most independent woman I know, and you will beat me severely with your explanations of how you can be even more independent."

"Turkish women aren't independent?"

"Yes, of course, but they are not reckless."

"I'm reckless?"

"Quinn, I am concerned about you being alone with the travels."

And now his broken English is back. This man is not who he appears to be. I quickly resume the conversation, hoping my hesitation hasn't given him a signal that I know something fishy is going on.

"Do women in Türkiye not travel alone?"

"The women of the village where I am from do not travel long distances alone, no."

This is the twenty-first century, not the Ottoman Empire. For some reason, he doesn't want me out of his sight.

"I have the business card for the bank in Istanbul, so I will just take the bus to Istanbul. Then I can take a taxi and give the driver the card. It will be easy."

"Show it to me."

I hesitate, but his eyes, like ink-black icicles, tell me he's not backing down. I pull the card from my wallet. He takes it from my hand. It's stupid of me, because now he knows exactly where I'm going. All this stress has turned me into an idiot.

He points to an address on the card. "This is in the Grand Bazaar. A taxi driver will not escort you inside the gates on foot. You will get lost inside. Although it is not a dangerous place, it is advisable to avoid going alone. It is like a maze for rats." He flips the card over, revealing a different address. "This one is just outside the bazaar. Equally confusing."

He looks at the calendar open on his phone and continues. "To which of these branches will you go?"

"Both."

"I will take you," he says, "and we will see which branch you need. What day would you like to go?"

His index finger hovers over his phone's calendar, ready to add an entry. His need to be the great protector, at the moment, is greater than my need for independence. Since I have a plane ticket coming, I'll have to deal with his anger later. I take the business card from his hand and smile.

"Any time convenient for you, Sedat, but not tomorrow. There is too much to do here."

He stays for another half hour until I plead exhaustion, but not before he makes sure I bolt myself inside the apartment.

I settle into a kitchen chair to check my email and have a cup of tea. The wall buzzer for the outside door sounds. Now what? Does no one use the telephone in this country? Not answering the buzzer, I head to the front balcony and look over at the top of Maynard's head. Irritated, I ignore the unlock button on my way back to the kitchen. The buzzing goes on for five minutes before all is quiet again. I've had one angry man harass me today. I don't need another.

The buzzer sounds again, and I stomp to the front door and push the intercom button.

"Maynard, just go away," I yell, not caring that the neighbors can hear my anger.

"*Affedersiniz, hanımefendi, kargonuz var.*" It's a cargo delivery.

"*Pardon. Gel.*"

I unlock the deadbolt and sign for the cargo delivery from the boy, apologizing. I close the door and re-lock it. Seeing Harris's name on the return, I rip the tab from the envelope so violently that the package hits the wooden floor with a *thud,* just as a thumb drive dislodges and lands next to it. I retrieve both the envelope and the drive.

Upon checking the envelope, I find a letter inside. Given his video, I sit at the table and unfold the page, terrified of what I might find. Harris's handwriting appears rushed, even more sprawling than normal. The lines curve across the page as if he were writing it in a moving vehicle.

Quinn,

If you are holding this letter, I am no longer alive. A lawyer held this letter and the contents in trust to be sent to you in the event of my death. Besides the disk I'm hoping you already have, I own nothing of value other than the money in the bank and this thumb drive.

If you don't want my things in the apartment, give them away. My parents disowned me years ago and won't want anything I've touched. The insurance policies for my mother were changed to you after we married.

This drive contains a ledger of every client's hidden account with their access information. You can spend this money or not. While the insurance policies are significant, these accounts are enough for you to live in luxury for the rest of your life. But I can guess how you will feel about dirty money.

The smaller disk, which I stuffed into the APO box, is the important one. I got the information from an old man at a card game. He says it is the original, and there are no copies. How I got there is a long and crazy story, but trust me—this information is crucial.

It would be best if you didn't try to read the small disk. There's probably some self-destructive code built into the login. The data concerns a unique EMP test. I don't know what form that test will take, nor the damage it will cause. Every nasty character in the world wants this data. If they cannot get the data, they cannot run the test, and the auction will fail.

DO NOT TRUST ANYONE. Please keep the disk in the necklace and on you at all times. My partner, Burt, turned on me. Stay away from him. I'm sure he'll try to find you.

I am sorry things turned out this way. You changed my life, and I promise you, I expected to use the money I won to travel the world and grow old with you.

Stay safe, Quinn.
All my love,
Harris

27

QUINN

I packed the night before, even before Arzu sent my ticket, taking no time to research what an EMP might be, but instead, sleeping off my jet lag. I tuck my hair under the colorful scarf the old woman gave me in Kemeraltı. For extra measure, I wear a baggy brown dress and carry a large plastic shopping bag concealing my backpack. With no makeup, my bathroom mirror tells me I will fade into the background.

Leaving the apartment, I shuffle, my body bent forward, and my shoulders rounded as I head for the taxi stand. After being chased twice, I imagine malevolent men at every turn, yet no one is familiar, and no one stalks me. I climb into a taxi, tell the driver to take me to the airport, and stare at my reflection in the taxi window. Sedat's angry face looms in my imagination. I can't shake the feeling that I am making a mistake by avoiding him, but it is too late once the taxi reaches İmir's Menderes airport. Arzu waits for me outside and grabs my bag as we head through the main doors.

"We are flying into the smaller airport on the Asian side of Istanbul, Sabiha Gökçen. It is easier to navigate and much closer to the city. Domestic flights, and half of those to Europe, generally use this airport. We'll ride the metro across the city to *Fatih*, the older section where the *Kapalı Çarşı*, the Grand Bazaar, is located. When we arrive, I'll show you how to get an Istanbul metro card with cash. You will use it for the metros, ferries, and buses, but be careful. You can be tracked this way. I bought the plane tickets with cash, and we should continue to do so."

"Where do we stay tonight?" I ask.

"My friend runs a small hotel just outside the bazaar. It is comfortable, don't worry, and it's a reasonable price. We will be off the books, as I don't think you want to broadcast that you are here."

"You're right about that."

Having Arzu with me makes the trip a breeze. I use the Wi-Fi on the Pegasus flight to research what little I can find on EMPs. An electromagnetic pulse is a brief burst of electromagnetic energy from the sun or a cluster of nuclear bombs, created when detonated high in the atmosphere. According to the Wiki site, these EMPs would disrupt communications at varying frequencies in modern warfare. The pulses would not affect the people, but if I understood correctly, they would zap all electronics in a certain radius. Fry them completely. On a larger scale, a single pulse could shut down air traffic control, financial systems, power grids, and water or sewer systems by damaging the electronics that operate them.

This is more science fiction than real life and way out of my comfort zone. Whether large or small, anything that creates an EMP in my mind originated through the military. Now Harris's insistence that I give the disk to someone high in his chain of command makes more sense if it contains information about a military weapon.

We arrive late in the evening at a small local hotel and enter our room through a rear door, unlocked by a boy who, at first, gives Arzu the standard Turkish kiss on both cheeks, then wraps her in a bear hug. We then climb a flight of stairs. In my room, while Arzu is searching for her contact here, I spend hours researching everything I can on EMPs.

The next morning, Cem Süleymanoğlu, a friend of Arzu's, whose first name is pronounced just like the American version of Jim, meets us outside the hotel. He walks with us to the Nuruosmaniye Gate, which is not yet open. Cem is stocky and short, with black curly hair and wide brown eyes. As he and Arzu clown around, I can tell they are close friends.

"Quinn," Cem says, "just so you know, there are twenty-four gates in the Grand Bazaar, and this is Gate One." I scan the large stone opening and see the original name forged in metal above the door. People mill around, waiting for the bazaar to open for the day.

"The indoor shopping center can be confusing until you learn your way," he continues. "If you go out of a gate, you can see its number." He stops and points to the top of the open doorway. "Then you can find where you are on Google Maps."

Arzu motions to my phone, and I pull up the app. My phone shows five bars, and I can see my location's blue dot on the map.

"I will show you other things along the way, but begin building your mental landmarks. Arzu says you recently moved to Türkiye, so I know you will be here again." He turns to show credentials to a security guard inside the gate, and we are waved inside.

I can't help but look up, a dangerous thing in a country with uneven streets and sidewalks. Inlaid tiles in blues and creams, with touches of red and yellow, cover a curved ceiling arching high above the jewelry stores lining the wide pedestrian walkway. The bling is explosive, and I grab Arzu's arm in amazement, then, embarrassed, let go. Nonplussed, she asks Cem to stop. I ogle over the rows and rows of gold, diamonds, and gemstones flashing in the jewelers' windows, a thousand times the volume of the small store where I worked in college.

I cannot help myself. I want to see and touch everything. Like the ancient shopping district in İmir, a narrow store with stacks of scarves beckons me. I run my fingers across the soft silk. The shop owner opens a large blue-and-green scarf and drapes it around my shoulders. It reminds me of Monet's Water Lilies, but I don't buy it. We are not here for that.

Cem beckons us to follow, and we slowly wind through the massive covered market built after the Ottoman conquest of Constantinople. The Iş Bank is just outside another gate, and I now understand Sedat's concern that I would get lost. We approach the bank branch just as it opens, and Cem takes the business card from my hand and goes inside, only to return seconds later.

"This is not the correct bank." The bazaar has opened, and the crowd is louder, but Cem does not raise his voice. I shift closer to hear him, avoiding the crowd that fills the narrow street.

"This business card address is correct, but the person you must see is at the other branch today. We will go outside the bazaar to a nearby location."

I must look concerned because he leans toward me.

"This is normal in Türkiye, Quinn. Sometimes, a bank officer is responsible for several branches. This is the correct address, but it is on the other side of the bazaar. There are a lot of people. Keep up, yes?"

I nod, and he looks at Arzu. She blinks in silent agreement as Cem hands me the bank manager's card.

We stride past several souvenir shops, then turn right. After two more blocks of brightly colored shops, we angle left, taking a narrow street lined with gold traders. At the next street, as we move quickly along store after store of carpets, I'm thoroughly lost.

Each carpet store window showcases at least one extravagant rug. I pause, looking at a small one about the size of a doormat. I turn to share my amazement with Arzu, but she and Cem are far ahead of me. His head turns to check on me, and he stops when he notices I'm gone. His face is alarmed as he alerts Arzu, and they return to me through the crowd.

"I see you can't resist," Arzu says, then laughs. "Quinn, there are too many beautiful things here. We will never get to the bank if you stop at them all."

I marvel at the small, intricately woven red carpet and its blue, daisy-like flowers. The carpet glows in the light.

"Why is this one so different from the others?"

"It is completely made of silk," Cem responds. "The back of the carpet has more than five hundred knots per square inch. Some of these are double-knotted, making them even more expensive. Others contain over a million knots per square meter."

He studies the side of my face. "We will plan another day for shopping, yes?"

Yes. There is no time for frivolities today. I fling my hand for us to proceed down the street packed with shoppers. After more carpet stores and then leather stores, we cross back into another section of gold jewelry.

Arzu trails behind me as we pass by men yelling in an alley, notepads in one hand and pencils in the other. Dozens of men are crammed in this narrow alley. Unable to help myself, I stop again. This time, Arzu slams into me from behind. She whistles for Cem to stop.

"What are they doing?" I ask.

"This is the gold market," Cem replies. "People buy and sell gold. It is like your stock market."

I remember the stock exchange photos on Wall Street in New York. This looks nothing like that.

"Without computers? In such a small alley with all these exposed wires?" This seems a ridiculously old-fashioned and ineffective way to sell gold.

He shrugs. "There are computers, but it has been this way for hundreds of years. If something is not broken, you do not change it."

"Don't their clients worry about being cheated?"

"These men will not cheat you. Their reputation is everything. I cannot say that for carpet sellers or other sellers, but when significant money is exchanged, you can trust it."

"Come, we must go," Arzu says, tugging the hem of my T-shirt. "At the bazaar, you wait hours if you do not arrive at the bank close to opening."

We flow out of the massive gate and into a busy street. The large blue Iş Bank sign looms ahead.

"This shouldn't take very long," I say as I reach for the door handle.

"We are not waiting." Arzu shakes her head. "We will find the person I told you about."

"You're leaving me in all this?" I motion to the crowds swirling around us.

"You will be okay," Cem says. He points to the lower side of the street. "If we are not back in an hour, or you want to explore, just follow the path of rainwater downhill, and it will lead you to the sea, where there are always taxis and ferries."

"Or you can take a taxi back to our hotel," Arzu says. "I will text you if there is a problem."

Cem looks at his watch. "Will an hour be enough time for you?"

"Sure." I nod my head.

They head back inside the bazaar. My hands grip my bag as I watch them disappear into the mass of people. They are doing this for me, and I shouldn't need a babysitter, even though my stomach is tightening into a knot. I turn toward the bank and squeeze through the waiting crowd to the door. A man bumps my shoulder, and I stumble in my haste. Several unknown hands reach out to keep me from falling.

I thank the people around me, then face the guard at the door and show him the business card. He speaks into a handheld radio and waits for a response. Like a golden key, the door buzzes, and the guard returns the card, letting me pass.

Alone in the outer entrance, a feeling of trepidation makes me pause. I'm already too accustomed to Arzu paving the way. Not this time. The hacker must be contacted manually as he refuses to use cell service. Either they will locate him, or they won't. They left me here, as the hacker refused to speak with a foreigner, a *yabancı*.

I must deal with Harris's mouse crumbs alone, even though I fear where they will lead. Nothing so far has been easy, and each new day has brought something worse than the one before. I'm almost terrified to find out what nasty things today will uncover.

An attractive woman in an expensive suit smiles at me through the internal doors. I don my invisible lawyer suit and take a slow breath. While I might not be Red Riding Hood, I know a wolf is inside this bank.

28

SEDAT

"You *lost* her again? Your only job was to track an American woman who turns every man's head on the streets of İmir, and you lost her?"

Sedat stands in the middle of the bullpen at eight in the morning on Thursday, twisting slowly in a circle as he makes eye contact with every one of the ten men stationed in İmir. He never has enough men, but one hundred men could not have done the job this time. Quinn is slippery.

In truth, he is angrier with himself than his men. How arrogant he had been to think that she would travel to Istanbul with him rather than alone. He reminds himself in this moment that there is a good reason he has never developed feelings for any woman and why he has never married. This beautiful American woman twists his heart unpredictably, and he hates himself for being powerless to stop it.

"You let that snake Robicheaux out of your sight in Sochi, and look what happened. Now you've let his wife out of your sight, and here we are again."

Sedat is typically calm to a fault in front of his men. Unwaveringly composed, he would never be caught showing signs of concern about how an operation is going, and unbeknownst to his team, he always carries a well-thought-out plan B in his back pocket should anything go awry. Not today.

"Do I terminate all of you?" His nose flares like a bull's. "What do you expect me to say to the chief? To the head of TNP, who watches us like a hawk?"

While Bora is used to Sedat's occasional rage, these men are not. Shocked expressions show on their faces. Several of the junior detectives hide behind their hands in embarrassment. Previously, he had always released his anger privately, but this time, his unbridled rage is a testament to how deeply this infuriating woman has woven herself into his psyche.

"Robicheaux stole ten million dollars at that card game, then walked away with the most valuable piece of intelligence in the world right under your noses. Two days later, they blew up his helicopter. When Aslan finds her, they will kill her." He is shouting, his men flinching with every word. "Must I do everything myself?"

Bora stands in the back, and Sedat sees him flinging his hand across his throat, signaling for him to cut his words.

"Our jobs are on the line, Bora, so do not tell me to stop shouting. She is unintended bait, and we cannot allow the Bulgarians to capture her; if they do, we will lose the information entirely, just as we lost Robicheaux. Our jobs are on the line here, so do not tell me to stop shouting."

Sedat glances down at his phone on the corner of the closest desk. At dinner the previous evening, he wedged a tracker in her backpack. It is smaller than the one he had planted earlier to listen to her conversations. He watches now as the blue dot on the map has stopped at a building outside the Grand Bazaar in Istanbul, and berates himself for assuming she would stay put and not check it more frequently.

"*Lanet olsun.*" He throws out the curse words without thinking. She is reckless and naive. Scanning the room, he sees each face and knows every man is as concerned as he is. There are no slackers in this room other than himself. He does not know how he has let this woman get the better of him. But it will not happen again.

"She is outside the Grand Bazaar." He zooms in on his phone, looking at the details of the tracking map. "She is in the İş Bank in Beyazıt."

He turns the face of his military-grade phone toward the room and displays it, then throws it at Bora.

"Call the Beyazıt station and see who is available. Then ensure everyone's SmartTrack is updated and get a team up there."

Bora silently nods as Sedat continues. "At least we can watch and hope no one kills her before we are in place."

Sedat leaves the bullpen and slams the door behind him. Turkish curse words drift over his shoulder as he strides toward the office of the chief of police. Dimerci will do anything to deport Quinn by Monday. He is running out of time.

29

QUINN

The ventilation inside İş Bank is glacial, and it reminds me of the ridiculous air conditioning I left behind in the southern United States. The woman in the expensive suit crosses the austere room, extending her hand in an American-style greeting.

"Madam, I am Isobel Turan," she says, her accent more Nordic than Turkish. "The man you requested is our manager, but he is out of the city now. How may I please assist you?" The woman is tall and blonde, unlike the many Turkish women who are olive-skinned and dark-haired.

I fish in my backpack for Harris's keys.

"My husband has a safe deposit box at this bank, I believe." I hope it is not the other branch, and I must walk alone back through the bazaar. "He is deceased, and I found these keys along with your manager's card. Is it possible for me to gain access to the box?"

"Your husband's name?"

"Major Harrison Robicheaux. He was with the American Air Force."

"I knew your husband a little, Mrs. Robicheaux." Her polite

smile and demeanor change instantly to concern. "I am very sorry he has died. This is such a shock for me, as he came to see us not long ago." She places her hand over her heart, her eyes filled with concern. "Please follow me."

Her four-inch heels click across the marble floor to a desk. She sits and opens a drawer.

"May I have your identification, please?"

I hand her my passport. She pulls out a sheet of paper and scans it. Her eyes shift to the passport, then to me. My heart skips a beat when I realize she is scowling at me. I grasp the keys so tightly they cut into my skin. There has to be a problem with my passport. My life would have been easier if the passport control officer had prevented me from entering the country the very first minute.

"We assured your husband there would be no problem," she says, her eyes pouring again over whatever discrepancy she has discovered between her sheet of paper and my passport. Isobel then flips the page to face me. The photo in my passport has been enlarged to fit the page.

"While you are the woman Mr. Robicheaux identified as his wife," she points to her computer screen, "I am concerned about a message flagged by your passport. The message has just arrived. One minute while I read it, please."

My leg begins its jackhammer. Isobel squints at her screen as my heart pounds in my chest. While I wait, it feels like only a minute, but it's probably ten. She sits back, arranges her face in a smile, and turns to face me.

"There is no problem. Just a routine note regarding your visa, as you are a guest in Türkiye. Please follow me." She lightly rubs the end of her nose with her fingers.

She just lied to me.

Without giving me a chance to respond, she stands and grabs a ring of keys. I follow Isobel down a stone staircase that takes me to what feels like a dungeon. She ushers me to a large barred door set into a curved stone archway that separates the safe deposit boxes from the rest of the bank.

"The large key, please."

She holds out her palm, and I drop the ancient key into it. It fits neatly into the iron lock. We walk into a carpeted stone room with gleaming metal safe deposit boxes set into three of the walls. Isobel takes the smaller key from my hand, opens the individual box, pulls the small box out a few inches, and then hands both keys back to me.

"You will be secure here." Isobel's face is flushed, visibly uncomfortable. "We allow only one person to be in this room. I will wait for you at my desk."

I nod my thanks, and she quietly exits the room. Something is happening. I need to finish here and get the hell out of this bank. The metal security box is large and heavy. I shift it to the small table in the middle of the room, almost dropping it. Given Isobel's concern, I'm afraid to open it. I start to return it to its slot, but stop halfway.

"Don't be such a ninny." The stone room dampens my whispered words. "There hasn't been anything yet that you couldn't handle. This won't be any different."

But it will be. I know it.

My face breaks into a cold sweat as I lift the lid. On top, Harris has stacked sleeved blocks of various currencies, several of which feature colorful ink and foreign languages. Arzu told me that there are people after me who want their money back, so I'm not surprised to see it, but it still makes me nervous. With sweaty hands, I place each type of currency in a separate stack on the table. I can't determine the exact amount of cash at a glance, but the stacks are enough to fill my backpack.

Next is a handgun. Uncertain how to check if the firearm is loaded, I lift it out of the box by the trigger guard with my thumb and index finger. I place it on the table next to the money, turning the barrel away from me just in case.

My breathing increases with the fear of what else is in the box.

At the bottom are passports from six countries, stacked neatly in rows. Fake credit cards and other documents for Harris and me, all using fake names with recent photos—the same photo as in my new U.S. passport. Now I know why Harris wanted to handle my passport and why there was an issue at the passport office at the air base. And possibly why there is a flag on it in Isobel's computer, making her so nervous.

Given the fakes in the box in front of me, there is no way my new U.S. passport is genuine. Hyperventilating, I collapse to the soft carpeted floor and struggle to get my breathing under control. On my knees, I bend over, mentally counting each breath until I slowly draw in larger and larger gulps of air. Once I can breathe normally, I lean against the table leg, my mind swirling.

Nothing legitimate requires so many passports. I certainly do not need them. Nothing could provide more substantial evidence of precisely what Harris had tried to do—disappear. There is no proof of Maynard's allegations of theft of assets or secrets, and there is also nothing here to clear my name, only Harris's gambling money.

I pull myself from off the floor to look at the stacks of currency. While I have my savings from the sale of my parents' home and my condo, it isn't enough to provide a decent retirement. I'll still have to work. But with this stack of money, if I live frugally, I can travel the world at least for a few years.

"Ignorance of the law is no excuse," booms the voice of Dr. Walthall, my law school contracts professor, in my head, as if he is in this alcove with me now. This isn't my money. I can't just take it.

Discovering fake passports in my name does not make me a criminal. I'm not a part of whatever this is. I think back to the red box, how it had been so readily unlocked and easy to find. He wanted me here, involving Isobel, to leave me an easy trail of crumbs. I wonder how truly "involved" she is.

Standing, I straighten my clothing and look through the contents again. This is too much for my backpack. Taking only the passports, I repack the box, return it to its place on the wall, and close the door. The massive door to the cage clangs shut on my way out.

I can hear Isobel frantically talking with someone as I reach the top of the staircase. I stop and hug the wall, listening. Her side of the conversation is too fast for me to understand. She is on her phone as I peek around the corner. The front-door security guard stands beside her, facing away from me. There is no way I can run past either of them.

So I wait.

30

QUINN

When the guard returns to his station and Isobel returns to her desk, I wait for the police to appear. After seeing only customers enter the door for ten minutes, I emerge from the stairwell. Isobel's demeanor is pleasant and professional, and I try to appear calm and relaxed as I give her a polite wave. Leaving to meet Cem and Arzu outside, I note the bank's opening hours painted on the glass front door. I will return.

"Did you find him?" I ask.

"We have an address," Arzu responds. "It took some time, but we believe this location is right."

"Let's do this, then." I look to each of them to confirm which way to go.

Cem whistles short and loud. A grubby eightish-year-old boy appears, his head closely shaved to a black stubble. He has a tea tray in his hand and wears a sly grin. In Turkish, Arzu asks him about the address she has written on her hand. He sets his tea tray on the sidewalk next to the bank's outer wall and sets off into the crowd like a ferret.

"Is this our new tour guide?" I look between Cem and Arzu. "Does he know where he's going?"

"It is the fastest way, I promise," she yells at me over her shoulder as we hurry to catch up with the boy.

We weave through boys with rolling hand carts loaded with barrels or baskets. Trying not to crash into workers and businessmen, we skirt around brightly colored tourists and speedwalk back through the gate. The little boy takes us deeper into the bazaar, through the leather district. A mass of shouting men in the street are arguing about something I can't understand. I pull ahead of Arzu and Cem, eager not to lose the boy.

Behind me, a crash explodes, followed by a roar of voices. A man screams in garbled Turkish and points at me. Fear triggers my adrenaline, and I run. The tea boy looks frightened as I catch up to him, and he also begins to sprint. I take off, not stopping to look behind me.

We run and run. After the bed linen section, stores of household goods, several city blocks of clothing, and rows and rows of shoes, I am desperate not to lose sight of the little boy in front. We are heading deeper into the bazaar, and there is no way for me to apply Cem's idea of memorizing landmarks. Realizing I am falling behind, the boy stops every ten seconds, looks back, and waves me to come forward faster. I check over my shoulder but don't see Arzu or Cem. Given the crowd, I'm sure they are behind me—somewhere.

Gasping through the winding market, I stop to catch my breath. Ahead, the boy turns to the right and through a gate with *Tacirler* curved over the top, then into an alley with a narrow corridor of shops. The boy looks at the paper in his hand and stops in front of a century-old wooden door twice my height, painted a dark green. The antique knob is as big as both my hands.

I turn to look, but the alley behind me is empty. Where are

Arzu and Cem? Unless the two friends conveniently bailed, the crash behind me involved them.

"Lady?" the boy asks, pointing to the green door.

I hesitate, not knowing what to do. I flick my hand for the boy to knock. I shift inside an adjacent doorway. The thick walls conceal me as I try to stop my knees from shaking. I hope the hacker speaks English.

The boy pounds on the door with a dirty fist and then waits. After a few seconds, I hear scuffling sounds, and the door cracks an inch, but I see only darkness. The boy begins his explanation with hand gestures toward me. The door closes, and the boy winks at me. He nods as if to say everything is going as expected. The door cracks wider, and I see a cheek and one eye, then a skeptical teenage face squinting at me. He holds his hand in front of his eyes to block the daylight.

"Do you speak English?" I look up the alley, desperate for Arzu to appear.

"Maybe." His voice was quiet and hesitant, but his word choice told me he could.

"Arzu sent me." Even though she told me the boy didn't use a cell phone, I didn't believe her. Every person on Earth under the age of thirty carries a cell phone.

His squinting face relaxes slightly as he blinks slowly. "Lady with a disk?" His English carries a thick accent.

I smile, hoping to put him at ease. "Yes. Can I come inside?"

"Give the boy lira to go, yes?"

I grab Turkish lira from my backpack and give the little boy ten lira. With an exaggerated bow, he flips me a two-finger salute and hurries off the way we—well, I—came. Arzu and Cem know I'm way over my head, as Maynard put it, and apparently don't want to be a part of whatever this is.

The wooden door's hinges creak as it opens. Clusters of acne cover the boy's ghostly white face. He wears baggy camouflage pants, red Converse tennis shoes, and a black wife-beater undershirt. I'm concerned that this boy might not be able to help me. He notices my misgivings and responds in kind with reluctance. I realize he misunderstood.

"Look, lady, you don't like what you see—" He moves to close the door.

"I thought you'd be older," I say as I block the door with my foot.

He looks to be fourteen. From an angry Russian to this, I wonder about Arzu's choice of business acquaintances. Sensing my indecision, the boy turns away, leaving the door open for me to decide whether to follow.

I step through into a dark entrance. His footsteps clomp heavily down a long, gloomy hallway, barely lit with a solitary, dim, naked bulb. We walk through a cramped passageway and come to a room. Daylight streams through a dusty window, and I see the boy's outline. He leads me to a circular plaza with a walled garden surrounding an ancient olive tree. To one side, a fountain softly splashes. Open doors surround the garden with shops converted into mini-warehouses and offices. Several men mill about, instructing middle-school-aged boys as they sort stacks of copper pots, the metal's sheen glinting in the sun as they pack them into crates. The garden and plaza are open to a cloudless blue sky. The boy trudges through the plaza, heading for the opposite side. He stops once he reaches a door.

"Arzu says trust you." Holding the door handle, he leans toward me and whispers. "No tell anyone where I live."

"I won't, but whatever you find on this disk stays between us." I shrug my shoulders at him. "Privacy is part of the job. Both for you and from you."

This chit-chat is making me nuts. I need to know what is on the disk.

"What is your name?" I ask him.

Hacker Boy ignores me and opens the door. The room is dark, the size of a single American garage, and the front window is painted black. The scent of boiled cabbage, stale cigarettes, and burnt tea accosts me. A low electric buzz makes my skin crawl. As my eyes adjust to the darkness, I see computer equipment, hard drives on racks, and the attached wires snaking across the floor.

He must live here, even though it's not an apartment. There is a kitchenette on the back wall, a single mattress shoved into a back corner with a dingy cover, and a bathroom, its open door revealing a glimpse of a floor toilet.

The boy motions for me to sit on a chair covered in cigarette burns. He sits at a new desk in an expensive ergonomic chair. I pull the memory card from the pendant and place it in his outstretched palm. Harris's warning buzzes through my brain, but I mentally slap it away.

"Arzu says you don't know this." He snaps on a desk lamp and peers at the disk.

"That's right."

"She says Alexandropov pissed with Aslan logo."

I think back to the Russian man in İmir, the lion logo message, and the video confirmation that Harris is dead. My stomach lurches.

"Yes," I respond.

"Damaged when ripped from computer." He flips the disk, inspecting it. "The information may no be good."

"You might be right," I hold up my hands as if in surrender, then point to the disk. "Find out."

"Leave with me. Self-destruct code take long time. You pay five hundred dollars U.S. when finish."

"I need this now." Given the safe deposit box, the money isn't an issue. The time, however, definitely is.

"You must wait." He looks at me with flat, bored eyes. "I guess several days, but...?" His shoulders rise, then drop. "Maybe we lucky, and it take one hour. Write where you stay hotel. I will leave a message for you when done."

He pushes notebook paper and a pen across his desk toward

The Expedient Wife

me. I hesitate. Hacker Boy gives me nothing in the way of trust, only a black, empty void. I may never see this disk again, but there is no time to find another hacker. I reach for the paper and pen, then write Arzu's and the hotel's names. He stuffs it in a drawer and stands, ready for me to leave.

"I don't know my way out. Can you show me on my phone?" I pull up Google Maps. There is no service since I am ensconced behind thick stone walls deep in the bazaar. "I guess I need a map."

He holds up his hand and walks away. A minute later, he reappears, a folded, colorful tourist map in his hand. He picks up a black pen and points to where we are, but doesn't touch the paper.

"No come here second time." His words are rapid. "Forget." He mutters a Turkish sentence, and I feel his frustration.

"I want your phone number." I jam my hands into my jeans pockets to keep them from twitching through my hair. He rolls his eyes.

"I find in hotel."

I hold out my hand. "Give me the disk. I'll find someone else."

"No one else. Arzu knows. Talk Arzu."

A flutter of concern runs through my stomach as Arzu is gone.

"She isn't here right now." I hold up my phone with no signal, "No way to call her."

I reach into my pocket and pull out two crisp hundred-dollar bills. "I'll give you two hundred dollars up front, but I want your name, a phone number, and an address for where you will be."

Hacker Boy's bored expression turns to hunger as he watches me wave the American dollars close to his face. Inflation in Türkiye is now in the three digits, and I am sure the boy is desperate for cash. I point to the notepad.

"Phone number."

Hacker Boy gives me his phone number, and after I press a bit more, he shares the address where we are, his mother's address, and his name. Artur Yılmaz. If I don't hear from him in twenty-four hours, I will find him.

I yank open the tourist map with one hand as the breeze curls the edges, and I realize I'm massaging my neck with my other hand, trying to ease the tension. I spin my head to the right, sure someone is watching. No one is there.

I focus back on the map. The tea boy led me in from the right. With my finger, I pinpoint the gate from this morning and move in that direction, recognizing several familiar things until I reach the Tacirler Gate. No one pays me any attention, and I take a breath of relief. Even though I am still on an unfamiliar street, I am inside the Grand Bazaar, and if what Cem says this morning about it being safe is true, I can relax.

After several wrong turns, I walk through the Mahmutpaşa Gate and stop at the street corner, flushed with happiness over my success. The road bends to the right, and the street is familiar. I pass the edge of the bazaar, the Nuruosmaniye Mosque, and come to a corner five minutes from the hotel.

Now, all I need to do is find Arzu.

31

SEDAT

The girl in front of Sedat is dressed in all black, wearing a hoodie, a T-shirt, and jeans. He wonders if she aspires to be an undercover spy or a goth rock singer. Her long, wavy brown hair is disheveled from her morning adventure. She does nothing to straighten her clothing or fix her hair. Expensive Doc Marten boots are on her feet, the shoestrings removed, per police procedure. Her hands are free, but she wears a chain belt and extensions hooked to the concrete floor.

She reminds him of the main character in the book he read this weekend, a female warrior in a fantasy novel. While he usually reads nonfiction, his inability to sleep most evenings has him reaching for anything that comes to hand.

A one-way glass window sits on his right. Bora is watching and listening. This case has become a minefield. Robicheaux's death has piqued the interest of the journalists, and before long, they will begin to hound Quinn if they can find her. If he is unlucky today, the head of the TNP will watch remotely via a private link to Ankara, and later Sedat will be drilled on why he failed to do certain things or asked specific questions.

His focus is critical. He sets aside all those concerns as he begins his interrogation.

"Hanife Arzu Tekin."

He reads from her file, but the girl remains still as if she is mute. He knows she is not. Bora sent him a video of her being detained an hour ago. The girl screamed and kicked as if she were a crazed banshee at two of his officers who hauled her to their vehicle. The two men shoved her into the rear seat of their patrol car. She beat on the rear door glass with her hands, then lay on her back to kick at the window. The patrol officers then held her down, bent her knees behind her, and then bound her hands to her feet, placing her on her side in the back seat. A female officer watched the girl's every move on the way to the station house.

A bruise stains her right eye. Another darkens the area below one of her elbows. Still, the video runs from the beginning of the operation to her placement in this interrogation room, and no one laid an unnecessary hand on the girl. His team had been taught that suspects and witnesses are to be unharmed. Here, the bruises are her fault.

If anyone is to harm a detainee, it will be him, but he detests that sort of activity and has only used it twice in his lifetime. He has found that words, photographs, and the insinuations of what they represent are much more effective. However, this girl may prove him wrong. While Durand is slippery, this girl is fierce. He decides to do something he has never done. Give information rather than get. In this case, it will serve him much better.

"Your father is Andreas Tekin, born in Spain to Turkish parents, who moved to Istanbul when he was five. Your mother is Dilek, a housewife activist, arrested several times in demonstrations." He returns his gaze to the girl's face, but she looks away. "At least you come by your activities honestly."

"Your arrest record is clean, surprising, given your computer's criminal history. My, my, the things you have done." He has measured his voice to show he is unperturbed by her silence. The girl again does not move, but her eyes widen when he mentions her computer, and he sees fear behind them.

A point for him.

"Your creative passwords were ineffective against my team. Next time, clear your history much deeper. We pride ourselves on finding anything, including every facility you hacked. We notified each company of how you accessed their system. Those back doors are now closed. The companies have been apprised of your habits and how to anticipate your next attempt to breach their systems. Thank you for your service. This type of example saves me hundreds of man-hours. If you need employment, Ms. Tekin, I will gladly discuss a legitimate position with you, even though you need significant training to curb your illicit impulses."

The girl raises one eyebrow. His belittling of her is a tactic only to see if she will talk, and it's clear she knows it from her stone-cold facial expression. She remains silent.

"Do you wish to tell me what you are doing with the Durand woman?"

The girl turns her head toward the wall. He studies her profile as her eyes slowly blink. He hopes she will not force him to arrest her and move on to other torture tactics that the idiots behind the camera will require him to perform.

"Quinn Durand," he continues, "is under suspicion as an accomplice to her husband's illegal activities. She has put our citizens at risk by stealing information that the Turkish state needs. Did you know this?"

The girl turns her head toward him but says nothing. Her face is a grimace, and he sees fire in her eyes. She has something to say, and he will push her hard enough to make her say it.

"We will find Durand, with or without your assistance. Tell me what you know if you value your relationship with your parents, university, and freedom. My team questioned your family and friends and is currently speaking with every one of your professors. After your little incident in the United States, your reputation already hangs by the merest thread, Ms. Tekin."

He, at this point, is bluffing. He only wanted to question her, not arrest her or conduct a thorough investigation into her life. If not for her violent physical behavior toward the officers, she would not have been detained for this long. But thanks to her wrath, he has removed an irritant from the digital world. He has eight hours to hold her, and if she remains silent, it will take them all.

Sedat leans over the table and pushes several photographs toward the girl. She turns her head. He stands, walks around the table, and takes her jaw in his hand, slowly turning her face toward his. He shoves her forward with his other hand, positioning her face directly over the photos.

In one of them, Cem is shown handcuffed to a drain downspout in an alley, flanked by two men with iron pipes in their hands. Of course, they will not beat him, but Tekin does not know this. Another shows rivulets of sweat and tears making tracks down Cem's cheeks as his eyes plead into the camera.

"Do you want him beaten? Which place should I instruct them to begin with first? His legs? His face? If we break his knees, he might never walk again. For a tour guide, that would be most unfortunate."

The girl jerks her head from Sedat's hand. "He doesn't know anything." Her words are sharp. "He's only a tour guide."

"Why did you hire him?" Sedat strolls back to his side of the table.

"He knows the Grand Bazaar well," Arzu replies.

"I will be happy to let him go if you tell me where you and the Durand woman were going."

"I don't know."

"*Saçmalama.* Stop talking nonsense." The girl is wasting his time.

"She was leading us this morning. We were not leading her."

Sedat lets his frustration show just a bit. "Nothing but shit comes from your mouth. Then why did you hire a guide? You know exactly where she is going, and I need to know where that is. You will stay here until you tell me."

Sedat heads for the door, turning toward her before he opens it. "You may think I will harm her, but I will not. Her safety concerns me most, so understand that if she is harmed by the others who are after her, it will be on your head, not mine. Equally, if Cem gets injured, that also will be on you."

32

QUINN

Concerned about Arzu, I jog across traffic, narrowly dodging a speeding car, and cross the street toward the hotel. Looking over my shoulder to see if anyone is following me, I slam headlong into a man, causing him to drop his briefcase and a package. Rattled, I am too embarrassed to look at him. He retrieves his briefcase as I collect the beautifully wrapped package, spouting apologies in my rough Turkish until I feel a hand lightly grasp my elbow. The familiar Turkish voice brings me to a halt.

"Quinn, *quelle surprise!*" Sedat's voice, spouting fluent French, takes my breath away.

It can't be.

I snatch my arm from his grasp, mortified when I look up to see him standing before me, a broad smile on his face. Sheepish, I stand mute, with no idea what to say. Sedat's right eyebrow raises slightly at my silent mental gymnastics. His hair is tied in a ponytail, a professional look that complements his navy suit, starched white shirt, and red tie. His black leather dress shoes shine. I can't see him teaching in this suit.

"Why are you here today?" he asks. "We planned to travel

together next week." His smile transforms for a second into a scowl, one a parent might give a recalcitrant teenager, before his face lights up again in his happiness to see me. I wish I felt the same. Flustered, I stand awkwardly, not knowing what to say, still holding the pretty package. I hand it to him.

"I was supposed to have lunch with a friend, but I can't find her, and she isn't answering her phone." I glance behind me, hoping to see Arzu's pixie face. "Would you like to go instead?" My lame lunch date lie is evident to both of us.

"But of course." He gives me a sly, I-know-you-avoided-my-question smile. "You read my mind. I know the perfect place."

Of course, he does. My brain seems to take a vacation around this man.

Sedat strolls toward a different gate of the bazaar, taking his time, and I follow. He introduces me to shopkeepers and friends. They are happy to see him, kissing each cheek and asking about his family. He's told me he lives here, but it is surprising to see how many people he knows in this city of millions. I have too many questions about him whenever I'm in his presence, and today is no exception. Maybe today I'll get answers.

The enthralling atmosphere of the bazaar envelops me, with its scent of spices and coffee, and the ebb and flow of people. It's like wearing a comfortable cloak. Walking beside Sedat, I am free from the threat of harassment, and I feel myself relax. I am a tourist for several minutes, enjoying the sights and sounds of Istanbul. He points out things that might interest me, such as the roof of the bazaar where a Bond movie was filmed and the spot where a motorcycle crashed through.

Deep inside the winding streets, we start down a stone staircase. There are no safety rails, and Sedat briefly grasps my arm, then snatches his hand away. Like at the apartment, he appears uncomfortable being physically close to me. I'm unsure whether this is a cultural issue or something specific to him.

Following a well-lit corridor, we duck under several low archways and arrive at a restaurant tucked into a cavernous room. The dining area is located on one side of the room, while the open kitchen is situated on the other. Sedat points toward a small table, and we sit. He is on his best behavior, and I feel foolish about coming to Istanbul early. Worrying about Arzu begins to niggle at me again, and I wonder if she bailed on me or if she's in trouble.

He watches me search for a menu. "In this type of restaurant, you go to the counter, see the food, and make your selections. They dish it and bring it to you."

I twist a strand of hair awkwardly, then stop, tucking my hands under my thighs. I'm not good with apologies.

"Look, Sedat, I'm sorry I ran out on you. You don't take no for an answer. There is no reason to worry about me all the time. I'm your tenant."

"Yes, and now you are my friend. And my friend is alone in a new country and should be grateful for my help."

I'm not sure how I feel about being his friend, especially when he orders me around like he's my boss.

"I am grateful," I say, hating the sound of my mother's voice reminding me to be polite.

He laughs.

"What's wrong?" I ask. "Is there something on my face?"

"You look as if you ate something terrible. Is being my friend so distasteful?"

"No, of course not." I twist my napkin under the table, uncomfortable that he can read me so well.

"Did you not believe me when I said you would get lost?"

"I got lost, but my friend was with me earlier. It didn't take long for me to find my way around."

He purses his lips, and I can tell he is skeptical. Without a word, he stands and motions toward the kitchen.

"Come with me to select your food."

I follow him to the counter. He greets the cafe owner, grasping the man's shoulders tightly. He laughs as they talk, and the man nods toward me, smiling. I do the same back to him.

Sedat selects several dishes, and I decide on mine. Then, he adds two more as an afterthought. A boy follows, bearing a tray laden with bread, salad, dishes, silverware, and water bottles. Again, there is enough food on our table to feed six.

I cannot figure this man out. This is more than friendship. He has made a point to see me every day. He is too much of a gentleman to pursue a recent widow, so I know he doesn't want a relationship. I don't want a protector, although after being followed by the men on the Kordon, I can see why he thinks I need one.

As Sedat sits and we eat, I decide I need an answer.

"I have a question."

His eyes cut to mine. "If you do not like my response, will you disappear again?"

I return his comment with a smirk and take another bite of food.

"Seriously," I ask. "You must see how this looks."

"How does *what* look?" His questioning expression borders on indignant as he looks around the room. "Eating together is not improper."

"You followed me to Istanbul. It makes me uncomfortable, particularly when you and I know other men are following me. Why?"

33

SEDAT

Sedat looks around the restaurant, then rests his fork on his plate. As he leans forward, he places his elbows on the table and steeples his fingertips. He cannot read anything in her expression, but the corner of her mouth twitches. Thirty seconds pass as he determines how to spin this before speaking.

"Why do you distrust me so, Quinn? Especially after such a difficult two days?"

He leans back in his chair, showing the annoyance he wants her to see. She isn't fazed, but instead leans forward, her intelligent brown eyes challenging him.

"Answer the question, Sedat. Istanbul is a big place. There is no way you ran into me by accident. I won't dance around it. Tell me why you followed me here."

He fiddles with his silverware beside his plate. This entire case right now rests on his ability to convince her that he bumped into her by accident. He is beginning to feel like the bumbling inspector in the Pink Panther movies he watched as a child.

"I promised Harris I would check on you until he came home. Now he is dead, and because of that promise, I feel responsible for your safety until you leave my country." He spits each word out like the bitter pit of an olive, wanting her to think that he is hurt and angry. "I am sorry if it is not what you wish me to do." To add to the charade, he violently twists off the cap of the water bottle and chugs half the contents.

"Your insistence on being independent is insulting. I am only attempting to help you." He pauses, as if trying to calm himself, opens another bottle, and adds water to her glass. "You must know, after yesterday, how dangerous things are for you in my country. I feel I must somehow protect you."

She spears a piece of lamb and eats quietly, not responding.

She knows the danger, as Harris made sure of it. From the video feed from her apartment, Sedat was able to enlarge the letter the cargo boy sent her. Arzu's face pops into his head, and he checks his watch. Round two begins at 2:00 p.m., plenty of time to glean as much as possible from Quinn.

And to get her to trust him.

He grabs a slice of bread from the basket and attacks his plate again. Constantly following this woman makes him ravenous.

"You ask why I am here? Today, there was a staff meeting at the university about next semester's classes. Before leaving this morning, I went to your apartment to see if you wanted to come early rather than wait until next week."

He looks away for a second and then back at her, openly indignant. "If you must know, I came to apologize for being difficult when you asked me about Istanbul and to be certain the two men from yesterday had not returned. I worry for you. Why? I don't know. You do not want my help. That is very clear."

As her face flushes with embarrassment, he continues.

"When you were not home, I knocked on your neighbor's door. Do you remember the lady across the hall who spies on everyone? She saw you leave with your backpack. Maybe the next time you wish to avoid me, you will not slam your door so loudly and disturb her."

He lets his words hang in the air. They don't explain how he found her among the hordes outside the bazaar in Istanbul. She will figure out the tracker soon enough. Relaxing, he continues more casually, knowing his story must appear logical.

"You showed me the business card from the bank." He waits, letting her mentally connect the puzzle pieces.

As she pops a black olive in her mouth, her body language tells him she is still skeptical of his story. Her long, black hair and light olive skin make her almost appear Turkish, except for the hint of something from the far east. While Arzu may think she is the warrior in this group, the woman in front of him is the true fighter. Regardless of the circumstances, he can see it.

"Isobel—yes, I know Isobel. She was in one of my economics classes several years ago. Her bank is not far from my office. She says you talked with her this morning, so I knew you were nearby. Most foreigners visit the bazaar in Istanbul, and my university is just behind it. It is not so surprising that we might see each other. You were only a block or so from the bank when you bumped into me."

He is unsure whether his story has convinced her, but she stays seated. If she were totally unconvinced, she would leave—abruptly and angrily. The busboy clears away the dishes, and Sedat orders coffee. The restaurant owner prepares the Turkish coffee tableside, carefully pouring the rich, dark brew into delicate espresso-sized cups. The smell is intoxicating, and, given her apparent coffee addiction, she immediately grabs the cup in front of her.

"Sip slowly," he instructs, "and do not drink the grounds at the bottom of your cup."

"Yes, I know." She smiles, and he wonders who taught her about Turkish coffee, suddenly jealous of that unknown person, wanting to be the one who teaches her everything. She takes a tentative sip of the hot coffee.

"The men did not come to the apartment," she says. "Thank you for checking on me." She takes another sip, and, mesmerized, I force myself to listen. "I had the opportunity to come early and took it, planning to tell you later. I didn't mean to make you angry. I just had things to do."

He nods, as if he understands, instead of being irritated that she scooted past the two men he had posted at her building.

"I need space to grieve Harris and determine what I will do next." She finishes her coffee and sets the cup on its saucer. "I trust no one at the moment, not even people from my own country."

"Why?" He takes another sip. Will she lie to him again as she did about meeting Arzu?

"They lie about Harris. And me."

Another embarrassing flush creeps up her neck. Everything about this woman is clearly shown either on her face or her body. Why did Harris select her for his latest conquest? There is no way he loved her, and Quinn is simply too inexperienced to play at that scoundrel's level of the game, regardless of how fierce she may be.

"Lie about what?" He leans forward, concentrating on her face.

"According to an Air Force officer, Harris was about to be charged with serious crimes by my country."

Maynard, the idiot. The man is so stupid that he threatened her with a prison that had been closed for years. He wonders if Quinn knows that.

"And you?" He raises his hand to the owner and orders dessert.

"He says they think I am his partner in crime. An accessory."

"Are you?"

Her eyebrow raises in question, and he senses she is hurt by his question. A magnificent step forward, but he needs more of her trust.

"No. But that will not stop them if they want to arrest me." She feels the full weight of the U.S. government resting on her shoulders. He knows because the weight of the TNP is on him. "I'm expected, according to this guy, to prove my innocence."

"Can you?"

"It's not possible to prove a negative. Yet if they criminally charge me, the government must prove my guilt beyond a reasonable doubt. I don't think they can do that. Until the trial, however, they can deny me bail, leaving me in jail, possibly here."

"In a Turkish prison?" He squints at her, leaning back in his chair, crossing his arms over his chest.

"That's what this guy says."

"Something is wrong with this, Quinn. Is this man lying to you?"

"Possibly. As I said, I can't trust anyone to tell me the truth." She looks away from him. Her profile reveals exhaustion and worry. After less than three full days of searching, being followed, and fearing the unknown, he expects she is tired of this life. He is tired of it as well, especially after two years. If he had arrested Robicheaux in Sochi, neither of them would be here. But then he would never have met her.

"How are the men following you involved?"

She faces him again.

"Harris stole money in a card game. I'm assuming those men are the ones who want it back." She shrugs her shoulders.

Dessert arrives, and they eat in silence. Even though Harris told her not to trust anyone, including him, that detestable bastard is no longer here.

She needs him. And he must make certain he is the only person she can trust.

34

QUINN

Sedat and I stand outside the bazaar, where I try to say goodbye. As expected, he is not having it.

"You must see my city," he says. "I will show you why Istanbul is the center of the ancient world."

"I'm worried about my friend." I shake my head. "I can't just leave her. She doesn't disappear like that or not answer her phone." I hope my face doesn't show that I think disappearing is exactly what Arzu would do when things get tough.

"You must come with me. I am sure she will understand." He smiles.

I squint at him, trying to decide why he completely ignored my words.

"My meeting is finished." He spreads his hands. "And my flight is, fortunately for you, not until tomorrow morning. You can see the city with a private guide—me. Your friend will be fine. I am sure of it."

He plops his briefcase flat on the ground with a flourish and sets the package aside. In the sidewalk's center, he lowers himself to his knees, clasping his hands in front of his chest. "Please come with me," he begs.

I feel the flush cover every inch of my skin with mortification as people on the sidewalk swarm around us, and several older ladies stop and stare. Others chuckle as they walk by. He throws out one arm and grasps my forearm.

"These fine people see that I am begging you. Please do not disappoint them."

I laugh and tug his arm to get him off his knees. "Let me see if my friend is back at the hotel. Then we can do whatever you want for the rest of the day."

If I mentally dance around Sedat's questions all day, it will distract me from Hacker Boy, especially if Arzu is at the hotel to wait for his message. She purchased one-way tickets since we didn't know how long the hacker would take, so I assume she is still here. The thought of waiting raises a mental picture of Maynard's ticking clock. Only four days remain to clear my name or devise another solution. Hacker Boy has to come through on this.

Sedat stands, and the edges of his eyes crinkle as he smiles widely and straightens his trousers. "I will go with you," Sedat says.

"Sedat—" I raise my eyebrows at him, "—remember what we just discussed? That I need you to give me a little space?"

He tilts his head like a confused puppy. "Yes, of course," he says, his voice conveying reluctance. "I will meet you here in two hours, in this same spot." He points to the ground. "Can you find me here again?"

"Of course. Two hours."

"And you will not disappear on me again? I am trusting you."

"I'll be here."

I give him my best smile, the one I use when the opposing counsel at a hearing thinks they are about to pull one over on me. I walk away, feeling Sedat's eyes boring into my back. Around the corner, I quickly find a shop with a bag large enough to hold the contents of the safe deposit box, then head back to İş Bank.

Isobel is still at this location, sitting at her desk as I arrive. My body is flooded with nervous anticipation at the thought of carrying all that currency.

"You returned." Isobel greets me with concern. "Is there a problem?"

"Since I will return to the U.S. soon, I decided I will need some of the things in the box." I offer her my passport again.

"Thank you, but your passport is unnecessary." She waves my passport away and frowns. "You know a man is looking for you?" Her nose scrunches as if she has smelled something disgusting.

"Yes, he found me," I respond, my lunch threatening to come up. "May I know what he asked about me?"

While Sedat admitted to coming here at lunch, hearing it from Isobel is unnerving.

"He was very polite, but his questions were too intrusive. I referred him to my manager because the things he wanted to know were none of his business."

"What did he ask?"

"About your money, how well I knew you, those things. I told him nothing. Those things are private." Isobel blushes as she turns to her computer, making me think she isn't telling me something.

Looking at her screen, her face screws up in surprise, then concern. I feel a trickle of sweat roll down my back. She will call the police. Isobel twists a lock of hair around her finger as her other hand works with the mouse.

"Isobel, is something wrong?"

My question startles her. She lets go of the mouse, turning to face me.

"Quinn, *hanım efendi*, you may wish to give me instructions on your accounts. The bank has many investments for these amounts."

I choke out a response. "Accounts?"

She nods. "Yes, there are several. They were not there earlier today. If you are leaving Türkiye, you may wish to transfer these funds to a bank in the United States."

"Can you give me the balances?"

She copies numbers on a small square of paper and slides it across the desk. There are three different accounts. One account has over five million dollars, and another five million is split between the other two accounts.

Ten million dollars. The men following me are after this money, not the cash in the vault. This has to be Harris's "winnings" mentioned in his letter. His lawyer, "holding things in trust," has been busy.

"My name is on these accounts?"

"They are listed in your name only."

I steel my courtroom face and hope my irritation doesn't show. "Will there be any problem with your bank if I transfer the funds to Citibank here in Türkiye?"

"No, of course not. It is routine. I will need your account information, but you are aware, of course, of your government's reporting requirements?"

"Yes." Damn you, Harris. Moving the money will trigger an IRS notification. Placing the accounts in my name requires me, at a minimum, to file an FBAR with next year's tax returns, even if I don't shift the funds. Any amounts over $10,000 require this disclosure form. And I am sure there are a number of laws I am about to break, other than this one.

"When were the deposits made into these three accounts?" I need to withdraw the money from this bank somehow. I may be beyond the filing or notification requirement if the funds are in this bank for less than twenty-four hours, but that's a guess on my part.

Isobel checks her computer. "The funds arrived this morning, wired from Sochi, Russia, yesterday."

Crap, this is even worse. Funds from Russia will be frozen at any minute due to the war in Ukraine. Harris created a dangerous paper trail, and I must either make this money disappear or risk being implicated. If I find the lawyer who set this up, I might strangle him or her for doing this to a colleague.

"I will need to withdraw all funds in cash," I tell her.

I am confident this is Harris's gambling money. I do not care who it belongs to; now it belongs to me. I need to hide it and play cat-and-mouse with part of it until I can determine what to do with the rest.

"Yes, you can do that, but will you take it all?" Isobel's eyes watch me with curiosity rather than alarm. "It may take time to arrange, but then again, it may not. One minute, and let me check the cash availability." She clicks through several computer screens.

"I am sure that in your country, cash on hand in amounts of this type in a standard branch is not found. However, in the Grand Bazaar, money changes hands frequently and in substantial amounts. We are supplied with ready cash weekly, although the transfers are irregular for security purposes."

I've never handled this much money, even from my wealthiest clients, and am amazed to think that the flow of money in these amounts is such a daily occurrence. But everything involving money seems unusual here, thinking back to the bazaar's Gold Alley, where the men yelled at each other to transfer gold.

"Yes, we have the cash on hand between our two branches," Isobel said, looking up from her computer screen. "But you should consider the possibility of other mechanisms rather than cash."

"Of course. How would I go about investing in gold?" I ask her. I cannot walk around with that much cash, but I cannot leave it here. Any money in a bank account will be frozen if the authorities get involved. I need options that hide my identity. "And if I deposit it with a trader in the bazaar, is it secure?"

"The price of gold fluctuates, but generally, it is a good investment." She taps her front teeth with the top of a pen. "There are many gold merchants in the bazaar. I can refer you to one. There are also private vaults if you prefer. Some of our clients use both options when they do not wish all their funds to remain in banks, particularly since the Swiss have been compromised, but you cannot access any of these options without a personal introduction."

Years ago, the IRS forced the Swiss to reveal the names of American account holders. I shudder at the thought of the IRS getting involved.

"Also, my brother is a diamond broker," she says. "That is another possible investment. Should I contact one of our internal investment managers on your behalf? Our bank also offers a wide range of international investment options. I would be happy to be your reference."

"I would like to talk with your brother." Diamonds are the perfect solution. Due to their size, I can easily conceal them. "Also, I will need a referral to a gold trader, one with a vault, please."

"Certainly." She reaches into her desk drawer and slides two business cards across the desk. "I must make arrangements for this amount of cash. It will take some time for the bank to collect these funds. You may need to return on another day, tomorrow perhaps."

"I understand, but if there is any possibility of doing this today, we should try." Less than two hours remain before I meet Sedat. "Thank you."

I pull out my phone to make the calls, then hesitate. Why would Harris give me these accounts and the funds in the safe deposit box? I will face criminal time if these funds are from the U.S. government. The prosecuting office will freeze every penny in my name if an indictment is issued. Harris did not know he was about to be under indictment, or he would have hidden the money himself. Wouldn't he? A slow burn begins at the base of my stomach.

"When was the last time you saw my husband?" I ask Isobel.

She taps her cheek with her fingers and squints at a calendar across the lobby.

"I think at least two weeks ago? I am not sure. One second." She swivels to face her computer screen, and the mouse clicking starts again. "Yes. Two weeks ago."

I feel like throwing up. Harris opened these accounts the minute he left me. We don't need this level of personal banking, and we planned to live in İmir, which is hours away from Istanbul. He intended to deposit his gambling winnings into this bank. And when he needed cash? He planned to send me—his gullible mule—to transfer the money.

My anger mounts, and I need time to think.

"Please let me think about all this while I go to the safe deposit box," I say to Isobel.

"Certainly."

I clean out the safe deposit box, placing the gun at the bottom of the bag. Then I hesitate. Since I cannot fly with a firearm, I will be forced to rent a car and drive if it is in my possession. The bank box is the safest place to keep it, especially since I have no experience with guns, or if there's a penalty for having one in Türkiye. I place it back in the empty box with Harris's fake passports and lock it up.

The cash and all "my" passports go into the bag. I would love to confide in Sedat and have his help to think through what I am about to do, but I can't. I already told him too much at lunch.

After what Harris has done to me, my trust meter is broken. He was only after the money, fun, and games. Today confirms that his video and last letter were lies—nothing but lies. The naivete of my actions over the past six months is glaring. I was—and still am for Harris, even in death—only an expediency, a means to an end, even if immoral or unjust.

Harris's expedient wife.

35

QUINN

Resolving to dig myself out of the hole Harris created, I lock the safe deposit box. Before I return to Isobel's desk, I call Sedat. This time, he answers.

"Yes, Quinn. Is there a problem?" Sedat's deep voice makes my stomach twist with the lie I am about to tell.

"Sedat, my friend just arrived at the hotel. Since you and I will spend the entire evening together, I would like to spend a few more hours with my friend. Will this be okay?"

"Of course, Quinn. Since you were unavailable, I am currently in a meeting, and the additional time will allow me to complete the task appropriately. I will meet you at the same spot as before. Yes?"

"Yes. Thank you for understanding. I will see you soon."

Given the ease of the conversation, my stomach relaxes, even though I am becoming a liar like my husband. I sit in front of Isobel as she returns the master key to the safe deposit box to me. She smiles and slides a paper with an address across the desk to me.

"The gold trader confirmed that his facility has a small private vault that might be helpful for you. I also called my brother. He is free now if you wish to make an appointment. His gallery is also nearby."

Gold is a good solution, but putting this much money in the hands of someone I don't know is risky. Yet there is no other choice. I will keep $100,000 in cash and divide the remainder. I will use part for a Bitcoin cat-and-mouse plan my subconscious is working on, another for diamonds, and some for gold.

My conscience fights with me. *Why are you keeping all this money? Let the government take it!* I can't. Harris went to great lengths to set up this elaborate scheme involving me. There is no way that any prosecutor will believe I had no knowledge of the money or the fake passports. He needed these funds for something, and I need to know what that something is. My husband thought me stupid, and I intend to prove him wrong.

Isobel uses my phone to contact the gold trader on WhatsApp and hands it back to me when the call connects.

"Hello, madam." I reduce the sound on the video call so the tellers across the room cannot hear. The man is young, with light red hair and hazel eyes. His English is perfect. "No names, please. Because this is a referral from our partner, we will not charge you a fee."

Now I see. For Isobel, this is an under-the-table transaction. She will explain to her boss that I insisted on withdrawing the funds. She will receive a small amount of gold as her fee from the merchant she referred me to. It's a win-win. He provides me with the current gold rate and details about his vault capabilities. I agree to the details of the exchange.

"We will handle this transaction and send you the deposit confirmation by WhatsApp on your Turkish phone, as that service is fully encrypted. There is nothing else you will need to do, madam."

"This transaction cannot be wired if that is what you intended to do for me," I say to Isobel, my eyes flicking back and forth from the gold merchant to the banker. "This must be handled with cash."

I look back at the man on the phone. "How will we transfer the funds?"

He does not hesitate. "I will send my team immediately. How much will you be transferring?"

I blink, realizing they are about to cart hundreds of pounds of U.S. currency across the busy Grand Bazaar. I swallow, hoping the third I am transferring will not disappear into the depths of the ancient market.

"Four million U.S. dollars," I reply. "Can I do transfers and wires for subsequent transactions once placed with you?"

"Yes, of course. We only need your account number, but there will be fees for this service."

"I understand."

Isobel pulls out several withdrawal slips. She slides one to me, and I complete the numbers. Then, she stands and walks to a teller's window.

The man continues. "We are just inside Gate Number One. Once your funds arrive, we will hold your gold in our vault unless you give us a different directive."

"How secure is the gold?"

"As you would say, like Fort Knox. The account is only numbers. We do not use names, keep photos, or remember faces. However, the Grand Bazaar is heavily monitored by cameras and undercover police. If you are concerned, you may wish to take precautions. Please be advised that if you lose or misplace your account number, you will be unable to retrieve your assets. Do you understand?"

"Yes," I reply. "I will accompany your employees."

"*Seni bekliyoruz*. We are waiting for you."

We end the call. Isobel returns holding the withdrawal receipts.

"You are lucky," she says. "The security truck arrived early today; otherwise, this much cash would not be available. Ordinarily, we must schedule something this large."

If I had been in the States, this would never have happened. In 2008, when the banks failed during the housing crash, I had trouble finding banks strong enough to handle my client's trust funds at one-tenth of this amount. I pulled cash daily, in $30,000 to $40,000 increments, not millions.

"My brother Remzi will meet you here in a few minutes. He will accompany you to the bazaar and then escort you to his showroom when you finish buying your gold."

"I need one million nine hundred thousand dollars transferred to this account, please." I write the account information for a cryptocurrency account on a withdrawal slip. It holds part of the funds from the sale of my parents' house in Georgia.

She finishes and hands me the transaction slip.

"I need to purchase a few items. May I step out for a few minutes?" I ask.

"Absolutely no problem," she says. "Browse the shops outside while we prepare your funds." She gives me a wink, and I wonder how many under-the-table transactions she has done. I look at the woman helping me and swallow my guilt. If the men following me learn where Harris wired the money, Isobel will be in jeopardy.

I can't think of that now.

When I return from buying a disguise, the gold merchant's team of five men and a heavy-duty wheeled box the size of a box freezer is ready. Isobel's brother, Remzi, arrives as the tellers prepare the money in large security bags. Within minutes, the black steel box is loaded with 200 pounds of $100 bills.

I follow them out into the street and through the crowds into the Grand Bazaar, trying to keep my nerves under control. As we do this, I see that I am not the only one transferring funds this way. Large rolling boxes are clustered around other gold offices. Once we reach the gold trader's storefront, my reflection confirms that my new scarf, glasses, and abaya completely conceal my identity from anyone or any camera—unless sophisticated facial recognition software is involved. I'll have to take that chance.

Inside, the trader counts out his share of the funds and hands me a sheet of paper listing the vault's cash, my account number, and the gold balance. Even with the fees, the price of gold has increased, as has my balance, in the last hour.

I shake the hand of the gold merchant, looking into his hazel eyes. The remaining four million gets transferred into a large black suitcase held by two of Remzi's men who met us at the gold office. One of the men carries the final one hundred thousand in my thick canvas shopping bag, where I've stuffed my backpack.

"Do you think rolling around all this cash is crazy?" asks Remzi, once we are outside the bazaar and headed to his showroom. He is tall and handsome, with white-blonde hair and ice-blue eyes, almost identical to his willowy sister, Isobel.

"Yes. This is a little insane."

"Isobel and I are from Norway, but we grew up in Germany, and have lived here since we graduated from high school. We were shocked by some of the things we saw in the bazaar. However, it only occurs here, not in other parts of the country. There is a rich history and tradition in the *Kapalı Çarşı*, particularly regarding money. Most Turks are unaware of how this is accomplished. Only those with a certain level of funds, such as yourself, are given access to these services."

I feel strange, as if I have physically crossed an invisible economic barrier that I shouldn't have. My conscience is still fighting with me. *This is jail time. You can't keep all this!* But I can. With these funds, I can live well just on the interest earned and never touch the principal, never mind the ridiculous revenge factor of screwing over my dead husband that continues to boil deep inside me.

We reach Remzi's private gallery in less than five minutes. We are buzzed into a small, conservatively decorated office with a smaller room in the back that appears to be a workroom. Cameras are visible in all four corners. He introduces me to his assistant, who disappears into the back room. After the traditional hot tea, we begin.

"You will be spending the entire four million U.S. dollars?" Remzi asks.

"Yes. I need something easy to carry and conceal. Maybe a small pouch of diamonds."

"A pouch of loose diamonds will be convenient, but not so easy to hide, and not useful unless you intend to leave them in a safe. Will you need to sell them individually for cash?"

"No, I don't think so," I respond. There is enough cash and gold to support me for the rest of my life.

"I think a piece of jewelry might be better," Remzi suggests. "Maybe a necklace or a diamond ring, perhaps, or several. And there are bracelets and earrings, of course. Over time, the value will increase. They traditionally are a good long-term investment."

"I don't wear much jewelry. Something hidden would be better, rather than a flashy diamond ring." Harris's cartouche has easily stayed hidden under my shirt. I think a string of diamonds would achieve the same effect. "With a necklace, can they be smaller-sized diamonds that hang a bit low?"

"Yes, of course. Let me show you some examples in your price range."

Remzi goes into the back of his gallery and returns with several black cases. I try on several longer necklaces until I find one that serves the purpose I need. The diamonds are all square, smaller at the top and larger at the bottom, with one slightly larger diamond serving as the centerpiece.

"I think this one."

"A nice choice. Will you be wearing it today?"

"Yes. But I will need paperwork for the eventual insurance."

"Of course. Will you need an escort back to the bank or your hotel?"

"Yes, I think that might be wise."

The rest of the transaction is uneventful. A security guard escorts me back to my hotel. On the way, I spot a *Kahve Dünyası*, the Turkish equivalent of Starbucks, only more luxurious. Unable to avoid the beckoning smell of coffee, I ask the escort to follow me inside.

An hour before I meet Sedat, the guard discreetly watching out for me at another table, I spend ten minutes under two-hundred-year-old plane trees getting over the shock of what I've learned.

And what I've done.

36

SEDAT

Sedat's lunch with Quinn Durand proved fruitful. He looks forward to the additional hours he will have to develop their fictitious relationship later that evening. On the phone, he wants to ask Quinn outright what she is doing, but he relies on the tracker to see that she has headed back to Iş Bank. He thinks of calling Isobel at the bank, but changes his mind. He frightened the poor girl sufficiently the first time.

Entering the interrogation room, Sedat sits across the table from Arzu. He nods at Bora behind the one-way mirror to begin recording. He stays silent, waiting. Finally, the girl becomes uncomfortable.

"I need a bathroom." Arzu sits as still as stone, her legs crossed with her distress.

"I am sure you would love to relieve yourself privately, but using your chair will suffice until you tell me what Quinn was doing this morning."

"This is torture. I will report you to the chief of police."

"To whom?" Sedat allows a smile to emerge. "You are not familiar with me?"

The girl glares at him, her hands clasped so tightly that her knuckles are white. Sedat moves to the window and uses the back of his hand to rap lightly. One of his men opens the door.

"Take her to the facilities. She is not to be out of your sight, then return her here to me." He turns to Arzu. "He will watch you relieve yourself, but if you are nice to him, I am sure he will turn his head. This is not the time to push back, Ms. Tekin."

Within ten minutes, the girl is returned to her chair and locked to the floor. Her stomach growls. At the noise, Sedat glances at the window and shakes his head. No food or water until the girl gives him an answer.

"Let me relieve you of the presumption that you can cause any problem for me whatsoever." Sedat leans forward, elbows on the table, as he steeples his fingers. "I am Chief Detective Sedat Özbek, and you are deep in the bowels of the Istanbul offices of the Turkish National Police. Quinn Durand is of utmost importance to my department. You will tell me where she went this morning."

Arzu's eyes grow wide, but she does not speak. He admires her fortitude, but it is a useless activity. He can trump up a charge to hold her if he needs to until her obstinacy breaks. Sedat waits for five minutes before he breaks the silence.

"Let me tell you a story I believe you will find interesting. A woman illegally disembarked at our airport, unaware that her passport was fake until she arrived. She was to meet her husband, but American military officers informed her he was dead, that his activities were under investigation, and that she was under investigation as a co-conspirator. She did not believe them. She has since learned her husband gambled with government money and then stole millions at an illegal card game."

Sedat looks at the girl as if she were a cockroach tacked to an entomologist's bug collection.

"The woman was told that U.S. investigations shifted to her, as they insist she is his partner in crime. They may charge her with conspiracy, but that is my guess, not a fact. She has a deadline to find information her husband stole, information that puts Türkiye at risk. The woman is on a mission to do just that, and whatever she finds will affect several countries, not just the United States.

"Let there be no mistake: this woman is naive and believes she can save the world alone. You are now a part of that scheme, and if she is indicted here and abroad, you will be indicted as a co-conspirator."

Arzu shifts forward and opens her mouth to speak. Sedat holds up his hand.

"Indulge me if you will, and allow me to finish. I know she carries critical information. You assist her in decrypting that information. You put yourself, your friend Cem, and anyone else involved into the orbit of multiple groups of aggressive people."

"Men whom we believe are Bulgarians are attempting to retrieve a large amount of money that Ms. Durand's husband stole from them. Next, the Americans, one in particular, are involved. Unidentified men followed Ms. Durand several times, and we believe a third group has hired them. Then, finally, there is me. I must complete this investigation, distribute the information to the organizations where it will do the most good, and, if possible, clear Ms. Durand's name. This is where you come in."

Sedat rises and carries his chair to the opposite side of the table. Clearing Quinn's name is not part of the chief's orders, yet he needs the lie to motivate Arzu to talk. And if he is honest, he wants that for himself. He carefully positions the chair, with its back facing Arzu. He straddles the seat and rests his hands on the back as he softly tries again.

"The people chasing Ms. Durand will not hesitate to harm her to get what they want. If she met with someone in the Grand Bazaar, Arzu, that person is most likely dead, or if not, will be soon."

He leans forward until he is directly in front of her. "Where did she go this morning, Arzu? Talk."

Arzu blinks, then looks at the one-way mirror before looking back at him.

"She went to see a boy I set her up with, but I don't know his name."

The girl places her hand on her throat, a classic tell. She has just lied to him. She knows this boy's name.

"What is the address?"

"It is in my phone."

Sedat looks at the window, and within a minute, one of his men brings in an iPhone. Sedat hands it to her, and she unlocks the phone, taps on it, and then shows him the screen. He takes a photo with his phone and sends it to Bora, then immediately removes her Face ID and password so they can copy her phone in its entirety. He hands it back to his officer and texts Bora to copy it.

"Who is this boy?" He looks at Arzu

"The only guy in this country who can open that disk for her."

"I need his name, Ms. Tekin."

"I don't know it."

This time, she covers her face with her hands. He must teach her how not to do these things if she works for him, which she will. He will give her no choice. Bora will have the boy's name in a few minutes, so he doesn't continue to pressure her with this point.

"What do you think is on the disk?"

"I don't know, and neither does she."

"Will this boy open it?"

"If he can't, then it can't be opened except by the person who created it."

"Thank you for this information. I hope it is not too late for the boy. Do not contact Quinn Durand for the remainder of the day." Sedat nods at the mirror before returning his focus to the girl.

"Since I know you will not do that," he says, "we must detain you until midnight, then you may return to İmir. The handcuffs and waist chain will be removed, and you will be given food. And Ms. Tekin—Arzu—honestly, I suggest you give Ms. Durand a wide berth for your safety and remind you that communicating with her puts your life in peril."

37

QUINN

I can't find Arzu. The hotel's desk clerk has not seen her, and there is no message. I call her phone and leave another voice message. Stuffing Turkish money in my pants pocket, I ask the desk clerk to place the canvas bag into the hotel safe. He locks it in front of me while I watch. I'm uncomfortable leaving it in the room or in the safe, but I don't want to wander around the city with all that cash.

Hesitating in the hotel lobby, part of me knows I should stay locked in the hotel room and wait for Arzu or a message from the Hacker Boy, Artur. But I promised Sedat I would meet him again. My desire to enjoy the city and forget about Harris and the mess he created overwhelms me. As I stroll to meet Sedat, the tips of the Blue Mosque's minarets reveal themselves. Just in front of them, he is there, waiting for me.

Sedat changed into casual clothes. His linen button-down shirt, jeans, and loafers make him look closer to my age.

"The first stop is your choice." He is wearing sunglasses, and for the first time since we've met, he looks as relaxed as I am trying to be. "What would you like to see?"

"The Blue Mosque, I think. Or the Hagia Sofia. They seem to be the most important places to see first."

"I planned to give this to you later, but you will need it to go inside the mosque." Sedat produces the beautifully wrapped package from earlier in the day. Inside is a silk scarf in Mediterranean colors, the scarf that looks like Monet's Water Lilies that the vendor in the bazaar had draped over my shoulders. I hide my apprehension as I admire its beautiful colors, imagining its softness sliding through my fingers. I hesitate to put it on.

"Here, let me show you."

He drapes the scarf over my shoulders, crossing it in front of my neck, then pulls it up to hide my hair and lets the ends trail behind me. I see in a store window that it makes me look glamorously French rather than Turkish. It is a thoughtful gift, and the colorful silk under my fingertips feels luscious, even though its very existence is conclusive evidence that we did not meet by accident.

I watch his eyes as he places his hands on my shoulders, checking each side of the scarf around my ears and trying not to touch my skin inadvertently. He is stalking me, and according to him, it is for my protection, but with this gift, I think it is something more.

Later, strolling down the hill from the Blue Mosque, Sedat points out more historical places. He paints a verbal picture of Istanbul, the of historic families on the European side, as well as those who now reside on the Asian side of the Bosphorus. I'm given pointers on the safe areas. Of course, the area where I was this morning is one he suggests I avoid, making me wonder if he followed me there as well.

We sit in an outdoor cafe under a large canopy and have tea. Sedat receives a telephone call and walks down the block, so I cannot hear. When he returns, his mood is lighter. Istanbul is his city, and we watch the passersby—tourists, locals, business people—and discuss how their lives must be. After several tulip glasses of tea, Sedat stands, ready to go.

"Come now. I want to show you two of my favorite places."

We wind our way through the twisting streets until I see the shimmering blue water of the Bosphorus, the large waterway that stretches from the Black Sea to the Sea of Marmara. Ferry boats cross back and forth between the European and Asian sides of the city, and a large container ship heads out to sea. Sedat touches my arm slightly, directing me into a building similar to the Grand Bazaar but on a lesser scale.

"This is the Egyptian Bazaar, what we call the *Mısır Çarşısı*. My parents often brought me here as a boy when my father needed to visit Istanbul."

We walk inside. In the first shop, large burlap bags are filled with intensely colored red and gold spices, each mounded to a peak. Walking along the passage, other spice shops display racks of bottles, decorative bags, and baskets with even more spices, a whirlwind of colors and smells. Cinnamon floats by in the air, and I get a whiff of fresh coffee.

Sedat tugs at my sleeve, and we peruse the shops, tasting olives, cheese, candies, and dried fruits until I'm stuffed. He explains anything unique to Türkiye, the region where the item was made, and its significance in the culture or cuisine, until I beg him to stop. My head spins when we step outside.

"I pushed you too hard," he says, his brow furrowed with concern.

"No. Just sensory overload. And a very full stomach."

"You are stressed because of Harris. I did not mean to add to this."

"No, Sedat, I appreciate your time. Even though I asked for space, I needed this time away. Thank you."

I squeeze his arm, but he flinches. I drop my hand and give him a genuine smile. The one he returns is the first authentic expression I've seen on his face, and something changes between us. Not friendship exactly, but a truce.

Stopping at a bench near the Bosphorus, we watch the ferries come and go as an old man throws food at hundreds of pigeons. The evening call to prayer begins, and because we are directly under the loudspeaker, I cover my ears with my hands. We shift toward the water and away from the mosque.

"Come, please listen." He directs me to the edge of the Bosphorus, and within seconds, dozens of mosques join in, and the entire city comes alive with melodious voices that echo across the water. I stare at the profile of the man stalking me, with more questions than answers.

38

QUINN

"When will you return to İmir?" Sedat asks.

He walks me to the front of my hotel, and I am thankful he hasn't asked to follow me inside. After dinner near Topkapı Palace, I am exhausted from avoiding his questions and frustrated by his refusal to answer mine.

"Until I can talk with my friend, I don't know. I'm worried about her."

"Please text me with any problem. I will be in Istanbul until tomorrow."

The elevator closes. As I reach my floor and step out of the elevator, I realize I've forgotten to check for a written message from Hacker Boy or Arzu at the front desk. I push the down button. There is movement in my peripheral vision. At the end of the hall, under a bright red EXIT sign, the heel of a man's shoe disappears into the stairwell, and the door slams. I shove away the paranoia and punch the elevator for the lobby.

There is no message for Arzu or me, only the desk clerk's assurance that he will call my room if he receives any message. After retrieving my canvas bag and backpack from his locked storage, I ask the desk clerk for a Turkish newspaper in English, watching the stairwell door to see who appears. He hands me today's paper, and I sit on a comfortable couch. No one walks through the stairwell door, and after fifteen minutes, I go back to my room, my nerves shot after the events of the day. After a shower, I give up waiting and surrender to my exhaustion.

The hotel phone rings at three-thirty in the morning. Groggy, I answer.

"My apologies, madam. There is an envelope here for you. Would you like me to send it up?"

"Yes, please."

Arzu's bed has not been slept in. She only brought a small backpack with her, and she had that with her in the bazaar. She is not coming back. My heart hurts with disappointment.

I open the door on the first knock. A sleepy bellboy hands me an envelope, and I tip him. Inside is a note in craggy handwriting and the wadded tissue I left on Hacker Boy's desk. The note directs me to the Spider Bar on Vapur İskelesi Sokak in Ortaköy. Checking my map, I see it's a thirty- to forty-minute taxi ride.

Inside the tissue is the disk, but nothing else. Either Artur has the report, or there is nothing to report. Or he's screwing me over once he gets the rest of his money.

Re-reading the cryptic instructions, I pull my hair back with a band, then jerk on a clean shirt over the sweats I'd worn to sleep in. I shove my clothes and computer into the shopping bag from earlier, putting only money in my backpack, and tuck the fake passports into the front zipper pocket.

At the front desk, I check out and grab a taxi out front. When we arrive, the driver points to a sign, and following his finger, I see the Spider Bar down the cobblestoned steps at the end of the block, close to the water. I am dropped off at an intersection bustling with people, even at this time of night.

College-aged students are everywhere, and they are loud, drunk, and happy. I push through a crowd of chanting yellow and red football fans with painted faces and shove open the door to the Spider Bar. I enter a dim, crowded room, but the sound level is much lower than outside. I visually plow through more red and yellow jerseys and find Hacker Boy in a booth at the back. The booth faces the bar entrance and is steps from the back door. Nursing a beer, he tips his head slightly as he recognizes me.

"*Bira*?" he asks when I sit across from him.

"No thanks." I'm not here to drink.

"Sorry about the nighttime," Artur says, as his finger taps the table impatiently.

"What did you find?" I see the fear in his eyes as he slides a folded piece of paper toward me, the disk on top.

"You have big trouble," he says.

On the paper is a list of number strings.

"What is this?" I sit back and stare at him. He takes a large gulp of beer.

"Arzu say about disk logo in Karşıyaka. Give disk back to Aslan. Will be better I think." He nods toward the disk.

"What is the logo?"

"It is from Aslan."

"Who or what is Aslan? Are they dangerous?"

"Big surprise you not dead." He points his index finger at my chest.

A shiver of fear runs down my back, and I don't try to hide it from him. "What do they do?"

"Anything for the money, legal, illegal, whatever. In all the world."

I need more information than this. Now is the time I truly need Arzu.

"The disk had just these numbers?" I look at the list again. It is either a list of bank accounts or something else entirely. The numbers of various lengths are grouped in sets of three. They fill the entire page.

"Some sectors corrupt with Russian who tried open

Karşıyaka'da. When data download, I erase disk. Then computer cooked."

Cooked. I blink, understanding how scared he is. His computer had to have been worth thousands.

"Your computer was fried?"

He nods, rubbing his fingers together to tell me I have to pay him more.

"You pay me now," he says, bumping my knee under the table. I reach under and grab a small, zippered fanny pack from his hand, transfer the $500, zip it back up, and thrust it toward him under the table. He counts the money out of sight, then looks up. "I burned computer for you. Four thousand."

His fanny pack bumps my knee again under the table.

Glad it isn't my money, I pull cash from my backpack and put it in the fanny pack. When satisfied, he orders another beer, but still does not relax, as evidenced by the vein throbbing at the side of his temple.

I fiddle with the disk, remembering Harris's instructions to leave it alone. He knew, however, that I wouldn't, and he also knew how much danger I would be in. Yet he sent this disk to me anyway, expecting me to do what he could not. My hands shake under the table as I try to carefully plan the next step, staring at the neon beer sign just over Artur's head.

"Important Aslan not to find you. Or Arzu," he says, breaking into my thoughts.

I force myself to focus on him as beads of sweat begin to roll down my spine. Given Arzu's disappearance, they may have found her already.

"Aslan very bad," he says, "You are stupid and causing a problem for me." His hand slams against his chest. "And Arzu."

He gives me a pained expression as he flicks one hand in the air as if swatting a fly, his mouth downturned. I stare at him. He knows where she is.

"Where is she?" I ask.

"Fatih police station, all day. Question about you, let her go tonight. At airport."

"What?" I am stunned, yet relieved. She is alive and not in jail.

"She call with *cep telefonu* five minutes before. Warning. She not talk you. She meet İmir, no by plane. Go bus, taxi maybe."

Sedat had no trouble finding me, so if any Turkish police wanted to find me, it wouldn't be difficult. I thought back to the man disappearing into the hotel staircase.

I point to the paper with the strings of numbers.

"Tell me what these numbers *are*." My voice reveals my exasperation, but I need him to spit it out.

"Coordinates, maybe?" He shrugs both shoulders.

I squint at him. "To what?"

He shrugs his shoulders again, his face an expression of innocence. "I do not know. You ask to open."

I glare at him, knowing he has spent time determining what these numbers mean for his curiosity, if not for his bank balance.

"I move apartment. My old apartment big garbage pile now. Do not know numbers. I no want know numbers."

He takes another drink of beer and looks around the room. Although he appears rattled, I know he is not being entirely truthful.

"Bullshit."

"Syria, Iraq, Türkiye, Russia, Switzerland, Albania." His brow furrows. "Locations? Do not know. Maybe humans off boats, drugs, guns…" His voice trails off as his shoulders continue to shrug. He doesn't look at me.

I swallow hard. Heat crawls from under my shirt up my neck. This is so far out of my comfort zone that I don't know how to think or react.

"If you had your best guess, what do you think these coordinates are for?"

"Guns. United States and Russia go to war. Nuclear."

"A world war? That's not realistic."

He rolls his eyes.

"Yes, nuclear war. You need leave country. United States bombs to Ukraine, Türkiye too close."

I take a minute to let that sink in.

"Ah, question," he asks.

"What?" I zip my backpack. I don't know where I'm going, but it's time I left Istanbul, and quickly. Artur waits until he has my full attention and leans toward me, his voice soft.

"Where list from?"

"What does it matter to you?" I ask, with no intention of telling him.

He points at me again.

"If you spy, then me, dead man," he pauses, "and you dead man also."

39

QUINN

I am in a taxi about an hour from İmir. The taxi driver has been as good as his word, going as quickly as possible without speeding or drawing attention to us. It's about seven on Friday morning. Maynard left six messages on my voicemail the night before, each with increasing concern.

Heaving a large sigh, I call him. He answers on the first ring.

"Quinn, where in the world are you? I was really worried something had happened to you."

"I'm fine, Maynard." I cannot suppress my irritation. "What do you want?"

"You fell off the earth for an entire day, so I wondered if you'd already left the country. Did you find the information we want?"

I am sure he used his Department of Defense or JAG source to check every flight manifest leaving in the past twenty-four hours. He doesn't fool me. He knows where I've been, I'm sure of it.

"Is Harris's body ready to leave?" He doesn't need to know what I've found, especially since I don't even know what I've found. I keep going. "Can I assume the Air Force will pay for my ticket to accompany Harris? Or is that something that I will be expected to pay since you guys don't think I'm legally married?"

"Soon, I think," he says. "I'll have to check on the transport costs. Why don't we get breakfast and talk about it?"

"Not this morning."

"Maybe lunch then?"

"Look, Maynard, you don't want breakfast or lunch. You want me to give you something I don't have. Once you tell me exactly what I'm looking for, then maybe I can help you. Let me know about Harris's body."

"I'll check on that, but—"

I cut him off. "You do that." I end the call and relax in the back seat of the taxi, confident that Maynard will be waiting on my front doorstep, probably with Sedat.

STARING out the window at the farms rushing by, I recall the first time I met Harris. In my mind, I replay his actions, trying to understand how, despite his charm, I could have missed this level of deception.

Trudy had met him through a cousin at some event in Charleston. For weeks, she insisted that he was "perfect" for me.

"Quinn, this man is meant for you, I promise. He's well-traveled, well-read, and is really easy on the eyes," she told me. "I really think you guys should meet."

"Trudy, I'm not interested. He's military, and he'll come and go, leaving me stuck here like always. Why would I want to do that?"

"He's not like that. He's an officer, and from what he's told me, he really wants a wife."

"I don't know about the wife part, but if it will make you stop badgering me, go ahead and give him my number."

At 167 Raw, my favorite Charleston restaurant, I sat that day nursing a deep red cabernet on a chilly Friday afternoon. Enjoying the bustle of tourists out the front window, I remember pondering for the umpteenth time how to move my law practice to Charleston and live with its charm and relaxation every day, far away from Glenboro, Georgia.

The empty chair at my table scraped the wooden floor, and I turned at the noise. A man dropped casually into the seat, his face sliding into a smile that forms a dimple on his right cheek. His eyes were a color of blue I've only seen in photos of the Caribbean. With a buzz-cut, it was apparent he was in the military. He offers his hand.

"Quinn? I'm Harris Robicheaux," he says, placing his baseball cap and sunglasses on the table.

"Quinn Durand." I shake his hand.

"Trudy described you well. But of course, with your looks, it isn't hard to pick you out."

I remember trying to decide whether he was commenting on my attractiveness or how unusual my one-quarter Asian heritage was in Charleston.

"May I order you another glass of wine?"

"I'm fine at the moment, just get one for yourself."

Trudy had been correct. He was very well-traveled, and his reading appetite was similar to mine. After dinner, we talked all night, leaving downtown and sitting on the beach at Sullivan's Island until sunrise. Harris was comfortable in an in-depth conversation about a country's political status halfway around the world, yet was quiet at times, reading my mood and adjusting accordingly. His next overseas assignment was Türkiye, and he was simultaneously concerned and fascinated by how the United States seemed to track that country's politics.

With long phone conversations every night after work, we fell into a routine where every weekend was an adventure to another city, play, or concert. I reminded myself to take it slow, even though Trudy was pushing me at him at every turn. We double-dated with her and Mark, her husband, and I remember watching one night at dinner, as they both were clearly captivated by Harris. It was a whirlwind, and I remember finally letting myself go to enjoy the fun.

And, without quite knowing why, I was hooked.

After several months of dating, I arrived home from work on a Friday afternoon and found Harris waiting in my living room with a packed suitcase.

"What is this?" I asked.

"A surprise. Get into something comfortable. We need to get to the airport."

"Where are we going?" I dropped my briefcase on the floor and struggled out of my wrinkled jacket, my lone symbol of conformity to the state's outdated courtroom dress code.

He reached out to help me. "I told you it's a surprise. Now, get yourself in there and get changed. I've packed everything you need. Leave that damned backpack. You won't need a computer where we're going."

"How long will we be gone?" I squinted at the new carry-on suitcase next to his knee.

"Quinn Durand. I know you work on Monday, *sha*. Quit being a killjoy. Git."

He refused to tell me where we were going, even when seated in first class for a flight to Atlanta. I waited impatiently through the one-hour trip. We changed gates in Atlanta, and our destination was Cabo San Lucas.

"What is this?" I stared at the information board behind the airline gate agent.

"Nothing you don't deserve. You need to get away from your job, the stress of that stupid judge, and that ridiculous telephone you refuse to turn off. That reminds me—give it to me." He extended his open palm.

"Harris, I need—"

"No, you don't need anything but me until Monday." He

snatched the phone from my hand and turned it off, shoving it into his leather carry-on. "You'll get it back Sunday on the flight home."

The resort was nestled along the hillside, creating a secluded, idyllic atmosphere. Rock-walled suites were decorated with four-poster beds and flowing white curtains dancing in the breeze. When I unzipped the carry-on, I found only a bikini, one pair of skimpy shorts, one set of matching lacy underwear, a T-shirt, and flip-flops. I blinked, then looked at Harris. Before I could protest the lack of clothing, he took me into his arms, and my anxiety floated away.

I close my eyes as the memories flood my mind. It was as if I were there again, seeing, smelling, hearing, and feeling everything.

A secluded plunge pool and hot tub overlook the Pacific Ocean. In the evenings, the waves crashed on the rocks below as we stayed wrapped up in each other. The staff remained discreet, quietly knocking only when they deposited our food outside the door.

Lounging in the hot tub Saturday night, Harris shifted back from me, searching for something in his towel on the pool deck. He extended his hand toward me in the dim poolside light. I recall feeling perplexed yet excited, like a character in a romance novel.

"What is this, Harris?" He handed me a black velvet box, and I opened it, careful not to drop the large diamond and emerald ring into the hot tub.

I look down at my hand now, still wearing the ring and its matching wedding ring. It is all I can do not to buzz down the taxi window and throw them both out onto the side of the road. I cannot stop the movie in my head. It is as if my mind wants to torture me.

Harris pulled me to him as my heart raced. I never expected to be the subject of a Hallmark movie.

"Marry me, Quinn. Come with me to Türkiye. Don't let us be apart."

But does he love me? The unexpected question popped into my head then, just as it had done numerous times since I'd arrived here. *Did he ever love me?* As if he could hear me that day, he continued with the words every person wants to hear, especially me.

"I love you, Quinn. I cannot live without you. Please say yes."

Every cell of my being cried out for me to say yes that day. It didn't matter that I wasn't entirely sure I loved him. It didn't matter that we'd only known each other for four months. He was offering me an adventure I'd craved for years. And besides, it was Harris, the most charming, romantic man ever imaginable.

"Yes," I say. And the whirlwind began.

Harris refused to wait. He wanted to get married right then, claiming he could call a priest to the hot tub. Over my laughter, he agreed to wait until the next day.

To my surprise, both then and now, Harris managed to pull it off. On Sunday at noon in a small chapel, we were married. The priest spoke only Spanish, and while I got lost in the ceremony, I was convinced that I had made the right decision if only for Harris's out-of-control happiness.

This was too fast, too risky, and too out of character for me, yet my romantic side pushed aside all my concerns. Finally, I'd had the wedding I wanted without being jilted.

What a fool.

After a sleepless honeymoon night, we returned to the States full of moving plans. I immediately notified my clients that my practice would be closing, began winding up the cases I could, and referred the rest to lawyers I respected who were happy to receive them. Our travel plans solidified as I rapidly and happily settled into marriage.

Then, two weeks later, Harris received emergency orders to leave for Türkiye.

"This isn't a big deal, Q," I remember Harris saying as he grabbed the small black duffel he used when traveling in uniform. "The Air Force will take good care of you, I promise. The paperwork is in order, and I scheduled the move. You'll travel solo under the original orders, and I promise I'll be waiting on the tarmac as your plane rolls up. Don't worry."

Now, here I am, a widow who sees so many problems with her whirlwind romantic wedding to the man of her dreams. I am not only expedient, but I am also an idiot.

40

SEDAT

"She will run again." Sedat's superior leans back in his leather desk chair, the private meeting taking place over the internal video system. While Demirci's demeanor is calm, Sedat detects an underlying irritation that only a looming deadline can bring. It is Friday, and Sedat is only marginally closer to Quinn's arrest or deportation than when he began.

"Yes, she is a challenge."

"What are you doing about this, Sedat?"

"I track her every movement. She cannot go anywhere, that I cannot see." Except for the untracked twenty minutes outside the Tacirler Gate, he has a map of everywhere she has been. His men have not found the hacker she visited, but it will only be hours before they do.

"Must I remind you of Monday's deadline? This woman must be out of the country quickly, and this information retrieved."

"I am well aware of the deadline, sir, but there are only so many things I can do short of imprisonment and torture."

"Yes, you believe that force is not always effective, but if necessary, I suggest you use it."

"Yes, sir, but I don't think—"

"Get me her confession or the information we want." Demirci's tone tells Sedat precisely what he intends even before the words are spoken. "Or I will."

The video call goes dark.

"He isn't fooling around, Sedat." Bora's words enter the room before he does.

"You aren't supposed to eavesdrop."

"It saves you from having to repeat everything." Bora sprawls into the chair in front of the desk. "Tell me you have a plan."

41

QUINN

I make it back to İmir in six hours, paying the taxi driver an excessive amount of dollars. Inside the apartment, I change, unpack, and then repack for the next trip. I am surprised but thankful that neither Maynard nor Sedat was waiting for me when I arrived.

I begin to search for hiding places, looking over every inch of the apartment. With my general practice back in South Georgia, I learned all types of creative things involving hunting, farming, and fishing, not to mention lying, stealing, hiding things, and, in a few cases, killing people. It was amazing the things people will do for idiotic reasons.

There is a small space in the bathroom, located behind the cabinet wall under the sink. I carefully remove the thin wood paneling, and even though there is no space between the wood and the cracked stucco wall, I use kitchen scissors and an empty wine bottle as a makeshift hammer to scrape out a hole. Fitting the passport, the thumb drive, and the diamond necklace bundle into the hole, I reinstall the wooden section of the cabinet and smear white toothpaste on one corner to hide the damage to the white paint.

Hiding the money is more challenging because there is a substantial amount. If Maynard or anyone else searches the apartment, the cash will be discovered if I'm not ingenious. I scan the apartment carefully, looking for any furniture that could create a false compartment or another defect in the wall that could serve as a hiding place like the one in the bathroom. I don't dare slit the mattress or hide the money inside the sofa. Those are the first places someone will look.

Again, I'm forced to return to the bathroom. The wall of cabinets is deep enough and looks to be the best solution. It is old and immovable, occupying one entire wall in the room. After removing the drawers, I get on my hands and knees and stick my head inside the empty frame. The interior is unfinished and matches the color of the cardboard shipping boxes stacked throughout the apartment. There is enough room to create a false back wall that, if done correctly, will only be detectible by someone who knows it's there.

I slide one of the packing boxes into the room, empty its contents, and study how I'm going to cut the box so that it will not look like what it is—a cardboard box hiding something. Too bad I couldn't call my former client, who'd done something similar to this to hide his porn stash. His wife never found it.

After a few false starts and several destroyed boxes, I neatly place the $900,000 in a thin stack behind the false cardboard wall. Using a roll of thin brown packaging tape I find in the kitchen, I securely attach the cardboard to the frame, reinsert the drawers, and then load all the drawers with towels and other bathroom items.

Next, using the funds Isobel sent to my cryptocurrency account, I implemented the process I carefully planned earlier in the taxi. I want the criminals chasing a computer trail rather than harassing Isobel or looking for me. One of my most significant cases several years prior involved a builder along the coast near Savannah who defrauded his clients and several banks. From that case, after being scared to death by the FBI that I'd lose my law license after the client had attempted to implicate me, I, through detailed forensic analysis, learned how he had transferred money to accounts in the Cayman Islands and to Switzerland. The feds never found the money.

Using what I'd learned while addressing the weak points the Feds had identified, I activated shell companies and established numbered bank accounts for them in the Cayman Islands. I'm not looking to hide the funds completely, but rather keep them moving anonymously through the system, splitting the approximately three-million-dollar balance into many smaller accounts and setting up automatic transfers for different days, times, and amounts.

I will shift the money into cash when life settles down. While I don't want the dirty money, many charities would be delighted to receive a large donation. However, until I understood exactly where the money came from and why my husband had stolen it, I would hold on to it.

Next, I pull out Artur's sheet with the sets of numbers. Opening an incognito Google Maps, which I know will likely not help me much, I use the numbers as coordinates. They are located in Europe, Asia, and the Middle East, but they don't exactly fit into a coordinate system. Six are in Türkiye. I pull up the satellite overlay. Each location is situated near either a storefront or a warehouse, but is otherwise unremarkable. Even if I had accurate geographical coordinates, there is no way online to determine how each specific location is being used.

I save my map for offline use, then send myself a screenshot on WhatsApp before wiping my search history. I want to explore the world, but this isn't how I thought it would happen. I pace back and forth, deciding the best way to see each place, how to get there, and what I will need for the trip. If Hacker Boy is right, I could be standing in a warehouse full of guns, bombs, or chemical tanks. I cannot just walk away and leave those things to the bad guys.

Harris wanted me to tell someone in the military. I pull up the Air Force site for İmir. It is actually part of the Incirlik base, miles away, and has little to no information about how İmir operates. No officers are identified, and only Turkish telephone numbers are provided.

Who do I tell? I still don't know.

After the trip to Istanbul, my confidence in navigating the country has grown, yet the fear of what people following me will do is impossible to ignore. I chew my ragged cuticles as I call Arzu's number, a nervous habit I thought I'd rid myself of after law school. The call goes to voicemail. Again.

The photo of Harris stares at me from the bookcase. Gritting my teeth, I stride across the room, and after removing the photo from the frame, I rip his face into shreds. Clutching the shreds in my hand, I head for the kitchen. Pulling out a metal pot, I toss the pieces inside and strike a match from the box next to the stove. I open the balcony door and set the pot on the floor as the photograph pieces curl and burn.

The photo in ashes, I grab the bottle of wine Sedat supplied, uncork it, and pour a glass. Whatever love I felt for Harris is gone, replaced by a roiling hatred and a deep desire to get myself out of my current predicament. There has to be someone I can trust other than Sedat. I swirl the wine in the glass and take another sip. While the man's controlling nature irritates me, I cannot find fault with his taste in wine. So, do I tell him?

No.

Arzu? While she is my best source of information, I need to know what she told the police before I share anything else with her. I grab my cell phone again and punch her number. This time, finally, she answers on the first ring.

"Come to the first place." The call is cut off immediately, and I am left staring at my phone. I look out the front window, but see no one watching me, even though I know they must be. I must leave rapidly before anyone outside knows what I'm doing. Grabbing my backpack, I blast out the front door and run down the hill to Mithatpaşa Caddesi, the mini-bus street. I am in luck. At my outstretched hand, a minibus glides in front of me. I step on board, hearing the door close as I pass my fare to the driver, thankful I blend in. As I look out the back window of the small bus, I see a man running into the middle of the street, a phone to his ear.

I get off near the Hilton and run the three blocks to the cafe. Although it is still morning, the temperature is already rising. Under a tree in the shade, Arzu is waiting. She sips Turkish coffee while smoking a cigarette, appearing unfazed by her run-in with the police.

When I get close, she turns her head away from me. Sena greets me and takes me to a table in the back. There are only a few customers at the opposite end of the room. Arzu joins me several minutes later, a sarcastic look on her face.

"You should exercise more, Miss America," she says, watching me as I wipe the sweat from my face. "You are getting lazy here in Türkiye."

She flips her long bangs away from her face, her mischievous grin making fun of me. I give her a scornful look, then grab the water bottle she shoves at me. I down half as she sits across from me.

"What happened to you in Istanbul?" I ask, placing the bottle on the table. "Hacker Boy says you got taken in by the police."

"Yes, I was detained but not arrested," Arzu replies. "Was it worth all the trouble I spent in that nasty place?"

"Yes. Artur told me that the information on the disk looks like a list of coordinates. I found them, sort of, on Google Maps. Four cities are not far from İmir, but I can't tell what is inside the buildings from looking online."

She leans forward, her face skeptical. "Where exactly are these places?"

I show her the offline map. After a few seconds, she looks up, surprised.

"You want to go to Syria?"

"No, Arzu," I respond, suppressing my irritation. "I want to go to these cities marked on the western side." I point to several locations on the coast with my finger. "Aren't all of these tourist places?"

She studies the map again, then leans back, tapping her fingers on the table while staring into the distance.

"Why would these tourist cities be on this list?" she asks, leaning forward, her voice a whisper.

I lean toward her. "I don't know. Artur says the locations could be used for anything."

"Like what?" Arzu asks, with two horizontal lines deepening on her forehead.

"Weapons, drugs," I respond, holding my hands up as I shrug. "And something he called Silk Road shipments."

"Trafficking," she says, as her nose wrinkles in disgust.

"Oh." A shiver runs down my back at the thought of opening a warehouse door to dozens of kidnapped women and children.

"You are crazy. I cannot help you with this." She slams back in her chair, a look of resignation on her face. "Not with the police watching me every minute. They flagged my residency card, and it caused me a delay at the airport."

"I don't know who else to ask, Arzu." I keep my voice low and glance at the other people in the restaurant. "Is someone watching you now?"

"Probably, but I don't know," she says as she looks me over carefully. "I just know I cannot go with you. They will arrest us both."

42

QUINN

Sena returns to see if we need something, and I order a coffee and breakfast. Arzu lights another cigarette as the waitress leaves.

"Please tell me why you must do this," she says. "Use your computer. Let me use mine. We can do any research you want from here."

"I've already done that. Each business is different, and they don't make sense. I'm not sure if they're still open or if the information on Google Maps is accurate. I need to see for myself."

"This is crazy." She shakes her head, not budging. "Let me see the numbers you say are the coordinates."

I pull out the page of numbers and hand it to her. She places it on the table and stares at the page, her eyes squinting as she concentrates.

"Wait a minute." She pulls out her cell phone and opens an app. "These are coordinates, but not how you think." She grabs a notebook and a pen from her backpack and begins creating the alphabet across the top of the page, then numbering each letter underneath.

"What are you doing, Arzu?"

"Just give me a minute." She takes the first set of numbers and translates them into words. Each set reveals they are not coordinates, but groups of three nonsensical words.

"This is interesting," she says. "They are coordinates using What Three Words." After transposing the first five sets, she turns the page toward me and slides her phone next to mine.

"Explain what I'm seeing. I don't know this app."

"What Three Words is a location app. If you want a delivery exactly to a specific door of a building, you can give the delivery driver the three words. For example, my apartment is in a building on the 74th *Sokak*. In İmir, there are multiple 74th Streets, as each neighborhood has its own. And many small streets or alleys in Türkiye have no numbers or names. But I can use What Three Words, and give my driver "fairly.brighter.nuance," using the Turkish version, of course, and he will be able to find my building's front door exactly."

"This is very cool. Why haven't I heard of it?"

"Maybe, Miss America, it's because your country is a bit behind on these things? It's very helpful when you are hiking and need to give your emergency location, or in the park and you want a pizza to be delivered." She gives me a sarcastic grin, then grabs the paper and her phone to translate the remainder of the numbers. "And they have created the app in each country's language." When she finishes, she looks up. "Ok, so now you have the real locations."

Grabbing my phone, I download the app. After opening her laptop and logging in, she identifies each location, and then I mark them inside the app on my phone. Although the places are distinctly different from those I created using numbers as geographical coordinates, the ones in Türkiye are still located in major cities on the western coast.

We checked them all, even the ones in other countries that are extremely far away.

"There are too many, even in Türkiye," Arzu says.

"I'll select four or five, in tourist cities not too far away."

"Don't do this, Quinn. He will come after you. And me."

"Don't go with me then. Just tell me what to do," I respond. Arzu silently stares at me, attempting to understand why I had to see these places in person. How do I explain this desperate need to know for myself?

"You must cover yourself," she says, resigned to my folly. "Maybe dye your hair. We need to get you Turkish clothes. You can't look American."

"Seriously? What color do you want it? Pink? I'm not dying my hair, Arzu. I must look like what I am—a tourist."

"Yes, I am very serious. It would be best if you looked different. They drilled me yesterday, even with questions about the color of your underwear, which I thankfully do not know. You need to blend in completely."

"Why don't I rent a car? That way, you could come with me."

"No. Be reckless with your own life. I will hide behind my computer, which, thanks to you, is no longer safe." She again taps her fingers restlessly on the table, her face tight with concern. "And what will you do in your rental car when the Jandarma flags you and questions you? They don't speak English."

I know that the Jandarma is a rural police force with military capabilities used in some countries, such as France and Italy. She snaps her fingers with an idea.

"Mustafa will help."

"Who is that?"

"He owns a tour company. He will help you blend in as a tourist. But his behavior is obnoxious. Please do not tell me later that I did not warn you."

"Arzu, I don't want to cause you or anyone else more trouble, like Artur or Cem. Do you plan to tell Mustafa what I'm doing?"

"No, you are a tourist. That is all he will know. Just pay him what he asks."

"Speaking of money, I guess I owe you."

Arzu throws back her head and laughs. "No amount of money in that bag will be enough for what I went through yesterday."

"What did you tell them?"

"You trusted me, remember? I told them nothing, only the address for Artur. After you met with him, he packed everything, hired a boy to help him with a cart for his things, and disappeared. I am not concerned about Artur. They cannot catch him."

She waves her fingers at Sena and pantomimes 'drinking coffee' before continuing. "For six hours, I said nothing, even when they wouldn't let me pee and made me starve."

"What about Cem?"

Arzu's eyes shift to the left and then down to the floor. Every body-language textbook I used to prepare for juries and trials included this as a classic sign of a lie about to be told.

"They missed Cem. He is too fast, but they know about him." She looks over my head at something behind me and then taps out another cigarette. "He made it home, then left the country by ferry for a several-month holiday in Crete. We both hope you will be back in America when he returns."

Looking around the now-empty restaurant, I zip open the backpack and begin counting one-hundred-dollar bills, stacking them on the table. When I get to a thousand dollars, I stop and study Arzu, my eyebrows raised in question. She shakes her head.

"Okay then, tell me when it's enough."

Arzu laughs when the stack reaches $5,000 and puts her hand on mine to stop me.

"This is enough. Too much, actually, but I will take it as it looks like a lot of money is in that bag and I need a new computer."

I zip the bag and drop it in the chair next to me. "What happened to yours?"

"They copied it, effectively trashed it. After that, they trashed my life. I'll have no way to get clients after this. I'm toast, as you guys say."

"I'm sorry, Arzu." I don't know what else to say.

Sena delivers coffee for Arzu, and we sit silently for a minute or two.

"With this, Mustafa person, is there a possibility of a private tour?" I ask.

"I am sure there must be, but you cannot hide alone. You need to be in a group." She is right. I need the cover of others.

"Thank you—and your friends." I sit back.

From the look on Arzu's face, my hiding in plain sight won't be easy. Yet I can tell it isn't me she is thinking about. She won't meet my eyes.

"What is it, Arzu? What happened to you yesterday at the police station?" My mind fills with thoughts of interrogation, torture, or worse from the social media news across America. I am sure those things also happen in Türkiye.

"Your friends are more important than mine, Quinn. I'm sure that is why you are still free." She taps her fingers on the table. I place my hand over hers to stop as Sena places cold water bottles on our table next to the Turkish coffee. I stare at the girl's back as she rushes away.

"You are acting like a fidgety cat." I open a bottle as Arzu crosses, then re-crosses her legs. I feel the same nervousness I felt last night with Artur.

"What friend are you talking about?"

"The man who comes to your apartment."

"Who?" I ask. The only men who visit my apartment are Maynard and Sedat. The first is not my friend. "Do you mean Sedat?"

Her head cocks to the side, a worried smile on her face. I stare at her as a nerve twitches in my neck.

"You are toying with Sedat Özbek." Her smile fades. "I thought you were smarter than this."

"He is just my landlord, and that's not the name he gave me." I search my backpack for Sedat's business card. After she reads it, she laughs, flipping the card back toward my face.

"Your professor," she air quotes the word, "is the chief inspector for the Istanbul division of the Turkish National Police. He's the third-highest-ranking police officer in the country and a specialist in organized crime."

"He what?" The water in my mouth shoots across the table. She moves quickly, avoiding the water that would have hit her directly in the chest. I start to call her a liar, then stop myself. Either this must be the biggest joke anyone has ever played on me, or she has just answered every question niggling at me about Sedat.

"You're joking, right?" I never thought of using the internet to search for Sedat or Maynard, for that matter. I take people at face value. How stupid I am. I trusted them both, just like I did with Harris.

Stupid, stupid, stupid. My lawyer brain deserted me once again.

Arzu thrusts her phone toward me, her face deadly serious. On the Istanbul University website, a photo of Sedat is to the left of his academic description.

"This is the man who questioned me for hours yesterday. Is this your professor-landlord?"

I feel the blood drain from my face.

"This man," Arzu continues, "scared the crap out of me. The reason he is so enamored with you? From what I learned at the police station yesterday, because your husband is now dead, you are officially his target."

She pushes at the cuticle on her thumb until it begins to bleed. I place my hand on her arm to make her stop, and she looks at me, her ocean-green eyes full of worry.

"He made it very clear to stay far away from you. He does not even want me talking to you."

I rise to leave, and she grabs my arm. "Did I say I would do that?"

She pulls two cheap-looking phones from her bag and hands one to me.

"Use one of these. I am sure he monitors your calls."

I take one of the burner phones. It is already programmed with a single phone number.

"We can only call each other. Do not use it for anything else." She holds up the other phone for me to see.

"What exactly did he say that scared you so badly?"

"After he chained my feet to the floor, he confirmed what I knew from the underground talk. Then he threatened to ruin my reputation. He wants information from you, and he intends to get it."

"But he can't do anything to me."

"Please tell me you aren't this naive. I'm quite sure this man has tortured people."

"That's what happens in spy novels and movies, and—"

"Well, Miss America, your world is one big spy novel now. Get used to it."

I clench my fists, my fingernails cutting into my skin. Sedat and I had spent the previous day together, with me mentally convincing myself to trust him throughout the entire afternoon.

It's official now. My trust meter is not just broken; it has been completely shattered.

43

SEDAT

While waiting at the apartment in İmir, Sedat lights a cigarette and, after placing a clean handkerchief from his pocket on the step, he sits. Twenty-four hours earlier, he had walked the seaside with Quinn in Istanbul, enjoying his time with her while recovering from unpleasant duties with her friend. He had gained so much of her trust, and to a certain extent, she had his. Part of him then wanted to throw the entire investigation into the Bosphorus and tell her how he felt about her. But as he has done his whole life, he kept his feelings to himself.

And he will do so today.

He is kidding himself. There is no trust between them. It is an illusion. His mind is only projecting a relationship he cannot have. She did not tell him about the boy she visited later in Ortaköy, nor the information he handed over. His afternoon and evening were only several hours of luxury with a foreign woman, for which he now punishes himself.

Quinn's conversation with Arzu, a half hour earlier, still burns a hole in his stomach. His first mistake was not detaining Arzu in Istanbul until he had Quinn in custody or had her deported. He miscalculated the budding relationship between the two women. His second mistake was handling Quinn himself. Her presence obliterates all of his training, and he knows better.

Quinn turns the corner two blocks from the apartment, her head held high, her body rigid. Sedat continues to smoke, seeing her anger at him even from a distance. She is livid. If he touches her now, his fingers will burn as if she were a hot stove. She stops before him on the sidewalk, her keys in her hand. He wonders whether she knows how to use them effectively as weapons.

"Are you here to escort me to jail?" Quinn's voice is sarcastic, her rage front and center at his deceit.

He has misplayed this, but because of Demirci, the absolute truth is still not an option.

"Jail? What are you talking about? I am here because I missed you today." He even sounds ridiculous to himself. He is now wary around her, uncertain if the angry feline will rip him to shreds verbally and physically. "I wanted to be certain you arrived home safely from Istanbul."

"We need to talk, Sedat." She will not face him, but side-eyes him with furious suspicion, exactly like his mother.

"Certainly." He stubs out his cigarette on the sidewalk and stands to follow her up the stairs to the apartment.

"No, not inside. We'll talk here."

"If you wish." He shifts his hands behind him, knowing full well that Bora is listening through the microphone in Quinn's backpack, even though Sedat insisted before he left the office that he turn it off. He did not want this conversation recorded, his error to be preserved for all to hear.

"Sedat, who are you?" She sits on the third step and motions for him to sit beside her, tapping her index finger on the marble step. He feels like a five-year-old about to be scolded by his teacher.

"What do you mean?" he asks, refusing to sit. There was no

time to plan for damage control. In his desperate need to see her, he had rushed rather than thinking this through.

"You are not a college professor but someone else. Or maybe a college professor *and* someone else." She refuses to look at him, her gaze fixed on the building across the street.

"Who told you this ridiculous thing?" He gives her what he hopes is a confused smile, batting away the internal tug demanding he tell her the truth. His job is on the line, a position in the Turkish National Police that he has worked to obtain since high school. No one can know how he feels about this woman, most of all her.

She doesn't respond, and he is surprised at her protection of Arzu. She could accuse the hacker of giving her the information, thus giving him an excuse to claim the girl lied. But she doesn't walk into that trap.

Sedat tries again, forcing his face into a mask of concern. "You believe this person?"

"Yes," Quinn answers. "There is no reason not to. Stop avoiding the question."

He can feel the anger rolling off her in waves, which tells him she must feel the same about their time in Istanbul as he does. Otherwise, there would be no need for such heightened emotion. The realization gives him hope, even though he knows he is a foolish, foolish man.

"Quinn, I am exactly who I told you. I don't know what is happening here."

Quinn finally turns to him, and he shifts to study her face.

"You ask so many questions about my life, but you've told me very little about yours. I know little pieces, but you seem to skirt around any substantive conversation about yourself."

"I am a very private person, Quinn. Discussing my life is difficult for me. I apologize if this has offended you."

"What's interesting is that your questions are only about me. Is there nothing you want to ask about Harris? About his work with the military? Everyone else seems to want to know. Don't you?"

"I am not interested in Harris." Sedat looks at her face, memorizing every millimeter of it, knowing this may be the last time he sees her until her arrest or deportation.

"Just admit the truth."

"What truth?"

"That you are very high up in the Turkish National Police. You investigated Harris and now are investigating me."

He laughs loudly. "You are serious? Investigating? How ridiculous. Quinn, please. Your friend is mistaken."

He rakes his hand through his hair, a nervous habit when he is at a loss for words. He feigns being insulted.

"I know you're spying on me," she says, smiling as she looks up at him, not letting it go. "I just don't know why. But I do know I've made you nervous. You do the same hand thing with your hair that I do when I'm caught off guard."

He steps back, surprised, and prepares for battle.

"I am not nervous. I have no reason to be."

Lie upon lie upon lie. He hates himself for this. He must stop this conversation before it destroys everything he has built with her, even though he knows it is already too late.

"I helped you in every possible way." He rips his glasses from his face, staring at the distrust in her eyes, and points them at her. "I thought we had a friendship after yesterday, but I will not stand for these accusations. Since you do not want my help, I will leave you to your life."

44

QUINN

Checking to be sure the deadbolt is locked on the front door, I head for the living room and grab my backpack from the couch. Before I can stop myself, I fling it across the room hard enough so that it hits the wall and crashes to the floor.

I allowed myself to trust him—such a glaring mistake.

Huffing out my disgust, I retrieve my backpack and the small purse I wore to dinner with Sedat. I empty both bags of their contents and inspect each item. Feeling every inch of the bag, I find a small lump hidden in the crease at the bottom corner. It is a small, round device, the size of an eraser on the end of a pencil. Another is inside the zipper pocket on one side. I find nothing inside the purse.

I look at the difference between the small gadgets. Inspecting my telephone for a bug, I find no new software or anything else unusual, but I probably wouldn't recognize such a program if it bit me on the nose. Arzu is right to use burner phones.

My anger boils over. This is worse than what Arzu told me. He isn't just tracking me; he hears everything I say. I scream openly and vehemently at Sedat, cursing the day I came to this country, and the day I met him, knowing full well he hears every word through one of the tiny devices.

But this isn't Sedat's fault.

That responsibility belongs entirely to Harris.

My hatred for Harris at that moment takes me over the top, and I feel almost sucked under with the raging tidal wave of anger. Going from room to room, I pick up boxes, flinging the contents across the floor, searching for something I missed that would tell me why my husband did what he did. Why he stole from the government, why he felt the need to drink, gamble, and whore around the world, and most of all, why he married me.

When I regain my equilibrium, I make a promise to myself. No one will take anything from me ever again—unless I am dead.

The doorbell rings, and I'm filled with dread. Sedat has returned, I'm sure, to arrest me. Through the peephole, however, I see two men I don't recognize in ill-fitting dark suits and ties. One's thinning hair is in a comb-over, and the other has a crew cut. From their facial structure, they appear neither American nor Turkish.

I do not know how they got inside my building, but whoever they are, they've finally caught up with me. I grasp the pendant under my shirt, knowing that even if Artur erased the data, I still cannot part with it. Instinctively, I flip the deadbolt lock repeatedly, hoping the loud clicking makes it clear I am not letting them in.

The thickness of the steel door, along with Sedat's assurances of its impenetrability, comforts me, and I go to the kitchen to make tea and wait them out, hoping they eventually will leave. Yet the men's discussion in an unfamiliar language, loud enough to come through the thick metal door, makes my nerves scream. Leaving the gun in the bank was a mistake.

Two solid raps against the steel door sound metallic, like a man's ring. I turn off the heat under the teapot and wait.

"Mrs. Robicheaux, we need to speak to you." The voice,

speaking in heavily accented English, booms through the door. I flatten my hands against the door to keep them from shaking. If these men are with the gang Artur had described, my minutes are numbered if they breach the door. My brain travels back to Sedat's lesson on the lock, and now I understand exactly what he was trying to tell me, how he was trying to protect me.

"What do you want?" I pray I've kept the fear from my voice.

"We are business partners with your husband. May we please enter to extend our condolences?"

"My husband had no business partners. Go away." If they don't leave, I'm not sure what to do. Call the MPs? If Maynard is correct, I am not the military's responsibility.

The strange voice tries again, a little softer. "Mrs. Robicheaux, please be reasonable. Open the door. We will not hurt you."

"I don't know you and don't want to talk to you. Go away before I call the police."

A snort of laughter floats through the door, and the softness is gone.

"Mrs. Quinn, you are an American. The police will not come for you."

Terrified he might be right, I grab my cell phone. Heading for the bedroom so the men can't hear my call, I dial the emergency number for the Turkish police I'd memorized from the military packet.

"*Alo. İzmir Emniyet Acil Hattı.*" A bored male voice answered.

"Please, I need help." I breathe a sigh of relief that someone answers. "Strangers are trying to break through my door. Send someone!"

"*Ben İngilizce bilmiyorum. Bir dakika lütfen.*" The disembodied voice doesn't understand English, and my hope for help fades. Maybe the strangers are right, and he won't help. Before I can speak, there is a click, and I hear a fuzzy sound telling me I am on hold. I wait, wondering what to do if no one picks up the call.

The men in the hall pound on the door. "Mrs. Robicheax!"

Another click and a woman's voice comes over the line. "Alo. May I help you, please?"

"Yes, thank you. There are two men at my front door. I don't know them, and I'm afraid to open the door. They refuse to go away."

"Be patient, madam. I promise you, they will go away."

"No!" My scream had to be heard outside the apartment. "They won't. At some point, if someone doesn't do something to help me, they will kill me. Listen to me! Help me, please!" I begin to beg. "Please, can't you send someone?"

"Madam, if there is no emergency, we cannot send someone. Are you injured?"

"No, they are outside."

"Is your door wooden or steel?" she asks.

"It is steel." I close my eyes, understanding where she is going with her questions.

"Then you will be safe. A police car will drive by your apartment and check your door. Can you give me the number, please?"

"This is an emergency, I promise you." I try not to shout. "I need the police car now, not later." I give the policewoman the address, and then she thanks me before disconnecting the call.

I am alone. All I can do is hope the steel door holds. Pounding on the door begins again, first one man, then the other. Then silence. I approach the door again when a loud clunk, like a metal box, hits the floor. The voice takes on a sing-songy nature as if he is talking to a child.

"Mrs. Robicheaux, we are not leaving. You will be trapped inside until we decide to let you out. Let us in so we can get what we came for. We won't hurt you, but if you don't let us in, we will drill the door." The sound of a drill revs, followed by raucous male laughter that makes me think they are drunk.

The police woman's polite assurances that these men will eventually give up and leave are now ludicrous. I know what these men want, and they will not leave until they get it. There will be lots of blood and broken bones—mine—if no one helps me.

The drilling noise blasts through the apartment, and when I place my hand on the door, it shudders heavily as they drill the lock. I punch Arzu's number, but then disconnect the call. She's already done enough for me. Besides, I cannot risk her life to save mine now.

I go to the balcony and look down at the street. I know Sedat is watching this building—if not him personally, then someone who works for him. I cannot call him, nor can I call Maynard. I am not interested in going to a Turkish jail or a stateside prison. Both men will take the disk and feed me to these piranhas.

The drill revs again, and my body begins to shake. I need help.

Sedat is *the* police, whether he admits to it or not. I call him, but the call fails or is disconnected. Is he rejecting my calls? I sit in the bedroom to escape the drilling noise that fills the apartment.

I punch in his number again. Again, the call fails. This repeats over and over again until, finally, I'm surprised when his voicemail answers. In my haste to leave a message, I hit the wrong button. The call disconnects. I scurry to the living room to find the two tiny devices that were hidden in my backpack.

"I know you can hear me, Sedat," I say to the devices lying on my bed. "Pick up the phone!"

I hit redial again as I pace the bedroom. The men outside my door won't stop pounding, shouting my name with laughter as they drill.

Can't my neighbors hear this racket? Won't they call the police?

After ten rings, Sedat's voicemail finally picks up again. I need him here. Now. I control my fear until I hear his voice, a recorded message in Turkish. Panic-stricken and crying, I begin to beg, not caring what he thinks or what the repercussions will be when he gets here. I just want to get away from the maniacs outside my front door.

Most of all, I don't want to die.

"Sedat, please, for God's sake, call me. I need your help." I wipe my tears on my sleeve and breathe in so he can understand my message. "There are men here. They claim to be Harris's business partners. I am sure they want the same thing you do, as well as the money."

The pounding begins again, accompanied by the drill's revving. With urgency in my voice, I try not to scream.

"Please! They are drilling the door. I've called the police emergency line, but they're no help. I don't know how strong this door is. I don't know where else to turn." My voice trails off to a whisper. "Please, Sedat, please help me."

I cut the call, knowing he might never receive my message and that, even if he did, he might not arrive in time.

45

QUINN

The drilling stops. I tiptoe to the foyer and peek through the peephole. The two men are leaning against the stair rail, smoking. I sag against the door, worried that Arzu is right. My recklessness has come full circle.

The drill starts again, and the vibrations shake my shoulders. I hope the massive lock holds long enough for Sedat to send help.

"Mrs. Robicheaux, this is your final chance." The heavily accented voice booms through the door. "Your husband had things he was to give us before he died. We are just trying to get them from you. Please open the door, and we will get what we need and leave you. We will not hurt you."

"What exactly do you want?" I look through the peephole. My neighbor is standing outside her door, shaking her finger at the men.

"It will be much better to enter the apartment and stop shouting in the hallway. We are making your neighbor frightened, I think. I would hate to hurt *her*." The man turns toward the neighbor

A door slams in the hallway. I look through the peephole again, and my neighbor is gone.

I stare at my phone, begging Sedat to call, but it remains silent. My mind whirling, I retrieve a chair from the dining room and place it under the doorknob of the steel door. I take another chair and retreat to the bathroom, locking the door behind me. The dining chair wedged under that doorknob, I wait.

The drill stops.

When it starts again, my entire body trembles; the fear is so intense that I shimmy off the toilet and wedge myself between the bathroom and the shower. I can't stop shaking. Everything is on overdrive: the pungent smell of my sweat, the drone of the drill, and the taste of the salt from biting my upper lip. I scan the bathroom for weapons and find only my orange plastic-encased razor blades next to a laundry basket.

My nerves are shot. I sit like a stone as I imagine the door splintering open. I don't move when the drill stops, not daring to make a noise. The silence ticks away, and I hear every sound in the old apartment: the squeaks and clunks of the building, the screech of my upstairs neighbors' dining chairs, and the kids outside running down the street.

At the front door, there is a sudden scuffling, shuffling, and slamming, followed by shouts in foreign languages and then silence. I sit through ten minutes of the unnerving quiet, then move the chair, unlock the door, and check the peephole. The men are gone, but the equipment remains. The lock still holds. I tiptoe to the end of the picture window and hide behind the curtains.

Sedat's BMW is parked at an angle, blocking the street in front of the building. Police cars with red and blue lights secure both ends of the street, lighting up the neighborhood with color, even in the middle of the day. I twist the hem of my shirt so tightly I can hear the stitches pop as I sit on the couch in the living room, rocking back and forth, the phone in my lap, my hands clutched together to keep them from shaking. When the phone buzzes, it startles me.

I swipe to answer the call.

"*Lütfen şekerim,* please open the door to the front. I am outside." Sedat's deep voice is solid, his Turkish accent thick with concern.

I run to the front door and push the security lock on the intercom. Placing my ear to the door, I hear his footsteps grow louder as they come up the stairs, and I begin turning the locks in the massive steel door, holding the last click until he gets close. When I see him through the peephole, I turn the final lock.

Opening the door, I launch into him like a rocket. He holds me tight, one arm around my waist and the other strokes my hair until I stop shaking. After several minutes, I release him and step away, embarrassed by my actions, even though the fear is a valid cause for me to seek comfort from another person, even someone who's about to put me in jail.

"Who were they?" I ask as we step over the drill and other equipment and move into the living room.

"The police have them. They are not talking, but they will." The vein running across his temple pulses with each heartbeat, matching the repeated grinding of his jaw. "What did they say to you?"

As usual, he wants information from me but tells me nothing. I immediately chastise myself. He just came to my rescue.

"Only that Harris had something they wanted. They didn't say what."

"Nothing else?" he asks.

I shake my head. He turns and walks out onto the balcony and lights a cigarette. I go to stand next to him. He pulls out his cell phone and opens an app, punching several things before closing it and returning it to his front shirt pocket.

"Is there wine left from the other night?" He doesn't look at me, but stares across the bay. Surprised at Sedat's request, I start toward the kitchen. "I'll get you a glass."

"*Teşekkür ederim,*" he says as I hand him the glass. His free hand runs through his hair. He takes a sip from the glass, and I wait, knowing that he will call someone, and they will come for me, taking me to a dirty, rat-infested prison to wait out my fate, all for a string of mysterious numbers that are actually words in disguise.

"I believed I could protect you," Sedat says, clutching the wine glass like a lifeboat in one hand, his cigarette in the other.

"From?" I stand.

"Bulgarians, Americans, the Director of the Turkish National Police, anyone else who is following you for money or information, or anything else your husband has hidden." He looks at me, his face haggard. "Your husband was the subject of a lengthy investigation by my office. Now that he is dead, you are my target. Initially, I wanted honesty with you, but my employer's methods require stealth."

"If your men were thorough," I say, "you should know I have nothing to do with this."

"My Director does not believe this. He feels strongly that you were Harris's partner."

"I am not now, nor was I ever." I turn and walk into the kitchen. Now that Sedat is finally being truthful, this might be a long conversation, and I need my own glass. Sedat is back inside as I return with the glass and the bottle, and I place them on the dining table as we sit.

"Tell me what you do know so I can prove it to the director and get you away from here."

"You are asking me to trust you when you've only just admitted that you've been lying to me the entire time?"

"I am the lesser of your multiple evils, Quinn."

"I'm not sure that is true."

"Quinn, if I wanted to arrest you or hurt you, I would have done so already. It is the Bulgarians, and possibly the Americans, you need to fear."

I cross the room to the coffee table and gather the two devices

I found earlier. I stand before Sedat, reaching out my closed fist. He opens his hand, and I drop them into his palm, one by one.

"Yours?" I ask.

"Yes." He has the decency to look chagrined. He turns them over, one by one, and turns them off.

"Were the two men who followed us on the Kordon part of your department?"

"No. Bulgarians, possibly connected to the men here today. I should know shortly."

"Is someone listening to us now?"

"No. There is only me this time."

"How can you protect me from this, Sedat?"

"Find what they want and return it to them."

"What if the money Harris won was stolen? Maybe mob money."

"Then I will confiscate it on behalf of the Turkish government."

"I'm not sure your country needs more ill-gotten gains, Sedat."

"We are not discussing politics, Quinn. We are discussing your life." His eyes stare at me, dark with intensity. "We believe your little disk is quite dangerous."

"What is on it?"

"Your teenager in Istanbul wasn't much help?" He leans back in his chair as his emotions shove him into a corner. I know how he feels.

"Locations. That is all I know." I don't feel comfortable sharing the details with him.

"Given your popularity, those locations must be important." He takes a sip of wine as he scrutinizes my face. "Another department of the Turkish National Police found various caches of chemical weapons in Türkiye. That department and another group are in the process of disposing of them. Most likely your disk—"

"*My* disk?" I ask with mock outrage. "This is Harris's mess, not mine. I didn't create this disk."

"No, but you aren't giving it up, either."

"Because I received a warning that no one could be trusted. And because of your lies, that includes you." I sit, crossing my arms stubbornly across my chest. "If I give it to you, how does that help me?"

"We, rather, I, will make it known loudly that the information is with the TNP, not you. It will change the game entirely for you."

"So what about the money?"

"We searched the accounts held in Iş Bank." He grins at me. "It is amazing the bond you create with women you hardly know. Even though she protested on your behalf, we gave Isobel no choice."

"And did you confiscate the money?"

"You know that we did not. It disappeared almost immediately after two transactions. The majority was withdrawn as cash, and the other was transferred to multiple offshore accounts we are still chasing."

I can't stop grinning as I stand to retrieve another bottle of the wine I purchased the day before to help me sleep.

"Quinn, what have you done?" His face is incredulous. "You are not even denying it."

Not responding, I go to the kitchen, bringing back the bottle to top off his glass.

"You'll figure it out, Sedat."

"There isn't time, Quinn. If you don't hand over the disk and the money by Monday, I will be forced to detain you indefinitely. And don't throw the American phrase of 'I know my rights' at me. In this country, and especially for crimes of this type, there are none."

"I'm useless to you in jail, and you know it."

"My director thinks otherwise, but would prefer you be

deported to save costs. He will ensure your remaining days in Türkiye are unpleasant if you are not deported."

"He'll torture me? The U.S. wants this information as badly as you, I'm sure. They won't let me stay in your prison."

"You may be right, but my country has one of the ten most notorious prisons in the world. Would you prefer to be held in one of them or an American black site?"

The thought of either sends a shiver down my back.

"There is an alternative," I say.

"And what is that?" Sedat gives me a wary look.

"Use me as bait.

46

SEDAT

Sedat twists his wine glass, counting backward from twenty to zero in French as he attempts to listen to her insane idea.

"I'm sure they will torture me a little," she says to him, "but you won't let much happen to me. And you can arrest the people who come for me and catch all the players simultaneously."

"You cannot be serious," Sedat says. She has lost her mind. And maybe, with the grief, shock, and environment, she has. "Are you naive enough to believe you will survive this little stunt?"

"Yes." Sedat shakes his head, making sure his disbelief is written across his face.

"It is not worth what may happen to you, Quinn. Before you believe yourself so noble, you should know the truth about your husband." He spits out the word 'husband' like a curse word.

"My husband—" she interrupts.

He shakes his head and holds up his hand. "He has never been honest with you, and you need to see the truth and make the right decision about what you are hiding."

"What makes you think—"

He holds up his hand again, palm outward, to stop her.

"No lies." He carefully measures his words. "It is time for the truth between us. You cannot continue this alone, Quinn."

"The truth. How can we talk about truth when I've been your target the entire time?" She is correct. He knows she can no longer trust him, if she did at all. He shoves away how she felt in his arms minutes ago.

"I had no choice but to include you as a target once you went with him to Mexico."

Quinn walks to the open living room door and stares at the bay for several minutes, watching the seagulls fly past the balcony. She turns to look at Sedat, and he watches her carefully as she returns to the table and sits.

"You pretend to be a professor at Istanbul University," she says.

"I am a professor." His voice is indignant. "I teach economics, Quinn. It is not a lie. For me, it relieves the stress in my life. However, due to this investigation and my temporary transfer to the İmir office, I am currently on sabbatical. The university president still requires me to attend staff meetings, such as the one yesterday."

"And your real job?" She asks.

"My main employment is to find nasty people like your husband and make sure they behave themselves in my country."

"What do you think Harris has done? I've heard Maynard's version. Let's hear yours."

At the mention of Maynard, Sedat's nose wrinkles as if he smells something disgusting. Quinn's questions attempt to ferret out all his lies, but that will be impossible, given her husband's past. Untangling Harrison Robicheaux's life is like unspooling a sticky spider web.

"I don't think, Quinn. I know. Unlike the idiot Maynard, I was assigned this case years ago. I watched your husband do many, many things—"

He hesitates, trying to sanitize his explanation rather than use Maynard's method for shock value. Truths are coming that Quinn will not want to hear. He leans toward her, grasping her hand between both of his. She tries to tug it away, but he refuses to let go. She will need him to be an anchor, even if she doesn't know it.

"Since I met you," he says, "what you told me about your husband is complete fantasy, as is your entire courtship and marriage." The color slowly drains from her face, and he releases her hand. Surely, she must know *some* of the things he will tell her. Did Harris lie to her about everything?

"Why didn't you tell me this initially?" she asks. "When you played my landlord and then took me to dinner?"

"What would you have done if I'd told you that first day? Slammed the door in my face. You are not good with the truth, Quinn. You don't want to hear it, particularly about your husband. And I *am* your landlord. I put you in my own mother's apartment to be able to keep you safe."

"Well, that makes me feel so much better," she responds with dripping sarcasm. "Especially when it makes it so easy to watch me." Her forehead wrinkles in concern. "Are you watching me here?" Quinn looks around the living room.

"There are cameras, yes." He admits this to her, even though he knows she will never find the hidden microscopic devices. His tech is too good.

"Are they filming now? In every room?" Her voice rises with alarm.

"My superior insisted we plant cameras in your apartment." Sedat looks down the hall. "Not the bathroom. And you should continue to dress there rather than in your bedroom."

She stands, takes a large drink of wine, and then walks to the balcony. He gives her a minute alone and then follows her outside.

"You can relax, Quinn. I turned them off when I was on the balcony before you brought me the wine."

"Okay, back to your version of the truth," she says, letting out a breath.

"Your marriage is a farce." Sedat decides not to hold back. She will never be free of Harris unless she faces the reality of her circumstances. "You were not married by a priest, and the paperwork you were given came from an online service that prints anything one can pay for. I'm surprised that, as intelligent as you are, especially as a lawyer, you let the lack of formalities in Mexico pass you by."

Quinn doesn't blink, and her eyes look like a deer in headlights. She has realized this by now. Sedat continues.

"The sham marriage was for a purpose I've not yet determined. It does not make sense, particularly given his past behavior. You know he has been married before?"

She nods again, her face still white, and he wonders if he should stop. This must be hurting her, and that is not his intention.

"More than one marriage. Several appear to be ruses, but for an undercover purpose, a job."

"What do you mean?" She looks at him quizzically.

"Ah, you don't know this. Your husband worked for people other than the United States Air Force."

After minutes of silence, Quinn finally asks the looming question. "Who?"

"Your husband made a magnificent living by stealing from your government. At first, I believe he was caught, but then, due to his superior talents, your government reassigned him to other purposes. For him, stealing was a game; no matter the assignment or risk, the employer was unimportant. It doesn't appear that money was a significant motivator. From his family history, he came from a wealthy background. Over the last few years, he continued to "up the ante" as you Americans would say, involving himself in much riskier but much more lucrative ventures, some with his superior's approval, some without, but all within their knowledge."

"Who is his superior?" she asks.

"In the U. S. Government? It's Maynard. Most of what that man has told you has been garbage."

She returns to the dining table and almost falls into the chair. Sedat is certain she is rapidly replaying every conversation she had with the man.

"How do you know this?" Her voice is a whisper.

"Our contact at one of the American agencies. Your husband was assigned to an Italian post but seemed to be in Istanbul more than Aviano. They wanted to know why. We owed them a favor and agreed to assist. We learned of Harris's gambling habit and his penchant for tall, attractive women, some of whom he passed off as wives, others as lovers. There were certain sex clubs and other sexual habits. He had a fondness for many deviant things, some very dark." He looks away to avoid her eyes, too embarrassed to tell her the disgusting sexual habits of her husband.

"Those, Quinn, I cannot bring myself to tell you."

47

SEDAT

She reaches for her wine glass, changes her mind, and then bolts down the hall. Sedat grabs the unsteady glass just before it hits the table. The bathroom door slams, and he hears the lock turn. Grabbing a dish towel from the kitchen in case she is sick, he heads toward the bathroom.

Standing outside the door, he hears muffled sobs. He starts to knock, but drops his hand. He has no idea what to do. Finally, the crying stops, and he hears water running into the sink. He knocks.

"Quinn, *şekerim,* please unlock the door."

"Go away, Sedat. I am too mortified ever to face you or anyone else ever again."

"We are in this together. Do not shove me away. Please, let me in."

After a minute, the lock clicks, and Quinn cracks open the door. Sedat pulls it open and reaches for her, taking her into his arms, holding her tightly as she begins to cry once more. He pulls her hair away from her face and pulls her to the floor. They sit silently together, he cradling her like a child, until Quinn nods, looking up at him, ready for him to continue. Pulling her to her feet, he leaves her to pull herself together.

She returns to the dining table, and he waits until she looks at him. Her eyes are red, and her face is puffy. He wants to pull her to him again and hold her tightly until this entire mess is finished. But that is not how this will go.

"Thank you," she says. "I'm ready now." She is too embarrassed to look at him. He gently reaches for her face, making her look directly at him.

"*Bu bir şey değil.* It is nothing. Are you sure you wish to hear the rest?" he asks.

"I need it all." Her face is stoic, but Sedat hesitates. She places her hand on his, nudging him to begin.

He drops his hand and lets out a sigh. She will hate him for this.

"Just before you were married, we received information that Robicheaux had been invited to a high-stakes card game in Sochi on the Black Sea. The members of this game were all men like him, risk-takers from various countries with dark habits. The stakes included money and other pieces of information worth much more than the cash on the table."

"What I will tell you now is something you should not know. However, it explains how we came to be here, and I believe you should know this. Your American friends would tell you this is 'classified.' Robicheaux was on some assignment. We do not know what type, only that the U.S. government did not sanction it; however, someone else did. Americans were involved, but not officially. That is all we know. He won spectacularly at the card game, and your disk was the, how do you say?" He rubs his hand down his tired face. "Ah, yes, the icing on the cake."

Sedat reaches into his coat for a handkerchief and begins cleaning his glasses.

"This card game was held just before your arrival. Afterward, he was accused of cheating. There was an old, drunken Israeli who gave him something in Sochi, something no one, until now, has been able to identify. Robicheaux paid the man through the card game, ensuring that enough games were lost to cover the correct amount. Your husband was brilliant, able to count the cards as they were played. I believe the entire game was a ruse, and your husband paid the old man for the disk's valuable information."

"Robicheaux disappeared immediately after the game. My men could not find him. Then, we received notification of the helicopter crash several days later. Our country's forensics department, at the request of the U.S. Air Force, confirmed your husband was the one who died from one of his teeth. We do not know who the other person in the helicopter was. They escaped and are still at large. In the two missing days, Harris secreted the disk to you."

Sedat leans forward. "I need you to give it to me. Quinn, it is dangerous for you. I beg you to take the money he won and return to the United States."

"I'm not giving the disk to anyone, especially not you." Quinn slides her chair back from the table. "No matter how nice you are being to me right now, I don't trust you. And I'm not going anywhere. I refuse to hand it off to someone I don't know, who will use whatever it is to line their fancy-suited pockets or wreak havoc on someone else. Once I determine the importance of this information, I will decide what to do with it."

She stands, pushing her chair under the table, her hands on her hips as if challenging him to fight. He stands and leans toward her, his face so close he can smell the mint from her toothpaste. He grasps her elbow.

"*Saçmalama*, Quinn, you are talking nonsense. Stop playing games that you cannot win. My boss will deport you, the Americans will jail you, the Bulgarians will kill you. Be realistic."

"This is my life, not yours." Quinn spits her words at him. "I must know what Harris was up to and why he pulled me into his mess of a life. He tricked me into marrying him, and I must know why. He is using me, even in death, to do something. It has to be important because I can't believe the man who told me in life—and in death—that he loved me would do otherwise. You can't stop me, so don't even try."

As she starts to push past him, Sedat grasps her arms, forcing her to stand still.

"Listen to me. I am everywhere, Quinn, and I excel at my job. I watched you when you landed at Çiğli Air Base in İmir, and I have been with you everywhere." His voice lowers. "The helpful man at the passport office, Mehmet? He is my partner. The man who rented the apartment to your husband at the Housing Office? Yes, he is mine."

He releases her arms and gives her a reluctant smile. "The man at the market, whom you think is a friendly neighbor? My investigator. Shall I go on? Hasan at the bank, perhaps? And, of course, I spent hours sitting and drinking *rakı* with your husband. He never knew, as you did not, who I was. Who I am. It was not until I made it clear to your friend, Arzu, when I interrogated her, that anyone knew. My mistake? She should have remained detained until this was resolved. And we would never have had this conversation."

When he looks at her again, she is like a statue.

"Is Arzu one of yours? Artur?"

"No, my sweet. You brought them into this lovely scenario alone." His voice is rising now, and he cannot stop himself. "Do not make me do this, Quinn. Give me the disk, tell me what you know. I am begging you. If my director takes control..." He trails off, unable to say what his boss will do to her.

He hides his face in his hands and takes a breath. Glancing toward the bedroom, he gives her a pointed look. "Sleep in pajamas. You certainly did not in Mexico."

Her eyes widen with his revelation, her face shocked as if he had slapped her. She walks across the room and drops onto the couch, staring out the front window.

Sedat continues his rant, unable to stop. "I tried to help, be pleasant, and protect you. What did you do in return? You lied to me, escaped my men, made me follow you to Istanbul, and made me lose my mind in the Grand Bazaar when you disappeared with the *çay* boy."

The thought of what could have happened to her causes him to stuff his hands into his jacket pockets to keep from hitting something.

"Do you realize how insane you are acting?" His voice rises along with his anger. "Have you no fear? You must stop this madness! Your friend, Arzu, should also be held responsible. Both of you are playing a game as if you are in a spy movie."

He stops, stepping outside on the balcony to stop his hammering heart. Sedat cannot remember being this angry in his entire life. This woman has upended him, and he feels like the world is spinning out of control. He can do nothing to stop it.

Quinn's soft voice is behind him. "For Harris, this was all a game. Can't you see that? To play this game, I must think as he does, or I will never get to the bottom of this."

"Harris was a spy, trained and experienced," he huffs. "You, şekerim, are not." He turns to search her face. "Why do you insist on doing this? Go home. Leave all this behind you."

Leave me behind as well before you destroy my life, he thinks to himself.

"No, Sedat. Harris married me for a reason." Quinn places her hand on his arm momentarily, then thankfully lets it drop. They are too close to the window and are being watched. "He sent me the disk *to hide* and enough money to help me do so. Help me find out why."

If only they weren't on the balcony with the eyes of his department on them. He would pull her to him, hold her, and try to change her mind. But they are, and he cannot. The stubborn woman refuses to hear the truth.

"They will try to kill you for it, Quinn. And as reckless as you are, I may be unable to save you."

48

QUINN

I get a wake-up call from Arzu at six and leave for the bus station on this quiet Saturday morning. I am hungover, feeling like a tractor has pulled me through a hayfield, but it is my fault. I will sleep on the way, and if I can't, riding south for five and a half hours is a suitable punishment for drinking so much the night before.

Despite Sedat's loud and angry protests, I am now officially bait. He insisted I stay locked in the apartment and let whoever was after me try again. I agreed to stay, even though I had no intention to do so. With Harris's concern about EMPs, I need to see these locations for myself.

Sedat will be livid when he finds out I escaped again, and I expect that to be soon. I wrap the microphone in the scarf he gave me, hoping he will not be able to hear my conversations with Arzu. I do not tell her that I am the bait for the big fish when I call her from the taxi.

"Quinn, you should stay home and forget about locating those coordinates. Don't be so ridiculous. Maybe they aren't locations. Maybe I just wanted them to be so simple that I forced them into What Three Words. They are probably bank accounts, and I can try to locate them for you." Her fear zips through the line like lightning, making me wonder if Sedat contacted her. She already believes I am mindlessly rash and impulsive. "I worried about this all night. They can kidnap you. Or worse. Let me search online."

Those were Sedat's exact words as we hashed out my plan. He disagreed with everything—every idea, thought, possibility. He wants me in the apartment where he says I will be safe, especially after the Bulgarians' visit. No, I will not wait at the apartment, even if it means risking my life. Arzu lets out a massive sigh over the phone and then waits for my response.

"I've already searched online, remember?" I say. "I need to see these places in person. Will Mustafa meet me?"

She snorts a laugh. "Yes. And he will be delighted to accept your money. He will meet you at the Otogar this morning at seven. Please do not remind me later of how obnoxious he is. I warned you, yes?"

"Don't get so twisted about this. There's a protector, remember? Sedat is there even if I cannot see him." I pay the taxi driver and follow the crowds toward the bus station. "Lighten up. When I get back, I will take you out for the most expensive dinner you've ever had at the restaurant of your choice."

"*Maşallah, Quinn'cim. Allah'a emanet ol.* May Allah watch over you."

I smile at Arzu's endearing term, the suffix at the end of my name that tells me we are friends, regardless of what I say.

"Thank you, Arzu. Keep your head down. I will call you if I discover something."

"No. I do not want to know. Just come back safe, please, Miss America. I do not wish the responsibility of your death."

The Otogar is filled with noisy, smelly buses and bustling with people. I don't know what Mustafa looks like, but I don't want to call Arzu back. Her stress levels are already elevated to an intensity that could launch a rocket. My appearance is unmistakable, and the boy should be able to find me.

I stuff the scarf Sedat gave me and tuck it into my backpack. I am on a tour and need to look at the part. Wearing the universal uniform of an American on vacation—tennis shoes, a T-shirt, and jeans—I hold the latest iPhone for taking photos. I scream tourist. If someone wants to find me, I have made it easy. After all, that is the point.

A young man strides toward me with glossy pamphlets in his hand and a car salesman's smile. He is a few years older than Arzu, dressed in black leather pants and a tight white T-shirt sporting a Turkish logo.

"Miss America! I am so happy to see you!"

I laugh at the man's use of Arzu's nickname for me. A pale, thin arm extends for a handshake, but it's a bluff, and I am greeted with an overly enthusiastic Turkish double kiss instead. I gag at the thickness of his cologne. The memory of another cologne from last night nudges at the edge of my mind, and I shove it away.

"We have a wonderful trip for you, full of history and anthropology, fascinating, just fascinating. I am very sure you will enjoy the hospitality of Turkish Vacation Tours. Please, let me take your baggage."

He reaches for my backpack. Hanging on to the strap on my shoulder, I step back and grin. Yes, Arzu, you warned me.

"Thank you, but I'll just hang on to it."

"Certainly!" His heavily accented voice booms in English over the din of the Otogar. "Let's get you to our luxury coach and make you comfortable. Other guests are waiting, and after I meet a few more, we will be on our way!"

He doesn't ask for my passport or any other identification, and I mentally thank Arzu again. The bus is half full of tourists like me, and the other half is Turkish vacationers. The closest coordinates Artur gave me are in a large circle in southwestern Türkiye. To explore each location, I will begin in Antalya, then turn west toward Marmaris on the Mediterranean coast, proceed further west to Bodrum on the Aegean coast, and finally head north to Kuşadası before returning to İmir.

Interestingly, both Maynard's and Sedat's deadlines are on Monday. An uncomfortable feeling rises in my gut at the thought of that asshole working with Sedat. Yet, neither of their deadlines is my concern, and I won't let them stop me. The bus is only to escape İmir without being followed. Arzu has prepared Mustafa, so once we reach Antalya, he has a guide who will rent a car and take me to the rest of the cities.

Antalya sprawls along the Mediterranean, with hotel towers lined along its beaches. The bus arrives just after noon, but unfortunately, our hotel is off the beach and near the old city, which is too far to walk to the first coordinate. After consulting the map, I catch up to Mustafa as he heads inside the hotel with the rest of the group, motioning him away from the other people.

"Is my private guide ready? I need to leave earlier than requested." Arzu and I had reasoned that two girls traveling the coast would be ordinary in the summer, especially if one of them were Turkish. She can also rent a car and deal with any traffic stops we might encounter. According to Arzu, the Turkish Jandarma is the law enforcement outside the cities that handles all matters, including traffic. The traffic stops are frequent, and the drivers can be questioned about anything, so going it alone isn't an option.

"Yes. You can pay to me now. As requested, Yasemin will meet you in the lobby at four tomorrow morning. In cash, yes?"

I nod. He holds out his hand for the money, but I ignore it. The girl may not get paid if I give it to him.

"I need to leave tonight. I'll pay Yasemin when she arrives." His smile flips to a petulant frown as he drops his hand.

"I will text you what time she can be ready." He begins

tapping on his phone as he walks to catch up with the bus passengers.

Rather than waiting for Mustafa to get back to me, I use the Turkish BiTaksi app to call for a ride. Forty-five minutes later, I am at the westernmost side of Antalya, near the shipping warehouses. I direct the driver through the tax-free shipping zone and past the first coordinate. The warehouse is adjacent to an electrical substation, surrounded by other warehouses and the marina. Most businesses are wrapping up for the day, and others look vacant. The What Three Words square I've identified shows no sign of any active business or building number, just a rusty warehouse.

The taxi driver drops me off at Beaver Coffee, several blocks away, after I give the impression that I am meeting a friend. Leaving the taxi, I stroll into Beaver and order a takeaway coffee. I then meander around the marina, wandering down each dock area without a gate and along the long U-shaped boardwalk that hugs the basin. When I reach the warehouses, I find no fences, gates, security, and only a few cars. I see no people.

The electrical substation buzzes as I pass. At the warehouse, the door has no lock. This is too easy, and it makes me nervous. Seeing no one around, I grasp the handle and pull hard. The door screeches as the metal wheels grind against the railing. I release the door and look around, but no one appears.

I step inside the gloomy space. It is roughly 100 square feet and two stories tall. The only items in the room are piles of clothing, shoes, baby toys, other paraphernalia, and trash. The odor of sweat, cardboard, and stagnant, damp laundry hangs in the musty air. It doesn't feel like trafficking, but rather like the Turkish version of Goodwill—a collection of abandoned things people no longer want.

I retrace my steps and walk the neighborhood. Besides the proximity to the marina and the substation, this place is a dead end. Frustrated, I walk toward the main street and call for another taxi. Waiting, my phone buzzes with a text from Mustafa.

CAR AND DRIVER ARE IN THE LOBBY

Heartened by his efficiency, I climb into the taxi, ready to keep moving.

49

QUINN

At the hotel lobby, I search for someone who might be Yasemin, but instead, I see Arzu chatting with the desk clerk, with large takeaway coffees in each hand.

I can't stop the smile from spreading across my face. "What are you doing here?"

She grins back and hands me a coffee. "I told Mustafa I would take over. He says my Miss America is too difficult. Are you ready to leave?"

"What? He didn't like me paying Yasemin directly?"

Arzu laughs.

"Why you?" I lower my voice. "You didn't want to do this."

"Well," she responds in a sing-song manner, "after you left, I called Mustafa. He was about to charge you double for changing the time. And I know the girl he would send you off with." She leans over and whispers as her nose wrinkles in disgust. "She's pretty stupid."

I laugh. "Did you get a rental car?"

"Of course. It is in my friend's name. With Sedat's flag on my *kimlik kartı*, my residence card, I can't rent it in my name."

"Always resourceful."

"*Kesinlikle.* Absolutely," she says. "Now you need a better disguise."

"I don't want one."

"Why?" she asks, concerned at the shift in my plan.

"I'll explain once we're on the way. Go get your bag." She motions toward the elevators.

"I never checked in." This is all I have. I motion to my backpack. She directs me to the hotel's back door and into the parking area.

"What happened with the location here in Antalya?" she asks.

"It was empty. Google Maps had no address for this W3W coordinate, so I had no idea what this place was supposed to be. The warehouse had only trash and clothes. The door was unlocked, and it was way too easy. Nothing close by other than a marina and a power substation."

"The police can still get you for entering a property that isn't yours."

"Yes, I know, but there was nothing for me or anyone else to steal, and no one saw me."

While Arzu drives, I pull out the newspapers I had bought for the journey, but hadn't had a chance to read. Skimming through the pages, my eyes catch a story about the murder of a young man in Istanbul. The body was found near the University gate of the Grand Bazaar. He was beaten to death. Although his name was withheld, something about the description tells me it is the Hacker Boy, Artur.

My heartbeats slam against my chest, and I think I might throw up. "Pull over."

"What?" She glances at me, then back to the road.

"You need to read this. Pull over now, please." She slows the car to the side of the road and puts on her emergency flashers. I shove the paper toward her.

She reads and then looks at me, fear etched across her face.

"It is Artur. It has to be. The location is accurate. I wish there were a photo to be certain."

"You're right, we don't know for certain," I say.

"But we do know. This is our fault," she responds.

"No, Arzu." I shake my head. "The only fault is mine." We sit, the passing traffic the only sound.

"This is real," Arzu whispers.

"Very real. And I wish you had not come. I should have stopped you back at the hotel and made you go home." I shift in my seat. "I talked to Sedat. I told him everything."

"You told him everything, and he did not arrest you?" Arzu's mouth drops open.

"I talked him into a better plan." I know she won't like this. "For me to be bait."

She squints at me. "Fishing bait? I don't understand."

"I refuse to be locked in any jail, whether American or Turkish, and the only other possibility is for me to run. This will flush out all the players at once."

"No, Quinn." Her eyebrows come together as her eyes glare at me. "This is too dangerous for you. If what Sedat told me is true, they will kill you." Her eyes glance at the rearview mirror.

"I don't want to look over my shoulder the rest of my life."

"Why didn't you just give him the stupid disk?" Arzu presses her lips together until they're flat. "We could be having tea now on the ferry instead of roaming around like chickens."

"Because I can't be sure he won't give it to someone else. Harris says—"

"Harris says?" she interrupts me, her eyes wide. "You are talking with a dead person now?"

I roll my eyes at her.

"I got a note through a lawyer who Harris arranged to send things after he died. He bought the disk from a guy in a card game. It has something to do with EMPs, but I only know a little about those."

"Electromagnetic pulse?"

"You know what that is?"

"Are you talking about huge nuclear bombs in the air?"

"Honestly, I don't know, but I don't think that is what this is about," I say. "Harris's note says that the disk will be auctioned after a sample is run. I'm assuming that these locations are the test sites for some new technology or military equipment." I give her a grin. "But without the disk, there is no auction."

She raises her eyebrows at me. "How do you know this disk isn't just a copy?" she asks.

"I don't, but Harris's note says this is the original, and the information is important and dangerous. Sedat says he got it from an Israeli in Sochi. Determining if these numbers are actual coordinates will give me a start at understanding what he was trying to do, and what this new tech or equipment might do."

Arzu sits quietly and thinks.

"Does Sedat know you are here?" she asks, her face full of fear at the mention of Sedat as she glances over at me.

I give her a pointed look, and she focuses on the road. I don't tell her about the tracking and listening devices. He handed them to me before he left, explaining what each did, and insisted I take them. The microphone is in my backpack, and the tracker is sewn into my bra.

"Sedat is dangerous, Quinn." She grasps my wrist. "How can you be sure he will save you once they come for you?"

"He wants the disk as badly as the others. He's watching me closely, I'm sure. He says his director wants to torture me for it, but Sedat wants it voluntarily and has until Monday before his boss takes over."

"So we are here to draw them out, make them follow you so Sedat can identify them?" she asks.

"Not just identify them, arrest them." I don't go into the legality of all this. That is Sedat's problem. I need to get her off this subject and back on the road. "I looked at all these places on the online map, but I couldn't identify anything. Like last night, they appear to be nothing, but there is something we are missing."

"Monday is the day after tomorrow."

"Yes. We need to get going."

Arzu, punching off the flashers, steers the car back into traffic, and we ride for a long time. She is correct about the level of danger, but according to Sedat, I should fear his director most. After being terrified yesterday by the Bulgarians, I can't entirely agree. The only person I am not concerned about is Maynard. He is a nuisance, acts like a spoiled toddler, but has done nothing to indicate that he will hurt me.

"You know," she hesitates a second, "bad things aren't always your fault."

"I know, but this time they are."

"No, this is your husband's fault—unless you are hiding something from me?"

I twist toward her. "You too? You think I'm part of his plan?"

"No," she glances at me, "you were pulled into something that is not your fault."

I stare at the blue waters of the Mediterranean, letting the scenery calm my anxiety.

"When I was little, we were beyond poor." Arzu checks the rearview mirror, turns on the blinker, and switches lanes. "We lived outside Ankara, near the back of the castle, in a *geci condo*, an illegal lean-to house. The house was little better than a barn and was built on government property, subject to being demolished at any moment."

I keep my gaze fixed on the windshield. I dare not interrupt.

"My father worked on a grounds crew maintaining the presidential palace and the neighboring *Atatürk Orman Çiftliği*."

I know that Kemal Atatürk was the founding father of the Turkish Republic.

"I don't know what a *çiftliği* is."

"It's the forest established by Atatürk, which also has a rose garden and an old farm museum. It's quite pretty." She glances out her side window for a second. "*Baba*, my father, drank up most of the money he made. *Anne*, my mother, cleaned several houses every day. She had to leave us alone after school to provide for seven children. We were always in trouble." She gave me a slight grin. "I was the only girl and the youngest."

"When I was five, all of my brothers, except for the youngest, went to an orphanage because my parents could not feed us."

"An orphanage?"

"Many Turkish families are forced to use the orphanages as a revolving system where they drop off and pick up months later." She draws in a large breath, then releases it as if I'm the first person who has heard this from her. From the little I know of her, I might be. "I got lucky. One of the families my mother cleaned for sponsored my brother and me."

"What does that mean?"

"They paid for our uniforms, school supplies, lunch money, and the bus fare to the best elementary school across town. My other brothers were a lot older and were not so lucky."

"Where are your parents now?"

"Dead."

"I'm sorry." Given her difficult past, I wonder about her siblings and their relationship with her now.

"Don't be. This is where being pulled into circumstances comes in. One day, I heard my parents arguing when I got off the school bus. My mother had reached her limit. She was throwing my father out of the house, and he refused to leave. They were in a raging battle. *Anne* tossed his things out the door, and *Baba* would retrieve them. He grew angrier each time he came out to get his things."

She stops talking, and from her forlorn expression, I'm unsure I want to hear the rest.

"It became quiet. After about five minutes, my oldest brother approached the front. *Baba* came stumbling out, a knife sticking from his chest and blood flowing down his clothes.

I reach out and touch her arm. She is gripping the steering wheel so tightly that her knuckles are white.

"My brother could not hold *Baba,* and my father fell face forward into the dirt. I will never forget that huge knife going all the way through my father's body, the tip sticking out of his back."

She pauses for several breaths, then continues. "My brother entered the house to find *Anne,* but he came out alone. He told us our father had killed her, but he would not allow us to go inside. He herded us away from the house and asked a neighbor to watch us."

"I sat in their yard for an hour as we watched. My brother dragged *Baba* into the house, emptying it of anything valuable or meaningful. Several men came by and helped. I smelled the smoke but didn't understand what they were doing. The neighbors made us help them fill water buckets to protect their houses as our house began to burn with my parents' dead bodies inside."

"Oh, my God. Why?" I feel sick to my stomach that such a small child had to experience this.

"No one wanted the police involved, and there was no way to pay for funerals. The land was not ours, but I didn't know that until I became an adult. My brother changed from a sixteen-year-old kid lighting that fire to instantly being an adult in charge of his six brothers and sisters."

"Where did you go?"

"The couple who sponsored us took my brother and me. The rest of my brothers lived on the street and did whatever it took to stay alive."

"Where are they now?"

"I don't know. The last time I saw any of them, I was twelve."

"What about your brother, the one who was with you?"

"He runs the hotel where we stayed in Istanbul."

I picture the older boy behind the reception desk who gave her the bear hug when we arrived. We drive through a small town. Arzu stops at a traffic light. Sadness radiates from her, and I wish there were something I could do, but the past is something no one can change. She grasps my hand and squeezes.

"So, Miss America, sometimes it is only circumstances. You must make the best of it, which I think is what you are facing now. But honestly? I think that you have lost your mind with this plan."

50

QUINN

"There's someone following us."

We have just reached the outskirts of Marmaris. The W3W location is listed as an auto repair shop on Google Maps. Arzu speeds up and turns into an industrial area. She weaves in and out of the warehouses, and a dark blue sedan follows each time. She finally loses them in the maze of narrow streets, and we head to the second location. From my map, I direct her to the one we need to see. We wait several minutes to see if the blue car appears.

"This is becoming dangerous, Quinn."

"Let me drop you somewhere safe and go by myself."

She shakes her head. "No, together." She points to the warehouse businesses around us. This is a *sanayi*, where the messy businesses such as car mechanics, tire stores, and furniture makers are located. This one is pretty big."

She grabs her phone and turns to me. "Sit and wait. Watch for that blue car that followed us."

I sit in the car with the doors locked and the window cracked for air, watching the people go about their business. My knee is jackhammering as I wait, expecting the blue sedan to turn the corner and head for me at any minute. Ten minutes later, Arzu returns.

"I talked to the owners of the nearby buildings. I told them I was a real estate agent looking for a space for my brother-in-law's auto mechanic business. This location has been vacant for six years. The owner's brother used the space as a car repair shop. He died, the company went out of business, and the widow's price was too high for the building to sell."

Arzu motions for me to get out of the car and walk with her to the building. "The doors are wide open, and the men say no one cares if we look. Let's go. Hurry."

I scan around me, searching for anyone who looks out of place or the blue car as we hustle toward the unit. I don't like being out in the open like this. Inside the building, I relax, but only a little. It is a rectangular room, fifty by one hundred feet, and empty except for a motorized winch and an overhead chain with a hook. I check the floor, but there is no proof of anything except a repair shop.

"Let me find the *kahve* and see if anyone else knows anything. Just wait for me here."

I occupy myself by scrolling on my phone and checking out the dirty window for the blue car. I am sure it is the Bulgarians or whoever tried to drill my deadbolt. Just as I am about to pull out my hair, Arzu comes back into the warehouse, and I breathe a sigh of relief.

"What took so long?"

"I told you. I was at the *kahve* getting information. Let's go." We return to the car and get in. "The wife did rent the space once, and that tenant used it to store ammunition. Once the surrounding businesses learned of it, they forced the wife to evict the renter. She rented it again six months ago, but no one has moved in. No one knows the status now. It's a dead end. Sorry."

"Another empty location," I mumble, not understanding where this is going.

My phone rings, and I put it on the speaker so Arzu can listen.

"Hi there." Maynard's cheerful voice fills the car. "I thought we might get lunch today."

"I thought I was clear that I don't need your help." Maynard can "go jump," as my mother used to say.

"You must eat. Let me pick you up." His voice is irritated.

"I'm not at home. And I'm not interested in eating lunch with you."

"Damn it, Quinn, you can't continue to avoid me." Maynard's voice is angry now. "You owe me something." He starts shouting, and I hold the phone away from my ear. "I want what Harris took from me."

Arzu mouths the word "American" and I nod my head. I keep my voice calm, even though Maynard makes me seethe. He's always pushing even though he insists he wants to help. I don't understand why he is so angry.

"I owe you nothing," I respond, "and if Harris took something from you, that's your problem. I'm hanging up now."

"Wait." His voice is now ice cold. "Command ordered me to tell you that Harris's body will be ready first thing Monday morning. I've been asked to plan for you to also leave on Monday. We must arrange for a moving company to pack your household goods and send them back to the U.S. I need an address to do that."

"That won't be necessary."

"Why not?"

"I'm not going back to the States. Contact Harris's mother and see what she wants done. Her address is in the document you gave me."

"Quinn, you cannot be serious." Maynard's anger is palpable.

"I am. And Maynard, even if I find whatever you're after, I

won't give it to you. I know who I can trust in this country, and you, my man, are not one of them."

I can hear Maynard screaming at me as I cut the call, grinning at Arzu like a madwoman.

"Quinn, what did you just do?"

"Kicked over a hornet's nest, I hope. If Sedat wants to see who comes running, let's ramp it up a notch or two."

51

QUINN

She looks at me like I've lost my mind and then gestures to the road ahead with a question on her face. I nod, and even though the sun is low along the horizon, we start toward Bodrum.

Harris got me involved in a wild goose chase, and so far, I've only found an empty warehouse and an abandoned auto mechanic's shop. This string of numbers has to lead to something, and I must determine what it is. From what little I know about electromagnetic pulse bombs, this will be difficult. I need an electrical engineer or maybe a nuclear physicist to help me.

"Wait. Stop. What is this?" I point to the other side of the fence from the empty warehouse unit.

Arzu squints at a building the size of two American football fields. She looks at the map on her phone.

"It is a water treatment facility."

"Do you think it supplies the water to Marmaris?"

"Probably. The freshwater would come from the mountains and maybe here." She points to the hills above the city that are part of a cross-country mountain chain. "What are you thinking?"

"I'm not sure. Last night, the building was next door to an

electrical substation. This one," I point over my shoulder to the empty unit, "is opposite a water plant. If I were going to test something, whether to destroy or disable, facilities like these would be what I would choose. Let's see what is in Bodrum."

We reach Bodrum by nine in the evening after a quick bathroom stop, where we also pick up a supply of caffeinated drinks to keep us going. The resort city is just ramping up, with three competing bands blasting at each other across the basin that houses the large city marina.

The location we are looking for is a dress store. We can tell even in the dark, however, that the small building my map has identified is empty, but of course, I must be sure. We haven't seen the dark blue car again, but I know it's still out there waiting, watching to see what we are doing. We wedge our car behind an apartment building, and we use our phone flashlights to confirm the storefront is empty.

"What else is around here?" I ask.

I freeze when I hear laughter behind me. We shift to stand in the shadows of the doorway, waiting. My heart is racing, and I almost laugh when two young boys cross the street, heading for a line of restaurants.

Back in the car, Arzu pulls up the map on her phone.

"It's the marina," I tell her. "Look. The empty storefront on Neyzen Tevfik Caddesi is directly across from the Bodrum Marina Yacht Club building."

"You are right." Arzu immediately picks up on my point. "The store is vacant, yet there are no signs for rent or sale. Sort of like the auto mechanic's place—empty, rented, but nothing is there." She starts the car and heads north. Our next stop is in Kuşadasi, an hour south of İmir and a two-hour drive for us. With the blue car out there somewhere, we are both wide awake.

"There were no signs on the other properties either," I say.

"You say the one in Antalya was also at a marina."

"Yes. So far, there are two marinas, an electrical substation, and a water treatment facility."

"You know, you could have figured that part out online."

"But there would be no blue car," I say softly, glancing at the traffic behind us. "I can't tell if they are behind us."

"How can they use these places to test an EMP?" Arzu asks. "This must be something very different from exploding large nuclear bombs overhead or short-circuiting a city's electronics." We are quiet for a few minutes to think.

"Each location is a specific building." I glance at her. "They are staging areas for the equipment, or testing places for small pulses to disrupt a single business, neighborhood, or city." I look at the offline map I'd saved on my phone. "There are two more locations in Kuşadası, one near the seaside and another outside town. We should look there when it gets daylight."

I look at Arzu. "I need to do more research. We also need an engineer or nuclear scientist to help us with this. It's complicated, and I don't understand how this works."

"I don't know anyone like that, but when we are back in İmir, I can ask around," Arzu replies.

We arrive at Söke, a town a half hour from Kuşadası. Tired and unfocused, I'm not watching for the blue car because of the late hour. Silent for almost an hour, we are heading to a twenty-four-hour Shell station just outside the city to grab coffee, get food, and take a rest break until daylight.

Arzu suddenly slaps my hand.

"Quinn, I think they're back." I stay behind the vehicle's headrest and turn slightly to look behind us. There is a single car, but it is within five feet of our rear bumper. I flip my visor and watch as the car behind us revs its engine, coming close enough to our Renault to give us a slight bump.

"They are toying with us." Arzu tightens her grip on the steering wheel and increases her speed.

"I don't think we can outrun them in this." I look over my

shoulder and watch as the BMW bumps us again, jolting our car forward. "We're too small."

Arzu adjusts her rearview mirror. "If they pull out and hit our corner, we will spin."

I can feel the adrenaline rushing through me. "They can't risk killing me."

"If they search your body, will they find the disk?" Arzu looks over, her eyes wide but determined to get us away from the car.

"Possibly." I grasp the necklace tightly through my shirt. "We need to lose them."

"I can do that in a few minutes when we get to Söke. There should be traffic, even at this hour, and more hiding places."

"At this close to midnight? Do you know this town?"

"All small Turkish cities are alike, Quinn. Don't worry."

We cross the city limits with the blue BMW on our bumper when Arzu swerves into the left lane, free of oncoming traffic, and skids into a left turn. The blue sedan does not turn behind us, but within seconds, I see it pacing us by one block. They will find us even if Arzu jerks into one of the narrow alleys to find a hiding place.

Our cat-and-mouse chase continues across Söke until we reach a main artery. Arzu turns left, heading toward Kuşadası on the four-lane highway, the larger car again on our tail. I look around me for anything I can use to slow the vehicle down. I spot the glass soda bottles in the back seat. The BMW is so close behind us that if I lean out my window and throw one, I'll hit the windshield.

I snatch the bag from the backseat. Four of the six glass bottles of Coke remain unopened, giving me some serious ammunition.

"Arzu, keep a steady speed. I'm going to try something." I pull my hair into a knot to keep it out of my way. After she nods, I buzz down the passenger-side window and climb to sit on the door.

"What are you doing? Are you crazy?" Her scream fights with the wind whipping around me, but doesn't stop me. "We can find a police station."

"There isn't time. Just drive steady and straight."

Aiming as best I can with the wind and Arzu going way over the speed limit, I grab a bottle and lob it toward the BMW. It flies end over end, and my aim is almost in the center of the windshield, but it is too dark for me to be certain. As we pass under a streetlight, I can see that the bottle did strike the windshield and crack it, but it is still intact. The wipers are working, trying to clear the soda from the windshield.

The car swerves slightly, then, as it speeds up and gets closer, I wrap my left arm through the seatbelt and hold on to the headrest as the BMW rams us hard this time. I grab another unopened bottle and lob it hard over the roof of our Renault.

This second attempt hits the driver's side, and the windshield splinters into a spiderweb. The passenger window in the BMW comes down, and I see a hand with a gun slide outside. I drop into the car and bend forward.

"Gun!" I scream. "Drive, Arzu!" Shots fly around us. The back window of the Renault shatters.

The car behind us is glued to our bumper, and I have a much wider field of view without a rear window. Scrambling to the back seat, I ignore the peppered glass that digs through my jeans. Hunkered down as she drives, Arzu is swerving as she tries to avoid the gunshots. There's no way I can hit the windshield with any power, given the awkward throw, even at this close distance to the car. I scramble back to the front seat.

I wait for the shooter to stop firing, signaling a possible need to reload. When the gunshots stop, I grab the third bottle, and, hoping that I don't get shot, I rise again out the passenger side window, and heave it toward the car behind me, using every bit of my strength. This time, I catch a glimpse of the windshield as it becomes almost completely white, the broken parts shattering even further. There is no way the driver can see now.

The car swerves. When the driver jerks the wheel to correct, he overcompensates, and just like in the movies, the car suddenly flips once, then twice, then a third time. In a shower of sparks, the BMW lands on its roof and skids off the side of the road and into a ravine. Our Renault slows, and I jerk my head toward Arzu and see her focusing on the rearview mirror.

"Don't, Arzu. Just drive."

Neither of us says anything momentarily as she floors the Renault and we head down the highway. The adrenaline is like a hurricane inside me as we wait for the police to be behind us at any moment. Within twenty minutes, we reached Kuşadası. We see no police, but I expect that won't last.

"We needed your Jandarma back there." I laugh, trying to break the strain in the air.

"If the Jandarma had been there, we would be on our way to jail. Your plan sucks, by the way. You have lost your mind. We were almost killed! What will I do about this car?"

"I will take care of it, Arzu." The Bulgarians' money can pay for it.

In Kuşadası, we find an all-night gas station with no customers. Arzu fills our tank, avoiding the cameras. Using a hoodie wrapped around my hand, I clean the rear windshield opening so that it won't be so noticeable to a passing car. We head to the W3W location as I open the remaining bottle of soda and share it with Arzu, preparing for the crash when our adrenaline hits its lowest point.

We are both surprised when the first location turns out to be in the busiest part of town. Arzu is familiar with the resort area, as it is conveniently close to İmir, and this location is also not far from her uncle's house. We reach the shop, where the roll-down door is locked tight.

"This is an expensive rent district," Arzu says, pointing to the stores and restaurants across the main boulevard from the cruise ship port.

"Yeah, but it is similar to the others, close to the port and several banks, as well as being in the busiest part of town. Let's go see the last one." We head to the highway and turn toward İmir. After several miles, we turn into another *sanayi* and head to the rear of the complex.

"This is a very shifty area, Quinn. It is technically outside the *sanayi*. You can't get out of the car. I shouldn't either, but one of us must check this place so we can go home."

"I'll go with you."

"No, absolutely not. You caused enough trouble." She crosses her arms over her chest. "You wait in the car. This should take me five minutes."

Not used to being told I can't do something, I watch the minutes count down on my watch as I wait in the car. After fifteen minutes, I make a small excursion down the block, but there's no Arzu. At the half-hour mark, I'm scared that something horrible has happened to her when she rounds the corner at a fast walk. She gets in the car and buckles her seatbelt to leave.

"The warehouse is full of old chemical tanks," she says. "And there's nothing else around here. Check your map."

I grab her arm to stop her.

"We can't leave. I need to see. There has to be a reason this is here." I reach for the handle to get out of the car.

"No," she snaps. "It is too dangerous. I called my uncle, and given the fear I heard in his voice, we're leaving now."

"I'm going." I'm halfway out.

"Quinn, don't. I was followed the entire time I was there. Followed in, followed out. Why do you think I was away so long? I had to lose them."

She starts the car and reaches for the gearshift just as a dark gray BMW turns the corner three blocks away. The vehicle slows after the second block and then pulls into an empty lot. A man steps out of the car, a phone to his ear.

A chill runs down my back.

"Quinn, look." The light from inside the vehicle reveals Sedat's familiar outline. A zap of fear trails across my shoulders and down my arms, and I shudder.

"I'm getting out now," I tell Arzu. "Slowly back the car away, then turn around and get the hell out of here."

"I can't leave you. You don't know what he will do to you." Arzu grabs the front of my shirt to keep me from getting out of the car. I push her hand away and reach into the backseat for my backpack.

"It's Sedat, Arzu. He won't do anything to me." I remember how he held me after the Bulgarians tried to break into my apartment, and then afterward, when I cried. Then I remember the day we were followed in İmir and how angry he got.

Well, one can hope.

52

QUINN

Sedat stands beside the sleek gray sedan, his broad back to me. He gesticulates wildly in the dark with a cigarette in one hand and the other arm bent, his cell phone still glued to his ear. His suit and polished shoes reflecting the car's dome light are significantly out of place in this rough section of Türkiye. I can tell he is infuriated, even though I don't understand the words he's saying.

I reach into my backpack, pull out the scarf he gave me only two days ago in Istanbul, and put the microphone in my pocket. Wrapping it around my shoulders like armor, I wait, standing terrified but erect and motionless as I hear Arzu floor the Renault and speed away. Turning at the sound, he sees me standing alone in the middle of the street. He stops talking.

Frozen, I watch him mouth several words. Then he jams the phone in his inside jacket pocket and strides toward me, a lion stalking its prey. When he passes under the streetlight, I can tell his olive skin is flushed, and his eyes are hooded. The closer he gets to me, the higher my fear escalates.

This man held me when I was terrified. He only wanted to

The Expedient Wife

help, he says, to protect me from his boss, Maynard, and the Bulgarians. Yet the anger in his eyes tonight brings doubt.

I touch the silk scarf at my neck, don my invisible lawyer coat, and prepare for the outrage. As mad as he might be, there is nothing he can do. I've been on my best behavior since leaving İmir, except for taking a few photos, possibly a little breaking and entering, and a few randomly tossed soda bottles. He agreed to the plan and, thanks to the bugs he provided that were on my body and in my backpack, was aware of my location the entire time. He wasn't paying attention if he expected me to stay locked in that apartment, waiting for someone else to dismantle the door.

He stops before me, his face flushed, his eyes black and cold as night. I can feel the waves of anger radiating from his body. Starting at my feet, his eyes crawl slowly upward until they are locked onto my face. He searches my eyes. His mouth opens, and then suddenly, he snaps it shut.

Sedat steps forward and carefully removes the scarf. He is so close I can see the muscle on the side of his face flexing as he grinds his teeth. He gently touches my face with one hand, softly fingering the scarf's fabric with the other as he looks over my shoulder into the darkness. Goosebumps rise on my arms as his coat sleeve touches my bare skin. My hands begin to shake as I start to touch him. He snatches his hand away from mine, flinging the sunglasses I'd forgotten on top of my head into the wind. They clatter onto the street, then clang against the fence.

His cigarette butt still burning on the sidewalk, he grinds it to pieces with the toe of his shoe. Still wordless, he pulls my hand through the bend of his arm. He drags me toward the BMW, my other hand holding on desperately to my backpack.

"Sedat? Why are you so angry? We talked about this." I try to jerk my arm free, but he captures it tightly in both hands.

"Do not speak to me about what we discussed." His voice is a strained whisper. He looms over me. "There is no way I agreed to this behavior of yours."

We trudge toward the car like an old couple out for an evening stroll, he pulling and I resisting. Staring at his profile, he is still apoplectic, and I wonder how long it will take before he explodes and whether Arzu has been arrested by now.

At the car, Sedat shoves me, bag and all, into the back seat and slides in after me. He slams the door, and the driver backs into the street and screeches away. No words are spoken between us for the entire trip. Following the main boulevard through the city, we reach the outskirts of town and park at a private airstrip.

My nerves tell me to run when the door opens, but Sedat senses it and locks his hand around my upper arm. He snaps an order to the driver, and the man stays inside the vehicle. I understand now why Arzu is afraid of him. It is the raw, feral energy he releases when he is angry. I feel like a trapped mouse about to be eaten as a snack by a furious lion.

Sedat pulls me into a small office in one corner of the hangar. Shoving downward on my shoulder, he forces me to sit in a ragged office chair as he sits across the table from me. Stuffing my hands underneath my legs to stop them from shaking, I feel my heart slamming in my chest with the fear. This man is seriously powerful, and I have no idea what he will do to me. I look toward the car, then out the office door into the night, and wonder when the police vehicles will arrive to take me away.

"Şekerim, look at me." His endearment is at odds with his anger.

"Where are we?" The bravado I'd felt with Arzu is long gone, but I'll be damned if I let him run over me, even if I am afraid.

After several taps, he places his iPhone silently on the table between us. He shrugs out of his suit jacket and, after folding it, places it on the table. I cross my arms over my chest and stare out into the hangar.

"Answer me, Sedat." Two can play this anger game. "Where are we, and why am I here? We agreed I would be bait."

A finger touches my chin and turns my face toward him. His black eyes are still angry, and his long black lashes blink slowly. I search his face, hoping he isn't my kidnapper or, worse, my executioner.

"We are in a place no one knows, with fifteen minutes before we must keep going." He points to his phone. "I turned off the microphone and the tracker."

"I'm not afraid of you." That is a lie, and I'm sure he knows it. Yet, part of me has this unexplainable obsession with poking the bear.

"You should be. I hold your fate in my hands." His voice escalates as he stands and leans toward me over the table. "Even more so, you should be afraid of yourself. Have you lost your mind? You should be glad the two men aren't dead, with you in jail in Söke. What were you thinking? Glass soda bottles?" He is shouting now. "Quinn, they had guns. I could hear them over the microphone. Thanks to Allah, you are not dead."

"They tried to run us off the road. Why are you so angry at me?"

"You were to be bait in the apartment, Quinn! You were safe there. I could watch you every minute. Here? You were almost killed. Can't you see this?" He slams into the chair and pulls out a pack of cigarettes. "I had to fire two of my men just now because they couldn't keep up with you." Opening it, he removes one and lights it. He offers me one.

I decline and stare at him, understanding dawning on me. He isn't angry but scared for me, especially when I can't seem to prevent myself from taking risks that he thinks are dangerous. He takes several long draws from the cigarette, giving himself time to calm down.

"The apartment was a controlled environment," he says. "Why did you leave?"

How can I explain my reckless fixation with learning what Harris was involved in? Even I don't understand it. It is so much more than clearing my name. I won't be physically or mentally freed until I know what this is about. I must trust myself and have the confidence to rely only on *myself*. My freedom—and not just in the physical sense—is at stake.

"Am I finally under arrest?" I ask. "Is that what we are doing here?"

Now, it is his turn to look out the window. I am sick of the lies from Harris, Maynard, and him. Only Arzu and Artur were truthful with me. Artur is dead, and Arzu is—where? Arrested?

A jolt runs through me. What has he done with Arzu?

"What I do with you will depend on what you tell me." His voice remains measured. "We are, as your American journalists say, off the record here. Now is your chance."

I shake my head despite my arms being covered in chill bumps.

"Where are you taking me?" I ask.

"Eventually, back to İmir if I can determine how to get you there safely. You made the head of the group in Bulgaria very angry. One of the injured men was his son. Several others followed Arzu, but they were underlings. They are in custody, as is she, for her own safety, but they are not talking."

"Where, specifically, is Arzu?"

"She's on the way back to İmir. A team is with her."

Relieved, I lean back in the chair and break his gaze. "She'll need help with the rental agency. The car is seriously damaged and was rented in her friend's name."

"You want my help?" Sedat lets out a laugh. "Not unless you talk to me. Tell me why you are running from warehouse to warehouse all over my country."

"Yeah, but no. Who owns the chemicals we just found?" I sit up. Is Sedat a terrorist in a professor's clothing? A weapons dealer?

"My government." Unhurried, he explains. "A cache of them was found in Syria, and we moved them to various locations. I told you this. We are systematically destroying them. As you have found, we are almost finished, but the process is slow due to the canisters' decay. This insanity cannot continue." He rises to his feet and begins walking around the small room. He stops behind my chair. "You will give the disk to me and stop this nonsense." His voice is dangerously soft.

He places his hands on my shoulders with a light squeeze, and a jolt of fear quivers through my body. I try to get my breathing under control as he continues to pat my shoulder. His anger seems to be gone now, but I feel a cold hardness in its place, which is much more frightening.

"I told you," I say, "until I know ultimately in whose hands this information will fall, I'm not giving it to you or anyone."

He is still behind me, and I cannot see his expression, but I can feel him shift closer to my back.

"Then you will not like the next step. I'm required to take you to İmir for interrogation. There will be spectators. I will do things you won't like. You cannot let them know we talked."

"Then let's go." I twist to look up at him. "I'm out of time anyway. Harris's body is ready, and I'm supposed to escort it out of the country first thing Monday morning. Once I don't show up, they'll be after me, too. I might as well get your group out of the way first."

He squats, now at eye level with me.

"Quinn, don't do this." Sedat looks at me as if I'm a belligerent teenager rather than a grown woman. "You won't be able to handle what is about to happen. I can only protect you for so long. Just give me the disk or its information, and you can be free of this. I can protect you, and the Americans will be unable to find you, much less take you back to your country."

I silently shake my head. Maybe I am acting childish, but I cannot let go of the strings of numbers or the disk.

"Maybe this will change your mind."

He stands, pulling photos from his jacket, spreading them in front of me like a curved hand of cards. I look away. Gripping my chin hard, he turns my head toward the photos, and I close my eyes in defiance.

"Open your eyes, Quinn." The hardness is back to anger now. "Look what your inquisitiveness has done."

When I do not comply, he shakes my head until my eyes open, instantly trained to the photos on the tray. Before me is Artur, the Hacker Boy, beaten and bloody.

Dead.

He was just a boy, evidenced by the pimples dotting his bluish-white face. The pain in my heart is abrupt, and I bend forward, covering my face with my hands as the guilt overwhelms me.

I killed him.

I feel Sedat's face next to mine.

"This is your fate if you do not give me the disk," he whispers. "Either give it to me voluntarily, or I will be forced to take it."

53

SEDAT

When she refuses to give him the disk, Sedat orders her back to the car. He knows she listens to him on the phone, but he ensures she can understand little of his curt orders and one-word responses. Being so physically close to her for an hour is excruciating for him as they blast toward İmir. The woman is twisting his insides.

He knows what Demirci will demand he do.

Yes, he is angry, he thinks, but not for what she thinks. She has backed him into an unnecessary corner. The director may take over the investigation or hand the file—and Quinn—to another deputy director. Sedat has handled the last twenty-four hours poorly by ignoring standard procedure and getting too close to his target.

It will all end soon. The deadline is in less than twenty-four hours, and unless Quinn hands over the disk, she will be jailed or deported come Monday morning, regardless of what the Americans want. Barring something extraordinary, he will never see her again. He must force her to understand what she risks by keeping the disk to herself. If he proceeds too lightly, it will cost them both—his current position and her freedom.

It is raining, a sudden storm that exactly mimics Sedat's mood. The rain does not let up, and within minutes of their arrival at his office in İmir, two uniformed policemen meet them at the BMW. Per his orders, they handcuff Quinn's arms behind her and take their time, as if oblivious to the rain. At two o'clock in the morning, there is very little activity in the station. He watches as she, wet and bedraggled, is roughly hauled into the building by his men and meticulously searched. She glares at him across the room as his men, per their training, touch every part of her body to be certain nothing is hidden.

She is lucky he did not demand that she completely strip. But if he had, he would never forgive himself. Or forget what her naked body looked like, wet and slick with rain. Such a difference a week makes—from a hopeful young woman flying to meet her new husband to an international criminal wanted by three different groups, to the woman, after her deportation on Monday, whom he would never forget.

The uniforms march her through the station house, and Sedat sends them to an interrogation room while he steps into the viewing room. One of the officers forcibly maneuvers her into a metal chair in front of a table and shifts her hands to cuff her to the table per Sedat's instructions. Alone, she is watched through a large, dark window on the wall in front of her.

Sedat observes Quinn through the one-way glass, deciphering the emotions that cross her face. This woman isn't very good at hiding things. Whatever she thinks is openly plastered across her face. He could have seen this if he had been more careful. He lets her take in the surroundings of the harshly lit interrogation room, wanting her imagination to lead her to a place of fear, a place where he can extract the information he needs.

The director will also be watching. Even though a live feed now broadcasts directly to Ankara, Sedat knows the man is not awake at this hour. Yet Demirci will watch the videotape immediately upon arriving at the office at seven. Sedat must be done by then.

"I'll get her a towel from my locker," Bora says, shifting toward the door.

"No, Bora. Leave her be. It will go faster if she is a bit miserable."

"You're a bastard, you know that?" Bora stands beside him, his arms crossed over his chest, and his irritation filling the room. "What happened when you were alone with her in the apartment? You cut off the cameras and the microphones."

Sedat glances at his partner. "You are too soft, Bora. You know this has to be done. And what happened is none of your business. Go through her things and get the boys to do their magic. I want a complete copy of her phone and an undetectable bug installed on it before I return it to her. I need a GPS in her shoe, another in her backpack, and the thin strip in her wallet."

They leave Quinn alone for an hour. The only sound is the steady drip of water from her clothing and, now and then, a sigh. Entering the interrogation room, he sits on one side of the table with Quinn on the other. She ignores him and stares at the camera in the corner, then at the one-way window. With him in the room, her expression is now locked down tight, and she shifts her gaze to focus on the empty chair beside him, as the sole of her running shoe hammers against the floor. They will sit here until she meets his gaze, even until Monday's deadline. For this to work, she must come to him.

After another half hour, he signals to Bora, waiting behind the window. The two uniforms return, drinks and cigarettes in their hands. They laugh and joke in Turkish while they enjoy their smokes. Sedat leaves and returns to the observation room, where Bora monitors the videotaping accompanying the director's live feed in Ankara.

"How long will you let her sit there, Sedat?" he asks. "I thought you would treat her differently. You're the one who criticized Maynard. You said she was intelligent and needed a gentle hand. Now you've started your PKK techniques on a woman who isn't a terrorist."

"You were not there for the past twenty-four hours, Bora. She could have died. Had the car not flipped outside of Söke, they would have shot her through the head had they caught her. She has to be here for her protection."

"Then protect her, Sedat. Don't do this."

Sedat tilts his head toward the video equipment Demirci is using to watch. "She has crossed a line. That is not possible now. And you know that."

It doesn't take long before the room is filled with smoke. Visibly uncomfortable, Quinn coughs several times but otherwise doesn't speak, even when the officers spread the photos of Artur on the table in front of her. Sedat desperately needs her to face the result of her actions. As Bora said, this woman is intelligent. She needs to take responsibility for her recklessness.

So he waits. He detests this treatment, but the director has ordered that she not be treated kindly. He wanted a videotape to ensure it. Now, on camera, Sedat has no choice. She had her chance at the airfield. And this is only the beginning.

It takes another half hour of cigarette smoke before she is in physical distress and breaks her silence.

"I need the bathroom, Sedat," Quinn spits her words at the window, "and water unless you want me to choke to death."

One of the men looks to Sedat behind the window, and a single knuckle raps from the inside. The two men open the door for her, and as she steps into the hallway, Sedat meets her silently. She breathes in the stale office air as he escorts her down the hall. Inside the ladies' room, Sedat motions her to an empty stall, turning his back but leaving the door open. Quinn relieves herself, then steps around Sedat to wash her hands. While it is difficult when cuffed, he can risk no chance of her escape.

Back in the empty interrogation room, Sedat begins.

"You married Harrison Robicheaux in Mexico. How romantic."

"Is there a question here, Sedat?"

Quinn appears bored, but he knows she is anything but. Her entire body shakes. Being inside the police station has caused the desired effect, but Sedat hopes she heard what he told her at the airport. Otherwise, all this will be wasted effort.

"Merely an observation. It is enlightening that you believed you were so in love with this man that you ignored what he involved you in. This is not the curious, reckless woman I know."

He selects one of the file folders before him and slides it toward her so she can reach it with her cuffed hands.

"Take it."

She opens the file to find copies of investigative reports. They are handwritten in English, with various sections redacted. She reads from the beginning of her husband's life to the day he died. Sedat knows every word of these documents, having pored over them, attempting to trap his target before he endangered the people of his country.

After the reports, there are photos of Harris in places he shouldn't have been, with women he shouldn't have been with. Quinn starts to flip the photos rapidly.

"Look at the dates on the photos, Quinn."

Even though she does not respond, she stops, and he watches her eyes flick to the bottom corner. He sees the moment she understands the photos were taken *after* her wedding day. First, the anger makes her face flush, and then there is the white-knuckled jealousy as women parade before her in these photos. She returns to the beginning of the stack and holds herself together, but only barely, as she scans the prints of raucous-looking parties, packed casinos, high-rolling Las Vegas card tables, and other wealthy European-looking places.

Her shoulders drop in relief when she believes she has reached the end. Sedat slides another file toward her. Quinn's eyes hit him with the hatred she feels at that moment, and he is sure that not all of it is for Harris.

More photos—also dated after her sham of a wedding. The number of secret trips Harris took behind Quinn's back is ridiculous. Sedat received this set from his contact in the United States. The first image is dated the week after their honeymoon, when Quinn was alone in Charleston.

Sedat watches her again as her eyes move to the date on the photo, one week after their wedding day. The image shows Harris sitting at a gambling table, with a stack of chips in front of him and a redhead in a sparkling green gown bent over his shoulder, her arms around him, smiling broadly for the camera.

Sedat struggles to control his own rage. He pulls out a cigarette and lights it, using the task to focus on something other than the woman across from him. He cannot decide whether his anger should be directed at Robicheaux for being a cad, Quinn for being monumentally naive, or himself for letting his emotions get out of control.

With more and more photos of different places and women, the lies are piling around Quinn like stinking, dead fish, and he hates being the head fishmonger. When she finishes the second folder, Sedat silently slides a third thin file across the table. This time, he refuses to watch her and turns slightly away, crossing one leg over the other as he smokes. Should he need to see, her reaction will be on camera.

Seventy-two hours of Quinn's honeymoon are documented in excruciating detail, both in and out of their suite. When he received the photos, he restricted them to himself and Bora, but Sedat knew, given his contact's salty comment, that the same was not done in the United States. After today, the director will also wish to review the files. A glance at Quinn shows her face in a rage so hot he thinks she would cross the table for him if she weren't bolted to the floor.

He uncrosses his legs and shifts to face her.

"This is an ultimate violation of my privacy, and you know it." She slams the photos on the table and attempts to stand, the handcuffs jerking her back down. "These reports are written in English, so I know you didn't create them." Her words are yelled at him, and he is sure her voice can be heard in Istanbul. "Where did you get them? And these photos."

The surreptitious photos of Quinn and her husband making love are indeed a violation of their privacy. He did not want to show her these. Yet Sedat needs her to feel the same rage he experiences each time he opens his investigation file. He wants her to feel what he feels every time he looks at her face and thinks about how badly Robicheaux took advantage of her. He wants her finally to know—and feel—the truth.

All of it.

54

SEDAT

Sedat continues his interrogation. By now, his director is possibly watching remotely, and Bora, joined by an American intelligence officer, is watching behind the observation window. Quinn is holding the thin folder tightly with her honeymoon photos. He attempts to move forward with his questions, but understands that her mind is still trapped by the contents of the file in her hand.

"I am not an expert on U.S. criminal law," he says, "but I know your law enforcement had enough information to indict him and needed to conduct surveillance for your connection, to know whether to add you to the indictment."

"For what criminal act? There are no charges or indictments in either folder. Maynard says the same thing. I found nothing when I checked the U. S. sites. I want to see the actual charges of something. Anything. What exactly did I do? Give me one specific event during my wedding weekend that involves me in this mess."

Sedat is about to tell her some of Robicheaux's deals in Mexico when he sees Quinn's eyes widen. At that exact moment, she understands the images of her lovemaking are in full living color on computers stretching from New York to Europe. She looks to the window, then back at him, her eyes panic-stricken.

"Who has copies of these photos?" Her voice is soft, but horrified, and a pink flush creeps up her neck. "Where are they stored, and on what servers? Are these all of them?"

Her petrified stare is a spear through his heart, and he looks away. He has more photos of her honeymoon, but the ones he included were enough. Interpol provided photos of other women in sex clubs and other similar situations that, if he can help it, she will never see.

He shoves another thick file across the table toward her, but she does not reach for it.

"Quinn, you need to see it all. Finish this."

She lets out a quivering sigh, reluctant to go on. Her face is white, and Sedat knows she is holding on to every ounce of her respect, given the photos before her. He prods her by pushing the last file closer, and she finally opens it. The originator's name has been redacted; however, Sedat is fairly certain it is Maynard. So much has been redacted that it makes for challenging reading. He watches as Quinn plows through, trying to make sense of the story.

The Air Force Office of Special Investigations had been monitoring Harris for the past two years, gathering as much information as possible from his career while building a case. He was assigned to Air Force Logistics overseas, yet according to this report, he used that assignment for personal gain, working with another officer in Procurement who dealt primarily with arms. Harris did not restrict himself to weapons but seemed to trade for anything he could find. Several things he sold are unnamed in the reports, designated only as high-value, classified items.

The reports track Robicheaux through his last five assignments, from Iraq to locations stateside, an intelligence school, an officer's school in Montgomery, Alabama, and then to Aviano Air Base in Italy.

Then, the gambling begins.

Harris participated in high-stakes, illegal card games. He won, lost, and partied with a different woman by his side each time. This report suggests that Robicheaux was using military funds to stake himself. According to the paperwork Sedat received from the Air Force Military Police, embezzlement was also suspected but never conclusively established. The Air Force report stops the day Harris intentionally meets Quinn in Charleston.

She now knows he never loved her. It was all pretend.

Sedat watches as she flips through the remainder of the file, the part she lived, then closes the folder and stares toward the one-way window. Her face and body are conflicted with so many emotions that he gives her time before he begins his next assault. He regrets taking this next step, but the camera light is still on over his shoulder. He must be convincing enough for them both.

Quinn touches something hidden inside her shirt just below her collarbone. He watches her closely until he sees the flicker of a gold chain in the light, something he hasn't seen before. Something rectangular lies beneath her shirt, hanging from the chain. At least now he knows where it is. If forced to search her, he will take that first.

Sedat begins his interrogation with a list of questions, which he asks repeatedly in different ways, testing whether she will give the same answer each time. If she says even a minor thing differently, he begins again with a barrage of questions on the same subject but in a different direction. He pushes and hammers her for an exhausting three more hours until she finally stops, puts her head in her arms, and refuses to say another word.

She only raises her head at the sound of the cap being removed from a water bottle.

"Drink, Quinn." He slides the bottle toward her.

"Don't tell me what to do, you bastard."

Her voice is raw from pleading her innocence and answering his hours of questions. From the teams following her, Sedat knows she is beyond depleted, having had no sleep for the past twenty-four hours and very little to eat or drink. But he must continue. At some point during the interrogation, he received a text message stating that someone from the U.S. was watching him through the one-way window. Nothing can be left to connect her to Robicheaux's transactions. The man duped her into marrying him, and that is all. Sedat intends to make that clear.

"Quinn, if you give me what I want, you can be free. If you do not, it will only get worse."

"I've told you everything I know." Her head drops back to her arms on the table.

"Where is the disk? The poor boy in Istanbul died for it, didn't he? Do you wish to risk Arzu's life or even your own?"

Quinn shifts to touch the necklace through her shirt as if whatever is there has magical powers, but catches herself in time. If the director has paid attention, a strip search will be next, and the man will not care about her privacy.

"There is no disk. Stop asking the same thing over and over."

"I can do things you will regret."

"You wouldn't dare." She looks at him, then speaks loudly toward the window, then shifts up toward the camera. "Thinking about torturing a grieving widow? This will turn into an international incident. I'll make sure of it.

"No, I would not do those things to you." He points to the window and leans forward. "But the director will. He is already demanding that I release you to him. He has already suggested things to make another trip to the lavatory unnecessary."

A rap from the window makes Sedat leave the room. Upon entering the observation room, Bora turns on a computer screen. Sedat looks at the American from the U.S. embassy, whose name he cannot remember.

"Will you excuse us for one minute, please?"

Reluctantly, the man steps outside the door, and Sedat closes it carefully. He hears Demirci clear his voice on the computer.

"Get on with it. Why are you stalling?" The director's gruff command grates on Sedat. If the man wanted to conduct the interview, he should be in İmir.

"Sir, there is nothing more to gain. This is not a trained operative but an average American citizen on foreign soil. We are heading to the fourth hour of this with no proof she is involved, only your suspicions. She has nothing on her—we searched. Patience will serve us much better with this woman than slapping her around. I've spent enough time around her to know that she will only go silent, and her threats of making an international incident are real.

"That woman is a nobody. What international incident?"

"She has legal contacts in her country that could make life tedious for us."

"She is bluffing, and you know it." Sedat hears shuffling paper over the computer as Demirci shifts off-screen, then silence.

"Sir?"

Demirci faces the camera again. "Do it your way, then. It is your career. But I believe this is a mistake. I'll give you another twenty-four hours, then you will send her to Ankara, and I will take care of her."

Before Sedat can protest, Demirci is gone, and the screen is black.

"Let's take her back to the apartment. Let her think for a while, then give it another go tonight," Bora says. "You're as exhausted as she is, and there's nothing to be gained by this. Unless you want to keep her here?"

"No, you're right. I'd rather have her at the apartment where I can watch her myself."

Sedat stands over a sleeping Quinn in the interrogation room, hesitant to wake her. But he must. As he unlocks the handcuffs, she sits up.

"You were given a reprieve." He doesn't try to hide the relief in his whisper.

"What?" Quinn's face is weary, her hair a tangled mess. "No torture today?" She attempts to straighten the tangles with her fingers, then gives up.

Sedat pulls her to stand so she can face him. He glances at the corner to be certain the red light from the camera is still off. His eyes are only an inch from hers as his whispered words blow across her face.

"You have no idea with whom you are playing, my sweet. I saved you again, and you will thank me one day. Demirci grants us only a twenty-four-hour reprieve before you are to be shipped to Ankara and subjected to his torture. Trust me, you do not want this. I am risking my entire career by getting you away from here. I believe it is your fear and grief that are causing you to do crazy things, but keeping you in a holding cell is not what you need. You will stay in the apartment under guard until I decide how to handle this."

He turns Quinn and marches her to the door while his hand stealthily shoves her phone into her back pocket.

55

QUINN

The sun has just risen. I step into my apartment and am met with chaos. Every drawer and cabinet is open, and the contents are on the floor. My suitcases are open, and my clothes are scattered across the bedroom. The mattress is ripped, and the stuffing is scattered all over the floor. None of the furniture is in the same place I left it. Holes are in the floors, walls, and ceiling. Would Sedat do this to his mother's apartment? No, unless her ownership is also a lie.

I remember the passports, the thumb drive, and the diamonds. Slowly, I head to the bathroom. It is the only room without cameras, and I need to cause no suspicion. Closing the door behind me, I look under the sink, knowing I will find a gaping hole. To my surprise, the wall is still intact, just as I had left it. Removing the backboard, I pull out the bag and collapse to the floor.

The storage cabinets and drawers are open, and their contents are scattered across the floor. To my shock, the false wall I created in the back remains in place. The person who did this was in too much of a hurry. This tells me that Sedat did not do this. He is too thorough, and his team, particularly the one that searched every inch of my body, would have found every last item.

Exhausted, I exhale, sit on the floor, and cry.

With no energy to clean up the mess, I right a dining chair, sit, and call Arzu. Sedat has probably bugged the damn thing, but at this point, I don't care. I hang up and call again. Nothing. I repeat this action ten times, as if the more I call, the more likely she is to answer. I give up, dig through the scattered clothing for something to wear, and head for the bathroom. The only thing I want right now, more than food, is a shower.

The intercom buzzes. Expecting Sedat and more interrogation, I go to the balcony and look over. I consider taking the eggs from the refrigerator with me to drop on his head.

But it's Maynard.

The intercom buzzes again, and I press the button to talk.

"Maynard. Do you know it's six in the morning? I'm not ready to have visitors. Can you come back later?"

"No. Tomorrow is your deadline, and I'm coming up. You can let me in, or I will get the MPs and force my way in. Enough, Quinn."

It's time to face his music. Besides, I know Sedat's men are somewhere near, as probably is Sedat. They are watching on the camera and listening through a bug that's most likely planted in my phone, or maybe through the cameras themselves.

I hide the passport bag inside a ripped pillow in the bedroom. The elevator dings, and I stride down the hallway to open the door for him. I extend my arm toward the living room, my body blocking him from the rest of the apartment.

"You've had visitors." He strides into the living room, turns a dining chair upright, then motions to another one. I stand.

He crosses his arms over his chest and starts again. "You might want to sit." Then he scrutinizes me. "Where have you been? Why do you look like a drowned rat?"

"I'm fine." I lean against the door frame.

"Have it your way. Let me tell you a little about your husband," he says. "When you see how corrupt he was, you'll see why I need that disk."

Maynard leans back in his chair and evaluates me, his beady eyes watching my face. I refuse to look away, even though I am about to drop. I've heard more about Harris in the past twenty-four hours than I could stomach already, but if he has his say, maybe I can get rid of him.

"Harris graduated from The University of the South in Tennessee. I know he told you Tulane, but that was a lie. He and I roamed Europe for a year until his daddy cut our travel money. When we returned to Nashville, his father expected Harris to run the family textile business like a good boy. The mother was an heiress to a cotton manufacturing business, the company handed down for several generations."

I don't move. Unfortunately, he has my attention.

"Harris joined the Air Force, and after Officer Candidate School, he got his first assignment as part of Desert Shield in Iraq. While most of the officers hated Iraq, Harris thrived. He studied the language, befriended the locals, and made a name for himself. His superiors reassigned him to intelligence school, and Harris's career took off."

Harris never told me any of this. He wouldn't.

"We both had TDY, a temporary duty, in Aviano, Italy, to track rumors of chemical weapons Saddam Hussein had in Iraq. That was the last I saw of him until ACSC, an Air Force school in Montgomery. By then, I wasn't sure who he was working for."

This is a lie, especially if Maynard was Harris's handler for whatever alphabet agency they worked for, as Sedat had claimed. I continue to lean against the door and listen, putting my hands in my jeans pockets to keep my fingers from cutting into my fists.

"Harris loved to gamble. As the years passed, he began receiving invitations to high-stakes gambling tables at the locations where he was stationed. Lately, he'd gone international. Those were fun times, let me tell you."

"Two nights before he died, we were in Sochi." Maynard cracks a smile. "He was at a table with some wealthy men and fleeced them substantially. An old man had thrown a miniature disk as part of his stake on the table. He was sick, wearing an oxygen cannula with an expensive portable tank sitting next to his chair."

"So what was it?" I ask, ready for this to be over.

Maynard drops the chair to the floor and walks toward me. When he reaches me, he grasps my upper arm and squeezes tightly.

"Don't play dumb with me." He leans toward me, his voice low and angry. "Where is the disk? Did you give it to Özbek? It's mine."

"I don't know what you're talking about." I shift from his grasp and step toward the front door. "I told the Turk the same thing. It's time for you to leave."

Maynard follows me to the door.

"Well, yeah, they're stalling me right now, I'll admit. That's why I'm here. To add a little fuel to the fire." He stands and holds out his hand. I open the door, and he slams it shut, pushing me toward the hall.

"Give me your passport," he sneers. "You need to quit gallivanting around the country."

"You aren't getting my passport." I let out an indignant laugh.

"I'm not leaving here without it." He grabs my neck, putting pressure on my throat. "It's either that or the Department of Defense will snatch you up, then plant you in a Turkish jail until they can deport you back to the U.S."

"And then your disk will never be found," I say, my voice a whisper as I struggle to breathe.

"I'm your only way out of this mess, can't you see?"

Maynard's face is manic, and a jolt of fear moves through my entire body. I struggle to swallow as his grip tightens on my throat, but it doesn't stop me. I take the spit in my mouth and blast it into his face. He drops his hand and backs away, cleaning his face with his sleeve.

"Why, you bitch!" he screams at me, and it is all I can do not to slap him.

"I'll give you my passport if you'll get out of my damn apartment."

Catching my breath again, I stalk into the living room and paw through my backpack. Grabbing my original passport, I return to the foyer, open the front door to the apartment, and hold out the little booklet. Maynard meets me at the door, and before he can snatch it from me, I toss it down the stairs.

He scrambles down the staircase.

"Without this," he yells up at me from the level below, "you know you can't leave the country." His whiny voice is cruel and sarcastic. "As an American, you can't go many places without it."

"Yeah, well fuck you."

I close the door and turn the new lock until I hear its last click. What a joke. I'm not worried about the fake passport. Thanks to Harris, there are six others.

And it's time to put them to use.

56

QUINN

Armed with a fake passport, my backpack is stuffed with the basics: several pairs of jeans, three clean shirts, a hoodie, sandals, and toiletries. My favorite running shoes are on. With kitchen scissors, I walk to the bathroom. As best I can, I cut my hair into a short bob. I will dye it at the first opportunity, but until then, I tuck the rest under a head scarf.

I don the black abaya I wore to the gold merchant, which covers me from head to toe. Checking my backpack one last time, I stuffed in an ugly hat, the scarf Sedat gave me, and a pair of square sunglasses I found from a street vendor in case I need them later.

I slump, imitating an older woman.

Sedat, or one of his men, added several new trackers to my backpack at the police station and another to my wallet. I ditch all the trackers that I find. I've had enough of Sedat right now and enough of his country. I need to go where I can regroup and plan how to move forward.

I try to call Arzu again. There is no answer. The possibility that she is dead cloaks me in a cloud of dread and fear.

Shuffling out the front door of the building, I am sweating

from the heavy abaya and the fear of being discovered. My backpack is a hump on my back, and the large shopping bag is on my front, under the abaya, making me look fat. Two men in plain clothes linger at the front steps, and I am sure they are Sedat's men, there to guard the building. When I step outside, they scrutinize me. Huffing down the steps, I feel my skin crawl as I get close to them. Just as I pass, one reaches into his pocket, and I freeze until I see the package of cigarettes in his hand.

They smoke their cigarettes and continue their conversation until I'm downhill and can no longer hear them. They will suffer under Sedat's punishment, but I cannot think about that now. He really should train them better.

I show the taxi driver the address of TNT Express, the closest FedEx agent to the airport. I don't speak. I don't want to reveal that behind my abaya and sunglasses is an American. He asks me questions, but I shake my head silently. When we arrive, the express mail office is busy, which is good for me. With what I have planned, if Sedat attempts to go through the packages, with luck, the clerk will be unable to identify which customer sent what.

Handling the packaging and addressing myself, I wrap the cartouche from Harris, the diamond necklace, the thumb drive, and the disk in separate FedEx envelopes, then address them to my virtual mailboxes in Savannah and Miami, both of which I had set up in the name of shell corporations the week before I left the States. I use the name listed on the fake passport as the sender of the envelopes, with a phony address.

I place the shopping bag full of cash into a FedEx box, address it to Remzi Turin, and include instructions to deliver it to the gold merchant for safety, along with an envelope containing a substantial tip for him. My instructions require that I receive the receipt directly via WhatsApp from the merchant. The sender of this box is a different name taken from my fake passports.

I speak to the clerk in halting English, using as few words as possible. The clerk tells me that the packages to the U.S. will be delivered in three days. I know they will remain safely ensconced in the U.S. virtual mailboxes until I pick them up or forward them to another address. The box for Remzi will be delivered within the hour, with a substantial tip to the driver to keep quiet. Will he? I have no idea.

The written list of coordinates from Artur is placed in yet another envelope for same-day delivery to Arzu, who is in the care of Sena at the restaurant, with several fake passports, a stack of cash, and a note asking Arzu to hide the passports and research the remaining locations across Europe. While I hate to involve Sena in this, she is my only option if something has happened to Arzu.

Once the packages are processed, I watch the entire process through the open double doors of the warehouse where the FedEx office is located. The envelopes bound for the U.S. travel on a conveyor belt to a young man, who adds them to a specific plastic box. The box is then closed, locked, and placed on a FedEx delivery truck that I watch leave for the airport.

The same-day deliveries to Remzi and Arzu leave immediately in a tiny white delivery van, as I have paid for expedited service in addition to the bribe.

A considerable weight drops from my shoulders. From the express mail office to the airport, I download the map with the coordinates into a file, then add a password before I wipe the online map. I cannot be too careful. I cannot think of anything else that I need to do before I leave the country. I've used fake names and addresses, and the deliveries are en route to locations only known to me.

I check my now-thin backpack for additional trackers and find nothing. Sedat may deduce that I've gone to the airport, but he will not be able to find my name on the flight manifest. He will search all the video feeds to find me, but he will still not know the name I am using. Even so, I look very much like a young Arab woman on her way back to the Middle East. It will take sophisticated facial recognition software for him to be certain it is me.

The taxi drops me off at the departure section of the Adnan Menderes Airport. Living in Türkiye is a traveler's dream. Only an hour or two from destinations in Europe or the Mediterranean, catching a cheap flight is routine for residents and visitors alike. With multiple fake passports, I can go anywhere. My eventual destination is Bangkok, Thailand, via Muscat, Oman; however, I must first arrive in Istanbul. I will stay in Muscat until I feel safe, then head to Bangkok. Or somewhere else. Anywhere but here until I can determine what will happen with these coordinates.

I approach the ticket counters, looking for Pegasus Airlines. While I would like to go to Sabiha Gökçen Airport on the eastern side of Istanbul, the earliest flight from İzmir will suffice. Standing before the electronic flight board, I search for a flight.

Finding an Ajet flight that leaves in thirty minutes, I turn to head for the ticket counter when a man steps in front of me, blocking my way. He smiles as I glance up at him, and I return the smile and move around him. From behind, the man catches up to me, and something hard presses into my side.

"Stop, madam. Otherwise, I will be forced to hurt you."

My mistake. Whoever this is, he confirmed my identity when I looked up at him and smiled. No self-respecting Arab woman would ever look a man in the face.

Damn it.

57

SEDAT

Quinn ran as Sedat expected. He had placed a man at the taxi stand to watch and report, but not to detain. Two others were sent to the Otogar, given her last escape. He chuckles to himself. She thought she had outmaneuvered him by removing the trackers and leaving them in the apartment.

Bora looks up from a report he has been reading. "Why are you laughing?"

"She thinks she has outsmarted me." Sedat turns the iPad toward Bora, pointing to the four blinking dots, each a different color. "She is in a taxi identified by our team, headed toward the airport."

"Why so many colors?"

"Red is her shoe, blue is the ratty backpack she takes everywhere like a college student, green is her wallet, and yellow is digital, the one inside her iPhone. This new technology is completely flat. If anything is lost or misplaced, at least one will always be on her."

"Unless she is naked," Bora responds with a grin.

Sedat raises one eyebrow. "Yes, there is that." He had considered a nanobot of some type, but requisitioning one would take excessive time and require the Director's approval, something he refuses to obtain.

"She has you spooked. And twisted around her finger. There will be no job if this goes on much longer."

"Possibly. This is the third time she has donned a disguise and avoided our men. She is making a fool of us. She can protest all she wants, but her skill at avoiding a tail and a security detail is superior, given that she is not trained." He wonders how he can use her to train his men in the future.

Sedat watches the tracking app's blinking lights on his phone. She may run, but she will never escape.

"Or just lucky," Bora replied. "I thought you didn't believe she was part of this."

"I didn't until now." Sedat turns away from Bora. "Maybe she has a natural talent for being a chameleon."

The dots travel from the apartment to a location near the Menderes airport, but outside the gates. After twenty minutes, they move again toward the airport.

"Find out what that stop is," Sedat points out the location to Bora, handing him the radio connecting them with the four men he had sent to the airport gate earlier. "Get someone there now."

The trackers continue their journey. He watches now as the four colored dots enter through the outer security of the airport, heading toward the ticketing counters. They turn and, after winding a bit, stop.

"What is she doing?" Bora asks, squinting at the dots.

"Another diversion, likely. Restroom possibly? She has too many tricks up her sleeve lately."

"Get the men from the front gate on her now. I need eyes."

58

QUINN

The man with the gun has brown hair, green eyes, a long Roman nose, and a face that isn't Turkish. He grips my elbow, acting proprietary like he's my husband, and pulls me to stand close to him.

"Hey, what the—" I fight to pull my arm from his grasp.

"Do not scream." His voice is heavily accented, making his soft-spoken English difficult to understand. "Act as if you know me and, more importantly, that you like me. If you do anything that causes alarm in any way, I will shoot you."

Something cold and hard again shoves against my side. I try to pull away from his grip, but he clinches tighter on my elbow and shoves the concealed weapon against me more forcefully. I freeze.

"Smile." His accent is like that of the men who drilled my door.

We stop in an open area in front of opposite rows of ticketing kiosks. I refuse to allow the fear under my skin to take over, even though there is no way I can escape this man. He has an air of distinguished detachment about him, and I am acutely aware that in the presence of this formidable man, the distressed outbursts of a hysterical woman will not be taken seriously by onlookers. He is over six feet, almost old enough to be my father, and strong. I feel the strength in his hand as he squeezes my arm, and I see it as his chest muscles shift under his tight shirt.

"Smile, I said. Do it now." The man keeps his threatening voice low. He pushes me forward, and I stumble. Catching me before I fall, he squeezes my elbow so harshly that I almost let out a scream. Instead, I weakly smile at him, then wince in pain as he shoves the gun under my backpack to hide it and into my back. A roll of fear flops in my gut. I'm all too familiar with the feeling now after Sedat's interrogation techniques, but this one is much worse.

"Now, you will act as if you forgot something. Stop, look into your handbag, and look back up at me." I comply, trying not to drop my backpack as it slides off one shoulder and almost hits the floor.

"Darling, I thought you had everything." The man's voice is louder this time, wanting others around us to hear. "We will return to the hotel. It is okay; please do not cry. Here, come, come. There is time before our flight takes off."

His voice is convincingly patient and loving; his gestures are soft and natural, as if responding with genuine compassion to my entirely authentic, panic-stricken expression. A woman passes us with a knowing smile. I start to say something to her, inadvertently shifting my body toward her.

"Don't do it," he whispers. "Let her keep walking." The man bends down, going through my backpack to keep the woman from seeing his face.

"Please don't hurt me." My mouth is dry with fear, and I struggle to form words. They tumble out in a croak. "Who are you?"

"No one you will see after today. Come with me." He retakes my elbow, pulling me in toward him. As my body brushes against him, I can feel the bulk of the gun somehow surreptitiously returned to a shoulder holster under his suit jacket.

"Where are we going?" I frantically look for a way out of this. "I don't know what you want from me." My body shakes with desperation. It is all I can do to stay upright.

He leads me out of the airport, grasping the crook of my arm as I stumble along. My eyes dart in every direction, frantically searching for a way to escape. He pulls the gun from his holster and shoves it so hard into my side that it takes my breath away.

We cross a lane of traffic to the outside parking area. A driver waits in a car at the end of the sidewalk, the engine running. A second man sits in the passenger seat. The back door to the car opens, and I am shoved inside, next to a third man who reeks of fish. I'm sure I know him, but it takes a few minutes to recognize him. Then it hits me. He is one of the men who chased Sedat and me down the Kordon.

The driver was his partner that day. The front passenger ignores me, and I can't see his face. The man who escorted me from the airport stays on the street, and the car takes off.

"What do you want from me?" I ask. I twist the hem of my shirt in my hands.

The men act like they don't hear me. Once we are outside the airport, the man beside me thrusts a black bag over my head, and I feel my hands being tied. I scream and begin to kick until a hand slaps me twice to shut me up, slamming my head against the seat. The bag smells like onions and rotten potatoes, and my gag reflex works overtime. I steel myself not to throw up in the bag.

The car turns right, and I begin counting to keep from screaming. Long after I've lost track of the seconds passing, the car stops, and the engine turns off. The door opens, and I hear the man next to me get out of the vehicle. I brace myself, and sure enough, he grabs the tops of my arms and drags me roughly from the back seat. I scramble to keep my shoulder from being pulled from its socket as I collide with the door on my way out. Once out of the car, I am released. A hand shoves me forward, and I lurch to keep my balance.

"Take this bag off my head," I say. "I won't look at you."

Out of nowhere, I am violently slapped across the side of my head, and my temple throbs. The top of my ear stings with an excruciating intensity. The man who hit me must have been wearing a heavy ring. A hard object is thrust into my back once again; this time, my kidney is taking the brunt. Unable to see, I can only assume it is the gun. I try my best not to fall or succumb to my body's urges to urinate and vomit simultaneously, as I am escorted forward with the gun still held firmly against my back.

We stop. A door opens. I hear scraping against concrete, and am propelled forward again. The bag is still over my head, and I listen intently. There is traffic and machinery nearby. An excavator bucket creaks. Its diesel engine growls as the bucket slams into something hard with a loud crack. I hear rumbling as a solid mass crumbles to pieces, then hunks of what sounds like concrete crash to the ground.

I'm ushered through a door. Inside, the exterior noise is muffled. There's a poke again into my back, and I take a step forward. The bag is finally pulled from my head, and I am shoved into a room where I slam into a wall and collapse to the floor.

Gasping for fresh air to cleanse the smell of onions and rotten potatoes from my nose, I see my backpack and phone scattered on the floor. I grab the phone and notice immediately that there is no cell service, and my heart sinks. Awkwardly grabbing the water bottle from my backpack, I take a drink. I scrounge for anything I can use to free my hands and pick the lock. There is nothing. I rip off the abaya. My t-shirt and jeans are wet with sweat, from both the heat and the fear.

The room has concrete block walls and a concrete ceiling, with a single shoulder-height barred window on one side, equipped with shutters. Security bars cover the window on the outside, and a sheet of plastic allows only diffused light into the room. There is no fresh air, and I can't reach far enough to break the plastic.

I suck in a deep breath and let it out slowly, repeating this ten more times until I can relax. The pounding in my head slowly eases, and I observe my surroundings, looking for a way to escape. Tonight won't be comfortable.

A single bulb suspended from the concrete ceiling sways slightly, indicating that air is entering from somewhere. I select a wall that looks cleaner than the others and sit, sliding down into a squat before finally giving up and sitting directly on the dirty floor. My stomach growls. I'm sure there won't be any food or access to a bathroom. A shudder grips my body, and I force my mind not to think about what *will* be.

I twist a strip of my hair around my finger until it pulls so tightly that strands come loose in my hand. The bag was meant to keep me from knowing where I was, not from seeing their faces.

They plan to kill me.

59

QUINN

There are voices on the other side of the door. The handle rattles, and my body breaks into a cold sweat. I stand up, backing myself down the wall and away from the door.

"Good evening, Quinn. Welcome!"

Maynard. Wait—*Maynard?*

"Maynard, thank God—"

My voice trails off when the man who attempted to drill my steel door walks into the room. My heart races. Standing almost six feet tall, he wears a light gray suit that contrasts with Maynard's cargo shorts and striped rugby shirt.

The Bulgarian's face beams, as if we are old friends, as he walks toward me, his arms extended as if to hug me. I shift to the side as I glare at him, and he drops his arms.

"We hope your accommodations are satisfactory." The heavily accented English reminds me of how terrified I was that night at the apartment.

Maynard grabs my left arm and cuts the rope that ties my hands in front of me. He twists my arm behind me, grabs my other arm roughly, and binds my hands behind me with plastic zip ties. He looks at the Bulgarian.

"Your men have already underestimated her."

The man nods, then gives me a winning smile. Maynard leaves my legs and feet unrestrained, but I wait to see what else happens before I aim for the place on either man that will hurt the most. I watch them, my eyes shifting from one to the other. There is no way I can strike either of them with my foot without making it worse for myself.

"I love your new haircut." Maynard reaches for my face, and I cringe. He grins at the other man, then back at me. "You have something we need," he says, stroking my cheek with his rough hand, holding me still with the other.

My body shudders.

"Come now, *cher*, I won't hit you. It would be a shame to hurt that pretty face of yours." Maynard laughs as he flips a hand at the Bulgarian. "But my new partner might."

With my eyes closed, I swear Harris is standing before me. Then it hits me. This is the voice from the video. I don't understand how Maynard can sound exactly like my husband, but he does. While Harris appeared alive on that video, there was no time to scrutinize it before it was gone. I've seen videos on social media where an avatar is artificially created to mimic a person, so I know it is possible.

Maynard steps away and extends a solicitous hand for the other man to approach.

"What do you want from me?" I lift my chin in defiance as I close my eyes, awaiting the slap. The Bulgarian leans so close I can smell garlic on his breath.

"Please, Quinn. May I call you Quinn?" The Bulgarian's voice is soft and pleading in his accent until he shifts abruptly into clipped British speech. "Let me get to the point. Your dead husband somehow sent the disk to you, but it did not belong to him. It belongs to me. Give it to me, and we will be on our way."

Neither man mentions the money. If they aren't concerned about ten million dollars, then the coordinates, or whatever they are, must be priceless.

"He did not send it to me." I hold the man's gaze and scowl at him, forcing my body to remain still as the shards of fear begin their relentless pricking.

"Please do not lie to me. It is the most important thing, you know." This new British accent reminds me of Sedat. I shove the thought away and focus, but not before a slug of despair shoots through me.

"There is nothing in my apartment," I respond. "I've been through everything Harris owned, and there is no disk. You're not the only ones looking for it, you know."

"Yes, there are others. Since you will be hounded until you give it up to someone, it is in your best interest, Quinn, to give it to me. Once you do, I will let you go. I promise you."

Given the huge drill they left at my apartment that night and the almost ruined door, his word is worth nothing. I don't believe him for a second, but I stay silent.

"Men are going through your husband's things again since you—and they—missed it the first time."

"Good luck with that." I can't conceal my contempt. Thanks to FedEx, all my envelopes are now on a plane, and the bulk of the money is with Remzi. I hope.

The Bulgarian's hand strikes my face so hard that I hit the wall behind me and sprawl onto the floor. I don't move for several minutes, seeing my face fade in and out in the glossy shine of the man's shoes with each heartbeat. When the pain begins to subside, I carefully sit, shifting away. After a glare at Maynard, I stare toward the window.

"Until next time," the Bulgarian says, leaving me alone with Maynard. I bite the inside of my cheeks to keep from saying exactly what I think of them.

"Take off your shoes and socks. You won't need them here, and I can't risk you trying to run."

"Fuck you," I respond. "My hands are tied behind my back if you've forgotten." If he wants something, he can take it from me. I'm not volunteering anything.

Maynard shoves me back on the floor as he snatches one shoe, then the other, peeling my socks off while I kick and scream, my anger and fear at a level so far beyond reason that I'm unable to control myself. He takes my backpack and the sweater tied to one of the straps, holding it up as he walks to the door.

"Let's see how you feel after a few hours on the cold concrete floor."

The door slams, and the lock turns. I close my eyes, thankful I've received only slaps to my face, but I know the Bulgarian, most likely, will ramp up his torture until he gets what he wants.

On the floor, I wedge my body into the opening between my arms and bring my hands under my knees. I need to contort my legs, get them over my hands, through my arms, and bring them to the front of my body. After several failed attempts, I give up. Too bad I'm not like my favorite male book characters and able to pop the cable ties apart with my brute strength.

While I detest my captors, this situation is, in part, my fault. Sedat tried to protect me, repeatedly warning me to stay in the apartment. My obstinate refusal to take the situation seriously led to this. I sit on the cold concrete and lean my head against the wall, closing my eyes and resisting the urge to relieve myself in my clothes, holding it as long as possible. Without food or water, a bathroom will soon be the least of my worries.

Most of all, right now, I hate my husband. It's a good thing he's already dead. Yet he isn't my husband. Because of the fake marriage license, according to Sedat, I'm still single.

I sleep at some point, and have fallen to my side. When I awaken, I am tightly curled in the fetal position, shivering in the cool night air. My shoulders ache from being stretched with my hands behind me. It would seem my bladder finally gave up during my nap, as my jeans are soaked. I have lost track of time, unsure whether it is late at night or early in the morning. I briefly consider calling out to the street, but I'm swiftly reminded that my cries for help would almost certainly be heard by my captors. I shudder at the thought of the severe beating I would receive.

Footsteps sound on the other side of the door. It's the Bulgarian, alone this time.

"Ah, you are awake, I see. And how was your sleep?" He may as well have been modeling for Armani, standing there smoothing the lapels of his coat and gently tugging his shirt sleeves, uniformly exposing an inch of starched cuff. The sight of him makes my stomach do a flip. He holds a small wooden chair in one hand and drops it in the center of the room. He continues talking, but not before I see his nose twitch at the pungent odor of urine.

"Let us pick up our conversation, shall we? I want to wrap this up and be on my way."

His cheerful speech is irritating, and every inch of me wishes I had a baseball bat and zip-tie-free hands.

"Now, Quinn. You don't want us to hurt you, do you? Tell me where you hid the disk."

I don't move except for the slight upward jut of my chin and a *tsk*, made with my tongue against the roof of my mouth, the Turkish non-verbal response for "no."

The Bulgarian laughs. "A bad habit after only six days?" He shoves me roughly into the wooden chair. "I'm sure you want to return home, yes? Home to your new Turkish lover? We expected him to rescue you long before now. But no matter, we are ready."

Talk of home is a fantasy. Their faces are never hidden, and I can identify them. I know they will not let me go now. The Bulgarian lets a large sigh float toward me, his face exasperated. Dread washes over me as he uses the back of his hand to rap on the door. I glare at him, daring him to do his best.

If they plan to kill me, they need to get on with it.

60

SEDAT

Sedat and Bora watch as the dots move to the outdoor parking lot. After a brief hesitation, the signals depart from the airport and proceed along *Akçay Caddesi*, the main thoroughfare through the Buca neighborhood. After more than twenty minutes, the signals proceed into an area of apartment buildings, where all four dots abruptly disappear.

"What is this?" Bora points to a line on the map.

"I have no idea," Sedat responds. "It encircles several blocks. Call TKGM and see what they know. See if the real estate title officer knows why this apartment complex has been delineated on the map."

Bora taps the number for his contact at *Tapu ve Kadastro Genel Müdürlüğü*, the office of deeds and real estate transactions. After a few questions, he ends the call.

"The city is demolishing the entire site to rebuild under the new earthquake codes," Bora says. "The clerk says a recent court case was resolved, holding the developer responsible for faulty construction. They are making that company take responsibility to avoid what happened in the Kahramanmaraş area."

Both men have memories of the Maraş area in Türkiye. It had

been the site of an earthquake one winter that measured 7.8 on the Richter scale. It struck southern and central Türkiye, as well as northern and western Syria. There were fifty thousand deaths, people they both knew, family and friends. The area was repeatedly bombarded with 30,000 aftershocks within a few months, and more continue to occur today. Sixteen percent of Turkey's population had been affected, and the entire country had ramped up efforts to demolish and rebuild buildings that did not meet earthquake codes. Or, as in this case, holding the developer who cut corners on construction methods responsible for rebuilding.

"Why did she go there?" Bora looks back at the map.

"You are assuming she went voluntarily, Bora. My question is, how did whoever this is know she would be going to the airport?"

The men looked at each other with concern.

"We have a leak," said Bora.

"More than likely, you are correct. There is nothing to do about that now."

"Once this is over, we will need to clean house if we cannot find out who it is. I'll check to see who was on duty today, particularly at her apartment. It was a big mistake, Sedat, to not keep her in a holding room."

"Agreed." Sedat lowered his voice to a whisper. "Except that she and I have our own agreement."

"What are you talking about?"

A sharp buzzing interrupts the men, and Sedat pulls his cell phone from his pocket.

"*Efendim?*"

"Sir, sending a photo of several men entering and exiting the building. There is no confirmation of the woman inside. They arrived several minutes before us."

Sedat wonders what else will go wrong with this investigation. "Send me the photos. What else?"

"The area is large, about a dozen buildings, each with six to eight apartments. According to the project supervisor, planned demolitions will be carried out over the next few days to level all the buildings.

"Stop them from demolishing any of the buildings. We need to establish a team and get them in place. Let me know when that is confirmed."

"Yes, sir. Will do."

"Relieve the men on duty. Pull new officers." Sedat cut the call as he stood, heading toward the door. "Let's go."

Bora scrambled behind his boss, jogging to keep up. When they reached Sedat's car, they squealed out of the parking garage, police lights flashing and siren howling.

"What agreement, Sedat?" Bora yelled at him. "Why are you so insane with this woman? I know she is attractive, but this is your career you are throwing away."

"I am not throwing it away. She agreed to be bait. In fact, it was her idea. Given that Demirci has given us only twenty-four more hours, it is our last resort."

"Bait?" Bora's face was livid. "How can you do this to a woman you care so much about?"

"As I said, it was her idea. She would rather take her risk here than to end up in prison or worse, at a U.S. black site."

"Demirci will just deport her on Monday. He no longer wants to fool with her."

"You haven't seen his face nor listened to the hatred in her voice, Bora. I have. He intends to take his frustrations with this entire investigation out on her."

"What if they kill her before we can get to her?"

"She knew the risks." *And I will hate myself forever*, Sedat thought to himself.

61

QUINN

Someone walks into the room. My head hangs as I'm too exhausted to continue sitting upright. Thirsty and hungry, I am tired from their constant haranguing.

"Look at me, Quinn." Maynard's voice is sharp and hateful.

I look up, having had enough of his games. The two men have played the roles of "good cop" and "bad cop" for the past hour, continually switching back and forth.

"What will you do with this disk you so desperately want?" The words spit out of me. "I know you are going to kill me after this, so there's no reason you can't tell me."

Maynard squints at me, and his raised eyebrows tell me I've surprised him. He crosses his arms over his chest and stares at me for a full minute before he responds.

"You are hiding the launch and location codes for a weapons test, along with the plans for the weapon embedded into the data," he responds. "The disk contains specific locations that will be used to test a new type of weapon developed by the German military, and they, along with the launch code, begin that test."

Harris's reference to the EMP becomes clear now, but I'm still confused. I cannot imagine how a large nuclear weapon can be scheduled to explode high in the sky and expect it to affect only a particular location. With my limited knowledge of EMPs, this doesn't make sense.

"Not everyone has nuclear weapons large enough to generate an EMP."

"This is something entirely different. A German group has perfected the weapon. It is hand-held and ultra-compact. They want the world to watch as they test it. The old man at the card game provided Harris with the coordinates as part of a deal they made. He's the one who thought up the weapon in the first place. He then sold the plans to the Germans, and Harris stole the plans. We, or now I, will auction the plans and the coordinates to the highest bidder. Even if the Germans have the original model, I have the only viable plans. And I have the only copy of the coordinates."

"No, *I* have the only copy," I said quietly, keeping my smirk to myself.

With the only copy of the code in transit back to the States, if I don't give it up, the rest of the world cannot suffer, regardless of what happens to me. Even if I'm dead, it will take a significant amount of time, if ever, before anyone could discover the code's hiding place. It doesn't mean, however, that whoever in Germany has this weapon won't try again.

All this is assuming that Maynard is telling me the truth.

I wait to see if he will elaborate further before I ask my next question, watching Maynard's eyes wander over my body. His silent leering instantly silences me. I imagine what I look like and hope my stringy boy-cut hair and urine-soaked jeans are enough to repel him. I scrutinize him for weapons, something I can hurt him with if I'm lucky enough ever to get my hands untied, but I don't see anything.

"A separate bidding process has already begun. Your husband thought he outsmarted his partner," he points a finger at his chest, "but he didn't."

"His partner was someone named Burt." And Harris's note told me to stay away from him.

Maynard gives me a wolfish grin. "Yes, that's me. Theodore Burton Maynard, III."

I'm about to be sick.

He taps the face of his watch as he leers at me. "There's less than twelve hours, but we won't need that much time."

How many hours will I last before he gets it through his thick head that I won't give him what he wants? Even if I tell him where the code is, he doesn't have enough time to retrieve it.

"Not very smart on your part, I mean, to sell something you don't have without making sure where it is." I've never been a good liar, and it's stupid for me to try to start now.

In less than a second, he has my throat in his hands, the chair careens backward, and my head hits the wall. One, two, three times, he slams my skull against the concrete until I am dizzy. I lost count of the number of slaps to my face, only the sensation of blood spurting from my split lips, and then the warmth as it oozes down my chin. I fall sideways, and just as I am about to hit the concrete floor, he catches the back of the chair and sits me up straight.

"Harris told me you aren't a daffodil but just look and act like one. Let's see if all your bravado is just a show." He moves behind me. I hear the snick of a switchblade knife, and brace for the stab I know is coming. "Let's make this a little less one-sided, shall we? I enjoy a woman who fights back."

The zip-ties snap, and my hands come forward. The rush of freedom simultaneously unleashes my fury. I swerve out of the chair and turn, but quickly realize my eyesight is impaired as my left eye is swollen shut. As Maynard grabs my T-shirt, I lean against the wall to regain my balance. He shoves me, and I fight back with every cell in my body.

Hoisting the chair, I use the strength of my shoulders and thighs to thrust it into him. One of the legs catches him directly in the stomach, knocking the breath out of him. Before he can push me away, I pull the chair up, slamming the back of it into his face. Blood spurts from his nose. I ram the chair into his face again, this time hearing the snap as his nose breaks.

Screaming, I lunge for him a third time, but in one motion, he has the chair tossed across the room, and my shirt ripped from my body as if it were made of tissue. He pauses, blood dripping from his face to the floor. I stand across the room now, in my running bra and pants, waiting for his next move. My body shivers with fear and rage, and my heaving breaths threaten to send me into hyperventilation.

Maynard leans forward, spitting blood on the floor. "If you'd just waited for me, *cher,* we'd be living that life I promised you. But you didn't." The taunting voice is identical to Harris's.

A cold rage detonates inside me, an intense hatred I've never felt before. The voice on the video wasn't Harris's. It was Maynard toying with me, telling me he loved me and wanted to change because of me. All of it was a lie. Before he can react, I'm across the room, digging my fingernails into his skin, leaving five claw marks down the side of his face.

He spins away from me, grabbing the chair and using it to block me from getting near him again.

"Serves you right for all the crap you two put me through. I got sick and tired of hearing about you from that bastard. He thought you were perfect. Glad I got rid of him."

"You killed Harris," I whisper.

"Harris picked you because, supposedly, you *weren't* stupid. Good old Harris, the womanizer of the world, could take any woman he wanted, but for some reason, he wanted you. He picked you for the sole purpose of putting the pieces together and *knowing in your heart,"*—his fingers make air quotes around the last four words—"the right thing to do. It was a part of this crazy plan he had. He said putting pieces together was part of your natural thought process."

He stops pacing, his hands on his hips. "I had to admit I was surprised when you did exactly what he told me you'd do—until you didn't. Those stupid Bulgarians should have blasted that damn door. I just told them to scare you, not to kill you, but of course, you didn't know that." He shrieks a high-pitched laugh. "Got your precious Özbek off track, didn't it?"

He paces the room, balling his hands into tight fists and then opening them again, closed, open, closed, open, over and over, eyes wild.

"Water under the bridge now. I want the coordinates and the plans. And yeah, the accounts, Quinn. They are also mine. And the money, of course, that Harris stole from me and those yahoos in Sochi. When I sell the data, I'll never think about Harris, you, or the good 'ole US of A ever again."

He pulls out a pistol and cocks it, aiming it at my right foot. "Let's see if I can move you toward the truth a little faster."

"Wait!" I scream and shift sideways.

Maynard sways to compensate, then grins and drops the gun to his side. "Yeah, I thought you'd change your mind. I have one question, though. Did you think he was in love with you?"

I don't know what to believe. While I now know the voice on the video was Maynard, the handwriting on the notes was still Harris.

"Did you?" Maynard screams.

His face is screwed up in anger and—jealousy? As he focuses on my face, I lunge to knock the gun from his hand. He slaps my right cheek, and I taste blood. He wants an answer, and I will give him what I think he doesn't want to hear.

"Harris loved me. And I loved him. Nothing you say will make me think differently."

"You are either the most naive woman in the world or the most stupid. He married you as part of the plan. Our plan." Maynard paces in circles. "He was *my partner*," he slams his hand on his chest with each of the two words, "and had been since college. We shared everything—women, profits, drugs. But then I knew something was wrong when he refused to share you. I loved him, and he, you stupid woman, loved *me*."

Sedat's reference to Harris's dark side rises to the light, and I feel as if I will vomit. Maynard's eyes latch onto mine; his pupils are tiny black points in a gray circle. He stops pacing, his hands flexing rapidly at his side as he speaks to the wall opposite me.

"We were making a fortune. He was a black-market genius, let me tell you. I've never met a better thief. He had this ridiculous plan to get that list from the sick old German and sell it to the highest bidder." He stops and whirls around, his face a picture of amazement. "And, by God, he did it."

"Then the Feds got too close, and he came up with an even crazier plan to fake his death. He held it together through every con, deal, and mark, even when drunk or stoned. But instead of giving me the disk to set up the auction, he sent it to you, a stupid backwoods hick without a brain in her head." His voice is now a whisper. "He was already in a body bag when I crashed the helicopter, but he wasn't dead; he was faking it. It was my pleasure to put him out of his misery. I guess I'm lucky to be alive after the gas tank exploded."

Before I can react, Maynard's right hook slams into my face. I hear his words as I crash backward in the chair, just before my world turns dark.

"Now it's your turn."

62

QUINN

Shoes appear in my field of vision, and a hand grasps my arm. Jerked to my feet, I gasp from the pain of my shoulder being wrenched in a direction it doesn't want to go, and the massive headache that has me spinning. I fight back, pushing, shoving, and letting loose a scream that I know has to be heard from the outside. The leer on Maynard's face makes the disgust rise from my toes and spread throughout my body. I lean back as far as the pain will allow, then hock a wad of spit into his face.

"Why, you little—"

Maynard lunges for me but is restrained by the meaty arm of the Bulgarian. I touch the side of my mouth and see the blood as I look at them coldly.

"Leave us. I'll take care of this." Maynard's words spat across the room at the other man.

With a slight nod, the man releases me, leaves, and slams the door. Maynard suddenly swings toward the door, wrenching it open. He shouts in Arabic or something else that isn't Turkish, into the next room.

My ears are still ringing from hitting the wall. I definitely have a concussion, as the nausea continues to come and go. I hate this. It is too easy for him to hurt me. I need to find a way to hurt him back.

The foul-smelling man from the back of the car brings a chair and motions for me to sit. He smells even more awful today, of body odor, the sour stench of too much alcohol, and something nasty I can't identify. Has he shit himself? The driver brings a tripod with a video camera mounted on top, placing it several feet in front of the chair, along with a harsh light.

Maynard re-enters and speaks to the men. My knowledge of languages is minimal, but it doesn't sound guttural enough for Arabic. One man roughly grabs my hands and pins me, straining the shoulder that had been injured, as another man holds my hands behind the chair. The second man holds a newspaper in his hand, then props it on my thighs, the top corners under my bra. Once Maynard is satisfied with how things look, he motions for the cameraman to begin. His voice booms.

"As you can see, Inspector, she is in relatively good health, no worse for wear, although I can assure you that this will not last," Maynard speaks loudly for the camera, but remains out of the frame. "She won't give me what I want, and I know one of you has it. Bring the information to the location I direct you to. Once you do, we will return her to you. We will be in touch with instructions."

"Don't do it, Sedat," I yell into the camera. "Don't give him anything."

Maynard laughs as he turns off the camera. "You make proof of life too easy." The car driver removes the camera, tripod, and lamp. I try to work blood back into my hands and arms. The stabbing pain is fierce now. I examine my body to assess the overall extent of the damage. A massive blue bruise envelops my shoulder, and others creep from under my bra and down my side. I tenderly swallow, and my throat hurts. I can feel pain under my chin, and when I touch my head, there is a bump the size of a small egg. It hurts to breathe, so I am anticipating a broken rib or two.

My ruined shirt is lying in the middle of the floor, but there's nothing left of it to cover me. I slump and try to stay calm, but it is impossible. I am practically convulsing with full-body shivers that won't subside. I don't know how much time has passed before I realize Maynard is standing before me.

"Time for communication with your lover boy."

He reaches for me, and I shy away. I scream, hoping someone outside can hear me, but the only sound in return is Maynard's hyena laugh. He pulls me out of the chair and, from behind, shoves me through the door. I stumble into a larger room with two windows, a door leading to the kitchen, and another to the outside. My heart leaps when I see my route to freedom.

I run to the opposite side of the room, toward the kitchen. When he comes after me, I hit him in the face, then dodge him and head for the exterior door. I don't make it. His grip on my left arm pulls my injured shoulder at such an angle that I am instantly on my knees in unbearable pain, unable to stop my cries, even when he releases me.

"Now, now, Quinn," Maynard says softly, wiping his face with his hand. "No need for that. You can't get out of here, so stop trying."

As I remain on my knees, whimpering from the pain, he punches in a number on his cell. Maynard speaks Turkish to an operator. Panting with the pain radiating down my arm, I stay on the floor, waiting for the next opportunity. He hasn't beaten me yet.

"*Sedat Ali Özbek, lütfen.*"

His eyes return to me while he waits. I turn my head, refusing to meet his gaze.

"*Ajan Özbek*, someone wishes to talk to you." Maynard smiles into the phone, clearly loving this. I hear Sedat talking, but the phone is too far away for me to understand what he's saying. Not responding to anything Sedat has said, Maynard hands me the cell phone.

"Sedat?" I hear a large breath being exhaled on the other end, along with expletives in English and Turkish in the background from someone else. Then his deep voice floats into my ear, strong, calm, and professional.

"*Şekerim*, do not talk, just listen. I will find you. You must believe me, I will find you, and I will kill the dog standing next to you, do you understand?"

A wave of relief washes over me. I relish what Sedat will do to this man when he catches him—if I can't get to him first. Hearing his voice gives me strength I didn't know I had.

"Sedat—" The phone is wrenched from my hand.

"You've had your proof of life," Maynard says into the phone. "No negotiation." I can't hear the response; I can only hear Maynard's instructions.

"Deliver the disk to the address I will give you, leaving it at the front desk in the name of Orhan Bey. Once I confirm the information is valid, you will receive the address to find your woman. But please know that for the next two hours, Özbek, she, and that body of hers, is mine."

Maynard cuts the call, setting the phone on the table. His face reminds me of a fifteen-year-old boy about to experience his first sexual encounter, all gloat and confidence. His eyes hold the fire of someone who thinks they are about to conquer.

"Now, that should give your lover something to consider, won't it? Let's see what we can do to make you more comfortable."

He reaches over and grasps my wrist, and before I can snatch it away, with a *click,* he has me handcuffed to the table in the middle of the room. Maynard strides into the kitchen, and I hear him banging around as if searching for something—a butcher's knife to hack me into small pieces, most likely.

When he returns, he brings tea instead of a knife or something worse. My stomach rumbles at the smell, but I need water, not food, yet I don't dare beg. He returns with a plate of Turkish tea biscuits and pulls up a chair beside me. Through the kitchen door, I eye the hot teapot. That would definitely do some severe damage.

"What would you offer me for a *bisquit*?" He uses the Turkish pronunciation.

"Nothing," I say. I'd rather eat dirt.

"When did you eat last?" He waves a cookie in front of my nose. My stomach rumbles, betraying me.

"I would rather starve." I turn my face away from the cookie and picture the plate of Turkish *mantı*, the ravioli swimming in a garlic yogurt sauce I'd had with Arzu in Bodrum. Sedat's rage at the airport in Kuşadası seems so long ago, and the returning thought that Arzu might be dead hits me in the chest. I refuse to believe it. I am alive. She must be alive.

And Sedat is coming.

Maynard's tone is playful, and it brings me back to my reality. "There is something that might change your mind. I'm going to get that launch code from you. It's up to you whether I take it slowly or quickly."

I ignore him until the snick of his switchblade causes me to look. An involuntary flash of fear rips down the back of my neck, causing me to shiver. His smile is evil, unhinged. His eyes are even more wild, if that is possible.

"Let's see what is under that ugly contraption you wear."

He takes the switchblade and slowly cuts through my running bra, making me worry he will slit me and not the bra. Sweat runs down my back, soaking my pants. The final piece of the bra falls, and I am naked from the waist up. I shiver.

"Ah, you are ready for me, I see." His voice is higher. "Your excitement is growing." His high-pitched laugh is unnerving, sending goosebumps down my arms. I stare at the opposite wall and pull against the handcuff, wishing I could cross my arms over my chest.

"Look at those firm nipples in the middle of those luscious breasts. I don't think that's from the cold."

Somehow, I must make him stop before he goes too far. I don't think I can take it if he does. He unzips his pants, and with my disgust, my gag reflex kicks in. He waits for me to speak again, his now childish face expectant.

"You are out of your mind," I say. I lean forward and whisper. "This game you're playing will be your last. If Sedat doesn't kill you, I will."

"Oh, it's not a game, I assure you. Your lover has no idea how to give you what you deserve. But I am sure you will want it repeatedly after I show you what I can do."

A deep shudder travels down my entire body as the revulsion increases.

"Hold on a little longer," he says, letting loose with another cackle. "Don't be so needy. There is plenty of time."

He eats a tea biscuit, dipping the last part into the tea and holding it over my right breast, making me flinch as the hot liquid drips onto my skin. As it travels downward to the tip of my nipple, he places the teacup on the table near his cell phone, then leans over to lick the drop.

He takes my right nipple in his mouth, the greasy hair on the top of his head so close to my face. Ignoring my disgust, I bow my head and bite into his scalp as hard as I can until I taste blood. Rather than backing away as I'd hoped, he bites my breast with all the strength of his jaw. Pain bursts through me as I shriek. The agony continues for what feels like minutes. When my screaming does not stop, he is forced to let me go to shut me up.

"You can scream as long as you like, but your tricks won't get you anywhere, I assure you."

I spit his blood on the floor. A purple bruise forms on my right breast. At least the nipple is still there.

"I see you are going to make this hard for me. Don't be this way, Quinn. Harris and I shared everything. I promise you he would want you to do this."

He retrieves my ripped shirt from the other room, stuffs it in my mouth, and then holds my free hand behind me. Taking the knife, keeping it far enough from me so that I can't do anything unexpected, he slowly cuts my pants just as he did the bra, piece by excruciating piece.

Afraid he is going to lose control and stab me, I force myself to be very still until, finally, he cuts the last piece away, pulling the remnants of my pants from under me. While I sit in my underwear, he steps back to admire his handiwork.

"There now, we can get down to business a little bit better, don't you think?" Lust grows in his eyes.

I retch, spit out my shirt, and throw up what little there is in my stomach. My vomit splashes on his shoes. With a disgusted sigh, he checks his watch and then looks at me, using the shirt to clean the floor. He tries to shove the rag back in my mouth, and I fight back, trying to bite him each time he gets close until he finally gives up and throws it into the corner on the floor. He checks his watch and lets out a chuckle.

"There's still over an hour. This is fun, don't you think?"

63

QUINN

I watch him take another tea biscuit, break it off, and dunk it into the tea. This bastard killed Harris, and my husband knew it was likely to happen. He'd known that his partner had stepped off the edge of sanity. Harris sent me the disk because he knew I'd do the right thing with it even if he couldn't. He didn't trust himself but trusted me. Did he know I would die as well?

Maynard's voice takes a reasonable tone.

"Quinn, unless you want me to beat you or start shooting you full of holes or give you what you don't want," his fingers fiddle with the zipper of his pants, "you need to tell me where the disk and the account records are."

I stay silent, and he squeezes the trigger under the table. The bullet misses my little toe by half an inch and ricochets into the far wall, either from his bad aim or my flinch. I'm lucky the bullet did not bounce right back and hit me. Or unlucky in that it did not hit him.

"How do you know I have anything in the first place?"

"Because, you stupid bitch, the idiot at the APO box saw you with the envelope."

The same clerk whom Sedat thought was working for him. If I ever make it back to İmir, I am going to strangle the lazy SOB personally, but of course, I'll need to outrun Sedat.

"I've gone through your things." He yells at me. "The Bulgarians searched that apartment twice. Where did you hide them?"

"I'll never tell you."

"Bullshit." He shifts his chair to face me, sliding it closer while he raises the gun and points it at my chest.

"Ever since I landed in Türkiye," I shout at him, "I've been followed, chased, and jailed. You stupid man, it's in the APO box in Alsancak. If you'd been a little smarter, you could have found it any time."

He looks at the ceiling and then back down at me while he mumbles curse words under his breath. The construction machinery outside has stopped working. Men's faint voices shout back and forth outside. I open my mouth to scream, but Maynard slaps his hand over it. Something hits the door, and I flinch, but Maynard is oblivious.

Sedat. He is here. My breath gets faster as my heart begins banging against my chest.

"What account information are you looking for?" I stall for more time. I already know what's on that thumb drive.

"Illegal ones." He looks at me with a twisted, cruel expression. "All the nasty people Harris and I worked with over the years. Each time we had to transfer money to or from one of these bastards, we kept the information, knowing we might be able to use it one day." Losing all that money might make me crazy, too. "Talk, talk, talk. There's no time for whatever game you are playing, Quinn."

Maynard raises the gun and squeezes off a round on the other side of my foot. Concrete shards blast into my body, and the pain is so bad I can't look to see if my toe is still attached. A bead of sweat trickles down the side of my forehead, heading for my eye.

Wiping the side of my face with my free hand, I hear the

distinct squeak of a door opening. Someone is here, but if Maynard hears the sound, he doesn't show it. If it is one of the other men, they will come into the room, yet no one enters.

"Quinn, I will count to three. This is your last chance." He raises the gun to my middle, then changes his mind, centering it on my heart.

"If you kill me, there'll be no way you or anyone else will ever find it. Absolutely no way." I jerk the handcuff hard and feel the table move.

"One." Maynard wiggles the gun, apparently trying to decide whether to shoot me in the head or my heart. If I can shift and throw him off, his shot might go wide.

"Please. Don't do this." We are at the end, and I know it. I don't dare look toward the door behind him. *Sedat, please, for God's sake, let that sound be you.*

"Two." He aims the gun at my knee this time, then my heart, then my head. He's playing with me like a child, but can't get to three. As he opens his mouth for the final number, I stand up and ram forward with everything I have in me. The overturned table slamming into him is so abrupt that he drops the gun, and it skitters across the concrete floor and into the next room.

Maynard falls backward and teeters, his arms shooting out from his sides for balance on the way down. His head slams into the concrete floor with a loud *thunk*. With one hand still attached to the dining table, I wind up tangled sideways on the floor, my arm stretched awkwardly upward, my shoulder screaming in pain. Because of the angle I've fallen, I can't see what happened to him.

There is only silence for the next few minutes.

I use my feet to scoot myself around, then my other hand to pull me upward to stand. I slip the handcuff off the table leg. Maynard is lying on the floor, his head in a pool of blood that is slowly spreading toward me. His eyes are closed, and every ounce of me wants him to be dead, but I can't wait to see. The Bulgarians will return at any minute.

The outer door opens another inch, and instead of the guns and uniforms I expect to enter, a tomcat lazily saunters inside. The confidence that I was to be rescued pops like a balloon. I rest my head against the wall as the last flicker of hope that Sedat is on the way dies inside me. He isn't. There is no one outside, no one coming to save me.

I must save myself.

There are no sounds, no construction, and no traffic. This is a busy city. For it to be this quiet, something is wrong. I need to get moving.

I move toward the door, and my head swims with dizziness at the exertion. My vision is blurred, and I see two doors to escape through, then three. I stand and lean against the wall again, closing my eyes, which worsens the vertigo. Cautiously, I make my way to the outside door, where I use the handle to steady myself. I wait a few seconds, but the only sound I can hear is the slam of car doors very close by.

Bulgarians.

Terror seizes me, and I think, for a second, my heart will stop beating. I can't go through another round of torture, and when they find Maynard dead, they will chop me into pieces and throw me into İmir Bay.

I use the filthy, cracked marble counter next to the door to steady myself as I pull the exterior door inward. I scramble up the steps to ground level as best as I can. As the glaring sunlight spreads across the ground before me, I realize it is midday, even though I don't know what day.

I am exposed, standing in the middle of an apartment complex dressed only in my panties. I need to hide. Fast. The building next door has overgrown bushes, and I head toward them as best I can, given the dizziness.

Halfway between the two structures, I suddenly am airborne,

light, like a balloon floating skyward. The air is hot, and there are no sounds. For a second or two, my body cartwheels through the air. When the explosion hits me, the boom is deafening.

A gray cloud rushes toward me like a freight train. I spin in the air. The hairs on my skin singe from the heat.

I can't breathe.

Upside down, I see the cobblestones of the sidewalk flying toward me, then the green of the park across the way. My brain is confused. There's a park? Why are there no children laughing?

Dropping like a rock, my body explodes with excruciating pain as my face hits the sidewalk and my side slams into the wall of the building. What little air is in my lungs is forced out of me. Then I'm shoved upward again by a second explosion, but rather than hear it, I feel it, as something warm oozes down both sides of my face. Debris rains around me, and I can see bone poking out of my thigh as the blood runs slick down my leg. A roiling cloud covers me with dust.

My world is silent, and I'm sure it is ending.

I'm so sorry, Sedat.

I gasp with pain as I slide down the rough concrete wall into a heap, unable to lift my head from the filthy sidewalk. Choking from the dust, I am desperate to catch my breath. When I am finally able to get a lung full of air, the pain is excruciating. Unable to fight the hacking coughs, I try to catch my breath.

Every inch of my body screams in pain.

I stare with one eye at what is left of the building behind me and see only a concrete pile. The bright blue sky shines through a break in the gray dust. Within seconds, it is covered in black smoke boiling up from the buildings. I blink in silence, unable to hear anything other than a loud ringing inside my head.

Then everything is gone.

64

QUINN

I float in and out of consciousness, pain coursing through my body each time I cough or move. I struggle for air. Trying to open my eyes, even with the harsh light, I see Sedat, the harried professor with baggy pants, an unshaven face, and his thick black glasses, beside me.

"Sedat, you came," I whisper, drifting off again, as nothing he says in response makes sense. I feel his hand touch mine. There is an incessant beeping behind my head. Maybe it is inside my head. I don't know. The world goes black.

Sedat's voice wakes me again, and the beeping increases as my heart jumps in terror. He is angrily making demands to someone I cannot see, and then I feel a warm sensation flood my arm. The pain subsides, and I float away.

In my nightmares, Sedat and Harris are fighting each other to the death, battling through angry Bulgarians, on ferries in a Southern hurricane, and bombs in the street. A breeze brushes my face. The bed is rocking, like I'm on a boat, and the roll is strangely sideways, not undulating as it should be. I open my eyes to ceiling tiles clipping along. Agitated, I grip the sidebars and try to pull up. One of my arms is in a cast, and I can't move my leg.

The pain is excruciating, and I hear a tearful sob. I blink. The sob is mine.

The bed stops, and Sedat's hand rests solidly on my shoulder, gently pushing me back down. His head appears in my blurry field of vision. The memory of the interrogation in İmir rushes at me with a vengeance. My heart is racing, and I try to sit up again. He holds me down. Frantic, I can manage only a whisper; my throat is too raw, and speaking is too painful.

"Please don't take me to the prison in Diyarbakır. Anywhere but that one." Something is wrong with what I am saying, but I cannot understand what. Shoving his hand away, I try to pull up again, but fail, desperate for him not to take me to prison this way. I won't be able to defend myself in this condition. I will die.

Nausea from the pain rises, and I feel the convulsions as I start to vomit.

The bed shifts sideways on its rollers, and Sedat faces me, the bedpan in one hand and the towel in the other. After I finish and my face is clean, he softly pushes me to lie flat once again, his voice low as he murmurs comforting words in Turkish. His face comes near mine, and I close my eyes and finally relax. He kisses my forehead, then my right cheek. The familiar scent of his cologne comforts me as he whispers in my ear.

"I am only taking you to a place more secure. You are not safe here. Please do not fight me, şekerim. Go back to sleep."

He speaks to someone behind me in rapid Turkish. Within seconds, my world begins to spin again, back into the darkness.

SEDAT PACES the width of the room. He is the professional Sedat today, the mean one in an expensive suit and Italian shoes. I wonder why my hands aren't cuffed to the bed since the IV has been removed from my arm. He will take me to jail, if I am not there already, I am sure of it.

Seeing that I am awake, Sedat steps toward the side of my bed. His hand caresses the back of my hand, and I am surprised at the gentleness of his touch.

"Where am I?" My voice is barely a whisper. It hurts to speak.

"My family home in the mountains. I moved you here to protect you."

His response shocks me. *He took me to his home?* "What happened? Why wasn't the hospital safe?"

"You were caught in an explosion. Do you remember that part?"

I close my eyes briefly, and everything rushes back—the Bulgarians, Maynard, the building collapsing around me. When I open them, I check my body for damage. My arms and legs are covered in bandages. Reaching to touch my face, the pain from my shoulder is severe, yet I have to know. My head and most of my face are also bandaged, and I am unable to touch my skin except for my lips and around my eyes.

Sedat's voice is soft, and his eyes observe me as he continues.

"You broke two ribs, and the remainder are bruised. Your right leg has a clean fracture just below the knee, and the muscle in your right thigh has been torn. That leg will be in a cast for some time. Your right arm is broken in three places. You came very close to having a punctured lung as you landed on exposed iron rebar. Your shoulders are bruised, and one was dislocated when I found you. You have a serious concussion, multiple cuts from falling glass and concrete, and too many stitches to count. Your face..." He falters and looks away.

"What's wrong with my face?" He hesitated, and I could see he didn't want to tell me. "Just tell me the truth, Sedat. I have to know."

"You landed on it after the explosion tossed you into the air. One side was completely crushed. They performed the initial surgery to save your eyes and make sure your breathing was not obstructed. But there will need to be more after you have gained some strength."

"How long have I been here?" I croak.

"It has been ten days since the explosion. I brought you here three days ago when I could no longer hide you in the hospital. You were in and out of consciousness the entire time. Initially, we were concerned that you would never wake up. You are alive, but..."

He trails off again.

"What? Am I missing something? What had to be removed?" I frantically begin tugging at the sheets covering me, ignoring the searing pain in my right arm, concerned that I am missing one of my legs. "Sedat, tell me!"

He holds my arms still, his face inches from mine. He leans toward me, his arms wrapping around me, and the familiar smell of his cologne makes me relax. When I'm calm again, he sits up, one hand stroking my hair, his eyes locked onto mine.

"As damaged as they are, you have all your organs and limbs. However, the world believes you died in the explosion, Quinn. Demerci believes you are dead. It is the only way I could protect you from him."

I blink at him, unable to speak. I died. But I didn't. I cannot grasp this new reality.

"Why?"

"He wanted you in prison. He refuses to be convinced that you did not have anything to do with Harris's theft and all the other things that continue to crop up since his death. It is the best way to protect you. The damage to your face is extensive, and as I said, you will need more corrective surgery in several places. The doctors tell me that you will look completely different than before when they are done. At the time, it was an opportunity."

"It's my life, Sedat. Was I not given a choice? Wouldn't it have been better if you'd let me die?" Sedat's face blanched then, as if I'd made his worst nightmare come true.

I am instantly sorry for being so abrasive. He doesn't deserve that from me. I reach my hand to touch his face. "I'm sorry. I'm just scared."

"I could not let you die." Sedat cannot seem to touch me enough now that I'm awake. "You were either sedated or in a coma. Someone had to make decisions, so we did. Your dying was not an option for any of us. You have no family, so we became your family."

"Who?"

"All of us. You will see. You will be cared for here. I have arranged for a physician to be on call for you on an indefinite basis. For your surgeries, there are places we have arranged out of the country."

"I will have a new face. Do I have a new name?"

"Emel Çetin."

"You made me Turkish?" I can't help but laugh, and then immediately regret it, as everything in my body hurts.

Sedat pulls a passport from his pocket and hands it to me. "There is no photo. We will finish the process after your surgeries are completed. The hospital had to have a Turkish citizenship number to treat you, so I created your new identity."

I am speechless at everything this man has done for me. Taking the time to check out my body with one hand slowly, I understand the body damage list Sedat gave me, and that the most important thing happening to me involves my face and the numerous surgeries that will be required. It is still a shock, though.

Relaxed again, I reach to touch Sedat's face again, and hold it with my less damaged hand. "Thank you. I didn't want to die.

65

QUINN

"It's a shock to wake up to all this," I tell him the next day. I've lost almost ten days. I close my eyes and try to remember every bit and piece since the explosion until now. He is sitting in a chair next to the window, reading a book.

"I am quite sure. But we will help you through this." He stands and then walks to my bedside.

"Who?"

"Myself, Arzu, Cem, Isobel, Remzi, Bora."

"Who is Bora?"

"Mehmet?"

"Ah, the passport guy who hated Maynard. I recall you mentioning that he was your partner. You guys should have told me how sadistic Maynard was. Is that asshole dead?"

"They are all dead. At least the ones we found, and yes, Maynard's body was one of them. I believe there were more *en route* who fled after the explosion."

"Am I truly safe now?"

His response is a simple blink of both eyes, the Turkish response for "yes." I reach my uninjured arm toward him, and he takes me into his arms again. I hold him as best I can as the tears begin to fall.

Once the fear that held me has drained away, Sedat lets me go. He stands and walks to the broad window, which shows the mountains dropping to a large body of water. Taking in my surroundings, I see that I am in a bedroom with an ornately patterned ceiling and a crystal chandelier. I lie on an antique wooden bed, wrapped in soft, white sheets and a fluffy, blue blanket. He spins around, and the bright sunlight behind him doesn't allow me to see his face.

"Thanks to Allah, you never found the additional trackers. Without them, we would never have found you."

I'm confused. "Additional trackers? Looking at all the damage here, I don't think you got there fast enough," I whisper.

"Yes, they had blocked all communications. For that part, you are fortunate. Without a block, the construction company planned to detonate all the buildings on the first day."

"You saved me?"

"You saved yourself, Quinn. I found you almost too late."

"So what happens next? How do I become this Emel Çetin person?"

"Only your name and your face have changed, Quinn. You can learn to live a new life."

I look out the window. "Where are we, I mean geographically?"

"The Black Sea. At my parents' *dağ evi*."

"*Dağ evi*?" I ask.

"A mountain house. This one was built by my great-great-grandmother. It is a fortress. Once you are better, you will see for yourself and understand why it is the best place to hide you."

"Who are you hiding me from if everyone thinks I'm dead?" I roll my head to the side. His look is incredulous.

"You want a list *şekerim*?" He slides a chair beside the bed and sits, reaching for my hand. Needing comfort, I let him take it as he talks.

"From whoever might hurt you. I neutralized the Bulgarians, but your country is after you. They want that disk. Even though your death was skillfully orchestrated so that even the best American investigators will never learn that you are alive, I must take precautions to be certain."

"Where is Arzu? What has happened to her? Is she dead?" I am frantic. Sedat was not in the room when I woke, only arriving after an hour, dressed for work. "Are you leaving me?"

"Why do you always think the worst, Quinn? Have the drugs completely ruined your brain?" He mutters to himself then. "No, you were this foolish from the beginning."

"You are in a foul mood this morning." My voice is a rasp as I find new energy to speak. "I never know whether something is the truth or a lie. You are a different person when you wear a suit. That man is the one who lies, pushes me around, and threatens me. Can you ask the other one to come? Please? The kind one?" A tear rolls from the corner of my eye.

He approaches the bed, and I see I've caught him off guard. Anger flares with the squint of his eyes and creases across his forehead. Does he not know he is essentially two people?

"I am not your husband, Quinn. I did not intentionally lie to you. I've only done my best to keep you safe. If that makes you angry, then so be it. I cannot always be a nice person."

"Where is Arzu?"

When he doesn't respond, I think that she must be dead. The heart monitor next to my bed beeps rapidly. I take a long, deep breath, count to ten, and then release it. The beeping decreases. I twist the sheets in my hand to keep my eyes away from his face and the truth. I wish the drugs would wear off, but

I know I won't be able to stand the pain if they do. First Artur, now Arzu.

Silently, Sedat stands and walks out of the bedroom. I hear only his footsteps cross the room, then him softly talking in the other room. When he returns, I turn away. I cannot stand for him to accuse me of Arzu's death the way he did Artur's.

Something hard bumps my hand, and I open my eyes. Sedat is holding out his cell phone.

"Take it. Someone wants to speak with you."

A familiar voice comes out of the speakerphone. "*Quinn'cim*. I am here. Everything is okay. Özbek says you are very upset."

"Arzu?" I look at Sedat as I reach for his phone, causing another spasm of pain down my arm. His head nods slightly, then he turns and leaves the room. I turn off the speaker and put the phone to my ear.

"Arzu?"

"Yes. I am here. I am fine, I promise you. Özbek is very upset with himself. He did not mean to make you think I was dead. That man can be so stupid sometimes."

"Where are you?" I ask.

"I am in a hospital in İmir. They brought me here yesterday. Your new friend got me a private room. I thanked him, but he should also hear it from you."

The sarcasm in her voice slices through my pain. This is the Arzu I know.

"I thought —"

"They saved me from the American; his men did."

"Who saved you?" I am still reeling from the knowledge that she is alive.

"Your new friend, Sedat *Bey*, had his men pull the American off me before he could kill me. They took me to the hospital instead of going after the man. They saved me, Quinn."

"What American, Arzu?"

"I don't know who it was. I never saw his face. I only

remember that he was a big blond man with a strange American accent."

I almost blurted out "Harris" until I remembered he was dead. It had to be Maynard. Yet he had also died two weeks ago. A ripple of fear went down my spine.

"Özbek refuses to tell us anything about the investigation. The television reports say they found several bodies, but the İmir police will also not give out more information. I assumed it was climate protesters about the demolition garbage until Özbek told me a little and said you were part of it. We have a lot to talk about, Miss America."

"And we will," I say, even though there is a lot I will never know unless Sedat chooses to share it with me.

"Why are you in the mountains?" she asks.

"You know that answer."

"Özbek." She cackles, then wheezes. I wait for her to catch her breath. "It must be nice to have such a high-ranking bodyguard. Too bad he is so ugly."

"And you will pay for that, you know." Even though it hurts to laugh, I cannot stop. I am so happy she is alive.

When Sedat returns, I hand his phone back to him. I grab his wrist before he sits and returns to his reading book. He gives me an expectant look.

"Thank you. She says your men saved her. She was lucky they were so close to her."

"Not lucky. They were there watching her."

"You've had her under surveillance?"

"Of course. After you escaped and ended up in an explosion, I take no chances, even with your friends." He stares out the window at the Black Sea. "Several of my men will pay for that."

"Don't punish them. It wasn't their fault."

"But it is their fault, and they will deserve the punishment. You escaped and headed for the airport. Without my trackers, you would have been lost until they recovered your body from the wreckage."

I shudder at the thought of lying under all the rubble. He places the book in his hand on the table and steps back to the side of the bed.

"You owe me something."

"Yes, my life."

"Do not play games, now, Quinn. Give it to me."

We stare at each other, each willing the other to give in. He is right. He saved my life—and, more importantly, Arzu's—so I blink first.

66

QUINN

I'm in Kadiköy, a neighborhood on the Asian side of Istanbul, sitting on a bench that faces the Bosphorus. It has been a year since the explosion. I watch a passing Moody sailboat, wondering for the thousandth time how I ended up here, in this new place, in this new body, in this new life. My mother would not recognize me; only my height is the same. Superficially, my hair is buzzed short, and today it is bleached white. Tomorrow, it might be red; who knows?

After a dozen surgeries and Sedat's relentless haranguing through my physical therapy, I can use both arms and legs, although my right leg ached this past winter. I lost thirty pounds of Southern fluff while in and out of hospitals for many months, and replaced it with hard-earned muscle. I run, I walk, I go to the gym. I must do something every day to calm myself and give myself strength to face the physical and mental scars left by my husband.

Yet, my face reminds me daily of my new life and who I am now—Emel. I will never get used to that name. This face looks nothing like the one before and still gives me a start in the bathroom mirror each morning, even after a year.

My eye color changes with contacts to green rather than brown. My nose was reset after the explosion and is now more slender with a slight upturn. Having been rebuilt and resculpted, my new cheekbones alter the width of my face, my expression, and the two surgeries on my eyes have all but eliminated any vestige of my Asian heritage. The startling new package was complete when my chin was replaced with a cleft in its center.

My face, while having no discernible heritage, no longer betrays me. I have been given the freedom to live, hidden in plain sight from those who still might find me. Harris's gambling money is still shifting in the Caribbean, and the gold is still protected in the private vault in the Grand Bazaar. The diamonds rest neatly under my blouse. I don't need the money and don't want it. But they—the ones who did not get blown to bits in the explosion—don't get a thing.

And I need the economic comfort of knowing I can run and hide.

The W3W coordinates and the launch code are now locked in a new safe deposit box with Harris's gun at Isobel's bank. They will stay there until I decide what to do with them. The money and the data are now the bait. As long as I have it, someone will be looking for it. And when they find it, I will make sure they pay, after I determine exactly what this is about.

To Sedat's disappointment, Artur's hack job erased the data from the disk. I will deal with his anger when he learns about the numbers the boy gave me on paper. But that is for another day.

Over the past year, there were more than just physical changes. Sedat insists I stay close to the doctors and therapists in Istanbul and, if he is honest with himself, close to him. We live thirty minutes apart by train; he is in Nişantaşı on the European side, and I am in Feneryolu on the Asian side. Arzu lives with me at the moment. My apartment is small yet comfortable, featuring two bedrooms and two bathrooms, and is conveniently located close to the Marmaray station, with a short walk to the waterfront walkway, similar to the one in İmir. I spend many days riding ferryboats back and forth across the water as I explore my new city and learn its language, people, and culture. The grand inquisitor checks on me daily, and occasionally, I see that I am being watched by men in suits who keep a careful distance.

Today, I think of Harris, something I rarely do. It is too painful. But his seduction, our marriage, and his death taught me that a trite expression can be a bitter truth: Actions do speak louder than words.

At first, lying in the ancient house in the mountains as I mended, I wanted it all to make sense. I wanted my life back, the hope of the fairytale I was promised, and clarity—to know precisely how Harris had felt about me. It took weeks for me to understand that I would never learn the truth about my husband and why he selected me as his patsy. Any happiness must come from inside me, not from someone else. And regardless of the answers, they are just words. They aren't real. The life I thought I missed isn't real.

I was always the "good girl" growing up, the one who always "did the right things." I was an honors student who would have made anyone else's parents proud. I became a lawyer in the hope that my community would look up to me, the ones who gossiped and never left me alone. I always followed the rules, trying to be an upstanding bar member, a "somebody" in my hometown, even though I hated my job. And finally, I married a man who said he loved me, sweeping me off my feet, the icing on a fairytale wedding cake.

None of those things was real.

With many nasty words thrown at Sedat during drug-induced, pain-filled sessions and others later when I was drug-free, I finally began to release who I used to be and embrace the person I am now. There is no resolution for the parents who never gave me love or revenge for a dead husband who deceived me. Nor can the satisfaction of killing his insane partner resolve the hatred I carry inside for so many hurts I've hidden for thirty years. Maynard's death and Bulgarians chasing me are nightmares I re-live over and over. Nightmares that, according to my Sedat-enforced therapist, might never go away.

My new life and body were all built with action, not words. Harris gave me all the right words, the right promises, and the right expectations. But those weren't the truth. The truth arises during the long nights of pain in a hospital bed with Arzu's hand firmly grasping mine. It comes with Sedat joining me on the thrice-weekly trips to the physical therapist, cheering, cajoling, and downright forcing me to move forward to walk again. And flowers from Bora, placed in a fresh vase every week, along with a different Turkish sweet or chocolate, delivered every Saturday by Isobel or Cem.

Most of all, it comes with hard conversations with myself, with the realization that I am not alone or unloved, and that I will only be unhappy if I let myself be. It comes with action: resolving all those hurtful things inside and letting them go, and loving my Turkish friends—my new family—with every ounce of the new me.

And to decide about Sedat. If I allow myself to remain close to him, it is his life I am risking, not mine. Everyone I've ever loved has died.

Today, I walk to the pier, take the ferry to Karaköy, then ride the tram up the hill, past the Blue Mosque and the Hagia Sophia, getting off at Beyazıt-Kapalıçarşı for the Grand Bazaar. I am meeting Arzu here for lunch during her break from teaching in the Computer Science Department at Istanbul University. I'm sure Sedat had something to do with that, and I also think she works for him on the side, but that's their business.

She is happy. That is what is essential now.

I reach into my pocket for my ringing cell phone. There is no identification, only *"Bilinmeyen Arama,"* the Turkish phrase for an Unknown Caller. I always let these calls go unanswered, as the carrier automatically routes them to voicemail. My friends insist that I am paranoid, but with as many broken bones as I have suffered, the paranoia is necessary. The call continues to ring incessantly, and my chest tightens as I wonder who might be on the other end.

No one has this number. I just got the new phone less than twenty minutes ago.

"Allo?" I answer, bracing myself for a voice I don't want to hear.

"Miss America, where are you?" Arzu has me on speaker. "We're starving, and Mustafa refuses to bring our food because yours will get cold." The melodic tone of her voice gives away her feigned whine. I can hear her smiling. "You know, Cem and Isobel only get a half hour for lunch. Sedat is getting irritated, and we don't want to anger the big man today. Stop gawking at all the crumbling zillion-year-old buildings and get in here, will you?"

I hear Bora laughing in the background.

"Arzu, did you hack my new phone?" I ask.

The sound of raucous laughter fills the air as I end the call and open the door to the restaurant. It is the truth. Actions always speak louder than words.

ACKNOWLEDGMENTS

Thank you to all the readers of this first international thriller, both in the United States and in Türkiye. A thank you to editor Barbara Burgess-Van Aken for her comments. The book is better for your thoughts. Thanks also to Rebecca Millar for her early editorial efforts. To the early beta readers, with special appreciation to Kimberly Brock, Marta Lane, and Rebecca Finley for their valuable comments. To Andrea St. Amand for her insights into white-collar crime. Any errors are exclusively mine for the benefit of the story.

A special thanks goes to Ayhan, Allison, and Aydin Uğur for all the reading required in the beginning to help me firm up the plot and understand the Turkish characters as well as the language. With family and friends, as Quinn has discovered, life is much easier.

ABOUT THE AUTHOR

R. S. Hampton is an attorney turned novelist, weaving suspenseful stories that unfold across various landscapes—bustling cities, quiet coastal towns, and places tucked just out of sight. With a legal career spanning three decades, her characters are often lawyers, their clients, and the people entangled in their search for truth—where morality is rarely black and white, and justice doesn't always follow the rules.

A lifelong traveler, she is drawn to places that spark curiosity, places with history, edge, and unexpected depth. Her stories are shaped by the settings in which they unfold, each becoming a character in its own right. Whether it's a courtroom in a city she once called home or a hidden alleyway in a country she's only just begun to understand, her novels reflect the intricacies of the worlds she explores.

She and her husband split their time between multiple countries, embracing a multicultural life that mirrors the layered complexities of her fiction. When she's not writing, she's usually on the move—seeking out the next place, the next story, and the next unanswered question.

For more books, updates, and contact information:
www.RSHamptonBooks.com

Help Indie Authors Succeed

Thank you for picking up this book! Whether you bought it, borrowed it, or stumbled upon it, I truly appreciate your time and interest. As an independent author, sharing stories with readers like you is a dream come true—and you're already helping just by reading.

If you enjoyed this story, **here are a few simple ways you can make a difference:**

1. Share your thoughts

Whether it's a quick review online or a conversation with a friend, your words help other readers discover this book.

2. Tell your community

Mention the book to fellow readers, share it on social media, or recommend it to your local library or bookstore.

3. Show your support

Pre-ordering upcoming books or attending events when possible can help small authors reach new audiences.

4. Stay connected

Follow me on social media or subscribe to my newsletter for updates and behind-the-scenes glimpses into my writing journey.

Every little action makes a difference, and I couldn't do this without you. Thank you for being part of this adventure!

With Gratitude,

R. S. Hampton

www.ingramcontent.com/pod-product-compliance
Lightning Source LLC
LaVergne TN
LVHW091700070526
838199LV00050B/2227